BABY CARTER

Dina Santorelli

Praise for *Baby Carter*:

"Dina Santorelli writes a terrific thriller."
—Andrew Gross, *New York Times*
best-selling author of *The One Man*

"This *Baby* really delivers! With loads of suspense, a page-turning plot, and twists and turns that will keep you riveted, *Baby Carter* is a very satisfying conclusion to this exciting series. Can't wait to see what Dina Santorelli is up to next!"
—Anne Canadeo, best-selling author of
The Black Sheep & Company Mysteries

"Dina Santorelli has once again crafted a riveting and twisty thriller that will be read late into the night. Fast-paced and filled with complex characters, *Baby Carter* is the perfect ending to the Baby Grand Trilogy."
—K.L. Murphy, author of the
Detective Cancini Mysteries

"Once again, Dina Santorelli delivers a well-written, thrilling book that will keep you on the edge of your seat—and up late at night. The storyline dives deeper into the characters of Don, Jamie, and Faith, taking you places you didn't expect and leading to the unexpected ending of the Baby Grand series. A must-read!"
—Eric Davis, former Navy SEAL and author of
*Raising Men: Lessons Navy SEALs Learned from Their
Training and Taught to Their Sons*

Books by Dina Santorelli

Fiction
Baby Grand
Baby Bailino
Baby Carter

Nonfiction (Author)
Daft Punk: A Trip Inside the Pyramid

Nonfiction (Collaborator/Contributor)
*Good Girls Don't Get Fat: How Weight Obsession Is Messing
    Up Our Girls and How We Can Help Them Thrive
    Despite It*
*Bully: An Action Plan for Teachers, Parents, and Communities
    to Combat the Bullying Crisis*
I, Spy: How to Be Your Own Private Investigator
*Raising Men: Lessons Navy Seals Learned from
    Their Training and Taught to Their Sons*
*Become an American Ninja Warrior: The Ultimate Insider's
    Guide*

Publisher's Cataloging-In-Publication Data
(Prepared by The Donohue Group, Inc.)

Names: Santorelli, Dina.
Title: Baby Carter / Dina Santorelli.
Description: Massapequa Park, New York : eLuna Media LLC, [2018]
    | Series: [Baby Grand trilogy] ; [3]
Identifiers: ISBN 9780997719154 (paperback) | ISBN 9780997719147
    (ebook)
Subjects: LCSH: Presidential press secretaries--United States--Fiction.
    | Mothers and daughters--United States--Fiction. | Intelligence
    officers--United States--Fiction. | Organized crime--United States--
    Fiction. | Wyoming--Fiction. | LCGFT: Thrillers (Fiction)
Classification: LCC PS3619.A586 B33 2018 (print) | LCC PS3619.
    A586 (ebook) | DDC 813/.6--dc23

dinasantorelli.com
elunamedia.com

Cover design by Books Covered
Interior design by Wooly Head Design
Production management by Stonesong Digital

For all the strong mommas, especially my own

BABY CARTER

Dina Santorelli

1

"C'mon, Faithy, you're it!"

Charlotte Grand slid across the White House floor in her socks as Faith Carter ran to catch up.

"Why do *I* always have to be it first?" Faith called.

Charlotte stopped abruptly and put her hands on her hips. "*Duh.* That's because I'm oldest."

"So?"

"*So???*" Charlotte rolled her eyes. "The oldest always gets to hide first. *Everybody* knows that."

"All right, you two, that's enough."

Jamie Carter filed the last of the memos into her office's new walnut cabinet and stood back to admire the room. The furnishing had been built by students at a local high school as a gift to the president, who had invited the senior class to the inauguration earlier that year. It was wonderfully imperfect, with a few nails sticking out and the left back leg shorter than the rest but obviously crafted with love and attention. It was the last piece needed to complete her office, which had taken six months to cobble together. Decorating never seemed to be a priority when part of your job was helping the person running the country.

"It looks nice, Momma," Faith said, standing in the doorway with a smile. Her voice echoed throughout the chamber.

"Thanks, sweetie," Jamie said, although she still felt some reluctance about taking up so much square footage, especially in the private residence. Because the room had originally been a meeting room for visiting guests, it was rather spacious—certainly bigger than many of the other designated office areas in the White House. However, the president had been adamant that she have a live-in work space, and Jamie was grateful. Trauma may not be the best way to begin a relationship, but, in part, because of what had happened to them, President Grand was not only Jamie's boss but had become one of her very best friends. The First Family was like a second family.

She placed a photo of her and her daughter on top of the walnut cabinet, twisting it so that it faced the room. "How was school?" she asked Faith. "Did you—?"

"C'mon, Faithy, hide your eyes!" Charlotte called, pulling Faith back into the hallway.

"It's just not fair," Faith pouted, chasing after Charlotte.

Jamie watched the girls circle around an accent table, piled with their school backpacks. They had become like sisters over the past four years and acted more like it every day—playing, arguing, sulking, teaching each other, confiding in one another. Her daughter's hair, which had grown long, trailed behind her as she ran, and Jamie could smell her raspberry-scented shampoo. Working closely with the president of the United States was certainly a highlight of Jamie's career, but it paled in comparison to being able to work where she was near her daughter.

Jamie slipped a manila folder into her briefcase and checked her phone. "Careful, girls. That's an antique."

"She's being bossy again, Momma." Faith stopped running and crossed her arms.

"I am not," Charlotte protested. "Just because you don't know the rules of the game doesn't mean there's something wrong with *me*."

Charlotte's eyes zeroed in on Faith with an audacity that Jamie recognized in the First Lady, who scared most of the White House staff with that look. Jamie placed her phone into her purse and threw the strap of her briefcase onto her shoulder.

"C'mon, girls, work it out." She left her office and bent down in front of both girls, pulling them in for a huddle. "That's what this house is all about, isn't it? Compromise? Moving forward? Progress?"

"I thought it was about getting the bad guys," Charlotte said.

"Well, that too," Jamie said. "But how do you think we get the bad guys?"

"With guns?"

"Not always."

"But you carry a gun, Momma," Faith said.

"Not when I'm at work, sweetie. And the way things are done best is with diplomacy. Violence should never be a first resort." She looked at her watch. The president was running late for his cabinet meeting, which had been rescheduled for that afternoon. The secretary of homeland security was a stickler for punctuality, so this wouldn't bode well for the president's attempt to get him on board with his proposed legislation to shore up the borders.

"Are you having a meeting with my dad?" Charlotte asked with obvious pride. "He's the president," she said to Faith.

"Yes," Faith said dramatically, "we *know*."

Jamie smiled and kissed her daughter's forehead. "Be a good girl for Mrs. Grand, okay?" She waved to President Grand's mother, who was sitting on a sofa in the next room and reading a book to Phillip Jr. The old woman had become a fixture in Faith's life ever since Jamie agreed to make the move to Washington with the Grand family.

"Charlotte, dear," the old woman called, "let Ms. Carter say goodbye to her daughter without you hovering about."

"Oh, that's all right, Mrs. Grand," Jamie said, "she doesn't need to—"

"Coming, Grandmother!" Charlotte called and ran to the sitting room, her blond curls tumbling beside her.

"When are you coming back, Momma?" Faith asked Jamie, her dark eyes wide.

"In just a few hours. This shouldn't take that long." She smoothed down her daughter's hair and adjusted her shirt.

Faith reached underneath the collar of her shirt and retrieved her gold cross, which she pulled so that the chain formed a V down her torso. The jewelry had become her most prized possession, especially after she misplaced her Hello Kitty watch several weeks ago. The rope chain had become all kinky from the little girl's constant fiddling, and, on cue, Faith began to rub the gold cross between her fingers, probably signaling her frustration with Charlotte. Every time she did, Jamie's mind's eye flashed back to the man who had worn the jewelry first—a man she was never sure if Faith remembered.

"Try to play nicely with Charlotte, okay?" Jamie whispered.

"But—"

"Try your best."

Faith sighed. "Okay, Momma."

"And be careful, okay?"

"Yes, Momma."

"Remember, always be on the lookout for anyone—or anything—weird or out of the ordinary."

"I know."

"And stay with Mrs. Grand."

"I *know*, Momma." Jamie sensed that Faith had the urge to roll her eyes but was too respectful to. "You tell me every day."

"I know I do," Jamie said, cupping her daughter's soft cheek with her hand.

The truth was that Jamie probably told her twice a day. Stranger danger was not the same for them as it was for other families—and not just because they spent much of their time with the leader of the free world. Although the events of early 2014 were long behind them and, true to his word, Don Bailino had done all he could to ensure Faith's safety, the circumstances surrounding her daughter's lineage would always make her a potential target, one way or another. People could forget, of course, but they didn't always, and organizations could have long memories. Would the FBI or NYPD one day make the child pay for the sins of the father? Were there other organized crime families lurking about and waiting? For what, Jamie didn't know. Would the paparazzi ever tire of Faith's salacious story of conception? President Grand's tenure as president may have been relatively calm, but Jamie's personal threat level would never be at green. And, unfortunately, neither would Faith's.

"I'm just double-checking," Jamie said, "because—"

"Because it makes you feel better."

"That's right." She pinched her daughter's cheek.

"I didn't forget … In an emergency I go right to the men in the suits." Faith pointed toward the Secret Service agent standing down the hallway. This afternoon, Agent Brandon Fuller had private residence duty. Brandon, who was young and handsome, was Faith's favorite and was one of several agents President Grand had brought with him from the FBI's team at the Executive Mansion in New York. Jamie knew the best security was layered security, and the White House was perhaps the most layered residence in the country. She thought that would make her feel better, but some days Jamie felt Faith was as exposed as she was insulated.

"Right," Jamie said, "and if you don't have time, you—"

"I hide in the hiding spots that you showed me."

"And if—"

"And if I don't have time or if there's big, big trouble," Faith got in close to whisper, "that's when I hit one of those red buttons." She pointed to various locations in the residence. "But that's only for real emergencies," Faith added, "not peanut emergencies. It's for when something's really, really wrong, but not because of food."

Charlotte had already gotten into trouble for hitting one of the panic buttons not long after the inauguration when Philly, who had a raging peanut allergy, had eaten a dessert that had been given to the president as a gift by a traveling dignitary; it had been manufactured in a plant that processed peanuts. As Philly began to lose his breath, Charlotte went straight for the panic button before anyone noticed. The Secret Service arrived just after Mrs. Grand administered the EpiPen, but the situation got out to the press and caused an uproar in social media circles. Jamie had spent the rest of the afternoon and the better part of the next morning in the press briefing room trying to explain what had happened. It was another of many President Grand moments to make it onto *Saturday Night Live*.

"Right." Jamie wrapped her arms around her daughter. "I love you so much," she said with a squeeze.

"I love you too, Momma."

Charlotte, who was standing by her grandmother's side, watched them closely, as she often did. It was no secret that the First Lady wasn't the warm and fuzzy type, and neither was the president's mother, for that matter, but Jamie knew that President Grand was a big softie and more than made up for it. Jamie winked at Charlotte, who smiled.

Secret Service agents appeared at the end of the hallway, followed by Phillip Grand's looming head, which tended to tower over most others in his proximity. His large eyes searched the hallway. "Jamie, are you ready? We're just about—"

"Daddy!" Charlotte squealed and ran into her father's arms.

"Hey, cookie." The president lifted Charlotte into the air. "How was school?"

"Great! We learned about fractions."

"Ah, very important," the president said, placing Charlotte on the ground. "I want to hear all about it later. Daddy has to go now with Jamie. You and Faith play, and I'll be back soon."

Jamie hurried back into her office and picked up a package of hard candies to smooth things over with the secretary of homeland security, who had a notorious sweet tooth.

"Remember, girls, talk it through!" Jamie called, joining the president and adjusting her jacket. "Pretend you're the ambassadors for two countries and that you need to resolve your situation through diplomacy."

"What?" Faith asked, puzzled.

"Be nice to one another," Jamie rephrased. "Be fair, and, most important, have fun!"

"We will, Momma!" Faith yelled as Charlotte grabbed her hand and pulled her in the opposite direction.

"Where are we going?" Faith asked.

Charlotte put her finger to her lips and tiptoed past her grandmother toward the presidential bedroom suite.

Faith dragged her feet. "I *told* you, Charlie. We're not supposed to play in here."

"You're such a scaredy-cat." Charlotte peeked into the president's bedroom. "I bet it has the best hiding spaces. Look how big it is." She waved her hands dramatically in the air. "You know all my spots in the other rooms. We've done them a gazillion times. A gazillion is more than a billion. You'll learn that in kindergarten."

"But I'm not sure—"

Charlotte pulled Faith around a small table with a lamp.

She turned it off. "Just this once, okay? You can listen to me. I have president's blood in me."

Faith shrugged. "I guess."

"It's okay," Charlotte said, patting Faith's head. "I know you really don't know anything about that. Having a daddy, I mean."

"You're being mean again," Faith said. She crossed her arms and narrowed her dark eyes.

"Don't look at me like that," Charlotte said. "It makes me feel weird." She peeked down the hallway where her grandmother was escorting Philly into another room. "Quick, here's our chance," she whispered. "Hide your eyes."

"Wait, what about *dipomacy*? What my momma said?"

Charlotte sighed. "Okay, you can hide first. We'll pretend that it's Opposite Day. Is that fair?"

"Yes!" Faith said, delighted.

Charlotte put her head into her folded arms on the table.

"No peeking," Faith said.

"I'm not." Charlotte squeezed her eyes shut. "You better hurry! I'm a really fast counter. One, two, three ..."

Faith ran into the large bedroom and stopped. She had never been in this room before, or if she had, she didn't remember what it looked like, and her eyes took in the large furnishings—desk, dresser, chairs, bed, curtains, rugs. She thought about hiding under the desk, but that would be the first place Charlotte would look. It always was. Behind the curtains would be the second place. Faith's eyes scanned the floor for some hiding places, and she noticed a space under the giant bed that was disguised by a little flowery curtain. If she got back far enough, Charlotte would never find her there.

"Seven, eight, nine ..." Charlotte called from the hallway.

Faith darted toward the bed and crawled underneath. It was dark, but the little curtain didn't hang all the way to the floor, so it let in a bit of light. She scooched back as far as she could when her hand touched something furry.

"*Ewww* ..." She pulled her hand back but realized it was one of President Grand's bedroom slippers—the ones he wore when he was stealing cookies from the kitchen in the middle of the night. She lifted the curtain and peeked out, hoping that Charlotte didn't hear her *ewww*.

"Thirteen, fourteen, fifteen ..."

Faith climbed over the slipper, and then its partner, making sure to place them neatly back where they were. As she scuttled farther back, the palm of her hand grazed something else, something big and hard—she ran her hand around it—and square. She thought maybe President Grand liked to keep a memory box under his bed like she did. She tried to push the box out of the way so she could hide, but it was heavy and wouldn't budge. She tried turning it, but it was wedged against the bottom of the bed. She lifted the little curtain facing the window, and the sunlight shined on it. Faith could see a little bit inside the top—it was filled with wires and smelled like a gas station and way down at the bottom she thought she saw her Hello Kitty watch. *What could it be doing in there?*

She could feel her arms start to get all bumpy like they did when she was cold. Her mother's words floated to her:

Be on the lookout for anyone—or anything—weird or out of the ordinary.

Was this weird, she wondered. Was it weird that

President Grand would steal her Hello Kitty watch? Weird enough to give up her hiding spot? Was this big, big trouble? Did big, big trouble come in a big, big box?

"Twenty-three, twenty-four, twenty-five …" Charlotte cheered. "Ready or not, here I come!"

Charlotte came charging toward the bedroom as Faith crawled out from under the bed.

"What are you doing?" Charlotte asked. "When I said *Opposite Day*, I didn't mean *this*. I can totally see you, and, yuck, you're full of dust."

Faith ran past her toward the hallway.

"Wait, where are you going?" Charlotte yelled, running after her.

"No-peanut emergency, no-peanut emergency," Faith whispered to herself, her speed across the varnished floor getting the attention of Agent Fuller down the hall.

"Faith, what is it?" he asked, but before he could get to her, Faith squeezed herself next to the bookcase outside Charlotte's bedroom, stood up on her tippy-toes, and slapped her hand against the red panic button, sounding the silent alarm.

2

Paul Wilcox gazed out his window at the view of downtown Arlington. It was a clear, crisp evening—or at least it looked like one from behind the thick window glass of the high-rise. Behind him, the flat-screen television played one of those fishing shows in which he had tried to take an interest over the past few years. Although once a favorite pastime, fishing no longer calmed and captivated him in the way it had. Not since the spring of 2014 when arguably Wilcox's biggest fish had gotten away.

That was Wilcox's theory, anyway. Everyone else—his colleagues at the FBI, the Grands, the Carters, the media—believed that Don Bailino was dead, and they had moved on to more pressing and exciting matters. And *why wouldn't they*, Wilcox thought, grabbing the remote control from the coffee table and turning off the television. Jamie Carter's own eyewitness account placed Bailino in a burning building that had collapsed before her very eyes. Wilcox's FBI team had discovered Bailino's severed hand, one of many body parts found in the old Barbara farmhouse in upstate New York that spring. Italian organized crime had gone quiet. Who was Wilcox to argue with the facts?

He grabbed a sparkling water from the fridge, crossed the living room, and set his drink on the ring-stained desk in his home office. All around him, on every wall, photos of organized crime members, from the Barbaras to the Cataldis, hung like fruit on family trees. He had gotten shit from his brother for rehanging all these mug shots after he had moved into the apartment, but the truth was, after decades in the Bureau, he probably felt more at home with these thugs than he did with members of his own family.

"What do you need all this crap for?" his brother Randy had asked. "Aren't you retired?"

Of course, *yes* was the official answer to that question.

Far from it was the unofficial one.

The men on the walls seemed to smile at him—even Gino Cataldi, who notoriously never smiled in photos because his younger brother Paolo used to torture him mercilessly about the space between his two front teeth. Wilcox tapped the side of his water bottle with his thumb. He had scrawled a giant X across every one of those faces except for one: Don Bailino, who stared back at him in defiance.

In what had become a daily ritual, Wilcox reached across his desk and retrieved one of the files from the Bailino case that he had copied from the Albany field office. He also pulled out several stacks of collated papers and copies of the photos taken at the Barbara farmhouse that night in 2014 and sat down. Wilcox didn't know why he went through the trouble of photographing the materials. Most of them mysteriously had become available on the Internet. These days, the FBI had more leaks than an old garden hose.

At the top of the pile was an image of Bailino's severed hand, hairy-knuckled and bloody. Although his team had pieced together the rest of the bodies discovered in the old farmhouse, like paleontologists reassembling a family of T. rexes, no other body part could be found belonging to Don Bailino. Wilcox picked up his loupe and scrutinized the hand, from wrist to fingertips, as he had done hundreds of times, each time leading to the same conclusion: The cut had been clean, like the others, and was likely to have been committed with the sword found on the premises.

However, Wilcox believed that the cut had been a little *too* clean. Whoever had sliced off Bailino's hand, right where the ulna and radius met the wrist, had been a bit too careful about it, whereas Paolo Cataldi had been sliced and diced like a side of beef. Wilcox leaned back in his chair and returned the photo to the pile. What this meant he still wasn't sure, but he knew that the photo represented what should have been the government's Exhibit A in an ongoing investigation of *United States v. Don Bailino* instead of what it was: a bookmark. After all, wouldn't it have been easy—at least, for a man like Bailino—to cauterize his wound in a burning building and use the farmhouse's large storm drains, as he had done before, to escape?

Yet, there was no evidence to prove that, and the Bureau's arson experts believed that the rest of Bailino had likely burned in the gas fire, which also ate up quite a bit of the farmhouse and the bodies that his team *did* find. Still, for Wilcox, no body meant no closure. Therefore, despite the DNA gumbo that was the Barbara crime scene and the racketeering radio silence, Wilcox believed that a dangerous psychopath was on the loose somewhere in the

United States, and he didn't much care if he was the only one who did.

His cell phone rang. He looked at the caller ID and swiped the screen.

"Wilcox," he said.

"Do you really have to answer the phone that way if you know it's me?" his brother asked.

"What can I say? Old habits die hard."

"You ever hear what they say about all work and no play?"

"What's up, Randy?" Wilcox said, impatiently.

"Against my better judgment, Ry asked me to call. She wants to know if you can make it for dinner tonight."

"Not tonight," Wilcox said.

"You said that last night, Paul. And the night before."

"I've got work."

"You're on the clock? Now? You're retired, remember?"

"Side work. Some consulting," Wilcox lied. "Thank Ry, and let her know I'll try for next week."

"All right, but, you know, we thought when you moved back we'd see some more of you."

"Tell Ry I'll make it up to her."

"Sure … Actually, I know how you can make it up to her," Randy said. "Ry's friend Bev is in town next week. It might be nice if we could schedule a dinner party. When's the last time you were within two feet of a real girl?"

"Very funny."

"I'm not being funny. Come. You'll have a good time."

"Is that all?" Wilcox said.

Randy sighed. "Yeah, I guess so. Get some air, man. You looked like shit the last time I saw you, whenever that was."

"I'll call you next week."

Wilcox clicked off the call and slipped the phone into his pocket. He had always assumed that environmental engineers like Randy were as busy as FBI agents, but his brother managed to spend quite a bit of time at his second job—trying to get Wilcox laid.

He pulled a box labeled *Organized Crime TD-1031* off a pile in the corner of the room, placed it on his desk, and opened the flaps. Wilcox often had remarked to FBI trainees that he could tell how long he had been in the organized crime game by the types of surveillance materials he had amassed over the years. This particular box was decades in the making; inside was an assortment of floppy disks, DVDs, digital recording devices, microfilm, Polaroid photos, and old cassette and VHS tapes. He spent a few minutes rummaging through it and picked up the DVD of the interview he had done with Paolo Cataldi at the FBI field office in Albany back in the spring of 2014. How smug Cataldi had seemed. Wilcox had watched it more than thirty times, and he always had the feeling that he had missed something. What, he didn't know, but he decided he would re-watch it later that evening.

Before shutting down his laptop, Wilcox logged onto his secure email client and browsed his in-box. Since his retirement, his emails—which used to number in the hundreds on any given day—had dwindled to a few Viagra ads and a bunch from Match.com, for which his brother had signed him up. This evening, however, one email stood out from the rest, and Wilcox was distracted by the sight of a familiar name: *Phillip Grand*. He clicked on the email:

Agent Wilcox—

Technically, Wilcox was no longer an agent, since he was retired, but he found that didn't matter much to any of his former colleagues and associates.

I have it on good authority that, should you accept the nomination, you will have the majority vote in the Senate when Director Randall's tenure ends next month. Still awaiting your answer. I need your decision.

Signed, Phillip Grand

Ten years earlier, there wouldn't have been a decision at all. Wilcox would have jumped at the chance to serve as director of the Federal Bureau of Investigation, the highest ranking member of the national security organization. What was stopping him now? He wasn't sure.

He shut down his laptop and leaned back in his chair. Phillip Grand was a good man. Wilcox believed that, as did the rest of the country—a whopping 80 percent of the voting population, including Democrats and Republicans, had voted for him in the last presidential election. However, Wilcox wasn't entirely convinced that Grand had come clean about what had transpired that night at the Barbara farmhouse, the night he managed to rescue Jamie and Faith Carter. The timing seemed off, his story too convenient.

Wilcox reached inside a manila folder on his desk and pulled out a photo of an antique bullet, the one that had been found inside Paolo Cataldi's eye socket, wedged against his cranium. The large, odd-shaped bullet was believed to have been fired by the antique pistol stolen, presumably by Bailino, from Phillip Grand's office at the Executive Mansion. And yet how did Bailino manage to get the pistol? Wilcox's thoughts again turned to Phillip Grand.

He pulled out the copies he had made of Phillip Grand's military records, which he had practically memorized. There was nothing remarkable about the president's military service other than his relationship with Bailino, whom he had met in army boot camp, the two of them older than most of the other cadets. Despite their many differences, the pair had become fast friends by virtually all accounts, and Bailino had even saved Phillip Grand's life in Iraq. Could Phillip Grand have known that Bailino would be in the farmhouse that night? Or had he, as was the official record, stumbled upon the burning building on his way to his housekeeper's?

Wilcox chugged the rest of his water and went into the kitchen, where the city was growing dark outside the windows. He tossed the bottle into the recycling bin as, one by one, street lights blinked on, illuminating the traffic below. He gazed at the men and women scrambling in and out of taxis and buildings. Apparently, nearly half of Arlington's population was single—or so his brother had told him practically every time he called. His brother also told him that it was impossible to meet anyone when he was fifteen stories aboveground. He had a point.

When his cell phone rang again, Wilcox had a good mind to let it go to voice mail. His brother and sister-in-law had a habit of tag-teaming him into submission, but the caller ID showed the call was Agent Brandon Fuller. Wilcox had been happy for the kid when he became a part of Grand's security detail. He was a smart agent who would serve the president well. Wilcox swiped the screen.

"Agent Fuller?" he said.

"Hello, sir."

Sir. As Wilcox told Randy, old habits die hard.

"What can I do for you?" Wilcox asked.

"Sir, the president asked me to contact you and ask if you might come to the White House." Brandon paused, which, Wilcox knew, meant that the young agent was about to deliver troubling news.

Wilcox felt the hair rise on the back of his neck. "What is it, Fuller?"

"Sir, we found an improvised explosive device in the White House."

"What?" Instinctively, Wilcox stepped away from the window and stood in the center of his living room. "Where?"

"Jamie Carter's daughter found it during a game of hide-and-seek with Charlotte Grand. It was in the president's private residence. It's been disarmed, and everyone is safe."

"Where is the president?"

"He and his family are in the PEOC. We're running a sweep of the White House now."

"When did this happen?" Wilcox's questions were coming fast and furious, and although Agent Fuller no longer reported to him, he answered every one.

"About two hours ago, sir. They're keeping it quiet right now, but word will—"

"I'll be there in twenty minutes," Wilcox said. "Tell the president I'm on my way."

Wilcox grabbed his car keys from the kitchen counter and was about to leave his apartment when he had a thought and hurried back into his office. Without really knowing why, he reached onto his desk and stuck the grisly photo of Bailino's hand into his coat pocket. As Wilcox made his way to his apartment door, his long-honed FBI sense was shooting information across his brain's synapses like a pinball, trying to make connections, trying to retrieve memories, and he couldn't help but wonder:

Was this the break he had been waiting for?

3

Phillip Grand sat with his head in his hands in the Presidential Emergency Operations Center beneath the East Wing of the White House. At the other end of the long conference table, his children were sitting next to their grandmother eating cookies and milk and playing on their iPads, trying to disregard the men in bulletproof vests with guns standing behind them.

Faith Carter's discovery of the explosive device in his private residence had sent the White House into what he could only describe as a subdued frenzy—Secret Service agents funneling onto every floor like insects, ushering staff out the door and he and his family downstairs to safety. In all the commotion, Phillip hadn't had time to think, but once everything quieted down it didn't take long for old fears to come roaring back.

Somebody wanted to do him and his family harm.

Again.

It was a lot to process. He looked around him at the familiar and unfamiliar faces of the joint-service military and noncommissioned officers whose job it was to protect him, and he was reminded of Charlotte's abduction and of Maddox's betrayal five years ago. He and Katherine had been vigilant about keeping a tight circle of trusted colleagues around them. Had they once again inadvertently exposed their family to harm?

"Daddy?"

Charlotte ran toward him, her curls bouncing around her face. His daughter had emerged from the abduction unscathed—she didn't remember it at all—but now that she was older and more cognizant of the dangers surrounding her family, Phillip worried that something might trigger a memory and how she would process what was happening now. She sat on his lap and looked up at him with her big blue eyes.

"When can we go back home, Daddy?" she asked.

"I don't know, pumpkin, but I need you to know you are safe. See all the men here?" He pointed to the security staff around them. "They're all here so that we can all be safe." He hoped his daughter didn't notice the uncertainty in his voice. There was a very real chance that the person who had placed the explosive device in the White House was standing in that very room. He pushed the thought aside. He had to.

"I know, Daddy," she said.

He touched her cheeks. "Are you taking care of your brother for me?"

She nodded. "He was scared, but Grandmother is reading him his favorite story." She pointed to the two across the table. "Where's Faith? The men didn't take her with us."

"She's not here right now, Charlie, but she's safe. She's with her mother."

"But why? Why doesn't she want to stay here with us?"

Phillip had wanted to know the same thing, but Jamie had been rattled—understandably so. Whatever Phillip thought he and his family had been through in the past five years, Jamie had been through far worse, and he wasn't about to put any demands on her. He trusted her judgment. "I asked, but her mother wanted to go someplace else."

"But Mommy said that this is the safest place to be," Charlotte insisted. "It's just not fair. Is it because I said it was Opposite Day?"

"Mr. President, a word?"

Josef Clark stood before him and smiled awkwardly at Charlotte, who stiffened on Phillip's lap. Charlotte had never taken to his chief of staff, which, normally, wouldn't set off any alarm bells for Phillip, but with the attempted bombing, Charlotte's small aversion suddenly seemed like a big deal. *Had Clark been in the private residence*, he wondered and then stopped himself. Why would Clark have reason to hurt Phillip? After all, hadn't he reclaimed the presidency for the Republican Party? Hadn't he brought Clark to the White House as part of his team? But did violence need a reason? He brushed the nagging fears aside.

"All right, button, go to Grandmother. I need to talk to Mr. Clark." He kissed his daughter's head, and Charlotte scampered toward Phillip Jr., running her hand along the smooth onyx of the conference table.

"Yes, Joe," Phillip said, standing up.

"Mr. President," Clark said, putting a hand on Phillip's shoulder. "How are you holding up?"

"I'm fine. Considering …" Clark's eyes were tired and puffy, as if he hadn't slept, which wasn't unusual. Clark was a night owl. Phillip had spent many a night burning the midnight oil with his chief of staff, who could outwork just about all of the White House employees, except Katherine.

Clark rubbed his stubbled chin and glanced around the Center. "It looks like everyone is all right," Clark said.

"Thank God," Phillip said. More than three thousand people worked full-time in the White House—people Phillip had brought with him from New York, people who had supported him throughout his presidential candidacy, all of whom had placed their trust in him. A good chunk of them were in this room. He had a responsibility to keep them safe as well. "How are you, Joe?" he asked.

"Me?" Clark shrugged. "I'm fine. Unfortunately, this isn't my first rodeo, Mr. President. These days, the Republican National Committee has experienced more than its fair share of bomb threats. It's what you might call the new normal."

Phillip shook his head. "Once upon a time, people could disagree without having to worry about getting into their cars—or into their beds."

"Times change, Mr. President." Clark leaned in closer. "But that doesn't mean our resolve has to. Whatever son of a bitch got to your private residence will get what's coming to 'em. I promise you that. We'll string him up old-school-like," he said with a wink.

Clark was a Louisiana native who had spent decades in the Senate. He was known in conservative circles as the Po' boy Pitbull, so while there was some humor in his comment, Phillip knew he meant what he said. The joke around the Capitol was that Josef Clark never showered—he only took blood baths. That wink alone could keep a gun control bill from passing the Senate.

Across the room, Rudy Ray Mitchell was talking with Katherine, who had been preparing for a presentation that evening for the League of Women Voters when the Secret Service agents brought her down to the Center. Her hair was still in an after-shower ponytail, her face shiny and free of make-up. Rudy Ray caught Phillip's eye and excused himself, and when he did, Phillip saw Clark wrinkle his nose.

The party hadn't been too happy with Rudy Ray as Phillip's vice presidential pick, claiming it had to do with his lack of political experience and not because he was black. The national committee had lobbied hard for Clark and a few other old-timers to be chosen as Phillip's running mate instead, but in the end, there was something about Rudy Ray Mitchell, a certified financial planner by trade, that made Phillip feel like he could trust him. He thought again of the explosive device. Had he been wrong?

"You all right, Phil?" Rudy Ray asked in his southern drawl, and Clark winced. Rudy Ray rarely called Phillip *Mr. President*, and while it was no big deal to Phillip, the conservative forums wanted to hang him for it.

"Yes, fine. Thanks, Rudy Ray."

Mitchell and Clark nodded politely at one another.

"Excuse me, Mr. President," Clark said. "I'm going to have a word with the First Lady." He stepped toward Katherine, who was talking now to the defense secretary. While most of Phillip's staff did everything they could to avoid going face-to-face with Katherine Grand, Clark seemed to relish it. Even with Clark's long and impressive resume, that alone should have qualified him for the position of chief of staff.

"Any word yet on what's going on?" Rudy Ray asked.

"No, but I expect a briefing from Agent Fuller any minute. It shouldn't be long now."

Rudy Ray nodded and surveyed the Center. Despite the circumstances, he appeared relaxed—but, then again, Rudy Ray Mitchell always appeared relaxed. "I don't think I've ever seen so many people in one room," he said. "Not even back when I was a boy in my gramma's small apartment for Thanksgiving!"

The Presidential Emergency Operations Center was a bunker that originally had been constructed for President Franklin D. Roosevelt during World War II. Phillip wondered how much the size of the government had grown since those days. "It is a bit tight in here," he said.

"In more ways than one," Rudy Ray said with his characteristic chuckle.

Phillip gave a small smile. His vice president was an outsider and, in many ways, the polar opposite of Josef Clark—he had few friends in the inner circles of Washington on either side of the aisle. Originally a Democrat, Rudy Ray had made waves in the black community when he jumped sides ten years ago, citing a lack of fiscal restraint in the Democratic Party. Since then, he had had to deal with being called an Uncle Tom by the NAACP and the Black Lives Matter activists while contending with the lingering racism of the Republican Party. Rudy Ray Mitchell might have been the only person in the Operations Center who wanted to bust out more than Phillip.

"The kids seem all right," Rudy Ray said. Charlotte and Philly were sharing a sprinkled donut with the secretary of transportation.

"They're tough kids," Phillip said.

"They take after their father."

"Have you met Katherine?" Phillip said with a smile.

"Ah, point taken. A strong family." Rudy Ray patted Phillip's shoulder. "You'll get through this."

Rudy Ray said the same thing during the election when the barbs had started slinging. Phillip had been accused by the media of placating to minorities with the appointment of a black man to the ticket, which Phillip thought absurd. Hadn't he stood side by side in the military with men and women of every race and creed, and, as governor of New York, established a legal roundtable filled with new and diverse voices? Yes, a black man would bode well for Phillip in the South, but it was also a risky move in other parts of the country. In the end, Phillip had chosen with his heart, and he hoped that he had "gotten through," as Rudy Ray remarked, because American voters had done the same.

A hush came over the room, and a bevy of Secret Service agents entered the already crowded bunker. Leading the pack was Brandon Fuller.

"I'll let you do your thing," Rudy Ray said and stepped aside as Brandon reached them.

"I just received word, Mr. President," Brandon said, without wasting any time. "It's all clear. It's safe for you and your family, and the cabinet members and the others, to return to the White House."

"Thank God," Phillip said and glanced around the Operations Center where just about every individual was looking at him expectantly. He took a step toward them and held up his hand. "Everyone, thank you for your patience," he said. "I was just informed by Secret Service that there is no longer a threat to the White House and that you may all return to your offices." A round of applause erupted. "Obviously, today's cabinet meeting will be postponed, and I will provide more specific details as I learn them. Until then, just know that you are safe, thanks to the hard work of Agent Fuller and all the members of our Secret Service and security staff." Phillip motioned to Brandon, whom he knew was not a fan of attention. Brandon cast his eyes downward and bowed his head slightly.

"Also," Phillip added, "I urge you to please exercise caution and not speak to anyone about what happened this afternoon until we know exactly what has transpired here. No need to get the rumor mill worked up. I appreciate your cooperation. Thank you, again."

As the crowd dispersed and made a move toward the exit, Katherine appeared at Phillip's side. "What do we know?" she asked Brandon.

"According to preliminary reports, it looks like it was a simple improvised explosive device," Brandon said. "Nothing complicated."

"For the love of God, how did such a thing get into the White House?" she demanded in a strained whisper, attracting a few stares from the people leaving the Center.

"It didn't," Brandon said.

"I don't understand," Phillip said.

Brandon's phone buzzed. "Excuse me, Mr. President." He picked up his phone. "Fuller … All right." He clipped the phone back onto his belt. "Sir, Special Agent Paul Wilcox is here."

The sound of Wilcox's name made Phillip relax in a way that reminded him of when he was a little boy and he heard his father's car door slam at the end of the day—as if the cavalry had arrived to shoulder some of Phillip's burden.

"Should I send him down?" Brandon asked.

"No." Phillip took Katherine's hand. "Let's get the kids. If we've got the all clear, I'd like to get out of here. The quicker we can get back to normal"—he thought of Clark and his mention of *the new normal*—"the better."

4

Bob leaned back on his stool at the restaurant's bar hoping someone would notice him. He was wearing his lucky deep purple business suit—the one he liked to wear on all the Sunday political shows as a symbol of nonpartisanship—but he didn't seem to catch anyone's eye except the butterface sitting at the far end of the bar whose heavily mascaraed stare he had been trying to avoid.

"Want another, buddy?" the bartender asked, sticking a white towel into a tumbler with his fist and swirling it around.

"Sure," Bob said, "and it's Bob."

"What is?"

"My name," Bob said with a confident grin, as if everyone should know it. "You must be new here."

The bartender gave a small smile and a refill on his gin and tonic and then walked down the bar to greet a white-haired old couple dressed for the theater.

Bob took a slug of his drink and slumped against the bar. It had been only five years since his book had come out about the abduction of little Charlotte Grand and Jamie—an international bestseller that had been the talk of practically every late-night talk show for a year—and he was starting to feel like he had little to show for it. Not so long ago, Bob couldn't walk down the street without being bombarded with autograph, selfie, and interview requests, which was virtually unheard of for authors, whose profiles usually hovered in the Howard Hughes range.

Even sales of the paperback had dwindled to only a few a week and wasn't doing much to get Bob's name back in the news these days. And now with Phillip Grand in Washington, his New York legal roundtable disbanded, and Jamie on television virtually every day, Bob had been left out in the cold.

His phone buzzed, and he pulled it eagerly from his jacket pocket, half-expecting it to be Chuck Todd from NBC, but his smile fizzled when he saw his mother's name. He placed the phone on top of the bar. He was in no mood for another lecture about leaving Worcester, Payne & Leach to start his own practice. "Don't you think you're jumping the gun? Who resigns after being made partner?" she had asked during Bob's last visit—a question to which his father had grunted, which was more than he usually said. *Like they ever had anything to do with his professional success.* If it were up to them, Bob would have had a "safe" career in his father's automobile parts wholesale business, driven a used car, and lived in some godforsaken middle-class neighborhood on Long Island, spending his days trying to remember what days to take his trash to the curb. The only thing he had ever done that his parents had approved of was marry Jamie—because she was safe, he knew. Safe and—surprise, surprise—a total bore.

Luckily, he and Jamie had managed to avoid one another

while they worked at the Albany Executive Mansion. It was not a surprise that she agreed with his parents about leaving Worcester, Payne & Leach. Like what she thought mattered. Bob had never listened to Jamie while they were married. He wasn't about to start now.

More patrons filed into the restaurant, the five o'clock crowd having worked up its usual hard thirst. Bob finished his drink and reached into his pocket to put a twenty on the bar when he saw Butterface heading in his direction. That was another thing he seemed to notice lately: There was a direct correlation between his profile and the beauty of the women he attracted—the less recognizable he had become, the uglier the chicks were who dug him. Talk about some *dog days*, he thought, quickly returning his phone to his jacket pocket. He nearly had his arms through its sleeves for a quick getaway when he got a whiff of wine, and Butterface whispered into his ear: "Wanna get outta here?"

"Actually, I do," he said, buttoning his jacket. "But not with you, hon."

"Married?" she asked, her smile too wide.

"Not anymore. Just not interested. I got court in the morning."

"Court?" she asked, pressing her breasts into the back of the barstool. "Judge, jury, or jackass lawyer?" She smiled again.

"The latter," he said. "Without the jackass."

"I'll be the judge of that," Butterface said seductively and put her hand on his forearm. "How's about I help relax you for your big day in court tomorrow?"

Bob rolled his eyes. "Listen … I'm trying to be nice, but

the truth is …" He pointed out the old woman standing at the bar with her old husband. "See that bitty over there? The one with so much foundation on her face that she looks like a cracked sidewalk and a wig that looks like she borrowed it from George Washington?"

"What about her?"

"I'd rather take her home than you. Actually, I'd rather take home George Washington."

Butterface poked her tongue into her cheek like a lollipop. "You don't have to be a dick about it," she said, stiffening. "I only came over here because you looked down in the dumps. My mistake."

"The only thing dumpy around here is you, hon," he said, turning his back on her and worming his way through the crowd.

At the other end of the bar, a television screen was broadcasting CNN, which was showing the front of the White House, and a pretty but middle-aged reporter was muttering something that Bob couldn't hear because the set was muted. He read the crawl at the bottom of the screen as he made his way toward the restaurant exit:

… unusual Secret Service activity at the White House. Sources say there may have been a security breach, but no word yet from the administration …

Outside the restaurant, the cold air whipped up some trash, and Bob pulled up his collar. He made a right and started walking toward Seventh Avenue, his mind on the words he had just read on the TV screen. *Fucked-up shit seems to follow that Phillip Grand wherever he goes like a bad penny*, he thought, even though Grand was quite possibly the most cautious person Bob had ever met. Bob couldn't blame the guy, of course, after what had happened to his daughter. *That middle-aged reporter better be ready to stand outside the White House all night,* Bob thought with a chuckle; that old stalwart Phillip Grand would spill his guts about whatever had happened today only when he was good and ready.

Bob debated whether or not to take a cab home but decided to duck into the subway instead—he'd take one last shot that someone might recognize him, maybe boost his mood. He descended the stairs and got on the R train, which pulled in just as he emerged onto the platform. Inside the train car, there were a few scattered seats, but Bob decided to stand, which made him look chivalrous, he thought. And also more exposed.

As the doors closed and the train car lurched forward, he caught the eye of a cute brunette who was sitting near the door. She smiled, just a little. So did he until he spied a large portfolio slanted against her knees. After being married to a writer, the last thing Bob wanted was another artist type in his life, although it was debatable whether what Jamie did was considered art. He unbuttoned his jacket, shifted his body, and faced the end of the train car, a big ripped poster for a medical alert company staring him in the face as more riders pressed their way into the subway car at the next stop.

He had seen on TV that the Metropolitan Transit Authority was finally planning on modernizing the subway system and rolling out open gangway cars, the city's way of packing even more sardines into these cans. The new cars were going to feature USB ports, flipped seats, digital displays, the works, but, knowing the speed with which things worked in New York City, Bob was doubtful he'd see them in his lifetime.

As the train pulled into Thirty-Fourth Street, he leaned against the grab pole, letting the passengers flow around him. Phillip Grand had been the impetus behind the MTA modernization when he was governor, an initiative spearheaded by that pushy broad he called a wife. "No great city had an outdated public transportation system," she had announced at one of the last news conferences the Grands gave before their move to Washington. Bob could still see Katherine Grand standing there like a queen—arms gesticulating around her, pearls tight around her neck like a noose. How Grand put up with that woman, he didn't know. As far as Bob was concerned, Katherine Grand had way too much access. Was it really necessary for her to attend every meeting of the legal roundtable? Phillip Grand wasn't one of those empty-headed politicians whose brains were filled only with the objectives of the people around him. The guy was Ivy League and a war veteran. What did he really need Katherine Grand for other than to pop out a few heirs? Bob had gotten sick of seeing Jamie at the beginning and end of every day; he couldn't imagine having to work with her all day too.

At the last stop in Manhattan, a horde of passengers got on, and Bob pressed himself against his grab pole as limbs, bodies, and backpacks leaned against him. Here he was, he thought, back in the subway again, amid the sweat and the urine stench, the last place he thought he'd be once Phillip Grand won the presidency. He had been as excited as anyone, not for Grand necessarily, but for his own prospects. Bob had been sure that Grand would ask him to be a member of his transition team after the roundtable had been disbanded and Grand announced he'd be taking a few of the lawyers with him to Washington. Considering all the help Bob had given him during Charlotte's abduction and his legal input over the years, he thought he was a shoo-in. Yet, Grand had gone all politically correct and hired two female attorneys— one Chinese American, the other black. Combined, they didn't have the years of law experience Bob did. Besides being poor choices, it was a slap in the face.

When the train got to his stop in Brooklyn, Bob got out with what seemed like half the subway car and jogged up the stairs, two by two, as if running an obstacle course with the guy next to him. The cold air quickly brushed away the subway soot, and Bob again buttoned his jacket and pulled up his collar. He had forgotten how this subway crap was for the birds. *Hot, cold, hot, cold*. He should have gotten an Uber.

"Excuse me?"

A woman hurried toward him from the subway station.

"Hi, I'm sorry to bother you, but we were just on the same subway car, and I saw you get out …"

Bob did his usual quick assessment: Judging by the light wrinkles around her eyes and mouth, the woman looked like she was in her midthirties. However, she was wearing a beanie, which pushed her blonde bangs into her eyes, making her look younger, but not young enough to fool him. Her carefully manicured hands were wrapped around a Starbucks coffee cup that had lipstick stains on the lid—signaling enough disposable income to get regular manicures and overpriced coffee.

"Yes," Bob said, suddenly interested. "What can I do for you?"

The woman hesitated, as if feeling foolish. "Are you, by any chance, Robert Scott? You know ... the author?"

A surge of heat ran through Bob's body. "Yes," he said with a smile. "I am."

"I thought so!" said the woman, her smile exposing a row of straight white teeth. "I googled you on the train when I saw you, and your Amazon page said you lived in Brooklyn, so I had a feeling ..." She took a breath. "I know you're going to think this is crazy ..."

"Not at all," Bob said. He tried to catch the eyes of the other people around him emerging from the subway station in order to draw more of a crowd. He took a step closer to the woman.

"Oh, good ... Well ... This is weird ... I don't really do this ..." She stamped her feet a bit as if she were cold. "But ... here goes ... I am part of a book club, and I'm not sure you do book clubs ... Not many authors do ... I mean, not many authors of your ... you know, caliber ... I mean, who doesn't know the story of Jamie Carter and Don Bailino? And you portrayed it so well. We read your book when it came out in paperback. We all loved it. I felt like I was there. Well, not really *there* ... You know what I mean."

"Yes, I do," Bob said. The woman was getting more attractive by the second. "And thank you."

"I mean, we're meeting this Saturday, and even though we're supposed to discuss another book, if you could, maybe, stop by … I don't know if you'd have any interest … We can't really pay you anything, but we do have wine and—"

"I'd love to," Bob said. He fished into his pocket. "Here's my business card. Email me the details, what time you're meeting, and all that, and I'll try and be there."

"Really? That's great!" the woman said, taking the card from his hand. "I'm Nadia, by the way. The girls are gonna flip when I tell them." She pulled down on her beanie, which smooshed the bangs against her eyes even more, and stuck out her hand. "Nice to meet you."

"You as well," Bob said, shaking her hand and noticing no wedding ring on the other.

"Okay, then …" She held up the business card and backed away. "I'll email you," she called.

Bob watched her go, her perfect thigh gap swaying between her jeaned legs. He practically jogged the three blocks to his apartment. His instincts had been good, after all—taking the subway, becoming an author, the private practice, divorcing Jamie. It all led him here. *Sure, a book club isn't as high profile as a national news slot*, he thought as he stepped inside the hallway of his building, *but it sure beats a butterface any day of the week.*

5

Wilcox was standing in the West Colonnade wearing his usual blue suit and starched white shirt, which surprised Phillip, although it shouldn't have. This was what retirement would look like for a man like Paul Wilcox, who had devoted his life to the Bureau. The longtime federal agent nodded as Phillip approached.

"Mr. President," Wilcox said. "It's good to see that you're all right. And the family?"

"Everyone's fine, thank you, Agent Wilcox."

"Mr. President, as you know, I'm no longer … with the Bureau." Wilcox gave a small nod. "Paul is fine."

It was clear by the expression on Wilcox's face that Paul was not fine. Phillip knew that Wilcox had been nudged into retirement. A new culture was taking root at the Bureau, one that relied more on technology than man power, and more on quantity rather than quality. This left no place for a veteran agent like Wilcox who believed time and teamwork is what solved cases, not hindered them.

"Thank you for coming." Phillip motioned toward the Oval Office. "Let's go to my office to talk."

Agents and staff members flowed silently around

them. Phillip held the door open for Wilcox and was about to close it behind them when Fred Collins came rushing forward.

"Mr. President? Do you have a moment?" he called.

Phillip didn't often work directly with his deputy press secretary, but with Jamie away he would need to. When Collins had been a reporter for a conservative news outlet in the D.C. area, he was known for his composure and coolness—with that smugness about him that journalists usually shared. However, the Collins approaching him now was of another sort—harried and sweating and looking as though he were going to pass out. Perhaps he was learning fast how much more difficult it was to make the news rather than deliver it.

"Mr. President, I think we need to go over your statement."

"There is no statement right now, Fred."

Collins looked astonished. "But, Mr. President, the press is outside the—"

"The press is always outside. I meant what I said in the PEOC."

"There are already murmurings, sir, about there being some kind of bomb in the White House, and I'm getting calls that—"

"You'll have to hold them off, Fred. I'm not in the business of giving misinformation, so until I know exactly what's going on, the press will have to wait." He motioned to Wilcox standing inside the Oval Office. "Have you met Special Agent Paul Wilcox?"

"No," Collins said, appearing dazed at the distraction. "Nice to meet you." He and Wilcox shook hands. "But, if I may, Mr. President … I'm not sure it's going to be easy to contain this and—"

"I'm afraid that's your job, Fred." Phillip thought he saw the color drain from Collins's face. He put his hand on his shoulder. "It will be all right. I will get you what you need as soon as I can. If need be, we'll cancel tomorrow morning's press briefing. Until Jamie returns, do your best."

"And when will Jamie—?"

"Thank you, Fred," Phillip said, stepping inside the Oval Office.

Collins was smart enough to take the hint and went fumbling back down the corridor, calling after the White House communications director as Phillip shut the door.

"Guy looks a bit green, no?" Wilcox said.

"He'll be all right," Phillip said, although he wasn't entirely convinced that Collins would be. "He's been thrown into the deep end of the pool."

He motioned for Wilcox to sit down on one of the mauve sofas that had been furnished by the previous administration. Clark had been getting on Phillip to redesign the room—"It's what new administrations do," he had said—but Phillip couldn't see the point of it. A couch was a couch. Maybe it was the conservative in him, but he couldn't rationalize the expense. He sat down on the other sofa facing Wilcox.

"You sent for me, Mr. President?" Wilcox asked.

Phillip nodded. "Agent Wilcox, we've had a long history together, you and I. You have helped me in very trying times in my life and in the lives of people I care about."

"I appreciate you saying that, Mr. President, but I was just doing my job."

"You went above and beyond, I think we both know that," Phillip said. "Other than Katherine and a select few, I trust you implicitly. I know you are a man of honor and a man of your word, which is the reason I would like to appoint you, as you know, as the new director of the Federal Bureau of Investigation—"

"Mr. President, I—"

"But that is not why I asked you to come today," Phillip said. He inched farther up on the sofa and leaned his elbows on his knees. "The list of people who have access to my private residence is short. Either there has been some breach of security or the person who has put my family in danger is very likely a member of my team or my staff, and that is a very difficult situation to consider, as you can imagine."

Wilcox nodded but said nothing.

"I need someone I can trust ... I know you've retired, Agent Wilcox, but I'd like to reinstate your credentials, temporarily, until we figure this out. You'd be working as a member of the Bureau but reporting directly to me. On special assignment. You'll have the full power of the office of the presidency behind you to do what you need. Agent Fuller and Katherine will be arriving shortly, and I expect Agent Fuller will be briefing me on the situation and next steps, and I'd like you to attend."

Wilcox stood, and Phillip thought for a moment that he was about to walk out the door, but instead the longtime special agent bowed his head and said, "It would be my honor, Mr. President."

"Good." Phillip stood up as well, and the men shook hands. "Again, you will have the full authority of the FBI, but will be reporting to me. Can you live with that?"

"I can," he said. "As long as you can live with me doing my job the way I need to do my job."

"I wouldn't ask for anything less, Agent Wilcox."

There was a double knock on the door, which was Katherine's signal, and she walked in with Agent Fuller. Katherine was the only one who would even think of entering the Oval Office without an invitation, which is why, Phillip believed, his wife had made a habit out of doing it—she liked the special privileges.

"Agent Wilcox," Katherine said and shook Wilcox's hand. "I'm sorry this meeting is due to such unfortunate circumstances."

"Mrs. Grand," Wilcox nodded. "You may call me Paul. Glad to see you are all right."

"Where are the children?" Phillip asked Katherine, who had changed her clothing and applied a bit of makeup.

"With your mother," she said. She sat down, and both Phillip and Wilcox returned to their places. Agent Fuller stood between the two sofas, his eyes on the four doors of the Oval Office and the windows. "You should know that Josef is inquiring about this meeting, as is Rudy Ray," Katherine said.

"We'll bring them and the others in shortly," Phillip said. "Right now, the information shared goes no further than the people in this room, the four of us." He leaned back and put his hand on Katherine's lap. "As everyone here knows, we've been, for lack of a better word, infiltrated, and we need to take that very seriously. I have trust in my staff and in my administration, or else they would not be working here, but I am also smart enough to know that trust only goes so far. I have the *utmost* trust in the people in this room, however. Is that understood?"

The three nodded.

"Good. Let's get started. Agent Wilcox, Agent Fuller was just telling us that he believes the explosive device was not brought into the White House. Isn't that right, Agent Fuller?"

"Yes, Mr. President," Brandon said. The young agent began rocking on his heels, reminding Phillip of a student giving a class presentation. "We believe that it was *made* here, in the White House, and brought into the president's private residence."

"Made?" Katherine said. "Like a cake?"

"In a sense, Mrs. Grand."

"What makes you say that, Agent Fuller?" Wilcox said.

"The IED was composed of found objects—baby food jars, metal utensils, a type of acid or gasoline, we'll have more specifics on that soon, but things easily collected and not readily noticed if they disappear. Improvised explosive devices usually consist of a few basic parts—a power supply, which could come from a flashlight battery, a detonator, a container to hold everything, and a trigger … It appears that portions of Faith Carter's Hello Kitty watch were even used as components."

"You can't be serious," Katherine said. "You can make a bomb from those things?"

"I'm afraid you can," Wilcox said.

"So what you're saying, Agent Fuller, is that this *thing* wasn't made overnight," Phillip said. "It was made over time."

"And right under our noses," Katherine added. She looked into Phillip's eyes.

"Yes," Brandon said grimly. "Carefully and methodically. The detonator was located under your pillow, Mr. President. It is a small miracle that little Faith Carter crawled under the bed and not on it."

Brandon's words hung in the air, and a feeling of violation sizzled through Phillip. His wife, his children, his family, his closest friends—they had all been in danger, and he hadn't known it.

"An individual, or individuals, crafted this, we assume, nearby and slid it under your bed, Mr. President," Brandon said. "But the good news—"

"There's good news?" Katherine asked.

"Yes, only so many people have access to the private residence. Right now, we believe it is highly unlikely that someone without clearance was able to get in undetected. Therefore, we are looking at only thirty or forty people who could have perpetrated this crime."

"Oh, is that all?" Katherine huffed with sarcasm.

Phillip agreed with his wife. This was far from good news. Perhaps the persons of interest could quickly be narrowed, but they were some of the people he trusted the most—and each had a veritable all-access pass to the White House.

"Cameras?" Wilcox asked.

Phillip shook his head. "Not in the private residence. Quite frankly, I didn't think I needed cameras. I do now."

"They're being installed as we speak, Mr. President," Brandon said.

Wilcox sat forward, his arms crossed. "Mr. President, I know that access to the private residence is restricted to immediate family, for the most part," Wilcox said. "Who else?"

"Some of the agents, such as Agent Fuller, have full access to the private residence," Phillip said, "as do some of the White House staff."

"And Jamie and Faith Carter?" Wilcox said.

"Of course. I already counted them," Phillip said. "Under family."

Wilcox nodded. "May I ask, Mr. President, where they are now? Jamie and Faith Carter?"

Phillip hesitated, and he wasn't sure why. "They're not in the White House," he said finally, almost defensively. "Jamie and Faith are off the premises."

"Mr. President, do you think that was the wisest choice for them, considering their history?"

Phillip could feel Katherine's and Brandon's eyes on him. It was a valid question.

"It wasn't my choice to make," Phillip said. "Jamie insisted on leaving. She was spooked. And I can't say I blame her."

"And yet she knows this house is probably the safest place that she could be," Wilcox said, "that her daughter could be."

"And, yet, there was an explosive device in this house, Agent Wilcox," Phillip said.

"What are you getting at, Agent Wilcox?" Katherine asked.

Wilcox didn't answer. His gaze remained on Phillip. "Where is Jamie going?" he asked. "To her brother's?"

"Actually, she's heading out west, I believe, for a few days."

"Did she leave an address?"

"What is this about, Agent Wilcox?" Katherine asked

again. It was clear that none of them were going to call him Paul. "I think we need to return to the matter at hand."

"With all due respect, Mrs. Grand, I am," Wilcox said.

The tension that had always existed between Katherine and Wilcox reared its ugly head, and Phillip held up his hand as if to defuse it. "She did not leave an address," he said. "And I didn't think to ask in all the commotion. Now … I'd like to return to Agent Fuller's briefing."

Wilcox appeared unsatisfied but settled back on the sofa and looked up at Brandon, who resumed his swaying.

"As I mentioned," the young agent said, "it looks like we're dealing with an IED, an improvised explosive device."

"What is believed to be its radius?" Phillip asked.

"As of now, we are guessing not much, only a few yards. It was rudimentary. Lethal, but rudimentary."

"Enough to harm us," Katherine said. Phillip squeezed her hand.

"Have you found anything other than the device?" Phillip asked.

Brandon shook his head. "No, Mr. President. Unfortunately, according to preliminary reports, the only fingerprints or hair samples we found belonged to little Faith Carter, members of your family, the Secret Service agents designated for the area, or the cleaning staff."

"Edna?" Katherine asked. "She's worked in the White House for years. For crying out loud, I never thought I'd miss Rosalia Garcia …"

"Let's not start a witch hunt," Phillip said. "Innocent until proven guilty."

"That being said," Brandon noted, "I'd like to begin questioning staff members, both those with access to the private residence as well as others who may have seen something unusual. Despite the limited persons of interest, I think it best to cast a wide net."

"Yes, go ahead," Phillip said. "Do what you need to. Agent Wilcox, any questions?"

"Just one," Wilcox said. "If Jamie Carter didn't leave an address, do you have any way of getting in touch with her?"

Brandon and Katherine looked at Phillip, who shouldn't have been surprised by the question. When Wilcox grabbed onto something, he had the bite force of a crocodile. He didn't let go.

"Katherine, Brandon, I'd like some time with Agent Wilcox alone, if that's all right. If you'll excuse us …" Katherine bristled, and Phillip could tell she was about to protest. "Katherine, please …" He put his hand on her knee.

She inhaled deeply and nodded, and she and Brandon headed for the exit. Phillip got up from the couch, poured two glasses of water, and handed one to Agent Wilcox. The longtime agent took it and moved to the window, looking out at the Rose Garden as Katherine closed the Oval Office door. Phillip drained his glass in one gulp and placed the emptied glass on his desk.

"You instructed me to do my job, Mr. President," Wilcox said before Phillip had a chance to speak. He placed his still-full glass next to Phillip's. "That's what I'm doing. I need to get a hold of Jamie Carter. Did she provide any contact information?"

Phillip let out a heavy sigh and sat back down on the sofa. "She gave me a phone number," he said finally.

"I believe you should contact her. There's something you need to consider. And I'm afraid you're not going to like it."

"What's that?"

Wilcox seemed to be thinking carefully about his words. "Mr. President, you know that there was a limit to the number of people who had access to your private residence. You just said so yourself."

"And?"

"I think you need to consider the fact that Jamie Carter is ... well, unfortunately, a suspect in the attempted bombing of the White House."

"A suspect?!" Phillip exclaimed, standing. "You can't be serious."

"I'm afraid I am."

"Agent Wilcox, you've known Jamie as long as I have, and you know damn well that what you're saying is crazy."

"I understand, and I agree with you, but, frankly, there's a short list of people who could have not only placed that explosive device in your bedroom but also put it together over an extended period of time. And she's one of them."

"This is absurd." Phillip raked his hands through his hair. "Her own daughter was here. Why would she do this?"

"I'm not saying she did. I'm saying she had the access, and we need to consider that."

"Does that mean the First Lady is a suspect, too?" Phillip asked. He could feel the scorn coating his tongue, his face aflame. "If access is the key, does that mean I am a suspect as well?"

"Mr. President ..." Wilcox, unrattled, crossed his arms

again. "You asked me here for a reason, and I believe it's to get to the bottom of what is happening. You said it yourself. You said you have a high degree of trust in me. However, in order to do my job the way I need to do my job, I need to speak with Jamie Carter."

Deep down, Phillip knew Wilcox was right, but his loyalty to Jamie was fierce. "She asked me not to give the telephone number to anyone," he said flatly.

Wilcox seemed unfazed. "And that doesn't seem odd to you?"

"In a word, Agent Wilcox? No. You were there with us. You *know* what that woman went through."

"I understand," Wilcox said, in his familiar calm, reassuring voice. "But even if she is innocent of any wrongdoing, and I suspect she is, she may know something that can help us. And … while we're on the subject of people who can help us, I'd also like to talk with Samuel O'Connell again."

"Samuel O'Connell?" The name made the hairs on the back of Phillip's neck rise. "You think he had something to do with this? He's a kid."

"He's the kid who took the video of you at the Barbara farmhouse. When I interviewed him three years ago, I got the feeling he knew more than he let on. About what, I'm not sure, but there's something there. I know it. He'd be a good place to start."

Phillip also believed that Samuel O'Connell knew more than he let on, and for that reason he had hoped to never hear from him again. "That is your decision," Phillip said. He reached for his jacket that had been hanging on the back of his office chair since he had been rushed down to the Presidential Emergency Operations Center. "You do what you need to. Your badge is waiting for you with security in the lobby. And about Jamie …" Phillip buttoned his jacket. "I will contact her and let her know what is going on and inquire as to when she will be returning."

"Thank you, Mr. President."

"Now, if you'll excuse me," Phillip said, heading toward the door. "I have to go give Collins—and maybe Katherine—some oxygen."

6

Jamie had been driving for nearly twelve hours, and after an eighteen-hour trip the day before, she should have been exhausted, but her adrenaline was still pumping. It was as if the near-explosion at the White House had awakened some kind of long-dormant plan, buried in the deep recesses of her brain, that kicked into action: *Get Faith to safety, and do it now*.

She looked through her rearview mirror at the backseat of the rental car where Faith was sleeping fitfully in her car seat, lulled by the constant drone of the motor. Her expression, although innocent, conveyed such a gravity that was beyond her years. How could Faith only have been four years old? While other parents were marveling at how quickly time was moving, Jamie, instead, felt like the years inched forward as if coated in mud. She imagined that's what happened when each day—each minute of each day—was fraught with worry:

Why is that man staring?

Where are the building exits in case we need to leave?

Is someone following us?

Constant vigilance was draining. And if the worries seemed to be putting the years on the little girl's face, Jamie could only imagine what they were doing to her own.

She checked her rearview and side-view mirrors. When she was a freelance writer, she had once written a feature story about a private investigator and had learned all kinds of useful tips about how to conduct a stakeout or spot a tail, but she never thought she'd ever use them—or remember them. Now, they were a part of her every day—varying her routes to the supermarket, driving a half hour out of her way to visit Edward, always carrying a change of clothing, including sunglasses and hats—all to make sure she wasn't being followed. Routine, the autopilot that gets most people through their days, would never be a part of hers. Or Faith's.

"Momma?" Faith stretched her arms and changed positions, the chewed-up straw that dangled out of her mouth dropping to the car floor. "Are we there yet?"

"Almost, sweetie. You want to watch another movie?"

Faith shrugged. She had already seen the movies they had brought twice. "I guess."

"I'll tell you what, just one more movie, and by the time the movie is finished, we will be there. Deal?"

Faith smiled. "Deal."

Jamie slipped *Finding Nemo*, Faith's favorite, into the DVD player as the little girl settled again into her car seat, and she pulled the wrinkled map that was lying on the front passenger seat onto her lap. Jamie bristled at how few ragged, zigzaggy lines there were in this part of the country. If there was one thing she learned on her first trip out west, it was that there was a lot of wide open space. The topography looked more like a tic-tac-toe board than a map, and she instinctively looked once again at her mirrors, missing the safety of the East Coast's tangle of roadways. Fewer routes meant that she and Faith would be easier to find if anyone was looking for them, not that Jamie was sure anyone was. At least not yet.

She put her finger on the city of Cody, Wyoming, which looked like a pencil point being swallowed up by white space, and she was overcome with doubt. Was she crazy? President Grand seemed to think she was, dragging her daughter away from the people who loved her the most as well as the Secret Service, arguably the best law enforcement in the world. She probably was, but the moment that silent alarm had rung, Jamie could think of only one place to go—an address she had kept secret for more than three years:

33 Cooper Court, Cody, Wyoming.

She put her blinker on and changed lanes. In her mind's eye, she could still see Bailino sitting in the driver's seat of Joey's car, intent on taking them to this place that he claimed could keep them safe. Yet, that was more than three years ago. Would they be safe there now?

After another hour, Jamie got off at an exit for Cody and brought the rental car to a stop on a desolate corner. A large billboard shouted that the town was named after Colonel William Frederick "Buffalo Bill" Cody, but there was little to see beyond the flat, unforgiving terrain, the mountains in the distance looking like stacked rocks. She stared at the map.

"Are we there, Momma?" Faith asked, looking out the window.

"Almost," Jamie said, but she was having second

thoughts. She felt more exposed than ever out there, and if she hadn't kept Faith cooped up in the car for all this time already, she had a good mind to turn back and come up with some kind of Plan B. She turned on her burner phone and checked to see if Phillip Grand had left her any messages. He hadn't. She turned it back off.

"Which way are we supposed to go?" Faith asked.

Jamie didn't know. She was reluctant to plug the address into an electronic device, which was no-no number one if you were trying to lose a tail. She decided to drive for a bit. Maybe she would come across a visitor or tourist center.

She put the car into gear and drove for a few minutes until she came upon an old man with a cane ambling along the side of the road. His sunken face was covered by flaps of skin and a ZZ Top beard. What were the odds that this guy was following them or was some kind of serial killer? She'd have to take her chances. Still, she reached down to feel for her pistol sitting in her calf holster before pulling the car next to him.

"Excuse me," she said, rolling down her window. In her rearview mirror, she could see Faith sitting upright in her seat, looking curiously at the old man.

The man slowed down but continued walking, as if afraid to stop because he might not start again. "Good afternoon, ma'am," he said. "Are you lost?"

"No, not exactly ..." Jamie said. She knew she probably looked lost, but it was no-no number two to say that to a stranger. She kept her hand on the pistol under her jeans.

"Figured you might be," the man said. "You don't look like you're from these parts. I'm guessing you're from back East?"

Jamie's hand squeezed the pistol tighter. "Why do you say that?"

"You got that anxiousness all about your face." The old man chuckled. "Plus, you got Virginia plates." He smiled. "Where you off to?"

"I'm looking for Cooper Court."

"Oh, the Carter place?"

Jamie stiffened at the sound of her name. "Um, I didn't …"

"Well, the Carter place is the only thing on Cooper Court, so that must be where you're off to, unless you've got your signals crossed. Most people from back East do." He chuckled again.

"Yes, I guess that's what I'm looking for." She glanced again in the rearview mirror at Faith, who was still eyeing the man closely. "The Carter place."

The man lifted his eyebrows in surprise. "Don't get many people looking to go there." He scratched his cheek and looked around as if trying to remember where he was. "Well, then, you're not far at all." He pointed down the road. "Just make a turn here and follow this road about three miles. Make a left when you get to Marge's store, which is the one with all the nice tables outside. She sells ices in the summertime. The kids love it." He ducked his head down. "Hello, little lady."

Faith smiled but didn't say anything.

"You mentioned Marge's store," Jamie said, trying to redirect the man's attention. She inched the car forward to keep up with him. "Is Cooper Court close to there?"

"*Yessiree*, just make a left and take that road all the way north to Cooper, and you'll see it there a ways down, on your right."

"Thank you so much." Jamie turned the steering wheel to get back on the road and sped in the direction the old man had indicated.

"Have a nice day!" she heard him call. "And, remember, no need to be in such a rush. You're in the West now!" He said something else, but by then Jamie had closed the window.

"Was that a nice man, Momma?" Faith asked when they had driven a few blocks.

"I don't know," Jamie said. "I don't really know him very well."

"Yeah, I don't either," Faith said, narrowing her eyes.

Jamie had been in Cody, Wyoming, for only a few minutes, but she felt like she had already seen everything there was to see. Yet, in another mile or so a small downtown appeared, resembling something out of a John Wayne western. Old-fashioned storefronts stood side by side and in various weathered colors, offering clothing and housewares, ice cream, beer, and leather goods. Then came the more familiar stuff—gas stations, banks, wireless telecommunications stores, a McDonald's, and a few museums, including the Buffalo Bill museum. Soon, Marge's store appeared, just as the old man had described. It was hard to miss. Colorful flags surrounded it on all sides as if the restaurant were being suspended like a hammock.

"Are we getting ices?" Faith asked, brightening.

"I'm not sure they're open, honey. It's not summertime anymore."

"Can't we stop and see?"

"Not today."

"Tomorrow?"

"Yes, tomorrow," Jamie said finally, and Faith sat back in her seat, satisfied.

Jamie made a left turn down a narrow road that took them quickly out of the downtown area and onto another barren landscape. After driving for twenty minutes, her internal antennae perked up. She was beginning to think that the old man had given her bum directions.

Out of the corner of her eye, she saw Faith's arms wave in the air.

"Momma, look, snow!" she squealed as tiny snowflakes began to dot the front windshield.

"I see it," Jamie said, putting on her windshield wipers.

The flakes became larger and more frequent, and Jamie's ears began to pop with the rise in elevation. They came upon a small intersection or what appeared to be an intersection—the cross street was barely a dirt road. Jamie stopped the car, the sound of the motor and the thump of the windshield wiper the only sound in the desolate landscape, where the snow was settling all around them.

"This can't be it," Jamie said, looking for a street sign. "Maybe I missed it?"

"Momma!" Faith pointed outside the window. "It's a sign!"

"Where?" Jamie leaned over and peered out the passenger window but didn't see anything beyond a line of trees.

Faith was pointing toward the ground. "Down there."

Jamie put the car in park, took off her seat belt, and moved closer to the window. Outside, on the ground, was a wooden street sign that read *Cooper Court*.

"Is that it?" Faith asked. "It begins with a C. Is that the one we're looking for?"

"Yes, honey, that's the one."

Perhaps the old man had come through. She put the car into gear and was about to make a right on the small road when Faith called out again.

"Momma, look!" She was pointing about ten yards down Cooper Court at a wooden post, and that's when Jamie saw it: a mailbox. She turned right and inched the car up to the post to read the name hanging on a small plank of wood:

Carter.

She caught her breath. This was it.

"Hey, that says my name," Faith said. "C-A-R-T-E-R. Carter. Why does it say my name, Momma? And why did that man say our name? Is this our house?"

"I'm not sure."

"But—"

"Hold on, honey, just let me think for a minute. I have to figure some things out."

Seeing her name on the tiny sign in the middle of nowhere was both reassuring and unsettling, as if she and Faith were being expected. She didn't like that. She tried to remember what Bailino had said about the man who lived there. He was an architect and lived alone, but so much could have changed in three years. Had the man married? Had he moved away and had someone else moved in? Why did it say *Carter*? Had that been the man's name? She looked around and saw nothing but trees and mountains, but the snow was really coming down now, hampering visibility. Was the Carter home even there anymore? Had the place been razed?

She pressed the gas pedal, and the car's wheels spun on the ice.

Shit.

"Momma, I'm getting cold," Faith said.

Jamie pressed the gas pedal, this time harder, but the wheels only spun faster. She quickly turned on the heat, threw the car into reverse, and floored it. The car bucked backward off the icy patch until they were back in the intersection. Still not a car in any direction.

"Are we going to Carter's house, Momma?" Faith asked.

The sun, now hidden behind a gray blanket, seemed to be quickly sinking. They didn't have much time before sunset.

"Yes, we'll see what's there, honey." She put the car back into drive, drove around the ice patch, and continued down Cooper Court.

The road was uneven, the rental car bucking up and down like a bronco. In her rearview mirror, Faith's little body bounced up and down in the car seat. They drove for five more minutes, the road curving into a patch of tall trees, and the snow disappeared entirely until they came out the other side. Now Jamie could tell she was on a hill. She was getting concerned—the farther they drove from the town, the longer it was going to take to get back, and it was already beginning to get dark.

"Maybe we should head back," Jamie said. She pulled the car onto a patch of clean snow at the crest of a small hill and caught her breath.

Below them, down a short roadway, was an enormous log cabin.

"Momma, look!" Faith said.

"I know. I see it, honey."

"Is that Carter's house?"

"I don't know."

She drove slowly toward the home, her tires crunching the snow along the pebbled driveway, and stopped just before the house.

"Are we here?" Faith said eagerly.

It was quiet, but Jamie's quickened heartbeat rang in her ears. The large house was three stories high and nearly identical to the contemporary-styled log cabin Bailino had owned in upstate New York. The home's large floor-to-ceiling windows faced west, and Jamie imagined whoever lived there had a stunning view of the sunset each evening. Behind it was a smaller house, which must have been the guesthouse Bailino mentioned to her, where he had planned on staying.

Jamie sat in the car for a few minutes to see if anyone would come out to greet them, but no one did. She threw the car into park, turned off the ignition, the silence settling on the car like a blanket, and opened the door. As she got out, her legs buckled beneath her, and she almost landed in the snow.

"Momma, are you okay?"

"Yes, sweetie." She stretched her legs as she opened the back door and Faith tumbled out of the car.

"My legs don't work either, Momma," she said with a laugh, landing in the snow.

"Careful, sweetie," she said. "Don't get too wet." She frowned at the little girl's sneakers and her own Mary Janes. Neither of them were prepared for this weather.

"It's so cold, Momma, but, look, it's melting in my hands." Faith dug her hands into the snow and scrunched up a handful into a ball.

Jamie smiled. It had been a long time since Faith had played in the snow. Washington, D.C., hadn't seen more than an inch or two since they moved there late last year.

"Kick your legs into the air a little bit," Jamie said. "You'll get the blood moving and also get some of that snow off your sneakers." The little girl hopped around like a bunny.

"C'mon, let's go see who's home," Jamie said. She took Faith's hand, and they walked toward the log cabin.

"It's so pretty here," Faith said. "Who lives here, Momma?"

"A man."

"His name is Carter too?"

"I think so."

When they got to the wooden porch of the main house, Jamie stamped her shoes—she could already feel the snow seeping through the cotton of her socks. She rang the doorbell. *Who did Bailino say she was supposed to say she was?* The owner's wife and daughter? She couldn't remember. Would the man let them stay in the guest house?

"There is so much space here, Momma, look …" Faith twirled around with her arms out. "Do you think I can have my own room here? There looks like there are so many rooms in the house."

Jamie wondered if she'd ever feel safe enough to let Faith sleep in a room by herself. "We'll see, honey," she said. She rang the doorbell again and knocked on the door.

The wind howled from a group of trees, making the

legs of a tiny porch accessory in the shape of a frog spin. No one seemed to be home. She peered into one of the windows, cupping her hands around her eyes. The rooms looked empty—no furniture, just clean, swept floors. It looked abandoned.

"Is anyone home, Momma?" Faith asked. The little girl had her arms wrapped around herself. Jamie had to get her inside somewhere fast.

"It doesn't look like it," Jamie said. She flipped up the welcome mat, thinking for some reason that there might be a key there, but there wasn't. She didn't see any car and thought maybe there was one in the garage, but there were no windows on the garage door, and the freshly fallen snow had covered any tracks that there might have been.

"Do you smell that, Momma?" Faith asked. "It smells like fire." She was trying to use her tongue to catch the falling snowflakes, which were piling on top of her dark hair like a crown.

Jamie inhaled and realized Faith was right. She feared it was a brush fire but then saw a faint plume of smoke coming from the guesthouse chimney. She took Faith's hand again, and the two walked the few yards to what was a miniature version of the main log cabin. She was about to knock on the door when a sound caught her ear, and she instinctively pulled her daughter toward her.

"Momma, what was that?" Faith whispered.

"*Shhh* ... sweetie. Let mommy listen."

Jamie scanned the snow-covered ground and didn't see anything but then heard the sound again—it was like intermittent heavy breathing and the sifting of snow.

She reached for the gun in her calf holster, thinking perhaps it was a bear, and tried to remember what to do when confronting a bear or other wildlife. She couldn't remember a thing, and in this weather, the damn thing was probably hungry.

She nudged Faith behind her as the sound grew louder, and clearer, like the paced breath of a runner. She pressed herself and Faith against the front door of the guesthouse when a giant animal pounced onto the far end of the porch, its large eyes on them, its breath turning to vapor.

Faith screamed and clutched Jamie's leg as Jamie pointed the gun at the animal, which resembled a big wolf of some kind. The creature shook the snow off its coat and then stood there, eyeing them curiously. One of its eyes was missing, the skin neatly flapped over the eye socket, as if it had surgery. She waited for it to attack, but it didn't show any signs of aggression when she heard the sound of crunchy footsteps again, and before Jamie could prepare herself for facing another animal, a large person in a black parka climbed onto the wooden porch and stopped short at the sight of them.

Jamie immediately pointed the gun toward the individual, who, based on his physical size, appeared to be a man. He stood beside the animal, a large pair of mirrored sunglasses wrapped around his eyes, and put his hands into the air.

"Hello," Jamie said. "I'm sorry. I don't mean to have this pointed toward you. I won't use it unless I have to. I'm looking for the person who lives here."

The wolf started to walk toward them, but before Jamie could move the gun, the man whistled and the animal stayed where it was and sat down. The man gestured at his parka hood.

"Okay, but, please, no sudden movements," Jamie said. "I'm faster than I look."

The man brushed the snow from his black hood, which he pulled down from his head, and removed his wraparound sunglasses. Jamie stared at his face, the weathered features slowly forming a familiar picture, and she gasped. Standing before her, with the sun setting behind him, was a bearded and sunburned Don Bailino.

7

There weren't many times in Don Bailino's life when he was stunned, but this was one of them. He assumed that the car motor he had heard while hiking with Lucky belonged to Goodwill and was somewhat pissed at himself for not listening more closely. *Damn country living was making him soft.* However, he had more pressing matters at the moment—particularly, the expression on Jamie Carter's face. He kept his arms raised, wondering if Jamie would lower the pistol now that she knew it was him. She didn't.

"I don't understand …" she said.

"Don't be scared."

"I'm not," she answered, although the gun was shaking in her hand. "You're alive? How? I saw that building come down."

"Put the gun down, please."

Jamie looked at the dog.

"She won't hurt you. Trust me, she wouldn't hurt a fly. She doesn't realize how big and terrifying she is." The dog looked up at him while he spoke, not sure of what to make of this detour from their routine. "I need to show you something," he said to Jamie.

She watched him carefully. "What?"

"Why the Feds think I'm dead."

Slowly, Bailino twisted his left arm upward, the sleeve of his fleece jacket falling until the stump of his left arm—the skin, hardened and scarred, where his hand used to be—rose above the cuff. "Does anyone know you're here?" he asked.

Jamie stared at his arm. After a few seconds, she lowered the gun. Her fingers worked the mechanism quickly, adjusting the safety. She had been practicing. The little girl, whose head was leaning against her mother's waist, watched him closely.

"I asked if anyone knows you're here," he said, lowering his arms. Her answer, he knew, was important: If she said yes, he would have to pack his things immediately and get them all out of there. If she said no, it meant that they had some time and also that she still trusted him, at least enough to drive cross-country to find the address he had told her. Unless, of course, she was lying, but despite that little hiccup in judgment with the car, Bailino was still confident he would be able to tell if she was.

"No," she said. "No one knows we're here."

"The president?"

"He only knows we're out west for a few days."

"Edward?"

She shook her head. "No. Not yet."

Bailino nodded and brushed the melting snow off his jacket. "All right, then. Let me get you inside before you both freeze to death."

He crossed the porch toward the front door as Jamie stepped aside. He could tell she was shivering, and he didn't know if it was because of the cold or because of whatever had driven her onto his doorstep—or maybe it was learning that he was alive. He turned the knob of the front door. "It's unlocked, by the way," he said. "You should always check." He motioned to the dog. "C'mon, Lucky."

Lucky stopped first to sniff their guests, and Faith let out a yelp, hiding behind her mother's legs.

"She won't hurt you, cupcake," Bailino said as Lucky scampered into the room and went straight toward the fireplace, curling herself up on the worn spot of the area rug. Bailino pulled off his jacket as Jamie and Faith watched from outside, their eyes glued to his left arm. Most days, he forgot that he no longer had a left hand. Moving to Wyoming from the East Coast had been more of an adjustment than learning to live without it.

"It's much warmer in here, you know?" he said with a smirk, but Jamie stood where she was. He let her be, and by the time he had a teakettle of hot water on the stove, she had stepped into the cabin with Faith behind her and closed the door. If Bailino harbored any lingering doubts about Jamie feeling safe with him, they dissipated as soon as she turned the deadbolt, locking them inside. He placed two mugs and a plastic cup on the table. "Can I take your coats?"

"We're okay right now," Jamie said, standing near the door.

Bailino nodded. "What happened?" he asked. "In D.C.?"

Jamie motioned to Faith, who was still behind her, staring at him.

"Hey, sweetie, do you want to watch some TV?" he asked.

She shook her head. "No, thank you," she whispered, her finger twirling a strand of her hair.

She had changed so much in the last three years. Her features had become more defined, and her hair was long and straight. Only her eyes were the same—a deep and piercing dark brown that sucked in her surroundings like a vacuum. Although the First Lady tended to parade her two children around like trained monkeys, Bailino never managed to catch a glimpse of Faith on television or in the papers. Jamie had always kept her out of sight. And he was happy for it.

Bailino's cell phone buzzed in his pocket. He looked at the caller ID, saw the name Ellie, and declined the call. "Do you want to play with Lucky?" he asked Faith, putting the phone back into his pocket.

The little girl eyed the dog, which was probably twice her size.

"What happened to her eye?" Faith asked.

"I don't know. I think somebody tried to hurt her, but I took her to the doctor, and now she's fine. Probably sees better out of that one eye than we do with two."

Faith's eyes appeared to soften, but she stayed safely behind her mother.

"Here," Bailino reached into a cabinet over the sink, "give her one of these, and she'll be your best friend." He walked toward them with his hand out, holding the dog biscuit, and slowly Faith reached out to grab the treat, her tiny hand red and cold from being outside. As she did, Lucky came running over, and the little girl recoiled.

"Her name is Lucky," Bailino said. "She's a nice dog." He petted the top of Lucky's head. "Go ahead, tell her to sit. Say, *Lucky, sit.*"

Upon hearing Bailino's command, the dog sat in front of them, her eyes on the treat in Faith's hand. Faith dropped the treat to the floor, and Lucky ate it in one bite. The dog continued to sit, her eyes looking up at the little girl, until Bailino said, "No more," and then returned to her place on the area rug.

"How about you?" he asked Faith. "You want something to eat? I have soup, some leftover pizza, blueberries ..."

The little girl's eyes opened slightly at the mention of blueberries.

"Here, come sit down, and I'll get them for you," Bailino said.

He opened the refrigerator, threading the stump of his left arm through the handle, grabbed a pint of blueberries, and ran it under cold water from the kitchen faucet. Faith was still watching him carefully, and his mind shot back to when he had served her blueberries at his father's old house in Pennsylvania. Although she had been distrustful of him at first, she hadn't been afraid of him. He wondered if she would be afraid now.

He placed the blueberries in a bowl and onto the table. "Go ahead, cupcake, they're all for you," he said.

Jamie took a few steps into the room, Faith hiding behind her, and pulled out a chair. "Want some?" she asked.

The little girl nodded and quickly climbed on the chair, her attention pivoting between Bailino and the dog. She reached into the bowl and placed a blueberry in her mouth, her other hand firmly grasping her mother's leg.

"Are you sure you don't want me to take your coats? It gets warm in here pretty quickly."

"All right, thank you," Jamie said. She unbuttoned Faith's coat and her own, and she handed them to Bailino—careful, he noticed, not to touch him or come too close. He brought the coats into his bedroom and laid them on a chair. He stood in there watching as Jamie brushed the hair out of Faith's face and planted a kiss on her forehead, something he had seen her do before, not only with Faith but with tiny Charlotte Grand. He would be lying if he said he hadn't wondered whether Jamie would show up on his doorstep out of the blue, either because she was in danger or out of some kind of curiosity about the place—or perhaps because somehow, intuitively, she knew he would be there. Sometimes he wondered if that was why he was still living there.

"How come you don't live in the main house?" Jamie asked when he returned to the kitchen. She was caressing Faith, who had now turned her entire attention to the dog.

"Yeah, never did make the move over there," Bailino said. "Guesthouse suited me fine."

"What happened to the tenant?"

"I got rid of him," Bailino said. "Stabbed him with an ice pick."

Jamie's hand stopped moving on the top of Faith's head.

"I'm kidding," Bailino said. "His job moved to Seattle about a year ago. Never had any reason to rent it out again. I like the privacy." He opened the fridge and placed a container of chocolate milk on the table. "I always keep a carton in the house." He smirked.

The milk got Faith's attention, and she tugged on her mother's arm.

"Would you like some chocolate milk too?" he asked.

"Yes, please," Faith said, sticking another blueberry in her mouth.

Bailino poured the milk into the plastic cup and set the carton back down on the table. "Do you have luggage in the car? Give me your keys, and I'll go—"

"It's okay. I mean, I don't want to mess you up. I really didn't know that you'd be—"

"You think I'm going to let you go now that you're here?" Bailino asked, and, again, Jamie's expression changed. "All right, relax … What I mean is … and I think you know this … you are safest here. With me. Right?"

He could tell Jamie was thinking. She stared at him, into his eyes for a long time, fingering the gun, which she had placed under the waistband of her jeans. She looked down at her daughter. "Is that okay with you?" she asked. "Do you want to stay here?"

Faith leaned against her mother's chest, her eyes looking up at Bailino and then down at the dog. She nodded.

"Good," Bailino said. "It's settled then. Are the car doors open?"

"Yes, but I can—"

"No, no, you stay here with the kid. Eat. Make yourself at home."

Outside, the air was clear, and although it was dark, the fallen snow made it appear like daytime. He followed the footsteps to the other side of the log cabin where Jamie's car was parked. Because the car's exterior was covered in snow, he didn't recognize the model right away, but he could tell it was a rental based on the color variation of the Virginia license plate tucked under the front grill. He opened up the driver's-side door and scanned the dashboard for an in-car GPS, but he didn't see one, only maps on the passenger seat.

Good girl, he thought.

He pulled the three bags of luggage out of the car, closed the doors, and searched the property. Other than Jamie and Faith's footprints and the rental's single set of tire tracks, the snow was undisturbed. By the time he got back inside the house, Lucky was lying on her back near the dining room table.

"She wants you to rub her belly," Bailino said, placing the luggage down and closing the front door.

Faith looked up at her mother. "Can I, Momma?"

Jamie said, "Okay, but be careful."

Faith stretched her hand toward the floor, but she couldn't reach far enough because she wouldn't let go of her mother's leg.

"You're going to have to get a little closer, I think," Jamie said. "Here, watch me."

Jamie got down on her knees next to the dog and began rubbing Lucky's belly. When she stopped, Lucky moved her front paws up and down.

"What is she doing?" Faith asked Bailino.

"She's telling you that she wants more, the big baby." Bailino smirked.

Faith bent down and, imitating her mother, rubbed the dog's fur. "It's so soft," she said.

"It should be. That dog gets more baths than an

infant." He brought the empty glasses to the kitchen sink and rinsed them. "Be careful, that dog might want you to do that all night. Here," he reached into the cabinet again, "bring this over there, by the fireplace, where it's nice and warm."

"Not too close, though," Jamie said.

"I know, Momma." Faith took the treat from Bailino's hand. "C'mon, Lucky," she said and wandered toward the fireplace, Lucky following behind. When they reached the rug, Faith said, "Sit," in a tiny voice, and the dog complied. She held out the treat, and Lucky pulled it into her mouth with her tongue. Faith giggled.

"She's good with her," Bailino said, watching them.

"She always wanted a dog," Jamie said. "But, we just … It's just not a good idea for us."

"Are you in danger?" he asked quietly, leaning across the table.

"I don't know," Jamie said.

"What do you mean? What happened?"

Jamie watched Faith pet the dog's belly. "There was a bomb threat," she whispered. "More than a bomb threat, really. It was an actual bomb."

"Where?" he asked.

"Inside the White House, in the president's private quarters."

"When was this?" He thought for a moment and remembered the unusual Secret Service activity. "On Monday?"

She nodded. "They're keeping the whole thing under wraps for now, but I'm sure it's only a matter of time before the media gets wind of it."

The day before had been an unusually quiet day at the White House, and Bailino hadn't thought much of it, even with the extra activity on Monday. Periodically, President Phillip Grand was known to take time for his family—a decision that generated some negative press early on, but was now praised by the media for his commitment to work-life balance. Go figure. Bailino wasn't surprised that word hadn't gotten out about the explosive device. That Grand ran a tight ship even back in their army days.

"Collins said you were on vacation this morning," Bailino said. "Taking a few days."

Jamie seemed surprised.

"One of the reporters from CNN asked where you were," he said. "You're very popular, you know."

"Not really," Jamie said modestly. "They only like me because I've got something they want. Access."

"Yeah, well, they didn't take too kindly to your replacement. They hammered him about Monday, and the guy looked like he was going to have a coronary." Bailino should have known that Jamie's absence from the briefing that morning meant something was up. *Damn country living*. "How did they find the bomb?" he asked.

"I can't believe you've been here all this time," Jamie said. "Has anyone recognized you?"

"No. You'd think a person who was once at the top of the FBI's Most Wanted List would elicit some stares, but most people around here put their heads down and mind their own business. In that way—and maybe the only way—this place reminds me of New York."

She was looking into his eyes now, and Bailino was trying to discern how she felt about his being alive—threatened or relieved. She was as beautiful as he remembered, but not quite as innocent. There was a weariness in her eyes that he recognized every time he looked in the mirror.

"Sweetheart," Bailino said, "I asked how they found the bomb."

"*I* found it."

Faith was standing near the dining room table, watching them.

Bailino looked at Jamie, who nodded.

"I hit the button, because it was big, big trouble," Faith said. "I was playing hide-and-seek with Charlie ..."

"Charlie?" Bailino asked.

"Charlotte Grand," Jamie clarified.

The little girl explained what had happened. She didn't appear troubled, and Bailino wasn't sure if that concerned him or made him happy. Most of the children he grew up with had learned to live with fear; they wore it like a badge that they forgot they had on.

"Can I watch TV now?" she asked.

"Of course, you can, cupcake." Bailino picked up the remote control from the table, pointed it toward the TV, which sprang to life, and handed it to the little girl. "Nickelodeon is channel twenty-three."

"Wow, it's different where we live," she said. "Can I take off my shoes?"

"You can do whatever you want," Bailino said. "This is your house."

"It *is*?" Faith looked at Jamie.

"That's just an expression, sweetie," Jamie said.

"But it does say Carter on the mailbox, Momma."

"She's got a point," Bailino said with a smirk. "When you're right, you're right."

Faith grabbed another blueberry and hurried over to the couch. Jamie's weary eyes followed her.

"You must be exhausted," Bailino said.

"No, I'm okay," she said, which he knew was a lie.

"She doesn't sleep a lot," Faith called. She was kneeling backward on the couch, looking at them, her chin pressing into the sofa back.

"Faith, no feet on someone's couch," Jamie said. "You know that."

"It's fine," Bailino said. "In fact ..." He got up, went to a closet, and took out some folded blankets and pillows. "Both of you should just relax. It was a long trip. I'll make up the bedroom for you."

"You really don't have to go to all this trouble," Jamie said. "I'm really not tired."

"I'll tell you what," Bailino said, placing the blankets and pillows next to Faith on the sofa. "I'll just leave them here." He unfolded the blanket, tucking the corners neatly between the pillows.

"C'mere, Momma, by me," Faith said. "It's comfy!"

Jamie walked over to Faith and sat beside her. She leaned back. "It is comfortable."

"The salesman talked me into a set that was double the price of the one I wanted."

Bailino took Jamie and Faith's bags into his bedroom and wheeled them into the corner. Then he changed the bed linens, cinching them tight, and fluffed the pillows. When he got back to the living room, Faith was sitting on the floor again and rubbing Lucky's belly.

"I told you," Bailino said. "You'll be stuck doing that all night."

"Is it a girl or a boy?" Faith asked.

"She's a girl," Bailino said.

"Look, Momma, she likes it," Faith said with a smile. "Momma?"

Bailino circled to the front of the couch. Jamie was sitting primly, her feet tucked underneath her, her head leaning on her hand. She was fast asleep.

8

Wilcox rang the broken doorbell of the split-level home in Albany, New York. The mechanism was hanging by a wire against the storm door, and he had to stick his thumb inside the device in order to press it down. It had been more than three years since his last visit to this house, and he tried to remember if the home had made any kind of impression on him then, but he couldn't recall. It certainly made an impression on him now, and not a good one.

The lawn was mostly yellowed and dry despite a sprinkler that had been on so long there were puddles all along the grass. Sections had been dug up by some kind of animal, and a stack of ceramic tiles, which stood in the center of the cracked driveway, had toppled over, leaving several of the blue-and-white-patterned squares scattered along the lawn.

No one answered, and Wilcox rang the doorbell again, wondering if the thing even worked at all. He thought about knocking, but, above him, a few shingles hung precariously over the doorframe, and the vibration might shake them loose. He was about to give it a try anyway when he heard a commotion inside: two people yelling back and forth, a man and a woman. He took out his badge from his jacket pocket. It had taken less time for Wilcox to become reinstated as an FBI agent than he spent at the Virginia DMV last month getting his driver's license renewed.

A woman brushed aside the browned curtains of a window next to the front door, and Wilcox held up the badge. The woman opened the door slightly.

"Ma'am, my name is Paul Wilcox. I'm a special agent for the Federal Bureau of Investigation. You may remember me from the spring of 2014. I visited your home regarding a video recording your son had uploaded to the Internet, containing images of President Phillip Grand, then New York governor Phillip Grand."

The woman blinked in either surprise or disbelief, or perhaps general weariness, which would match the mood of the home. Her eyes looked at Wilcox's badge and then back at him. "We already told law enforcement everything," she finally said.

"May I speak with your son, Samuel?"

"Is this about the money?"

"Money?" Wilcox asked.

The woman shifted her feet. "I told him it weren't right for him to be making money on it."

"You mean the video?"

"I knew when that Phillip Grand became the president and all he'd finally come after us."

"Ma'am, monetization of a music video is perfectly legal. I'm not here for that. I just need to ask him a few questions. There has been further development since the last time we spoke."

The woman huffed and closed the door. Wilcox heard the chain guard slide, and she opened it wider this time and folded her arms. Her hair was a darker shade of brown than he remembered and her midsection appeared plumper, hanging over the waistband of her jeans, but he recognized her.

"Samuel doesn't live here anymore," the woman said.

"His registered address is here, ma'am."

"Yeah, he says my husband plays the TV too loud, and he can't think."

"May I ask where he lives now?"

"He's been staying with a friend near the college. I think he was in France or something—the friend, I mean—but now he's back. I don't know for sure 'cause Samuel don't tell me nuthin'."

"May I have that address, ma'am?"

The woman shrugged. "I don't know it, but I can tell you how to get there."

Wilcox took out his cell phone, and she detailed the directions, not by route numbers but by landmarks. Wilcox entered the information into his phone—a Hooters here, a Sunoco gas station there—and then asked, "Do you know the name of the person he's living with, ma'am?"

"Of course. Alex Campos. A Greek fella. Why, is he in trouble too?"

"No, ma'am, no one's in trouble. Thank you."

Wilcox stepped back down the path and worked his way across the lawn, careful not to step in any puddles.

"If you see him, can you please tell him to call me?" the woman said. "He's terrible with his phone. Teenagers … You know how they are."

Wilcox gave a short wave and got back into his car. It took only a few minutes for the Bureau to track down Alex Campos's address, and he plugged it into his GPS and got back on the road.

He drove for about fifteen minutes and found himself on the route alongside the property that once belonged to Upackk, Don Bailino's award-winning factory. The land still looked untouched, the burnt-out factory remaining as it was last time he drove by, and Wilcox imagined it would remain so indefinitely until Faith Carter was of legal age. Out of the corner of his eye, he saw an animal run into a patch of trees and imagined Bailino hiding out somewhere on this property in some kind of cave or forest area like an Al-Qaeda operative. However, Wilcox knew that wasn't Bailino's style. If Wilcox was right, wherever Bailino was, he was living it up.

The GPS directions led Wilcox to a two-story home on a block of row houses just outside the SUNY Albany campus. The street was filled with parked cars and students playing catch and Frisbee, and Wilcox parked in front of a fire hydrant, which elicited some comments from a group of students sitting on a nearby porch. He walked a few houses down and up the short flight of steps matching the address he had on his phone. He couldn't find a doorbell, so he knocked and pulled out his badge once again.

"Can I help you?"

A young man, whom Wilcox recognized as one of the students sitting across the street, approached him.

"Yes, I'm looking for Samuel O'Connell. I was told he's staying here."

"Yes, he's staying with me. I'm Alex Campos." The

young man was tall and wiry with thick, bushy eyebrows and a square jaw. He stuck out his hand, but instead Wilcox held up his badge, and the young man dropped his arm to his side.

"Do you know where Samuel is?" Wilcox asked. "I'd like to speak with him."

"Is he in trouble?"

"Do you know where Mr. O'Connell is, young man?"

"He's in class, I think," Alex said, suddenly appearing nervous. "I heard him in his room when I got back this morning, but didn't see him leave. I had to get to class."

"When's the last time you saw him?"

"I was away for the weekend. Before I left, I guess. It must have been on Wednesday."

"May I?" Wilcox asked, motioning to the front door.

Alex nodded and walked past Wilcox, opening the door. Wilcox imagined all the students' doors were unlocked—all of them living in some kind of safe, youthful cocoon. Alex held the door open for Wilcox.

"How long have you known Mr. O'Connell?" Wilcox asked, stepping inside the tiled entryway. A corkboard with advertisements and notices hung near two mailbox slots, and a basket of fake flowers was arranged on a radiator. Alex picked up a newspaper from the floor and started walking up a flight of stairs.

"A couple of years, I guess. We're both majoring in biology." His answers were measured and thoughtful. "I used to hold video-game challenges when I was a freshman." He turned back to look at Wilcox. "They're these—"

"I know what video-game challenges are, Mr. Campos."

Alex smiled the way a child does when he's humoring

a parent. "Well, Sam was a pro. He won so many of them that I had to ban him from participating, but he liked to watch, so he came anyway and used to crash here." They walked toward the apartment door at the top of the stairway. "He said he had to get away from his mother. I don't think they get along. I let him stay in the apartment while I studied abroad, since he was always over anyway, and he just kind of never left."

"Where did you study overseas?"

"Germany."

Alex opened the door to his apartment. It was a mess, as Wilcox had expected a place inhabited by two male college students to be. The sink contained so many dishes that another pile had been started on the stovetop to handle the overflow.

"I refuse to do them," Alex said, motioning to the pile. "The rule is: *You use it, you clean it.* I was gone all weekend." He pointed to a room in the front of the apartment. "That's Sam's room there."

The door was closed, but the sounds of the television show *The Price Is Right* could be heard through the door.

Wilcox crossed the room and knocked on the door. He waited, but no one answered.

"Yo, Samuel," Alex called, standing beside Wilcox. He banged on the door so loudly that the woodwork peeled away from the wall. "Man, you need to open the door."

Wilcox put his ear to the door and listened. He tried the doorknob, which was locked. "You have insurance for this place?" he asked, taking a step back from the bedroom door.

"Yeah, why?"

Wilcox pulled out his gun, and Alex put his hands in the air as Wilcox kicked the doorknob, and the door flew open, the sound of Drew Carey's voice filling the apartment.

"Stay here, Mr. Campos," Wilcox said and slowly peeked into the room.

"No problem," Alex said, backing away from the bedroom.

A redheaded man was sitting at a computer station at the far end of the room near the window, his hand on a mouse. He didn't move.

"Mr. Campos?" Wilcox said.

"Yes," Alex called. Wilcox imagined the young man's hands were still in the air.

"You better call the police."

The computer screen facing him showed a game of solitaire—Samuel O'Connell appeared to be two moves away from winning his game. Wilcox kept the pistol in front of him as he circled the room until he was looking directly at the young man, whose hair had grown longer since the last time Wilcox had interviewed him. Long, scraggly bangs were now flanking the small bullet hole lodged in the center of his right eye socket.

9

ToniAnne Cataldi sat on the couch painting her toenails and watching the end of *Judge Judy* as a teaser aired for the upcoming local news.

"'Zo, I think they're gonna show it." She blew on her big toe, the hot air grazing her bent knee, and ran her finger along the top curve of the nail, wiping the excess deep red nail polish onto a dinner napkin that was crumpled on a paper plate next to her. "'Zo, did you hear me? *Renzo!*"

"*What?*" Lorenzo emerged from the bedroom in a pair of tight gym shorts. "I'm working out."

"Do you have to do that shit in the bedroom? It's gonna stink in there for hours now."

"I thought you loved my smell," he said, sitting next to her, his sweaty arms grazing her leg.

"Watch the toes, idiot," she said, scooching toward the armrest. "I love your cologne. That's different. Right now, you smell like a pig—and so will my sheets ... Great. And what the fuck did you do to your chest?"

"What?" He ran both his palms down his torso, the sweat smearing onto the top of his shorts. "It's the new thing. It's called manscaping."

"Well, I think you *scaped* too much off. You should let some hair grow back. I don't want to feel like I'm committing statutory rape every time we fuck."

"Yeah, yeah, whatever. What do you want? I have to do a few more reps."

ToniAnne pointed to the television as the staccato theme music of the news sounded and two anchors appeared on screen. "It's the top story, I think." She twisted the cap closed on the nail polish and put the paper plate and small bottle on the coffee table. She wiggled her feet in front of her, airing out her toes, as the words *Breaking News* floated in front of them.

"They really need new graphics," Lorenzo said.

"*Shhh …*"

"We have breaking news …" said the Hispanic woman sitting behind the news desk.

"Yeah, no kidding," Lorenzo said.

"Jesus, are you gonna watch or what?" ToniAnne said.

"Our top story tonight …" the anchor said, putting on a serious face. "Samuel O'Connell, a college student from upstate New York, was found dead in off-campus housing outside of SUNY Albany. Our investigative reporter Seth Campbell has been following this story all day. Let's go to him now. Seth?"

"I can seriously do this job," Lorenzo said.

ToniAnne threw the crumpled up napkin at Lorenzo as Seth Campbell appeared on screen. The reporter nodded to the camera before he too put on a somber face.

"Thank you, Susan." Seth cleared his voice. "Samuel O'Connell's mother said her son came to SUNY Albany to study biochemistry and molecular biology with dreams of becoming a forensic scientist ..."

ToniAnne paused the broadcast with the remote control. "Oh, brother ..." she said, rolling her eyes. "That kid could barely string together a coherent sentence, and now he's a brainiac?" Before Lorenzo could respond, she unpaused the television, and Seth continued.

"Those who knew him referred to him as a gentle giant, a young man who kept to himself but had close friends. O'Connell gained international fame when he uploaded a video to YouTube a little more than three years ago of President Phillip Grand, then governor of New York, racing into a burning building to save Jamie Carter and her daughter, Faith—the same burning building that killed mobster Paolo Cataldi as well as Don Bailino, who had been at the top of the FBI's Most Wanted List."

ToniAnne paused it again, reached for the napkin on Lorenzo's lap, and dotted the corners of her eyes with it. "Yes, we know all this. How can we forget? You keep reminding us," she said.

"I thought we weren't talking," Lorenzo said.

"Shut up." She unpaused the television.

"Although law enforcement has not yet released information on how Mr. O'Connell died, sources tell us that foul play is suspected."

She paused it once more. "I'd say a bullet through the eye counts as foul play, wouldn't you?" ToniAnne said with a laugh.

"Gimme that." Lorenzo swiped the remote from her hands. "I'm getting seasick." He unpaused it.

"Both APD and the FBI are on the scene, interviewing

witnesses and friends, and, we're told, persons of interest. The FBI asks that anyone with information contact them at Bureau headquarters."

Lorenzo pushed the pause button. "Should I pick up the phone?" he asked snidely, nudging ToniAnne with his elbow.

"Very funny." ToniAnne grabbed the remote back.

"We'll have more as the story develops," Seth said with a nod. "Back to you, Susan."

ToniAnne lowered the television volume and put the remote down on the couch cushion.

"It's about time they found him. I'm sure he stunk," Lorenzo said, pushing down on the muscles of his biceps.

"Just like you do." She pushed him away.

"Oh, you love it, baby," he said and nuzzled his face in her breasts.

"*Ewww* ... Get away from me until you shower. Seriously. And you have to get going anyway, don't you?"

Lorenzo got up and stretched, interlocking his fingers and pushing his hands toward the ceiling in a Mr. America pose.

"Jesus, you really did shave *everything*," she said, motioning to his armpits.

"Want to see where else I shaved?" he said, pulling on the waistband of his gym shorts.

"I'd rather not."

"Why are you in such a pissy mood?" he asked. "It sounds like they know nuthin'."

"And they *won't* know anything," ToniAnne said. "Like my father always said—God rest his soul—APDs, NYPDs, any PDs, are a bunch of dum*mies*." She laughed. She missed the old son of a bitch and his weird expressions. She wished he would have let her visit him more in prison.

"Can you make me a snack?" Lorenzo said.

"Jesus, do you ever *not* eat?" She got up and walked toward the kitchen on the heels of her feet, bending down to tighten the toilet paper twined around her toes.

"You better hope the Feds aren't on to you. You can't run too fast like that." Lorenzo laughed and disappeared into the bedroom.

"Please, there ain't no one alive who can connect me with that college asshole," ToniAnne called with a dismissive wave of the hand. She pulled leftover fried chicken cutlets from the fridge and set them on the counter. "Of that, my hairless friend, I can assure you."

10

Bailino stared at the little girl lying next to her mother, with the covers pulled up to her chin. All that was visible were her eyes and nose and her right hand, which dangled toward the floor and onto the belly of Lucky, who had figured out that if she lay directly beneath the little girl she could enjoy a belly rub for most of the night.

"Aren't you tired?" Bailino asked. "I made the bed up in my room for you."

"No." The little girl shook her head. Her dark eyes were bright and blinked at the television. "Anyway, me and Momma like to sleep together."

"She keeps you safe?"

Faith nodded. "And I keep her safe."

"Are you hungry?"

"No, thank you." She shook her head again and rubbed her nose against Jamie's cheek. "Is something wrong with Momma?" she asked.

"What do you mean?"

"Usually Momma hears me when I talk or feels when I do this"—she rubbed Jamie's cheek again with her nose—"and her eyes open, but now her eyes are closed."

"She must be very tired," Bailino said. "She traveled a long way."

"I know, she drove miles and miles to see you." She looked around the house. "Do you live here all alone?"

"No. I have Lucky." He smirked.

"Does Lucky have a last name?"

"That's a good question. Do dogs have last names?" he asked.

"I think so."

"Well, then her last name must be Carter, like mine."

"And mine." The little girl's face opened into a wide smile, lifting her cheeks and making it heart-shaped like her mother's. Bailino couldn't believe how grown-up she had become in three short years. She was articulate, smart, and thoughtful. Also like her mother.

"What's your name?" she asked. "Your first name, I mean."

"Don," Bailino said.

"Don Carter?" Faith asked.

Bailino shrugged. "Well, that's what they call me around here."

"I'm Faith Carter. That's what they call me where I live."

"I know."

"How do you know? Did Momma tell you?"

Bailino hesitated. He didn't want to contradict anything that her mother had told her. He was unsure of what she knew—if anything—about him. "Yes, she told me your name a long time ago when you were a little girl."

Jamie shifted in her sleep, her arm poking out from under the blankets and absently settling on the covered outline of her daughter.

"You know Momma for a long time?" Faith asked.

"Well, not too long."

"Do you know my Uncle Eddie too?"

Bailino nodded. "We've met."

"His last name is Carter too."

"I know. Did you know there's a president that was named Carter?"

"Yes, he was president when my mother was born."

Bailino looked at Jamie, who suddenly seemed so young. That sap Lyndon Johnson had been president when Bailino was born.

"But the president's name right now is Phillip Grand," Faith said. "He's Charlie's dad."

"Tell me about this Charlie. You like her?"

"She's nice, but sometimes she always interrupts me when I talk. She says I talk too slow."

"Is that right?" Bailino asked. "Meanwhile, you could recite the Gettysburg Address during the pauses in her father's campaign speeches."

Faith laughed politely, although Bailino was sure she had no idea what he had just said. She cuddled next to her mother.

"Is that real?" she asked, pointing to the antique gun on the wall.

Bailino was impressed by how quickly her mind processed information and at her natural curiosity. It had been a long time since he had been around young children, and he had forgotten how refreshing it was. They usually said what they meant and meant what they said. His kind of people.

"Yep, it's an old antique pistol."

"Why do you keep it up there?"

"That's a good question …"

"Maybe it's one of your favorite things."

"Yes, I guess it is."

"This is one of my favorite things …" Faith reached underneath her shirt and pulled something out. "It's my necklace." She held it up.

For the second time that day, Bailino was stunned. He stared at the familiar gold cross that Faith held between her tiny fingers, the cross that had been given to him by his paternal great-grandmother when he was a baby. He had figured the necklace had gotten confiscated by the Feds and was being stored somewhere in the annals of the Bureau. He never imagined it would ever get to the person for whom it had been intended. "It's very beautiful," he said.

"My dad gave it to me when I was a baby."

Make that three times.

The little girl said the word so naturally. *Dad.* And she looked at him with calm, confident eyes. Bailino wondered what Jamie had told Faith about her father, but he didn't have to wonder for very long.

"My dad died," Faith continued. "He died trying to save me and my mom. He was a hero."

"Wow," Bailino said, "just like you."

"Me?" Faith pointed to her chest.

"Yeah, you saved everyone at the White House."

"Does that mean I have hero's blood in me?"

"I think so."

"Is hero's blood better than president's blood?"

"I think so," Bailino said, and the little girl smiled.

Jamie murmured something in her sleep and turned slightly, tightening her hold on Faith.

"You must spend a lot of time with your momma," Bailino said.

"Yes, we're like this." Faith tried to wrap her pointer finger around her middle finger, but it got stuck, so she helped it along with her other hand. "Charlie thinks we spend too much time together. She said Momma should be finding me a new daddy."

"That Charlie sounds like a piece of work."

"Charlie *never* does her homework. She thinks she doesn't have to because her dad is the president."

"Is that right?"

"Anyway, Momma says she doesn't really want to be with other boys anyway."

"She's a smart woman, your mother," Bailino said. "Most guys are jerks. What else does Miss Charlotte Charlie Grand have to say?"

"She says that she always should get to hide first in hide-and-seek, because she's the oldest, and that's the rule."

"Well, I never heard that rule," Bailino said. "And I know everything there is to know about hide-and-seek."

"Serious?" she asked.

"Serious." He rubbed his beard. "It sounds to me like she's just being bossy. Like her mother."

Faith's eyes opened wide. "I thought only Momma and me knew that."

"That the First Lady is bossy? Trust me, it's no state secret."

Faith giggled. "I like talking to you. You're funny."

"I like talking to you too," he said, and his mind flashed back to when Joey was a little boy—how shy he was, but so incredibly smart. Faith reminded Bailino of him. Unfortunately, the kid had been born into a family of nitwits. Bailino had almost gotten him out. *Almost.* "Why don't you try to get some sleep?" He pointed to the wall clock. "Are you comfortable?"

Faith nodded. "You goin' to sleep?" she asked.

"I think so."

"All the way in there?" She pointed to the bedroom.

Bailino smirked. "Well, I might stay up for a little while longer. Is that all right?"

The little girl nodded and laid her head on the pillow next to her mother's.

"Okay, good night." Bailino flipped the television station to CNN to see if there were any new developments he should know about, but there was a commercial, so he turned off the set and headed into the kitchen. He could feel the little girl's eyes on him as he pulled out a chair at the dining table and sat.

He *was* pretty tired. Damn country living was turning him into an old man. Plus, his biological clock never seemed to reset from Eastern Time. Even after more than three years.

He pulled his cell phone out from his back pocket and his reading glasses from his shirt pocket, and he scanned the national news websites. They all had the same headline about the kid in Albany who had posted the YouTube video of Grand who had been killed. Bailino scanned the CNN story—no mention of how O'Connell died, but it looked like Wilcox was back in action.

"Momma says it's not a good idea to be on your phone right before bed." Faith's little head popped up from the sofa. "It's not healthy."

"Your momma's right," he said, looking at the little girl's tired face over the rim of his glasses. He placed the phone on the table. "Try and get some sleep now."

Faith's head disappeared, and Bailino leaned back in his chair. If the death of the YouTube kid and the planting of the White House explosive device were connected, it complicated matters. It meant that some powerful people were involved—people who had access to the White House's inner sanctum and, quite possibly, New York State law enforcement. And Bailino knew of only a few organizations that could pull off stunts like that.

He glanced over at the sofa, which was now still.

She drove miles and miles to see you.

That remained to be seen, but Bailino was glad that Jamie's instincts brought the kid to Wyoming, whether she knew he would be there or not. Because if what he saw on his phone was any indication, the little girl was right. None of it was healthy. For any of them.

11

Phillip was sitting on the Truman Balcony off the Yellow Oval Room, one of his favorite spots at the White House. It offered the best—and most secluded—views of Washington. In the east, the sun rose, casting a reddish glow on the grounds and making the carefully cut lawn appear like crushed velvet.

Across from him, seated on white wicker chairs, Agent Fuller and Agent Wilcox, looking tired from his long day in upstate New York, were exchanging notes. The murder of Samuel O'Connell had been a development that had stunned Phillip. The thought that the young man he met back in 2014 could be involved in an attempted bombing at the White House was almost laughable. His impression of O'Connell at the time was that of an aloof college student of few words and even fewer aspirations, one who had simply been in the right place at the right time when he stumbled upon Phillip coming out of that farmhouse.

"How is Samuel's mother?" Phillip asked. Like her son, Phyllis O'Connell had left a lasting impression on Phillip. During her 2014 visit to the Executive Mansion, she had had a strange preoccupation with the building's array of artwork, on loan from some of New York's museums.

When Phillip had inquired whether she was a fan of art, she replied with a guffaw, "No, but I'm a fan of all the money it's worth." Still, the woman had lost a child. "I should call her," Phillip said.

"Frankly, there's no need, Mr. President," said Wilcox, whose lanky frame seemed to overpower the petite wicker furniture. He took a sip of water. "Mrs. O'Connell has no reason to believe what happened to her son has anything to do with the White House. I believe your calling her would only raise suspicions."

"But *you* believe there is a connection?" Phillip asked.

"I do, Mr. President," he said. "However, I can't provide you with any proof other than a hunch at this time. When everything went down at the Barbara farmhouse three years ago, some puzzle pieces didn't fit, something didn't feel right, and in my time as an agent for the Bureau, I've learned that when something doesn't feel right it often isn't."

Brandon flipped through a report. "When did O'Connell's murder take place again?" he asked.

"Coroner put the time of death sometime between Tuesday and Wednesday morning," Wilcox said.

"So *after* the attempted bombing?" Phillip asked.

"Looks that way," Wilcox said. "Any word from Jamie Carter, Mr. President?"

"Not yet." Phillip had put off calling her in the hopes that she would check in. He had to admit: It was strange not to hear from her. In the time she had worked for him, he didn't think a day had gone by that he didn't speak with her or get an email or text, but it had been three days since Faith discovered the explosive device, and as much as he wanted to give her space, he was becoming concerned. Plus, Edward had been calling and asking about her. Apparently, she hadn't checked in with him either. "I will call her," he said finally. "Today."

"That's a good idea," Wilcox said just as Phillip's phone buzzed.

He looked at the caller ID, hopeful that it was Jamie, but instead it was Collins. Since his disastrous press briefing the day before, Collins had become a bit unhinged and was calling upon Phillip regularly for direction.

"It's Collins," Phillip said to the FBI agents. They returned to their paperwork, and Phillip swiped the phone screen. "Yes?"

"Mr. President," he said, in what had become his usual panicked voice. "I just received a call from a Jim Olsen at *The New York Times*. He said you know him."

"Yes, I know him well." Olsen seemed to have gotten a promotion along with Phillip, moving from local to national politics as Phillip moved from New York to Washington, D.C. "What is this about, Collins?"

"He says he has some information that he needs confirmed about what happened on Monday."

"Did he mention the IED?"

"Not directly," Collins said, "but I have a feeling he knows something."

"The briefing is in a few hours." Phillip had put off the press long enough—there was too much speculation and fear-mongering—and he had decided that he, himself, would address the media that morning and give Collins a break. "Tell him to wait."

"I told him that," Collins said, "but he was adamant about getting confirmation now."

"What exactly does he know?"

"I don't know. He wants to talk with you directly."

"That's not how this is done, Collins."

There was a pause on the other end of the line. "I know that, sir," Collins finally said, sounding a bit injured. "But Olsen said he's ready to publish online and would like confirmation from the White House—the president—immediately."

Phillip sighed. Olsen was playing hardball. "All right, Collins, thank you. I'll handle it." He placed his phone on the glass table. "Sorry for the interruption, gentlemen. You were saying?"

"We were talking about Jamie Carter," Wilcox said. "How it's best that she returns, for her safety as well as yours. I hate to press, but the sooner you can reach her, the better. At the very least, she can deal with the press. It would be helpful to have your full attention on this matter."

"Agreed." Phillip looked at his watch. It was probably an hour or two earlier where Jamie was staying, wherever that was. He took out his cell phone, scrolled to the number Jamie had given him, and dialed. He got up, stretching his legs, as Wilcox too stood and picked up his cell phone.

The line rang on Phillip's phone several times, but Jamie didn't answer, so he left a message. When he was through, Phillip placed the phone in his shirt pocket just as Wilcox was sliding his phone back onto the clip on his belt.

"She wasn't there," Phillip said. "I left a message. Brandon, how about your team? Anything new?"

"Unfortunately, no, Mr. President," Brandon said. "I've personally interviewed all of the staff, with the exception of Jamie"—he glanced at Wilcox—"and, unfortunately, we don't have anything usable. Several kitchen workers identified the utensils and other things used in the device, but couldn't recall when they had gone missing. In some cases, they thought months, which means there was a lot of time for the perpetrator to piece this thing together." Brandon began to rock slightly in his seat in the way Phillip had seen him do on his feet. "And, unfortunately, Mr. President, because we are talking about a long period of time, there's really no 'alibi' to speak of. Whoever did this was stealing a few minutes here, a few minutes there."

Phillip leaned back in his chair. "What are our next steps?" he asked.

"Once we get the final coroner's report on the death of Samuel O'Connell—and we hear from Jamie Carter—we'll figure out next steps," Wilcox said as his cell phone buzzed. He picked it up, listened, and put it back into his pocket. "Let's reconvene here tomorrow."

"Is everything all right?" Phillip asked.

"Got a lead, but I'll know more in the morning, Mr. President." He left quickly, and Brandon gathered up his paperwork.

"Will you be escorting me to Walter Reed today, Brandon?" Phillip asked.

The young agent shook his head. "I believe Agent Summers is on duty, Mr. President."

Phillip hadn't seen Agent Summers since the funeral. "Is he back at work already?"

"Actually," Brandon said, "he hasn't taken any time off at all."

"What? He's been working all week?"

Brandon nodded. "He's been working in the mornings so that he can get home to pick up his youngest daughter from the school bus. I haven't seen very much of him myself, except briefly, when I passed him in the hall outside the Oval Office yesterday."

"How is he?"

Brandon shrugged his shoulders. "As you might expect, sir. He keeps to himself. Says he prefers to focus on the job. Says it helps him not to think about it."

Charlotte had been asking about Agent Summers earlier in the week. He and Brandon were her two favorite agents. Phillip didn't have the heart to tell Charlotte about what had happened to Summers's young daughter—the two had gotten along so well at the summer picnic. A hit-and-run death was a lot for an adult to comprehend, let alone a child.

"Any leads on who did it?" Phillip asked.

"Not really," Brandon said. "Witnesses say it was a black SUV, and PD has a license plate number, but the plate was stolen. It doesn't look good."

"Thank you, Brandon. Keep me posted on any developments," Phillip said as the young agent left the balcony. He picked up his phone. "Janice, can you get Jim Olsen from the *New York Times* on the phone for me? Thanks." He held the phone to his ear and looked out at the view again. A soft breeze blew, reminding him of the night he surprised Katherine, on that very spot, with a candlelit dinner to celebrate their first hundred days in office. It seemed like a long time ago.

"I've got Mr. Olsen, Mr. President," Janice said into his ear. "I'll put him through."

Phillip waited through a few clicks until he heard Olsen's gruff voice say, "Hello."

"Well, well, well, Jim Olsen, is that you?"

"Yes, Mr. President," he said with a laugh. "Did you think I'd let you go down to Washington without me?"

"Nah, I know you better than that." If Phillip closed his eyes, he could imagine he was back at the Executive Mansion in Albany, overlooking the Hudson, Olsen at his ear digging around about some new state initiative he had vetoed. "How are you?" he asked.

"I'm good, Mr. President. I appreciate your call."

"Well, as you know, I'm not in the business of calling up journalists," Phillip said, trying to keep his voice light, "but Collins tells me you've got something and won't talk to anyone else here. You do know, Jim, that normally I hold the same position with journalists as I do with terrorists—I don't negotiate."

Olsen laughed. "Yes, I do know that. To be honest, Mr. President, I'm not quite sure what I've got. As I'm sure you heard at yesterday's press briefing—and have seen in newspapers across the country today—sources are telling us that there was an explosive device found at the White House on Monday. Is the White House ready to confirm that?"

"As I believe Collins told you, we will address that at this morning's press briefing."

"I understand, Mr. President," Olsen said, "but there is something specific I'd like to have confirmed." The familiar sounds of the newsroom—the tapping of keyboards and hurried voices—echoed in the background. "We get a lot of calls on our tip line, most of them, unfortunately, crackpots who find it funny to see journalists getting the runaround and chasing down bad leads. Makes for some real nice YouTube videos."

"I know a thing or two about YouTube videos myself ..."

"Yes," Olsen said. "I imagine you do, but there was one tip this morning that I thought was somewhat specific and strange."

"Oh?" The skin on the back of Phillip's neck prickled, and a strange feeling came over him—the same feeling he got when he was in the army and was about to be ambushed. "Jim, I'm afraid I don't have much time. I—"

"Mr. President," Olsen took an audible breath, "does a Hello Kitty watch mean anything to you?"

12

Jamie awoke with a start and instinctively felt around for Faith. When she didn't find her daughter's sleeping body next to her, she reached for her pistol, which was still in the waistband of her jeans—a discovery that both surprised and relieved her. Bright sunlight was streaming through the windows, making it difficult to see, and she blinked her eyes a few times until the furnishings of the log cabin came into focus.

The room was empty.

Her heart began to pound. *How long had she been asleep?*

Jamie pushed off the blanket that she didn't remember placing on herself and stood up quickly, holding the gun in front of her. She scanned the room. The fireplace was roaring, just as it had the night before, and everything appeared normal. No signs of a struggle. She glanced downward and saw a sheet of loose-leaf paper on the coffee table with a note written in crisp, block-letter handwriting:

Don't worry. She's with me. —Don

Worry shot through Jamie's body.

As Jamie made her way across the room, a flicker of movement outside the front window caught her attention, a contrasting of light and dark, like a shadow, and as she got closer, she heard a sound and realized it was Faith's voice.

She was giggling.

Jamie ran to the window, with the gun by her side.

Outside, Faith was standing on the front porch. She was watching Bailino throw a stick into the snow, and Lucky, whose fur was caked with snowflakes, run after it. When Lucky retrieved it, Bailino handed the stick to Faith who took a turn throwing it—a smile of pure joy on her face. Bailino spotted Jamie at the window and glanced at the gun in her hand, which Jamie moved down and out of view. He motioned to Faith, who turned toward the window and started waving and shouting.

"Watch me, Momma!" she shouted, her voice barely audible through the thick glass.

The little girl was wearing a black longshoreman's knit cap that practically covered her ears and her eyebrows and a winter coat whose sleeves were so long she had to keep pushing her little hands out. Faith took the stick again from Bailino, tossed it a few yards into the snow, and immediately turned around for Jamie's approval. Jamie put the gun between her thighs and raised her hands high so that Faith could see them, and she clapped.

Lucky returned the stick and shook off some of the snow clinging to her thick coat, which landed on Faith's face causing her to cackle. Bailino handed her the stick once again, and Faith threw it as far as she could, with Lucky dutifully chasing after it.

Under normal circumstances, this would have been an everyday scene—a father, his daughter, and his dog playing in the snow—but Jamie knew the situation was anything but everyday. She had the urge to go out there. It was not like her to leave Faith unattended or with someone else, and it was unusual to see Faith interact with a man other than Edward or Phillip Grand.

Bailino was standing close to Faith, but not too close. He was just enough away so that, if he needed to, he could reach her in an instant—a distance Jamie, herself, would have measured had she been out there. His gaze drifted, like a sniper, from Faith and Lucky to the land around them—snow-covered flatlands that stretched at least an acre or two until it reached a line of snow-covered trees. When the arc of his gaze landed back on Jamie, Bailino nodded and returned his attention to Faith.

For the first time in a long time, a wave of calm came over her, and she decided, for once, not to argue with it. She took one last look at her daughter, who was petting Lucky with the sleeve of her coat, and left the window. She placed the gun back into her ankle holster and began exploring the guesthouse.

The home was essentially one great room with what looked like several rooms in the back—a pair of bedrooms, perhaps, and a bathroom. Although it was much smaller than the log cabin Bailino had had in Albany, it reminded Jamie of it—the décor, the sense of place, the tidiness of the furnishings. Above the fireplace, the antique gun that had saved her life hung with distinction.

She walked toward the kitchen and opened the refrigerator for no particular reason and then the freezer, which had some frozen dinners, bags of vegetables, and a pair of large icicles laying side by side where the ice cube tray was supposed to be. She reached in and touched the sharp tip of one of them.

I got rid of him. Stabbed him with an ice pick.

Images flashed through her mind of Edward hogtied in the trunk of a car and of Paolo Cataldi's sliced-off body parts landing beside her at the Barbara farmhouse with a *thud*. The dark memories, one by one, pushed forward, but Jamie pushed back, focusing instead on the muffled sounds of Faith's giggling voice coming from somewhere outside. She closed the freezer.

A couple of glasses and bowls sat overturned in the dish rack, washed, and the dining table had been wiped, the placemats in line with the sides of the table. Faith's coat hung neatly on one of the table chairs. Near the back bedrooms, a baby grand piano stood in the far corner of the room. As she got closer, she realized it looked identical to the one that had been in Bailino's bedroom in Albany, and a feeling of déjà vu washed over her as the front door to the guesthouse flew open, and Faith came stumbling inside, her face aglow.

"Momma, Momma! I saw a gray wolf!"

"You did?" Jamie asked as Faith barreled into her arms, her skin cold, but her breath warm.

"And did you see me throw the stick?!"

"I did," Jamie said, helping her out of the large men's jacket. "That was great."

Lucky bounced through the door next and shook the snow off her coat as Bailino entered, stamping the snow from his boots. He closed the front door.

"Don says I'm a natural!" Faith squealed.

Don.

Her little body freed itself from the coat like a butterfly from a cocoon, and she joined Lucky on the area rug in front of the fireplace. She was still wearing the black knit cap on her head.

"She asked me for my name," Bailino said, hanging up his coat. "Hope it's all right."

"Of course," Jamie said, although she wasn't sure if it was.

"This is the best vacation ever, Momma!" said Faith, running her hand along the wet fur of the dog, who circled the area rug a few times before plopping down next to her. "Don says I need to get proper boots, though. And a proper coat. Can we buy proper boots and a proper coat for me?"

"Yes," Jamie said, "but, sweetie, I'm not sure how long we are going to stay."

Faith's bright mood darkened. "*Awww ...*" She put her arm on Lucky, who turned onto her back so Faith could rub her belly. "Can't we stay for a lot of days?" she asked in a small voice.

Strangely, the official word to the press was that Jamie was on vacation, and somehow it was turning out to be a real one. "We'll see," Jamie said. "And not so close to the fireplace, please?"

Her daughter shimmied a few inches away from the fire. "Momma doesn't like fireplaces," Faith informed Bailino.

"I'm not too fond of them myself," he said. He was running water into a tea kettle.

"Can we go for ices soon, Momma?" Faith asked. "You said yesterday that maybe today we could."

"I don't think it's open," Jamie said. She glanced at Bailino.

"Marge's? I'm afraid not until spring," he said, "but we can make some snow cones here, if you like?"

It was as if Bailino had said he was going to buy Faith a pony.

"Snow cones!" Faith cheered, standing up and startling Lucky, who got up too, her tail wagging. "Charlie would be so jealous!"

Bailino smirked, placed the teakettle on the stove, and lit the front burner. He pulled a mug out of the cabinet and held it up. "Tea, hot chocolate?" he asked Jamie.

"Hot chocolate, please," Faith called. She was twirling like a ballerina around the dog.

Jamie nodded. "I guess it's two hot chocolates," she said.

"Coming right up." Bailino placed three mugs and spoons on the table with a few packets of hot chocolate mix, all deftly with his right hand, as if he never needed the other one. "Did you sleep all right?" he asked as she slid onto one of the dining chairs.

"Too long," Jamie said. "Thank you for the blanket."

Bailino rubbed his beard, which was still speckled with snowflakes, and leaned toward her. "You remember that kid who posted the YouTube video of Grand?" he asked.

Sudden changes of conversation, delivered in quick, direct jabs, were Bailino's forte. While five years ago Jamie may have been caught off guard by them, she was ready this time—probably because she made it a habit to be ready for anything. "Yeah, the kid from upstate New York," she said.

"He's dead."

"Dead?" She wasn't ready for *that*. "How?"

He glanced again at Faith, who was hopping on

one foot while Lucky, appearing puzzled, followed her. "They're not saying," he said in a low voice. "But my guess is that it was a gunshot."

"Why do you say that?"

"Instinct," he said.

"Do you think it's related to what happened at the White House?"

"My instinct tells me yes."

"Why? What's the connection?"

"Don," Faith asked, coming near the table, "may I put the TV on?"

"Yeah, sure, cookie, you know how to do it. The remote is over there." Bailino pointed to one of the coffee tables.

"Is it okay, Momma?" Faith asked.

Jamie smiled. "Of course, go ahead. I'll call you when the hot chocolate has cooled."

Faith gave her a quick hug and ran toward the coffee table.

"She's so polite," Bailino said. "It reminds me of you walking through Bryant Park that day." He sat down in a chair and leaned back. "I can still see you, trying to find a place to sit, balancing your water on your resume."

He seemed to recall the memory fondly as if it weren't the moment of her abduction, the moment that had changed her life forever. "Easy pickings, right?" Jamie asked.

Bailino shrugged. "Yes and no."

"I'm not that same person anymore." She ripped open two of the packets of hot chocolate at the same time and poured the contents into their respective cups.

"No," Bailino said, staring at her. "You're not. But also you are."

The teakettle whistled. He turned off the burner and poured water into the three mugs.

"How did you get out?" she asked, stirring one cup of hot chocolate, then the next two. "Of the old farmhouse?"

"Sewers. Same way I got into the Executive Mansion in Albany. And the Little Flower Hotel." Bailino sat down at the table again. He seemed slower than she remembered, a bit tired, and she thought perhaps it was due to the elevation.

"You did that to your hand?" she asked.

"Yes," he said. "I hope you don't mind, but I had to go through your purse to see if you had a phone."

"Burner," Jamie said, "and it's off. No more rookie mistakes."

"Momma," Faith called, "is it cool yet?"

"Not yet, honey. A few more minutes."

The little girl leaned on the top of the couch. "Are you sure we can't stay a bit more? I like it here."

"No, honey, we'll probably have to leave soon."

"Leave? You just got here," Bailino said. "It's probably a good idea to stay until you know what's going on."

"I know. I need to check in with the president," Jamie said. "And with Edward."

Faith walked toward the window by the fireplace, and Jamie was about to call her back when Bailino said, "It's okay. The windows are bulletproof glass and locked. She's fine."

Lucky stood next to her, looking like a horse. Faith rested her hand between the dog's ears as if they had been friends for years.

"Where did you get the dog?" Jamie asked.

"Damn dog …" Bailino took a sip from his mug, the steam of the hot chocolate wetting his face. "A dog was the last thing I wanted, trust me." He placed the cup on the table. "About six months ago, I was out getting firewood, and I heard this tiny screeching. I followed the sound and came across this little girl." He motioned to Lucky. "She looked like crap—malnourished, like she had been dropped there by someone off the road. She was so much smaller than she is now, like a baby. I carried her back and wrapped her in blankets and fed her. I don't know why. Instinct, I guess. I didn't think she was going to make it anyway. One morning, I was lying on the couch there, and I woke up to her licking my hand. It was the first time I had ever seen her move. She had walked by herself. She hasn't left me alone since."

"You don't seem to mind." Jamie said with a smile.

"Damn shit machine."

"And you named her Lucky?"

"Not very creative, I know—I don't have your writer's mind—but it seemed appropriate. I took her to the vet to get that eye fixed. I had these grand ideas of turning her into a watchdog—especially after she grew to this size. But she was having none of it. Look at her …" Jamie glanced toward the window where the dog had apparently grown tired of waiting for Faith to return to the area rug or the couch and had plopped down next to her. "I guess you can't change a dog's nature," Bailino said.

An engine sounded, and instantly Bailino and Jamie stood, reaching for their respective guns.

"Momma, there's a car coming," Faith said, pointing out the window.

"C'mere, sweetie," Jamie said, running toward Faith. She pulled her away from the window and out of sight. "Who is it?" she asked Bailino.

Bailino walked toward the front window, holding his gun in such a way that Faith couldn't see it, and peered out. After a moment, he stuck the gun back into the waistband of his jeans.

"I'll be right back," he said, grabbing his wet coat from the hook near the front door. He went outside and closed the door quickly before Lucky could follow him.

"Who is it, Momma?" Faith asked.

"I'm not sure. Go have some of your hot chocolate. It's cool now."

As Faith ran to the table, Jamie stood next to the front window, peeking through the glass as Bailino trudged through the snow toward a large truck with Wyoming plates. The vehicle was about to pull into the driveway before Bailino stepped in front of it. The car's window rolled down, and Jamie could see a woman sitting in the driver's seat. She had long brown hair and sunglasses, and was smiling widely when Bailino leaned onto the window to talk to her. She put her hand on his, but he pulled away. Bailino pointed to Jamie's rental car, and the woman pointed toward the window, and Jamie hoped she hadn't seen Faith.

After a few moments, the truck made a U-turn. As it drove back up the driveway, Bailino watched it go until it was out of sight. He stood there for several minutes more, and then he turned back toward the house. He entered without saying a word, closed the door, locked it, and hung his coat back on its hook.

"Who was that?" Faith asked, breaking the silence, and Jamie shushed her.

"It's fine," Bailino said, returning to his seat at the table. "It's a lady that I know here. She works at the pet store in town."

"What's her name?" Faith asked.

"Ellie."

"Is she your girlfriend?"

"*Faith,*" Jamie said firmly.

"It's fine … No, she's not my girlfriend, *Detective Faith,*" he said, which made Faith giggle into her hot chocolate. His cheeks were red, probably from the cold, but Jamie had the sudden and strange thought they might be red from embarrassment. "Do you have a computer with you?" he asked Jamie, changing the conversation once again.

"No, I didn't bring it."

"Good," he said. "Any web activity you need to do should be done through my laptop, which is connected to an anonymizer. This way, your IP address can't be traced. Same goes for phone calls. If you need to make a call or retrieve a voice mail, you need to use one of my phones, like if you need to call Edward. Or Phillip Grand, like you mentioned."

Jamie knew she probably needed to call Edward first. News about the attempted bombing of the White House was going to get out, if it hadn't already, and she didn't want him to worry, but she wasn't sure what to say to him. Where would she say she was? And why did she bring Faith someplace far away? Edward, like the rest of the world, thought Bailino was dead, and she couldn't tell him otherwise—for Faith's safety, and also Bailino's.

Bailino handed her a phone. "Here, use this," he said. "Do what you have to do." Then Bailino shifted gears once again. "Hey, cupcake," he said to Faith. "Do you know how to make an omelet?"

Faith placed her empty mug on the table. A wet chocolate moustache glistened on her top lip. She shook her head no.

"You like peppers?" he asked.

She nodded.

"How about onions?"

Faith wrinkled her nose.

"Okay, get your coat, and we'll go get some peppers outside."

Faith stood up. "Where?" she asked, puzzled. "Out there?" She pointed to the window.

"Yep. C'mon, I'll show you. And your mom can come too, if she wants."

Jamie reached for Faith's coat that was hanging on the chair, but her daughter was already putting on the men's coat Bailino had given her.

"Where are the peppers? In your car?" Jamie asked.

"You want to know, you have to come." Bailino smirked, and Faith giggled again. It was clear that she liked him. Jamie remembered how Faith had taken to Bailino years before. She wondered if there was a small piece of her that somehow remembered him. Bailino zipped up Faith's coat and folded up her sleeves until her tiny hands poked through.

Faith pulled down her knit cap until her eyes were

barely visible. "You coming to get peppers, Momma?"

Bailino held up another one of his coats. "It's up to you. We'll only be a few minutes. We're not going far."

For some reason, Jamie felt like this was another one of Bailino's tests. In her mind's eye, she was back at the river at his Albany log cabin with little Charlotte Grand in her arms, getting an earful on the lessons of loyalty. Was Bailino testing her loyalty now, or was he simply asking her to go and get some peppers? She shrugged.

"I guess I can't miss out on a pepper adventure," she said, to her daughter's delight. She placed the phone on the dining table and took the coat from Bailino's outstretched hand.

When Bailino opened the door, the wind had kicked up and blown more freshly fallen snow on the front porch. Faith took hold of Balino's hand with her left hand and then grabbed Jamie's with her right, and the three walked down the snowy steps with Lucky tagging along behind them.

13

Phillip knew Clark was talking because his mouth was moving, but all Phillip could hear was Jim Olsen's question ringing in his ears: *Mr. President, does a Hello Kitty watch mean anything to you?*

Phillip had lied, of course. That was not information that was to be released, and all through the morning's press briefing he could feel Olsen's eyes on him like laser beams. Phillip and Agents Fuller and Wilcox decided they should give only the most general of details about the attempted bombing, and most of the journalists seemed content with finally getting some confirmation, with the exception of Olsen.

Phillip glanced absently at the pedestrians along the area streets gawking and pointing fingers at his tinted windows as the motorcade, a black metal caterpillar, turned right on Wisconsin Avenue, crossing into Maryland. The fact that Olsen had gotten that information meant one of two things: Either there was a leak in his administration, in addition to what was possibly a security breach, or the bomber had contacted the newspaper.

Phillip's cell phone rang, and he looked at the caller ID.

"Excuse me, Josef," he said and put the phone to his ear. "Yes, Agent Fuller."

"According to the phone records, it looks like the anonymous tip was made to the *Times* from a burner phone, Mr. President," Brandon said without wasting any time. Even after all his years in public service, it always astonished Phillip how quickly the Secret Service and FBI were able to attain information.

"So we've got nothing," Phillip said.

"Well, it looks like the call was local and made after business hours. That's something," Brandon said, and Phillip knew the young agent was trying to be positive. "But, yes, we don't know if the call was made by someone working inside the White House or by someone outside. At this point, it can still be anyone."

"Thank you, Brandon. Keep me posted," Phillip said and placed the phone on his lap.

"Bad news?" Clark asked. He held up his arm to hold onto the top of the automobile—affectionately dubbed "The Beast" by the past two administrations—as the car made a wide turn.

"Well, it's not good news," Phillip said. Like the press, Clark, and just about the rest of Phillip's inner circle, knew the general details about the explosive device but nothing about the Hello Kitty watch or the phone call to Jim Olsen. That information hadn't been made available to anyone.

"Mr. President, if you're not feeling well, we can put off—"

"I'm feeling fine, Josef," Phillip said. "Really, I am, and I'd rather not put off this visit."

Phillip never liked to cancel his "well wishes" visits

to Walter Reed National Military Medical Center. He knew how much the wounded service members receiving medical care there looked forward to them—as did he. And with the holidays approaching, it was an especially difficult time for them, particularly those who were away from their families. If Phillip could offer a smile or a handshake, it was worth it.

It was not so long ago that Phillip was a patient there. As was Bailino. A random image of the two of them watching *Roseanne* in Phillip's hospital room popped into his head, although Phillip couldn't recall Bailino ever smiling or laughing at the sitcom. He tended to watch television like he did everything else—with a laser focus.

"Strange how Vice President Mitchell isn't visiting with you today, Mr. President," Clark said, his voice coated with the usual disdain whenever he uttered Rudy Ray's name.

"I told him he could sit this one out," Phillip said. "His daughter is in a school play this morning."

Clark raised his eyebrows in obvious disapproval.

"Now, don't get all judgmental on ol' Rudy Ray," Phillip said. "He's as devoted to the military as I am, but family is what's most important. He can schedule another visit to Walter Reed."

"Just strange, is all," Clark said, his Louisiana accent permeating every word, a habit he had when he was trying to infer a point without actually making one, which was most of the time. His staffers knew that, when it came to Clark, the *Po' boy* always preceded the *Pitbull*.

"Why do you say that?"

"Well," Clark chuckled, "it's nothing, really …" which is what Clark usually said before he launched into a story.

"Last night, around midnight, I guess, I was packing up my gear to head home and was about to dismiss my interns, Ben and Brad ..."

Poor kids, Phillip thought. He knew that Clark worked his interns *hard*. He imagined that Ben and Brad hadn't had a decent dinner since the inauguration. Clark thought that the best way to know if someone was cut out for the business of politics was to work them until they nearly passed out from fatigue. It was like his own little version of Navy SEAL Hell Week. It was not Phillip's way, but Phillip couldn't fault the guy's work output. His office was a machine. And those interns who *did* make it through had an in with Josef Clark for life. Perhaps that was worth the price of exhaustion.

" ... I overheard them talking about having enough time to get to the pool. Well, curious, I asked them what swimming pool would be open that time of night." Clark looked Phillip straight in the eye. "You would have thought I asked them to brand their arm with my initials! They looked plum scared to death. I could tell they were up to somethin', so I said, 'All right, out with it.' And that's when they told me."

"I don't understand," Phillip said. "Told you what?"

Clark looked out the window at the passing storefronts. "They weren't talking about a *swimming* pool. They were talking about a betting pool."

"A football pool?"

"Not quite. Mr. President, it looks like our intern staff has some thoughts about who is involved with the attempted bombing of the White House."

Phillip adjusted himself in the leather seat. "Are you

telling me that there is a White House intern *pool* about the attempted bombing of the White House?"

"And the odds of it being good ol' Rudy Ray Mitchell is two to one, apparently. He came in second among the most likely suspects."

Phillip let out a long exhale and ran his fingers through his hair.

"Now, now, no need to get concerned," Clark said. "You know how young people are with their conspiracy theories and social media surveys these days. Can't do a damn thing unless it's been crowdsourced and they've taken an online quiz about it. I don't like it none either, but, still, I believe it's rather harmless."

"Not for poor Rudy Ray," Phillip said. "So let me get this straight … Rudy Ray's big plan was to get rid of Katherine and me and just ease into the presidency?"

"I agree. It doesn't make much sense, which is why I think you should disregard it."

"But you said yourself you thought it was strange that Rudy Ray wasn't here."

Clark adjusted some file folders on his lap. "The *timing* of it is strange is all, Mr. President. Me finding all this out, and his canceling on this morning's trip."

"And just who exactly did my crack team of interns come up with as the primary suspect of the attempted bombing? And please don't tell me it's Katherine."

"No." Clark shook his head. "The First Lady was ranked sixth. Edna Wyatt was number one."

"Edna?" Phillip asked, louder than he intended to. He glanced at the agents in the front seat and then lowered his voice. "A fifty-three-year-old housekeeper with grandchildren? A woman who was kind enough to help us through the transition and stay on?"

"Word has it that she is loyal to the previous administration."

Phillip leaned his head back against the headrest. He was tired of all the social media chatter, the conspiracy theories, the way people who have absolutely no knowledge of the facts somehow have the loudest voices in the room.

"What could Edna believe killing Katherine and me would do?" he asked. "It would only make Rudy Ray Mitchell the new president. It wouldn't bring back the old one. For Pete's sake," Phillip said with disgust. "I want you to squash this nonsense, Josef, however harmless you think it is. I'll have none of that speculation and innuendo in any part of my administration."

"Yes, Mr. President." Clark made a notation on his tablet and looked out the window.

Phillip did the same. It had begun to rain, the drops smearing the red taillights of the other cars in the motorcade. An awkward silence had settled upon them, and Phillip was glad when Agent Summers said from the front of the vehicle, "Five more minutes, Mr. President."

Even in the rearview mirror, Phillip could spot the sadness in the agent's eyes. He had wanted to say a little something to Summers before they started the trip, but the agent had been all business. And Phillip couldn't blame him. There was no getting over the death of a child. Although Phillip hadn't lost his daughter, he had come dangerously close, and that was close enough. He offered a small smile, but Agent Summers's gaze had already returned to the road ahead, and Phillip noticed a little girl's pink plastic ring on one of the agent's fingers.

Normally, the trip to Walter Reed took about a half hour, but a bit of road construction along Rockville Pike seemed to have stalled traffic flow. Phillip didn't mind. He preferred riding in the car rather than the helicopter, which they took from time to time. He was glad to be outdoors, on the ground with his fellow Americans, and away from the White House, which was beginning to resemble Fort Knox. Over the past few days, there had been a doubling up of FBI and Secret Service agents, particularly in the private quarters. As much as Phillip and Katherine tried not to let that spook the children, it was hard to convince them that there's no such thing as monsters when there was a Secret Service agent checking under their beds every night.

"Should be moving shortly, Mr. President," Agent Summers called.

Phillip glanced out the window, trying to recognize his surroundings. For security reasons, his routes varied each time he visited, so he was never quite sure through which entrance the motorcade would go. All he knew was that today he would be visiting Ward 57, the amputee ward, and getting a briefing on some of the newest advances in prosthetics, an area for which he was eager to find funding. When his Republican colleagues talked about beefing up the military budget, they were usually referring to tanks and guns and weapons of warfare. However, Phillip was just as interested in the medical technology that would make sure American veterans were taken care of long after their service was over.

He gazed up at the buildings of Walter Reed National

Military Medical Center when they came into view, the looming campus a reminder of the good that was still in the world—thousands of doctors, nurses, and hospital staff all tending to those who had devoted their lives to protecting the nation. Phillip wanted to do all he could to help them while he was in office and perhaps when he was out of office as well. He couldn't think of a nobler endeavor.

On the sidewalk, outside of what he now recognized as the north gate, a small group of men, women, and children had gathered. Phillip's visits weren't publicized, so there generally wasn't much fanfare, aside from a few families of the wounded and some random passersby who, by luck, would manage to get a quick glimpse of the president.

A little boy was holding his mother's hand and waving an American flag high in the air with the other hand. The boy was wearing jeans and a camouflage jacket, and his hair was so blond that it looked almost white.

"Stop the car a moment, Agent Summers, please," Phillip said.

"But, sir, they are waving us to turn and to go through the gate up ahead," the agent said.

"Just for a moment, Agent Summers." He met the agent's sad eyes through the rearview mirror again.

The car stopped, and Phillip pressed a button on his side control panel. Instantly, as his window rolled down, there was the sound of doors opening and slamming, and bodies of Secret Service agents appeared, surrounding his vehicle. The men and women on the sidewalk, surprised by the sudden photo op, pulled out their phones as Phillip directed his attention to the towheaded boy.

"What's your name, young man?" he asked.

The boy appeared bashful and hid partially behind his mother, but after being prompted by a girl who looked like his older sister, he said, "Buzz." He had a lisp, making the name sound like *Buth*.

"That's a great name," Phillip said and was about to ask the young man if he had been named after an astronaut when a sudden blast shook the Beast, followed by fire and smoke, knocking Phillip back into his seat and sending the little boy standing on the sidewalk into the air, his miniature American flag falling from his hand.

14

The greenhouse was located on the other side of the main log cabin, partially hidden by a large shed, which was why Jamie hadn't noticed it when she pulled into the driveway. Its large glass panels were covered with condensation and ice, making it look like an igloo. When Bailino opened the door, a burst of moist, warm air greeted them as they stepped inside.

"Wow!" Faith said, her eyes taking in the greenery. "Are you growing a forest in here?"

"Not quite," Bailino said with a smirk. "Go ahead, cupcake. Go look around. See if you can find the peppers."

Faith wandered off down a center aisle between two rows of crates, each one carefully segmented into equal-size boxes built from wood and labeled with Bailino's unmistakable handwriting, even and precise. The squared, side-by-side arrangement resembled his garden back in Albany, and an image rushed into Jamie's mind: stumbling upon the small bush of blond hair, buried in the dirt, belonging to the woman she had witnessed Bailino beat to death.

Bailino put on his reading glasses to examine the leaves of a plant, looking less like the shovel-wielding monster she knew he still was and more like a harmless middle-aged man with a green thumb. In the years since she thought Bailino had perished in the farmhouse that night in 2014, it had become less difficult for Jamie to reconcile his Jekyll and Hyde persona. Wouldn't anyone born into Bailino's world, she reasoned, have been thrust into similar circumstances and forced to make similar choices? Bailino was a survivor, and, as Jamie had learned, that entailed a blurring of morality. Or was she simply making excuses for him because now he was on *her* side and because they were connected through the person who meant the most to her in the world?

"You like oregano?" Bailino asked, running his fingers along the spiky, purplish flowers of a plant and pulling off a sprig. "Can't get it out here. The Italian food is the pits." He held it up.

"Sure," she said, again sticking her thoughts into a box in the corner of her mind, since they would do her no good now. "Reminds me of my mother. She put it in just about everything she made."

"A woman after my own heart," Bailino said, tucking the sprig in the crease of his left arm. "They mainly grow wheat, barley, and corn here." He ran his finger along another plant and adjusted an electronic thermostat that was suspended from the roof. "Not my cup of tea. Give me some oregano, some eggplant and zucchini, and I'm a happy man. Well, *almost*."

Jamie read the names of the various vegetables on the small placards Bailino had made. "You built this yourself?" she asked.

Bailino nodded. "Mostly. Now and then, I hire some

locals, like my paper boy. His parents don't give him much of an allowance, if you ask me. And there's also a veterans' organization in town. I give them a few bucks to do some small jobs—replace a pane of glass, do a little weeding. Gives them something to do. Makes them feel useful." He fiddled with a knob on something that looked like a radio. "They say greenhouse farming is the next big thing. Lots of technology involved. I built this about a year ago, and now spend most of my time in here."

"Found them!" Faith cheered. She was standing at the far end of the greenhouse, pointing to one of the crates.

"Good girl!" Bailino called and walked over to her.

Near the door, Lucky had made herself comfortable on a small area rug that resembled the one near the fireplace in the guesthouse, as if they were a set. Jamie gave the dog a pat on her head; Lucky's ears flipped down in appreciation.

Jamie wiped a small circle in the condensation of one of the glass panes of the greenhouse and pressed her face to the cold glass. Outside, the fallen snow reflected the sunlight like a mirror, making the world look bright and pristine, like a painting.

"Look, Momma!" Faith said, rushing toward her with two plump green peppers in her hands.

"Wow, those are big," Jamie said.

"Look, Lucky, look!" Faith said. When the dog heard her name she jumped up and knocked over a box of clothing that was stashed near the door of the greenhouse.

"Uh-oh," Faith said.

"No big deal," Bailino said. He was walking behind Faith carrying a few more sprigs and placed them in a basket. "It's just clothing. For charity. For Goodwill and the

University of Wyoming, which offers support services to veterans with disabilities who are attending. I leave it in here so it doesn't get wet, and this way I don't have to be home when they pick it up. They just come in here."

"Oh," Faith said with a nod.

Jamie wasn't sure if her daughter understood anything that Bailino had said or what the word "charity" meant, but she seemed to want them to think she did. Jamie picked up one of the shirts that had fallen on the ground.

"This shirt still has the tags on it," she said, folding it.

"I don't have much to donate, so I just buy a few things here and there and give," Bailino said, picking up the rest and folding it neatly. "Some of these guys have nuthin'. And no one."

He opened the greenhouse door, and Lucky took that as her cue to run out into the snow.

"Lucky, wait for me!" Faith called, dropping her peppers into Bailino's basket and scampering after the dog.

"Careful, Faith, don't fall," Jamie said, but in an instant her daughter came running back.

"Don, do you know how to make angels?" Faith asked, her eyes half covered by the black cap he had given her.

"Hmmm … I've made a few angels in my day."

"A snow angel?"

"Not for a long time."

"Here, watch this." Faith ran out again and stopped abruptly when the dog came toward her. "You sit here," she said to Lucky, and to Jamie's amazement the dog sat down as Faith ran a few steps more and plopped herself down in an untouched portion of the snow. She laid back and flapped her arms and legs.

"See?" she said, her black knit cap now covering her eyes completely. "It's easy. Don, you try."

"Faith," Jamie called, "I don't think—"

"All right," Bailino said. He placed the basket down on a tree stump. "Where should I make mine?"

"Right here." Faith patted the snow next to her.

As Jamie closed the greenhouse door, Bailino got on his knees, flopped backward, and began flapping his arms and legs. Lucky, who couldn't contain herself anymore, ran around them in laps, barking at them, not knowing what to make of what they were doing. After a few more flaps, they both stood up and stared down at their handiwork, and Jamie stood next to them. The weight of their bodies and the movement of their arms and legs had displaced so much snow that the dirt below was visible, making the snow angels look more like large brown butterflies.

"I'm hungry," Faith said. "Are you hungry?" She looked up at him.

"I could eat," he said.

"Last one in is a rotten egg!" she said and made a beeline for the guesthouse, with Lucky behind her. Bailino picked up the basket.

"You forget how much energy kids have," he said with a smirk, but Jamie could detect that he was slightly out of breath.

They started walking toward the guesthouse, their footsteps echoing in the quiet—the kind of isolated quiet that Jamie had learned to avoid in the past five years.

"She likes you," Jamie said. "And she doesn't like many people."

"She's a good kid. Smart." He looked at her with those

dark eyes she had become accustomed to seeing on her little girl's face. "Like her mother."

"I have to call the president," Jamie said, avoiding the urge to return the compliment. She stamped her feet on the front porch of the guesthouse and then walked inside.

"I know you do," Bailino said, following behind. "Just keep in mind that," he placed the basket on the table, "if he tells you that it's safe to go back, that doesn't mean you have to."

His face held that same look it did when he had first suggested in his log cabin five years before that they run off together. The notion had seemed so absurd to Jamie, like something a child might say or the suggestion of someone who truly did not understand the consequences of his actions. That was the thing that always confused Jamie about Don Bailino. In some ways, he was the smartest man she had ever met; in others, he was the most naïve.

"Momma, look, Charlie's daddy is on TV," Faith said, pointing the remote control at the television.

Jamie stepped closer to the set, which was tuned to CNN and showing what looked like cell phone footage of President Grand, hidden behind Secret Service agents, sitting in what Jamie recognized as The Beast. A headline popped off the screen:

Attempted Assassination

"Oh my God," Jamie said.

"What does it say, Momma?" Faith asked, looking concerned, but before Jamie could answer, an explosion knocked the video upward amid screams and shouts.

Bailino quickly grabbed the remote control and

changed the station to Nickelodeon. He placed it on the coffee table.

"What's going on?" Jamie asked as Faith hurried toward her and grabbed hold of her legs.

"I don't know," Bailino said, as the high-pitched machine-gun laugh of SpongeBob SquarePants filled the room. "But what I do know is that, whatever it is, you're staying with me."

15

Katherine held the compress to Phillip's head as Secret Service agents hurried through doorways and congregated around the large marble-topped island in the White House kitchen, which was covered in electronics, paperwork, and several opened bags of potato chips.

"I'm fine, Katherine," Phillip said. "It's just a bump."

"You are not leaving this House again," she said, pressing harder into the wound.

It took a lot to rattle Katherine Grand, but Phillip could tell this second assassination attempt had perhaps done more damage to his wife than it had to him. He gently took her hand away and placed the compress on the kitchen counter. "I'm all right. Really," he said.

She tilted her head up, her expression soft and worried, her veneer of unflappability compromised. He caressed her face, but she pushed his hands away. "I don't think you're understanding what is happening here, Phillip." She crossed her arms, the softness vanishing. "The one time, in our home, our private area, was alarming enough, but it appears this isn't a one-off. Whoever is doing this … is …"

She took a breath. "This person isn't going to stop."

"I know—I do—but this is not the time to panic, Katherine," Phillip said in a calm voice that surprised even him. It had been a long time, not since his military days, that he had been so close to a blast, but a steeliness had come over him as if by muscle memory. "We will find whoever is behind this. We will."

Katherine seemed unconvinced. More agents filled the kitchen, and she moved closer to him and whispered into his ear. "We have been compromised," she said.

Phillip nodded and sat on a stool at the counter. Only a select number of people knew of the day's visit to Walter Reed—both at the hospital and on his staff—including just about every person standing, right at that moment, in the White House kitchen. Phillip needed to speak with Agent Wilcox, but Brandon had been unable to reach him. Until then, he and Katherine would just have to maintain a united front and keep their eyes and ears open.

Collins appeared at the west entryway, looking flustered, but Phillip waved him away for the time being. He would deal with the press later. He leaned over the counter to check on Charlotte and Philly, who were coloring with their grandmother at a small kitchenette table. Philly was dutifully trying to stay within the lines, but his daughter seemed distracted. She was watching the men and women come and go, and kept glancing at Agent Brandon Fuller, who was talking on his phone a few feet away. Phillip knew Brandon wanted him to return to the Emergency Operations Center with his family as a preventative measure, but Phillip wouldn't hear of it. He didn't want to bring the children down there again. He wanted to keep things as normal as possible, but he was beginning to see that that would be an implausibility.

Dr. Stapleton, who had put her hair up in a ponytail since she had examined Phillip a few minutes before, returned with medication. "Take this if you feel any pain, and let me know *immediately* if you begin to experience any dizziness," she said, placing the tiny bottles on the kitchen counter. "I still think you need a more thorough examination."

"So do I," Katherine said, digging her hands further into her crossed arms.

"I'm fine." Phillip stood up and immediately felt dizzy, but he kept that to himself. "I've had worse." He shook the doctor's hand.

Dr. Stapleton gave him a short, disapproving look, but left the kitchen without another word, passing by Collins, who appeared again at the entryway. Phillip shook his head, and Collins disappeared once more.

Across the room, Brandon placed his phone on the clip of his belt, smiled at Charlotte, who was still watching him, and crossed the room toward Phillip and Katherine.

"This is what we know," he said. "It was a similar device to what we found in the private residence—not exactly the same, as the perpetrators were not limited to whatever found objects they could piece together in the White House. But they were similar, in ways I'd rather not go into now, and we believe made by the same individual or individuals."

"How did it get there?" Katherine asked.

"We don't know the answer yet," Brandon said. "It appears to have been hidden in a child's backpack near the crowd of onlookers. Security camera footage at the gate and on the street are being examined now."

"A child's backpack?" Katherine asked.

Brandon nodded.

"Hadn't the route been cleared?" Phillip asked.

"Yes, Mr. President, both by local PD and Secret Service. As I said, we'll know more when we watch the footage—a command center has been established at the site—but I have a strong sense that the perpetrator was either on or near the scene during detonation."

"You think the person was *there*?" Katherine asked.

"It's a hunch, but yes," Brandon said. "This would have allowed him or her to place the IED at the last minute, perhaps just moments before the president arrived. Whoever that was may have been standing on the sidewalk with the others."

Phillip thought of the people who had lined up to greet him, the innocent families waving and smiling. He couldn't remember seeing anyone suspicious, although he had focused only on the little boy. *The boy!* "Tell me about the injuries, Brandon. Were there any casualties?" he asked.

Brandon hesitated, and Phillip's heart sank.

"Several spectators," Brandon said. "The ones closest to the backpack."

"What about the little boy?" he asked.

"What little boy?" Katherine asked.

"I stopped to talk to a little boy …" Phillip remembered the towheaded young man's round cheeks and bashful eyes. "We were cleared to go through, but he looked so full of pride standing there …"

"The doctors say he's going to make it. He's cut up and

bruised from the shrapnel, and may have fractured his leg as, I believe, others had fallen upon him. Again, most of the injuries of the people near him on the sidewalk were minor, since they were far enough away from the point of detonation."

"And the others?" Phillip asked. "My men?" Following the blast, it had been pandemonium. He had had the sensation of his car speeding, he and Clark bouncing around the vehicle's interior like pinballs. Agent Summers must have had the sense to turn around and get them back to the White House. Phillip looked around the room. Nearly all of the Secret Service agents who had escorted him to Walter Reed were there. "Where is Agent Summers?"

"Agent Summers is all right," Brandon said. "He's on his way back to the command center. Again, most of the agents were far enough from the blast not to sustain critical injury. Just some bumps and bruises. But ..." Brandon rocked slightly, looking down at his toes. "Those closer to the gate weren't so lucky. The agents seated in the first car of the motorcade were hurt badly. One was critically injured."

"How critically?" Katherine asked.

"Frankly, we don't know if Agent Chodat, who was driving, is going to make it through the night. And a Walter Reed security guard sustained grave injuries. He was declared dead at the scene."

Phillip's eyes met Katherine's. Not since Mark Nurberg, when Charlotte had been abducted more than five years ago, had a member of law enforcement or security been killed while trying to protect Phillip and his family.

"Frankly, Mr. President," Brandon said, "had you not

stopped to talk with that little boy, your vehicle would have been positioned exactly in the same spot as Agent Chodat's."

Katherine reached for Phillip's arm as that familiar feeling of vulnerability crept back under his skin. A chance decision had changed his destiny. His head began to throb. "Have you gotten through to Agent Wilcox yet?" he asked.

"Not yet, but he must have seen the news," Brandon said. "I'm sure I'll hear from him as soon as he is able."

Collins, looking white as a ghost, appeared at the entrance to the kitchen again. This time, Phillip waved him in. "What is it, Collins?" he asked.

"Mr. President ..." Collins hurried toward the counter and placed his tablet on the kitchen island. "The press has been all over this and is demanding a statement from the White House. The phones won't stop ringing ..."

"Collins, let them demand." Phillip stood up, and the room blurred slightly. He leaned on the table for support, hoping that Katherine wouldn't notice. "We will let them know what we can when we are ready," he said. "We control the news. Not them."

"Mr. President, I'm afraid it's already gotten out of control." He pushed the tablet toward Phillip, and he and Katherine read the blaring headline on the screen:

Target: President Grand

In a second assassination attempt on the life of President Phillip Grand, a bomb exploded outside the gates of Water Reed National Military Medical Center, killing a hospital security guard and critically injuring a Secret Service agent. Sources say ...

"What sources?" Phillip asked.

"They're all anonymous," Collins said.

"Word is leaking out, Phillip," Katherine said, turning the screen toward her. "It was only a matter of time. Collins is right. We have to get in front of this."

"And there's more …" Collins said, his eyes wide with worry. "The *Times* has gone with a story … something about a Hello Kitty watch."

Dammit, Phillip thought. He pivoted the tablet toward him and skimmed the article that Collins pulled up, pinching the screen to adjust the text size. This wasn't good: If Olsen had run with the story, that meant he must have received confirmation from elsewhere, another reliable source. And from what Phillip could glean it was another anonymous source. If that didn't point to a leak in the White House, Phillip didn't know what did.

"Mr. President," Collins said, picking up his tablet, "have you heard from Ja—"

"I want you to work with the First Lady on this," Phillip said.

Katherine's head whipped around, and she frowned at him. "We have entire staffs dedicated to press and communications, Phillip," she said.

"I know, but Jamie isn't here, and this requires your expertise. I need you now," Phillip said. He also needed his wife to keep busy so she wouldn't worry about him. He would rather Katherine be grumpy than scared.

She let out a long exhale, one that was pointedly filled with dissatisfaction. "Oh, all right," she said, dropping her arms. "Let's go, Collins."

"Thank you," Phillip said, reaching for Katherine's hand. She squeezed it quickly and then let it go. "See if you can find out anything on Olsen's source."

"I'm not your damn press secretary, Mr. President," Katherine whispered as she walked away. "But I'll do what I can."

As Phillip watched them leave the kitchen, his eyes met Charlotte's. She was staring at him with a troubled look. He smiled, and although his daughter's big blue eyes showed concern, she smiled back.

"Mr. President, is there anything that you can tell me, anything unusual, maybe, that you remember from what you saw at Walter Reed, just before the explosion?" Brandon asked. "Did you get a good look at all the people standing on the sidewalk?"

"You really think he was there?" Phillip asked.

"It's a definite possibility."

Phillip tried to remember, but his head was beginning to throb again. He had led a public life for so long that faces tended to blur into one another. Only the little boy stood out. "I'm afraid not."

"How about right before the explosion? What can you remember?"

"Well ... I asked Agent Summers to stop. He said they were waving us through, but I was pretty adamant. We stopped. I talked to the little boy, whose sister prodded him to engage with me ... Is she okay? The sister?"

"Yes," Brandon said. "Just a few cuts and minor lacerations."

Phillip nodded. "And then moments later was the explosion."

"Security was waving you through, you say?" Brandon asked.

"Yes, is that relevant?"

"It could be."

"Why? You think someone knew?"

"At this point, I'm simply taking note of the facts, but, yes, it *is* possible. And if that's true, then whoever did this didn't seem to care very much about injuring his or her fellow security staff—or any of the innocent people on the public street. Let me make a few calls." Brandon unhooked his phone from his belt. "If you remember anything else, please let me know, and, with all due respect, Mr. President, until you get the all clear from me, please don't leave the White House, under any circumstances."

"I won't," Phillip said. "Thank you, Brandon."

From the corner of his eye, Phillip saw Rudy Ray Mitchell enter the kitchen, and for the first time since he had met his vice president, the sight of him filled Phillip with trepidation. Rudy Ray searched the crowded space, and when he spotted Phillip he crossed the room in a hurry.

"Phil! Phil!" His large frame glided like a barge. "Are you all right?" Rudy Ray eyed Phillip's forehead. "Dear Lord ..."

"I'm fine, Rudy Ray, thank you," Phillip said. He tried to focus on Rudy Ray's sincere eyes and not Clark's words whispering inside his head: *He came in second among the most likely suspects.* With all that had happened, Phillip was feeling inclined to believe that Clark had a point: Rudy Ray ducking out of the Walter Reed visit at the last minute—even with a legitimate reason—seemed suspicious. At the moment, though, it was too much to consider. "How was the play?" Phillip asked.

"The play? Who gives a damn about a school play? What can I do?"

Phillip looked around the room. The agents were all either on their phones or talking privately to one another. Unless they instructed him otherwise, Phillip had learned that it was best to stay away and let them do their job.

"I'm afraid there's nothing we can do at the moment," Phillip said.

Rudy Ray put his hand on Phillip's shoulder. "I should have been there," he said. "I should have been in the car with you."

The comment surprised Phillip and then burrowed under his skin. He studied Rudy Ray's genial expression, the one that had helped Phillip get elected, and shrugged. "How could you have known?" he asked, wondering if he'd see any kind of reaction in Rudy Ray's eyes. He didn't.

"Well," Rudy Ray let go of Phillip's shoulder, "I'll stick around anyway, in case anything turns up." He stuck his hand in one of the crinkled potato chip bags and said, "Please call me if you need anything," before wandering to the other side of the kitchen.

Phillip touched the bump on his head. His vision was becoming blurry—not enough to alert Katherine or Dr. Stapleton, but enough to tell him that he needed to rest for a bit. He crossed the room to where his mother and children were sitting.

"You should lie down," said his mother, who was sitting primly between Charlotte and Philly. "I think you *know* that."

Phillip couldn't remember how many times he had come home with black and blues or bumps as a child and his mother would glance at him coolly and say, "You should lie down." It was her answer for just about any situation—injuries, accidents, chaos, a bad grade on a spelling test. Phillip was sure he got his penchant for thinking things through from all those times he was told to lie down in his bed as a boy.

"I know, I will." He glanced at his children. "How is everybody here? You guys all right?"

"*Yeth*," Phillip Jr. said, pressing down on a stumpy white crayon. Charlotte simply shrugged. She was looking at her coloring book, with a crayon in her hand.

"What's the matter, cookie?" Phillip ran his hand through her curly hair. "Do you want to come with me to the Oval Office? I'm going to rest for a bit. You can play with your tablet and keep me company. Would you like that?"

She looked up at him, her blue eyes wet. "Are you gonna die?" she asked, looking at his head.

"What?"

Her eyes were wide, waiting for an answer, and Phillip reached down and scooped her up. Charlotte wrapped her legs around his waist, and he pushed back the curls from her face. "Not a chance. Look around at all the men and women who are here to protect us."

Charlotte didn't look around. She appeared skeptical, an expression that mirrored her mother's from just moments ago. She touched the bruise on his head. "Abraham Lincoln got hurt on his head too. My teacher said so."

"Ah, sweetheart, Abraham Lincoln was shot. That was something different. And that was a long, long time ago when they didn't have the people to protect the president like they do now. This is just a bump. Look." He moved his forehead closer so she could inspect it. "This will heal and get better. Do you know why?"

She shook her head.

"C'mon, you're with me every morning, right? What do I eat?"

"A healthy breakfast?"

"That's right. And that has made me strong and smart. Just like you."

Charlotte gave a reluctant smile.

"I'm as healthy as a horse. Right, mother?"

"A horse that needs to lie down," his mother said firmly, adjusting Philly's grip on his crayon.

Phillip could always count on his mother for some plain talk. Most people had considered his father the rock of the Grand family—with his distinguished military career and tough guy persona—but while his father provided a source of strength it was his mother who provided the voice of reason.

"I'm going, Mother. Philly, would you like to come too?"

"No, dank you," he said, grabbing a blue crayon.

"I'll stay here with him until he finishes," his mother said.

"Thank you." It had surprised even Phillip how much he had come to rely on his mother when his family made the move to Washington. While they were known to check in with one another often, mostly during their weekly get-togethers at Taryn's Diner back in Albany, he wouldn't consider the relationship they had to be *close*. He had mostly brought her along so that he could look after her and so she wouldn't be lonely after his father's death, but the truth was that he didn't know how he would have gotten through the past year without her.

"Well, it looks like it's just you and me, cookie," Phillip said. Charlotte wrapped her arms around Phillip's neck and laid her head on his shoulder, which made him feel wobbly again, but he adjusted his grip on her and carried her out of the kitchen.

It took them twenty minutes to get to the Oval Office, since practically every member of Phillip's staff, upon seeing him, came out of their offices to offer him kind words and well wishes. The only noticeable omission was Clark, whom Phillip could see was, not surprisingly, back in his office. His chief of staff—who had sustained a broken nose after the explosion—was standing in the middle of the room, bandages across his face, thundering something to his interns who were by his side, typing feverishly on their tablets.

Phillip closed the door to the Oval Office and placed Charlotte on one of the sofas.

"Are you going to sit with me, Daddy?" she asked.

"In just a minute, Charlie." He took out one of the tablets he kept in his desk for the kids and handed it to her. "You play for a little bit, okay? I need to make a phone call."

As Charlotte inched back on the sofa, Phillip sat behind his desk. It took several big breaths before the dizziness subsided. He hoped that these episodes passed, because what he needed now was to focus. He picked up the phone.

"Janice?"

"Yes, Mr. President?" his secretary said in her kind, gravelly voice.

"Janice, can you connect me with Walter Reed? I want to check on my agents."

As Janice patched him through, the images played again in Phillip's mind—the little boy waving his flag, his sister urging him forward, Rudy Ray putting his hand on Phillip's shoulder, Edna offering to stay on as his housekeeper, Clark talking about intern pools and suspect lists. They were all circling like hands of a clock. He rubbed his temples.

"Mr. President?" a voice said on the other end of the line. "This is Dr. Ortega, head of emergency medicine."

"Dr. Ortega, how are my men?"

There was a pause. "I'm afraid I have bad news, Mr. President. Agent Chodat succumbed to his injuries just moments ago. He didn't make it, sir."

The dizziness reared its ugly head, and with the phone to his ear, Phillip laid his head on his desk, watching a sideways Charlotte poke at her tablet. He closed his eyes.

What is going on, he wondered as the tinny voice of Dr. Ortega spoke in his ear, *and where the hell is Wilcox?*

16

Wilcox stepped off the aircraft at Yellowstone Regional Airport and hurried down the airplane stairs to the tarmac.

"Agent Wilcox?"

A regional federal agent with slicked-back blond hair stepped forward from a sedan. Wilcox nodded, tucking his tie into his jacket.

"I'm Agent Gannon. Right this way, sir," the agent said and opened the back door.

Wilcox got into the vehicle, joining two other agents, one of whom was driving, and the car sped out of the airport. He had had second thoughts about traveling to Wyoming and had almost turned the plane back when he received word about the second attempted assassination of the president, but with Agent Fuller on the ground and Phillip Grand and family safely back at the White House for the time being, he wanted to see this through once and for all.

"What have you got?" Wilcox said. He had been able to track Phillip Grand's call to the number of a burner phone. Although his voice message had not yet been accessed, the phone's last activity had been the night before somewhere within the vicinity of a town called Cody. Wilcox knew he was probably overstepping by tracking the president's phone call; however, President Grand had reinstated him to investigate the attempted bombing at the White House, and to do that Wilcox was sure he needed to contact Jamie Carter.

Gannon held up a paper map from the front seat of the sedan. "This is the area in question," he said.

"What's there?" Wilcox asked.

"Nothing, really."

Wilcox looked out the car window at the flat land around him and the mountains in the distance. He wondered why Jamie Carter was there. On the plane, he had done some research, and of all the properties Faith Carter had inherited from Don Bailino across the United States, none were in Wyoming. Also, based on Jamie Carter's phone records and what he knew about the Carters, she had no friends there—these days, she seemed to have no friends at all. Since her abduction five years ago, she had virtually kept to herself.

"Any hotels in the area?" Wilcox asked.

"About forty," Gannon said.

"Forty?" Wilcox asked incredulously. It would take days to go through them all. Gannon handed him a piece of paper. "What's this?"

"You asked about large pieces of property in the area. These three listings are the largest."

"Are they some kind of rental or hotel property?"

"Not that we're aware of, sir," the agent said.

"Who owns the homes?"

Gannon pulled up the data on his laptop. "One is

owned by a Silicon Valley corporation. It looks as if it is used as a vacation home for the CEO."

"And the others?"

"The second is owned by an old rancher whose family has lived in the area since the late eighteen hundreds. And the last is an old coal mining camp."

"Coal mining?"

"Coal mining was crucial to this territory's development going back about a hundred and fifty years," Gannon said with pride.

"Who owns it?"

Gannon checked his tablet. "A company by the name of Inlaid Boon."

"A tile company?" Wilcox asked. "In a coal mining facility?"

"Unfortunately, not likely. Many of the coal mines have been shut down in this region." Gannon consulted his tablet. "Don't know what the company does. It doesn't seem to be doing much of anything."

"Who runs the company?"

"Hmmm …" Gannon scanned the screen. "Looks privately held. The owner is listed as a D. Carter."

Carter.

Perhaps Jamie has a relative out here, Wilcox thought, although Carter was a fairly common surname. "Do you have any images?" he asked.

The agent lifted his tablet from the seat and showed Wilcox the screen. "These are images of all three properties," he said. "We got these from Google Earth."

Wilcox studied the digital photos, none of which looked remarkable in any way. "When were these taken?"

"In the last ten years or so," the agent said. "Hard to say."

"Anything more recent?"

"I'll get a current satellite image."

Wilcox glanced at the other men in the car, who remained silent. The only sound was the tires charging across the roads, which were slick from the melting snow.

"Here you go, sir," Gannon said, handing Wilcox the tablet. "These were taken just a few minutes ago."

Wilcox looked them over and brought the screen closer to his eyes. Two of the images looked virtually the same as the ones he had seen from Google Earth, but one of them looked vastly different. "Which one is this?" he asked, pointing to the image.

"That one? That's the old coal mining property. Inlaid Boon. D. Carter."

A three-story home had replaced the mining facility. A smaller structure had been built beside it, next to what looked like a large greenhouse. Although the property was covered with snow, Wilcox could see a compact vehicle was parked on the premises and the tracks of what looked like a large animal, perhaps a wolf. He zoomed in on the image using the tablet's touch screen and examined the structure more closely. It appeared to be a contemporary-styled log cabin. A few feet away were two brown patches in the shape of human bodies in the snow, one big and one small.

The skin on the back of Wilcox's neck began to prickle.

"This one," he said, handing Gannon the tablet. "Let's go here first. And step on it."

17

Bailino washed his hands in the kitchen sink while keeping his eyes on Jamie, who was sitting on his bed dialing the phone he had given her.

"Don, is this right?" Faith asked, trying to fold a linen napkin.

"Yes, you have to make sure the sides are right on top of one another, like the bottom side is hiding under the top side."

"Okay," she said, positioning it carefully on the table. "Where did you learn how to do this?"

"In the military, the army." Bailino glanced again at Jamie, who still had the phone to her ear, listening. "Do you know what that is, the army?"

Faith nodded. "Sometimes they come to the White House. They do this." She saluted with her right hand.

"That's right. They're very important people. They protect this country from the bad guys."

"Is that what you do too?"

"Sometimes," he said, turning off the water. He reached for a dozen eggs in the fridge as Faith climbed onto a step stool and stood next to him.

"Don, I was thinking …"

Bailino cracked open an egg and tossed the shell into

the garbage pail. "What about, cupcake?" He glanced again at Jamie.

"Well, I need to talk to Momma about it, but remember how we talked about Momma doesn't want to be with boys, and you said boys are jerks?"

"Yes, I remember that."

"But Charlie says Momma needs a daddy to love us."

"That Charlie is being influenced by her conservative Republican surroundings, if you ask me," Bailino said. "Nowadays, there are all different kinds of families—two fathers, two mothers, no fathers, no mothers. A family can be friends, if they care enough for one another." He cracked another egg.

"But I was thinking that … maybe *you* could be the daddy."

He held the broken eggshells in his hand on the side of the bowl and looked down at her. The little girl's dark eyes were focused and clear before she took the cracked eggshell from his hand, tried fitting the pieces back together, and tossed it into the garbage pail.

"What makes you say that?" Bailino wiped his hands on a dish towel.

"Because," she shrugged, "you already love us."

Before Bailino could respond, Jamie was back in the kitchen. "Phillip wasn't there," she said, placing the phone on the table. "But I checked my messages, and he left one."

"What time?" he asked.

"Early this morning, around six. He said he needs me to come back."

"That was before the second"—Bailino glanced at Faith—"attempt."

Faith pulled on his sleeve. "Don," she said, "you didn't answer ..."

He crouched down so that he was face to face with her. "I am honored that you asked me," he whispered, putting his hand on her smooth cheek. "I can't think of anything else I'd rather do." She smiled. "But I have to talk to your momma first about something. Here," he held up a green pepper. "Can you wash this for me?"

She nodded, and he turned on the faucet. As Faith brought the pepper under the stream of water and scrubbed it with her hands, Bailino leaned toward Jamie. "What did he say exactly?" he asked.

"What was that about?" Jamie asked, motioning to Faith.

Bailino shook his head. "It can wait. What did Grand say?"

"He said it was a rudimentary explosive device that they found, the one in the White House."

"I figured that. No way anything remotely complex could get in there. Anything else?"

"They're still trying to figure out how it got in there. They've questioned everyone who has access to the private quarters. That's why I need to go back."

"It's routine, sweetheart. Doesn't mean anything." He handed a paper towel to Faith, who began drying the pepper. "Did he mention anything about Special Agent Paul Wilcox?"

Jamie's eyes widened. "How did you know that? That he was on the case?"

"What did he say?"

"But how did you—"

"Sweetheart ..."

"Only that Wilcox needed to speak with me."

"What *exactly* did he say?"

Jamie hesitated. "He said that Agent Fuller and Special Agent Wilcox wanted to speak with me, which I thought was strange, because Agent Wilcox retired."

"That son of a bitch never retired. Not when it came to me. Where's Wilcox now?"

Jamie shrugged. "I don't know, but I got the feeling that he was there while Phillip was leaving me a message."

"Why?"

"I don't know, just a sense," Jamie said.

"When was the last time you turned your phone on, your burner?"

Jamie thought for a moment. "I checked to see if Phillip had left me a phone message."

"When was that?"

"When I got off the highway," she said. "When I first got to Cody last night."

"Grab your things," Bailino said, turning off the water faucet. "We gotta go."

18

The sedan skidded to a stop, and all four agents jumped out of the car.

Wilcox drew his gun and listened. The quiet was palpable, the log cabin standing tall before them like a monument in the snow. About ten feet ahead of their sedan was the compact car Wilcox had seen in the photo looking like a deserted island. Snow covered its hood and roof, but some had been wiped from the windows; a pair of footprints tracked back toward the log cabin. Wilcox approached the vehicle cautiously and peered inside the driver's-side window. Nothing—and no one—was there.

He motioned to the agents, and, together, they walked toward the cabin, a sprawling three-story building that appeared newly renovated. As he got closer, Wilcox saw how much the building resembled Bailino's Albany home. The two were almost identical. Had this proof been standing out there—in the great wide open—all this time?

Up ahead, footprints of various sizes canvassed the property, including two sets of footprints, one big, one small, on the front porch. He walked up the stairs as the agents dispersed—Gannon behind him, the others circling around the perimeter of the home. He knocked on the door.

"FBI," Wilcox said, his breath turning to smoke, and waited.

Large icicles lined the edge of the porch roof, dripping water, the drops falling into the snow and making a line of small indentations resembling bullet holes.

"Doesn't look like anyone lives here, Agent Wilcox," Gannon said, peering in a nearby window. He wiped a small circle with his hand, next to another circle that had been smeared at an earlier time. "No furniture. Doesn't look like anyone's been in there in years."

The other agents returned, reporting similar observations. Wilcox tried the doorknob, its metal cold and unforgiving, but it wouldn't budge.

"What's that smell?" Wilcox asked.

Around the side of the log cabin was the smaller building—a guesthouse of sorts—and the remnants of a fire rose from its chimney. Wilcox remembered that there was also another structure on the property, according to the satellite images Gannon had pulled. A greenhouse. He would check one and then the other.

As the agents approached the guesthouse, the snow became more disturbed, and Wilcox tightened his grip on his gun. The footprints included an animal's as well as fresh tire tracks that led away from a garage and toward the woods.

"*Dammit,*" Wilcox muttered. He turned the corner of the guesthouse, stepped onto the front porch, and was immediately greeted by warm air from an open front door. He peered inside. A light over a kitchen sink was on, illuminating a bowl and a pair of green peppers lying side-by-side on a cutting board. The television was playing a cartoon of some kind.

"Hello?" he said, leaning in. "FBI. Anyone here?"

He waited a beat before crossing the threshold, followed by the other agents who quickly fanned out. Wilcox peered out the kitchen window, which provided an incredible view of the mountains. A stainless steel chopping knife lay on the cutting board beside a dishcloth. Wilcox touched the cloth. It was still wet.

He eyed the carefully placed cloth napkins on the dining table and the way the sheets and pillows were neatly stacked on a nearby sofa. He opened the refrigerator—the labels of the jars and bottles all faced forward. Inside the cabinets, the view was the same—the cans, bottles, and bags all lined up like little soldiers.

As the other agents muttered directives to one another, Wilcox crossed the kitchen and peered into a back room, a bedroom. A black-and-white bedspread was neatly folded at the foot of the bed on top of a striped flat sheet that was tucked, military style, around the corners of the mattress. Agent Gannon came up beside him.

"It's all clear," he said. "No one's here. Do you want to check the other two properties?"

"There's no need to," Wilcox said, running his finger along the smooth and dust-free surface of the bedroom dresser.

"What do you mean?"

"This is it."

Gannon surveyed the room. "How can you be sure?"

Wilcox stepped farther into the bedroom to examine a

neat stack of Frankie Valli and the Four Seasons CDs on a nightstand. He crouched down and looked under the bed. "I just am."

"Should I send for backup?"

"No need," Wilcox said. "They're not coming back."

He opened a closet and examined a few dark-colored suits before walking into the main room.

"Well, they couldn't have gotten far," Gannon said. "I'll call it in and recommend checkpoints on a fifteen-mile radius."

Wilcox nodded confirmation, although he was sure it was too late, his eyes falling on the fireplace. The last remaining embers were glowing like cigarette ashes, and he walked toward it until he was eye to eye with the antique pistol hanging on the wall above it—the same antique pistol that had been stolen from Phillip Grand's Executive Mansion office in Albany. He would have recognized it anywhere.

"I knew it," Wilcox muttered, a feeling of satisfaction flooding through him. "He's alive."

19

The motel's broken neon sign blinked *Va_ancy* as Bailino pulled into the parking lot. They had been driving for nine hours, and although she could tell he wanted to keep going, Jamie felt it was best to stop. About halfway through the ride, Faith had grown lethargic, her voice sounding hollow and weak. Jamie was afraid her daughter was on the verge of getting sick. She needed to rest in a proper bed, at least for a few hours. Bailino didn't argue.

"Here," he said, handing her a hundred-dollar bill. "Get the room on the far side of the hotel, over there away from the manager's office."

Jamie looked in the direction Bailino was pointing. "What if it's taken?" she asked.

"It's not," he said with confidence. "I'll watch the kid."

Faith was staring at her with droopy eyelids. "I'll be right back," Jamie said. "And then we'll get you into bed." Faith nodded, which confirmed Jamie's suspicions. Faith never protested about going to bed when she was under the weather.

Jamie quickly ran toward the small office located near the entrance to the motel. The lot was mostly empty, except for a few teenagers drinking beer behind a pickup truck—they stared at her, joking among themselves.

When she opened the door to the office, a harsh bell rang, and a scrawny man, probably about sixty, appeared from a back room.

"Yeah?" he said. "We ain't got any extra towels."

"I'd like to check in for the night," Jamie said. "I'd like the room on the end, please."

The man eyed her suspiciously. "Which end?"

Jamie pointed out the door. "The room back there, near the dumpster. Is it available?"

The man looked out to where she was pointing, and Jamie noticed a security camera positioned right above the front door and aiming straight for them.

"Let me check," the man said, pulling out a large book the size of an encyclopedia and plopping it onto the counter. He flipped it open and made like he was consulting its pages but mostly just flipped a few of them back and forth. "It is," he announced. "Available, that is. But that's one of our premium rooms." He smiled crookedly.

"How much?" she asked, crossing her arms.

He took his time answering, as if he were sizing her up. "One twenty for the night. Including tax."

"I'll give you a hundred in cash," Jamie said and put the bill on the table.

The man stared at the hundred-dollar bill—which, despite being in Bailino's pocket, was crisp and flat, as if it had been ironed—like he hadn't ever seen one before. She expected a negotiation, but, without a word, he poked out his hand and snatched the money like a frog's tongue capturing an insect. Then he reached into his pocket and pulled out a key, unlocking a cabinet behind him. He ran his fingers, his nails cracked and dirty, along a line of colored keys and stopped at a brown one. He put it on the counter.

"We ain't got no extra towels," he said, sticking the hundred-dollar bill in his front pocket. Then he returned to the back room and disappeared.

Jamie took the key and hurried back toward the car.

"Any problems?" Bailino asked when she got into the passenger seat.

"No," she said. "Guy was a bit creepy."

"In a place like this?" Bailino said with a smirk. *"Shocker."*

He pulled the car to the end of the motel. In the backseat, Faith was still awake. Snot was running down her nose, pooling just above her top lip. Jamie wiped it with a fast food napkin.

"She'll be okay," Bailino said, putting the car into park. "Wait in the car." He took the key from her hand and strode toward a brown-colored door marked *Room 115*, prompting Lucky, who had been lying next to Faith, to sit up and observe.

Even from the parking lot, Jamie could see the doorknob wobble as Bailino stuck in the key, but the door quickly opened, and he disappeared behind it. Instinctively, Jamie put her hand on the pistol resting in its holster under her jeans.

"Are we staying here, Momma?" Faith asked weakly.

"Yes, I think so. For a little while."

The motel door opened again, and Bailino emerged. He returned to the car window.

"We're good." He opened the back door and pulled out the luggage. "Take the kid. I've got the rest."

Jamie helped Faith out of the car and held her hand, which felt limp in her palm.

"What about Lucky?" Faith asked, her glassy eyes looking back at the dog.

"She'll be fine, cupcake." Bailino whistled, and Lucky hopped out of the truck and onto the flatbed. "I'll call her in once we get situated."

As the three of them walked into the motel room, the group of teenagers near the office hurled empty beer bottles at one another, producing the rhythmic sound of broken glass hitting the pavement.

"I don't expect them to be any trouble," Bailino said, ushering her and Faith inside the motel room. He closed the door.

Although, as Jamie expected, the motel room hadn't been remodeled in decades, it was surprisingly clean. Bailino put the luggage down on the shag carpeting next to a squat night table as Jamie made her way to the second of two queen beds—the one farthest from the front windows and door—and pulled down the orange bedspread.

"Momma, do they have Nickoledeon here?" Faith asked softly as Jamie removed her coat. She had had some trouble walking from the car and was now leaning against Jamie's side.

"I think we'll be lucky if they have electricity in this dump," Bailino said, putting a duffel bag onto the floor near the door.

"I'll see, but first I need you to get into bed," Jamie said, and the little girl climbed on top of the mattress. Jamie pulled the covers up to her neck.

Bailino stood next to the window, peering out into the parking lot. "It's safe. For now," he said.

The motel was in the middle of nowhere. About a quarter of a mile north, there had been a gray overpass buzzing with highway traffic, and a few gas stations and food joints were scattered about, their neon signs appearing to suck up all the light in the area. It was clear Bailino hadn't chosen the place idly—it was far enough from the highway and any pedestrian traffic to ensure privacy but close enough so that they could make a quick getaway should something go wrong. In the past three years, Jamie had learned quite a bit about hiding.

Bailino opened the front door and gave a short whistle. Lucky jumped from the back of the truck and came running toward the motel room, stopping abruptly to pee next to the dumpster. Bailino closed the door as soon as the dog was inside.

"Lucky," Faith said in a voice that she probably intended to be a cheer but came out as a whimper. The dog went to her immediately and licked the snot from her face. "Where are we?" Faith asked, giving Lucky a pet on the head.

"Somewhere in South Dakota." Jamie tightened the blankets around her daughter. "Get some sleep. It's nice and comfy." She turned on the small television set with the remote control on the night table, and a staticky hum filled the room.

"I'm cold, Momma," Faith said, rubbing goosebumps that had appeared on her arms.

Bailino fiddled with the thermostat attached to the

wall near the door, but the lever moved too easily. He gave it a hard bang with his fist. "You want another room?" he asked.

"No, it's all right. It's only for a few hours." Jamie unzipped Faith's Hello Kitty luggage, fished around, and took out one of her wooly nightgowns. She pulled the covers down and placed it over her daughter's head, on top of her short-sleeved shirt, and pushed her arms through the sleeves. Her daughter complied wearily, her glazed eyes fixed on Lucky, and Jamie pulled the covers up once again.

"Am I sick, Momma?"

"No, I don't think so." She felt her forehead. "No fever. Probably just really tired and rundown. Too much fun in the snow." Jamie pinched her daughter's cheek.

Faith gave a small smile and looked absently at the television, which was tuned to an old movie channel. Lucky curled in a ball next to her.

"Momma, I think my eyes are sick," Faith said, placing her hand on the dog's thick fur. She pointed to the screen.

"No, the channel is just fuzzy, honey." Jamie grabbed the remote control and surfed around, but only one station came in clearly: National Geographic. "Here, watch the deer. Do you see them?" She pointed to the side of the screen.

"Yes, I see them. They're running away from the lions."

"They always do," Bailino said. He pulled a panel of the drapes aside to peer out the window again, his pistol at his side.

Jamie fetched some bottles of water and snack bags out of her luggage and placed them on a round Formica table next to two chairs in the corner of the room. She held out a bottle of water to Bailino.

"No, thank you, sweetheart. I'm fine."

"Do you see anything?"

"No, but it's a good idea for you to stay away from the window," Bailino said. "The light behind you is creating a shadow."

Jamie nodded. She held up the bottle of water to Faith, but the little girl was already asleep with Lucky under her arm.

"Would you look at that," Bailino said, glancing at the two of them.

"I don't know how I'm going to pry her away from that dog," Jamie said.

"Who says you have to? You saw them in the car. Like two peas in a pod."

"I don't think Lucky will like living in our apartment after getting to roam free in the woods."

"You'd be surprised at what an animal can get used to."

Bailino checked his phone, which he had been doing frequently since they left Wyoming. Nothing new had been reported, other than the *New York Times*'s story about Faith's Hello Kitty watch—a development that, while curious to the press, had been jarring to Jamie. She knew that Faith had come dangerously close to the explosive device in the White House, but what she hadn't considered was how close her daughter had been to the person who had planted it. Had the Hello Kitty watch been swiped from Faith's backpack? From Jamie's desk? From her little girl's wrist while she was napping in her office?

"Turn off the light, would you, hon?" Bailino said,

pointing to the light switch. Jamie complied and watched him lean back against the wall, almost disappearing into it. Many times during the long car ride she had thought about telling Bailino to drop her and Faith off somewhere, at a train station or a hospital. Her showing up at his home unexpectedly had put him back on the grid. She wondered if his log cabin in Wyoming had been discovered; if it had, she didn't know if he had other places to go, although she figured he did. He seemed to have a backup plan for every backup plan. Yet, he had already risked his life to save her and Faith—in fact, until a few days ago, she believed that he had *lost* his life for them—and she would rather he, or anyone else, not do it again.

"What do we do now?" she asked.

"I'm still deciding," Bailino said, although if Jamie knew him as well as she thought she did, she was sure he had already decided. He took out his phone again and scrolled, and his expression shifted slightly. "You talk to your brother yet?"

"No, why?"

"He filed a Missing Person report. For you and the kid."

Shit, Jamie thought. "Where did you see that?"

"Take your pick. It's everywhere. One vulture finds a prize, they all want it." He shook his head. "No matter. Here …" He reached into his pocket and gave her one of his burner phones. "Call him."

"What do I tell him?" she asked.

"Tell him that you're fine."

"What if that's not good enough?"

"It's going to have to be. We can't have every law enforcement agency looking for you. It'll slow us down."

Jamie dialed the phone. It barely rang one time before Edward picked up.

"Hello?" he said, his words in a rush. "Who's this?"

Jamie took a breath. "Edward …"

"Jamie, *Jesus*, thank God," Edward said. "Where are you?"

Jamie could hear Trish and the kids in the background yelling into the phone. "I'm fine, Edward. I'm fine. Sorry I didn't call you. It was a spur-of-the-moment decision, and I just needed some time."

"Time for what? Do you know how *worried* I've been? I've been calling Grand, and all he's saying is that you were fine and on vacation out west."

"That's right," Jamie said.

"On *vacation*? Are you *kidding* me, James?" Edward's voice was a mix of fear and anger. "Do you *see* what's going on in the news?"

"I can do without the sarcasm, Edward," Jamie said. "Listen, I can't talk, I—"

"Why can't you talk?"

"Edward, I just can't right now. I—"

"Are you in trouble?"

"I'm fine. Faith's fine."

"You don't sound fine."

"No, I—"

"Say the codeword if you're in trouble."

"I'm not."

"Just say the word, James."

"I don't need to say—"

"When are you coming home?"

"I don't know yet."

"What do you mean—"

"Edward, *enough*," Jamie said louder than she meant to. Faith was still asleep, but her voice had startled Lucky. The dog raised her head, her one eye watching Jamie keenly. "Edward, I'm a grown woman, and I don't have to report to you on every move I make." She took a breath, bracing herself for what she knew she had to say. "President Grand understands that I need some time, and you will have to too. I will let you know when I am coming home when I *know* when I'm coming home."

She waited for him to say something but there was nothing but silence on the other end of the line.

"Are you still there?" she asked.

"I'm here," he said in a low, injured voice. After Charlotte Grand had been abducted, Edward had tried to give her space, but he had served as her protector for so long that it was a part of who he was, which is why he moved down to Virginia after she agreed to stay on with Phillip. Jamie had learned that it was nearly impossible to make people change who they were.

"Please rescind or retract or whatever you have to do about the Missing Person report," she said. "There's no need for it, and the president has enough to worry about. I'll be home soon, okay?"

Again, silence until Edward finally said, "Fine. Whatever, James."

"Edward, you don't have to be—"

He clicked off the call.

Jamie sat down on the edge of Faith's bed. "Well, that went well," she said, placing the phone on her lap.

"He's just worried about you," Bailino said. "That's

a nice thing, a thing people take for granted. He'll come around." He checked out the window again. "How about that ex-husband of yours? He ever check in on you?"

"Bob? Are you kidding?"

"He ever try to get back with you."

Jamie shook her head. "I barely hear from him. Once in a while, when he needs something, he texts, but since Faith and I moved to Washington, not really. He's busy trying to figure out how to get back into the news. Ever since the legal roundtable was disbanded, he's been out of the limelight."

"Talk about a public service," Bailino said with a smirk.

"Listen …" Jamie handed Bailino the phone. "Once we get to Washington, do you have a place you can go?"

"More than enough. Where we both can go. Until we know what's going on, you need to stay with me."

"Isn't it dangerous for you to be with us?"

"Not any more than a typical day." He smirked again.

"I'm serious. Once we get to Chicago or Pittsburgh, maybe Faith and I should take a train back."

"Alone?"

"Yes. It will be safer for you."

"Not so safe for you."

"We don't know that. At this point, we can't know for sure that Faith and I are in danger. I think the second assassination attempt showed us that. Whoever it is is after the president."

"Maybe, but something tells me there's more," Bailino said. "I may have been out in the boonies for a while, but I still have my gut, and it's telling me that you're safest with me."

"I don't want to involve you any more than—"

"I'm already involved, sweetheart." Bailino adjusted the window curtains. "I've always been involved."

His intense eyes stared at her in their familiar way, but they seemed older, weary. "You should sleep," Jamie said. "You drove the whole day."

Bailino waved his hand dismissively. "I've slept enough. I'm done sleeping."

"I mean, I won't run off or anything, if that's what you're worried about."

"I know you won't. Because I'd find you."

She crossed her arms, feeling somewhat offended. "You sure about that?"

Bailino appeared amused, but then his face changed. "You told Faith her father died trying to save her?"

Jamie had been wondering what the two of them had been talking about at the log cabin. She nodded. "I did."

"Why?"

"Because I thought it was the truth."

He seemed to consider this. He rubbed his beard with the stump of his arm. "She called her father a hero."

"He was," Jamie said.

"I could argue otherwise."

"Faith would have died in that cabin if it weren't for you. We both would have."

"Grand saved you. He's the hero."

"He was there because of you," Jamie said. "He told me about your meeting at the abandoned playground."

"Who knew the old guy had it in him?" Bailino looked back out the window. "So the two of you are ... close, then?" It was the first time Jamie could remember that Bailino didn't look at her when he asked her a direct question.

"I'd say so. I trust him with my life, and with my daughter's."

"That's not what I meant," he said.

"I know it's not."

Bailino's eyes shifted back to her. "You're different," he said.

"If you mean I'm not weak and easily manipulated, then you're right. I'm not that girl anymore."

Bailino looked back out the window. "You never were," he said.

It was quiet for a few minutes, the hum of the television the only sound as Jamie watched Bailino and Bailino watched the world outside the window. Without Faith as a distraction, the room felt small, intimate, and she had a sudden desire to spend a few minutes alone.

"I think I might take a quick shower," she said, gauging his reaction. It had been days since she had touched a bar of soap.

"Go ahead," Bailino said, without taking his eyes from the window. "I'll watch the kid."

She stood there awkwardly for a few more minutes, not knowing if that was the reaction she had been expecting, and then she tiptoed toward her luggage. Faith was still lying in the same position in which she had fallen asleep, and Lucky had settled in next to her again, the animal's eye watching Jamie fiddle with her suitcase's zipper. Jamie picked out a few articles of clothing.

"I'll only be a few minutes," she said.

"No rush." Bailino's attention was still out the window.

She padded quickly to the bathroom, the floor squeaking under her feet, and closed the door. She thought of all the bathrooms she had been in with Bailino on the other side and hesitated before turning the bolt—she knew that if he wanted to get into the bathroom, he would, locked or not. She turned it anyway.

The space was small, and it was difficult to move since the shower stall took up most of the room. The floor was sticky, so she placed her clothing, shoes, and holster on the sink, which had a large crack in the porcelain. She carefully undressed, balled up her dirty clothing, and placed it also on the sink, slipping inside the shower. Her plan was to be in and out in minutes, but the water was surprisingly hot, and the moment she stuck her head underneath its stream she found she didn't have the strength to remove it.

She took a deep breath, feeling as if she hadn't taken one in years. The water ran down her body and circled around the rusty drain, dripping through its small holes. It had been through a storm drain that Bailino had escaped a burning building—and kidnapped a child. So much was taking place underneath what people saw every day. She had learned too that Washington, D.C., had all kinds of underground passageways and hiding places. Over the past five years, Jamie had learned it was important to live life not by what people saw, but by what they didn't.

She quickly shampooed her hair with the tiny vial of product located in a broken soap dish and got out of the shower. One small hand towel was all that hung on the towel rack, and she used it to dry herself as best as she could before getting dressed and strapping her gun in place on her calf. She opened the bathroom door and was surprised when everything looked the same—Bailino standing by the window and Faith lying in bed, like a still-life painting. Only Lucky had moved, from under Faith's arms to the bed closer to Bailino. Jamie crossed the room and could feel Bailino watching her; she almost had to check to make sure that she had gotten dressed.

"The bathroom's yours, if you want," she said as if the words would break his gaze. "The water is hot. It's nice."

If Bailino heard her, he didn't move. Lucky's tail wagged back and forth.

"I can stand watch for the few minutes you're not there," she said, trying not to sound too eager—like a student trying to impress her professor.

Bailino took one last look out the window before putting his pistol in the waistband of his jeans. He reached into his duffel bag, took out a dog bowl, and poured some of Lucky's dog chow into it. Then he opened a bottle of water and poured some into a companion bowl and placed them both on the floor near the door. The dog jumped off the bed and hurried toward the food. Bailino eyed the bathroom.

"If there's anything at all," he said to Jamie, "just—"

"We'll be fine," Jamie said. "I'll watch the *kid*." She smiled.

He looked unconvinced but nodded and grabbed a few items of clothing and toiletries from his duffel bag. As he walked toward the bathroom, Jamie stood in his place by the window. She heard the bathroom door close behind her, but not the lock, and the bathroom water clank on.

Jamie peered out between the two curtain panels.

The parking lot was quiet with the same few cars scattered throughout. The teens at the far end were gone, as was their truck; a few broken beer bottles were all that remained, glistening under a nearby streetlight. The sky had become gray, and large clouds had moved in, signaling rain. The man she had spoken to in the motel office came through the office door wearing an overcoat that hung on his gaunt body, waving to someone inside. Although he walked in the other direction, Jamie placed her hand over her holster when the water pipes clanked again and the bathroom door was suddenly open.

"You all right?" Bailino asked, his head outside, steam pouring through the crack between the door and the wall. He was holding the small hand towel against him.

She nodded. "Yes."

He ducked back inside and closed the door, leaving it slightly ajar. When he emerged, he was wearing a fresh pair of jeans and a white T-shirt.

"I'll take it from here," he said, placing his old clothing, which had been neatly stacked under his folded socks, into his bag.

"But I was barely here."

"You really should get some sleep." He motioned for her to move.

She remained where she was. "I'm fine."

"I'll tell you what …" Bailino said in the way she'd seen him talk to Faith, like he was placating her. "We'll go in shifts."

"Perfect."

"I'll go first," he said.

"But I'm already here. You can sleep first."

"Are you seriously going to argue with me?" He crossed his arms.

"Okay," she said, moving away from the wall. "One hour. Then I'll watch."

"One hour, it is."

Jamie checked on Faith who was sprawled across the top of her sheets horizontally. She felt her dewy forehead, which was cool to the touch, and kissed her check, adjusting her blankets so that they were on top of her again. She tried crawling in next to her.

"There's no reason to wake her," Bailino said. "There's a perfectly good bed here that's not being used."

"We usually sleep together."

"Suit yourself. You're only going to have to crawl back out again when it's your shift," he looked at his watch, "in fifty-eight minutes." He smirked. "Although if you fall asleep, I don't mind—"

"I'm not tired," Jamie said. She got up and pulled down the orange bedspread of the other bed. She sat down on it with her back against the headboard and watched the television, which was showing another nature show, this one about the disappearing honeybees. As soon as she was settled, Lucky jumped up onto the bed and circled a few times before plopping beside her, her back against Jamie's leg.

"Lucky, get down," Bailino said.

"It's all right …" Jamie petted the dog's head. "I don't mind."

As soon as the dog felt Jamie's touch, she turned her belly up, and for the first time, Jamie noticed the faded scarring on her underside—long, ragged marks, where the hair didn't grow, stretched from her neck to her tail.

"Oh, my God," Jamie whispered. "Somebody did this?"

Bailino nodded. "Someone left this dog out in the woods to die." He petted Lucky's head. "But we showed them, didn't we, girl?" Lucky nudged Bailino's arm with her snout, and Bailino began to rub behind her ears.

The dog's single eye blinked with satisfaction, and Jamie continued caressing Lucky's belly, running her palm along the long, faded scars. She had been surprised once at how cruel people could be, but not anymore. Faith's breath was blowing idle strands of hair away from her mouth, like a windsock, and an intense weariness overcame Jamie.

She turned her head so that Bailino couldn't see her alertness begin to fade. She closed her eyes and continued to run her hand across the dog's soft, tender skin—round and round—until her fingers grazed Bailino's hand, which was kneading the fur around the dog's neck, and her hand stopped. He put his hand on top of hers and squeezed gently, their stacked hands rising and falling with the dog's resting belly.

It was drizzling now, and the pulsating sound of raindrops pushed Jamie's eyelids open, and she looked toward the window. The lights of the motel parking lot, blurred by the rain, silhouetted Bailino, who was looking down at her, the grooves of his forehead, made shiny by his shower, softened, his dark eyes—Faith's eyes—staring. She tried to focus on his face, but there didn't seem to be enough light, so she sat there, still, watching him, feeling his large calloused palm resting on the top of her hand.

Once upon a time, she had thought it was so simple—love, hate, live, die. Bailino was right. She was different, but so was he, and she wasn't sure whether something had changed in him or in the way she saw him, but in the end, it didn't matter. She turned over her hand, letting Bailino's palm rest inside hers, and that was all the signal he needed. He shooed Lucky to the floor and slipped under the blanket beside her, and as he reached across her body and pulled her to him, she knew she was giving him exactly what he wanted, what he had always wanted, but perhaps what surprised her most was that the older, tired, and damaged person that she had become wanted it too.

❂

"Momma!"

Jamie opened her eyes, looked toward the bed next to her, and nearly panicked when she saw that it was empty.

"Momma, over here!"

At the foot of her own bed, Faith was dancing in front of the television to the jingle of a commercial. To Jamie's right, Bailino was at his place by the window.

"How are you feeling, Faithy?" Jamie asked. She rubbed her eyes.

"I'm great!" Faith said. "Much better!" The top of her lip appeared crusty, but her nose had stopped running.

"C'mere, let me feel your head," Jamie said.

Faith jumped onto the bed and crawled toward Jamie's hand, pushing her forehead into it. "Am I good, Momma?"

"You're good," Jamie said with a smile.

Outside, the sun was low in the clear sky, the

storm clouds having scattered. "What time is it?" she asked Bailino.

"What time is it, cupcake?" Bailino asked Faith.

Faith hopped over to the digital clock on the nightstand. "It's six-o-six," she said. "Oh, no, wait, it's six-o-seven." She hopped back over to the television.

"You were supposed to wake me after an hour," Jamie said. "That was six hours ago."

Bailino waved his hand. "Not necessary."

"Don said that we can have pancakes for breakfast, Momma," Faith said. "Here, Lucky!" She held a treat in the air, and the dog hopped up onto her hind legs until Faith dropped it into her mouth. "Can we? He said it's up to you."

Jamie looked up at Bailino. He was dressed in the same clothing he had put on after his shower and standing in the same spot. She reached under her blanket and felt her yoga pants and underwear still on her, her gun and holster in place. For a moment, she thought she had dreamt what had happened until she spied her bra neatly folded on the nightstand.

"Can we, Momma, huh, can we?" Faith asked, climbing on top of her bed again and jumping. "When will we be back home?"

"In a few days, I think, sweetie," Jamie said.

"Maybe sooner," Bailino said. "There was some news while you were sleeping."

While you were sleeping. His voice suddenly carried images with it, his hand upon her, his breath on her neck. "News?" she asked.

He swiped his cell phone screen and faced it toward her. "Some details about the YouTube guy's shooting," he said, and Jamie read the headline: *Famous YouTuber O'Connell Shot in Eye with a Single Bullet.*

Jamie took Bailino's phone from his hands and kept reading:

Sources say O'Connell's body was discovered during an FBI investigation into the attempting bombing of the White House. O'Connell had been staying in off-campus housing with fellow SUNY Albany student Alex Campos, who was present when the grisly discovery was made. O'Connell had risen to fame for capturing President Phillip Grand saving Jamie and Faith Carter from a burning building more than three years ago. So far, there has been no comment from law enforcement or the White House regarding the possible connection between the two events.

Jamie sat up in bed but remembered her bra was off and pulled the blanket over her. She returned the phone to Bailino. "You think O'Connell planted the IED?" she asked.

"No, I'm pretty sure it was someone else."

"I don't understand," Jamie said.

"Momma, watch!" Faith was jumping high on her bed and touching the ceiling with the tips of her fingers.

"Be careful, Faithy, and don't touch the ceiling," Jamie said. "It's dirty."

"O'Connell was shot in the eye," Bailino said as Faith took one last bounce off the bed and onto the floor.

"Why is that significant?"

"Paolo Cataldi was a stickler for one shots—one and done, he used to say—and taught his people to aim for the forehead."

"But Paolo Cataldi is dead." Jamie's eyes grew wide. "Or is he?"

"No, that son of a bitch is gone."

"So you're saying this was one of his guys? You think the shooter was aiming for the forehead and missed?"

"Not at all. I think it was a perfect shot."

"I'm sorry, but I'm lost," Jamie said.

"No, you're not, Momma," Faith said, twirling in front of the television. "You're in South Dakota."

"I used to know someone who liked to shoot people in the eye," Bailino said softly, his voice sounding like a low growl. "Saw it done twice." He got up and reached for his duffel bag. "C'mon, we need to go. And you need to call Edward."

"Uncle Eddie!" Faith squealed. "Lucky, you're going to meet Uncle Eddie!"

"Why?" Jamie asked.

"Call tomorrow morning when we're closer to the East Coast. You need to tell him to pick you up at Union Station tomorrow evening. Ask Grand to do a sweep of Edward's house, make sure it's safe, and then you and the kid should stay there."

She got out of bed, making sure her back was toward Bailino, picked up her bra, and went into the bathroom. When she came out, she quickly gathered her things.

"Momma, I think Lucky has to pee." Lucky was circling near the door.

Bailino opened the door, and the dog ran toward the dumpster.

"Where are *you* going?" Jamie asked Bailino.

"To talk some sense into the person who started all this nonsense."

Jamie helped Faith put on her jacket. "And you're sure he's the one who did it?"

"I'd bet money on it," Bailino said, zipping his duffel bag and throwing it over his shoulder. "And if I'm right, it's not a he. It's a *she*."

20

ToniAnne Cataldi sat on the deck of her backyard listening to the oldies radio station and watching Lorenzo, who had his head under the hood of his '83 Trans Am. It was amazing how much that man loved his car—besides her, it was the only thing he paid any attention to. And, yet, even with all his constant fiddling, he still hadn't gotten it to run in years.

ToniAnne had more in common with that damn car than she realized.

She gazed down at the paperwork on the glass table that her real estate agent had given her. She had four offers on her Aunt Mary's house in Brooklyn, all of them more than what she had asked for and probably ten times more than Uncle Paolo and Aunt Mary had paid for the dump after they got married. She didn't want to deal with any of it, but, unfortunately, she was the only one left. Everyone else was dead—or batshit crazy.

"Lorenzo, should I pick *eenie, meenie, miney,* or *mo*?" she called out.

"What?" Lorenzo called, sticking his head out from under the hood, oil smudged across his face.

She didn't know why she even bothered asking him

anything when he had his head buried in metal. She always had to repeat herself. "Just pick one: *eenie, meenie, miney,* or *mo.*"

"*Miney,* of course," he said. "*Duh.*"

"*Miney,* it is then." She pushed the papers away from her. "Well, that's that. What time is it?"

Lorenzo looked at his watch and frowned. He rubbed its face with the back of his hand and looked again. "About a quarter to five."

ToniAnne watched the news more times in the past week than she had in the past few years. She didn't expect to see or hear anything earth-shattering—so far there had been no sign of Lorenzo or of her car on any of the coverage of the second assassination attempt, and if Lorenzo knew what was good for him there wouldn't be any—but her father had said it was important to know everything the cops knew. Therefore, she had to plop herself down and watch those two know-it-all anchor bitches smile their way through the day's murders, rapes, and thefts.

She reached into her handbag and pulled out one of her burner phones. She typed:

What's the ETA on the next one?

She waited a few seconds, starting to get impatient, when the phone pinged.

Should have everything in a few days.

Not good enough, she texted. *Speed it up.*

She put her phone away and stood up. "You coming or what?" she asked.

"In a minute. I just want to finish this."

"Finish what? That thing hasn't run in seven years."

"Just go inside already." Lorenzo ducked his head back under the hood. "I know what I'm doing."

ToniAnne slid open the screen door and shut it behind her. She poured herself a glass of red wine and sat on the sofa, pushing aside all the sales orders for her at-home hair salon business, which was more of a hobby than a business, but what the IRS didn't know wouldn't hurt it.

She turned on the television with the remote control. Before the screen even warmed, she could hear Judge Judy laying into a landlord who had turned off the heat on a single mother with three kids. *That Judy is a badass*, she thought.

As the credits rolled, Lorenzo came trotting in and was about to sit next to her, but ToniAnne put her hand on the sofa cushion. "Wash your hands, please," she said, setting the wine glass down on the coffee table. "And your face."

Lorenzo huffed in his usual adolescent way but did as he was told. When he returned, an open soda can in his hand, the logo of the local news hour floated across the television screen, followed by the words *Breaking News*.

"There's breaking news every day," Lorenzo said, plopping down next to her. "What the hell?"

"I know," ToniAnne said. "It's a constant false alarm, it's ridi—"

ToniAnne's words left her as an image of Don Bailino filled the screen.

"We have breaking news," the anchor to the right said solemnly but excitedly as the anchor on the left beamed with fake anticipation. "Sources have told News 4 New York that organized crime boss and prominent businessman Don Bailino, who was believed to have died in the spring of 2014, may actually be alive."

ToniAnne sprang up from the couch. "Get ... the ... fuck ... outta ... here!"

"Bullshit," Lorenzo said. He laid back on the couch and crossed his arms.

"The Federal Bureau of Investigation has told the Associated Press that there is strong evidence to believe that Bailino has been living out west—and out in the open—for the past three and a half years." An aerial photo appeared on the screen showing a log cabin standing in the snow with Feds swarming the property like insects, followed by an old mug shot of Bailino. ToniAnne paused the television.

"Fuckin' Donny, man," she said, tracing the outline of her lips with her finger. "Never ceases to amaze."

"I'll believe it when I see him."

"Don't be jealous, hon."

"Jealous? Of that old guy? Please ..." Lorenzo stood up and stretched, a telltale sign, ToniAnne knew, that he was annoyed. "Can I borrow your car again? I'm gonna head to the gym."

"What's wrong with your caddie? You didn't want to drive it on the Belt Parkway on Monday because of the potholes ... You didn't want to drive it to Maryland yesterday, because you didn't want to put all the miles on it. Now what's the excuse?"

"It looks like rain. I don't want to get it wet. I just got it detailed."

"Oh, heaven forbid." She went into the kitchen, opened her handbag on the counter, and handed him the keys. He left without a good-bye. Another telltale sign he was pissed. *Sayonara*, asshole. ToniAnne hurried back to the television, sat in front of it, like a child eager for her favorite show, and unpaused it.

"Authorities have not discussed what evidence has been uncovered, but law enforcement officers nationwide have been instructed to be on the lookout for Bailino, who once topped the FBI's Most Wanted List and is believed to have only one hand. Sources say that he sawed it off," the reporter made a face like she had sucked on a lemon, *"when making his escape. We'll keep you posted as more updates occur. In the Bronx, a four-alarm fire broke out ..."*

ToniAnne paused the screen. Her blood was sizzling, her pulse hammering her ears. She hadn't seen Bailino since the day he had come to bring Joey upstate, not long before her father had been executed by that no-good Phillip Grand, but the mere mention of him on TV, and the flicker of a blurry photo, had brought him back in all his glory. The deepness of his eyes. The firm hold of his calloused hands. She could even smell his cologne.

Lorenzo was wrong. He *was* alive. She knew it, and something awakened in her that she thought had died three years before. *But why hadn't Donny contacted me*, she wondered. *I could have helped.* But she knew he wouldn't have. That wasn't his style. Donny protected the ones he loved. He always had.

She hit rewind on the remote control until she was back at the beginning of the news story and settled back into the couch. Then she pressed *play*, picked up her glass of wine, unbuttoned the top of her jeans, stuck her hand inside her underwear, and watched the news segment again and again.

21

"That's impossible. Bailino is dead," Phillip said, lying back on a chair in the presidential bedroom suite, a cold compress on his forehead. He felt a bit undignified, but he was trying to make two people happy—Katherine, who insisted he rest, and Wilcox, who insisted they meet.

"I'm afraid not, Mr. President," said Wilcox, who was all business, dressed in a suit and tie, and appeared out of place in the usually casual private area. He pulled a folder from the hands of Agent Fuller, who was standing beside him, and held it out for Phillip.

"Can't we do this at another time?" Katherine said, standing between them. She adjusted the cold compress. "Phillip really needs to rest."

"It's all right, Katherine." Phillip sat up slowly. He had had enough of lying down and should never have told his wife about the dizzy spells. He handed her the compress, opened the folder Wilcox had given him, and pulled out a stack of photos.

"The first one there is of Bailino's log cabin in Albany. The second is of the log cabin in Wyoming. They're identical, sir. Everything about the place, as you can see from the additional photos. The groceries ... the sheets ... All of it has Bailino's name written all over it."

Phillip flipped through the photos. "Is this really enough to prove he's alive?" he asked. "The way the news media is talking about it, you would think we found something more substantial."

"It's him, sir," Wilcox said. "I'm sure of it. My guess is the leak to the media was from someone at the field office out west. Local reporters were beginning to snoop around just as I was heading back to Washington."

"So you think he was *there*?" Katherine asked. "That he's been *living* there?"

The question made Wilcox appear tense. "He must have gotten tipped off, somehow. Unfortunately, we don't know what type of vehicle he's driving or where he is. What we do know is Jamie and probably Faith either *are*— or *were*—with him."

"Jamie?" Phillip asked. "What makes you say that?"

Wilcox took in a long inhale as if trying to fortify himself. "Mr. President, when you reinstated my credentials, you did so under the assumption that I would do everything in my power to find out who was responsible for the attempted bombing in the White House, correct?"

"Yes, Agent Wilcox," Phillip said, placing the photos on a side table.

"And you know I would do everything in my power to get that done."

"Yes, of course. What is this about?"

"Yesterday morning, while we were talking on the Truman Balcony, I traced the phone message you sent to Jamie Carter. I discovered it had been sent to a burner phone that—"

"You *traced* my private message?" Phillip asked, pain shooting like a thunderbolt across his temples. "Under whose authority?"

Wilcox straightened. "Yours, Mr. President."

"I didn't reinstate you so that you could spy on me."

"I think we're losing focus, sir," Wilcox said. "Your message is what got us here, to the location of Bailino. It had been sent to a phone that was not far," he pointed to the photos, "from the location of that log cabin. Jamie was *there*."

"I understand that part." Phillip reached for a glass of water, trying to stave off another dizzy spell. "I understand that Jamie was staying at a log cabin in Wyoming that resembled Bailino's log cabin in Albany. My concern, Agent Wilcox, is in your investigation you invaded an American citizen's privacy. And that's crossing the line."

Wilcox reached into his briefcase on the floor and pulled out a clear plastic bag. He handed it to Phillip.

"What is this?" Phillip asked, examining its contents, when his pulse quickened. Inside was his antique pistol, the one his father had given him, the one he believed to be buried somewhere under the rubble that was the old Barbara farmhouse and never expected to see again. "Where did you get this?" he asked.

"At the log cabin in Wyoming. It was hanging on the wall like a trophy," Wilcox said with disdain. "Forensics has already gotten Bailino's fingerprints from it—along with yours, of course."

"Mine?" Phillip asked, his voice cracking. Katherine sat next to him and put her hand on his knee.

"Well, it was your gun, Mr. President. It's understandable that there would be partial fingerprints of yours on it."

"Oh, of course," Phillip said. "How did it get there?"

"I'm sure you would agree that there is really only one way that pistol would show up in a guesthouse on property in Cody, Wyoming. The only question is … How did Bailino get it out of your office at the Albany Executive Mansion? The place was crawling with agents."

Phillip felt the weight of Wilcox's gaze, the same gaze that nearly pierced holes in him back at the hospital in Albany after the farmhouse incident—as if he knew there was more to the story and that Phillip could provide the answers.

"We know Bailino used this gun to shoot Paolo Cataldi …" Wilcox rummaged through his briefcase again and pulled out a photograph. "This is a photo of the antique bullet found inside Cataldi's eye socket. It's a match for this gun."

Phillip reached for the photo. It showed Paolo Cataldi's decapitated head with a prominent bullet hole through the eye socket and a small bullet beside it, next to a ruler and various markings. Wilcox then handed Phillip a similar grisly photograph of Samuel O'Connell.

"It may not have been a coincidence that both men were shot in the eye," Wilcox said.

"You think Bailino murdered O'Connell?" Katherine asked. Phillip handed both photos to her; his wife studied the gruesome images.

"I don't know, but it's worth noting," Wilcox said.

"There's something very Cataldi-esque about it. An eye for an eye, perhaps?"

Phillip rubbed his temples. He didn't know if it was the dizzy spells, the attempted assassination, Wilcox's stares, or the years of worrying that he would one day be found out that had finally put him over the edge, but he had had enough. "It's not worth noting," Phillip said. He took the photos from Katherine and handed them back to Wilcox.

"What do you mean, Mr. President?" Wilcox asked. The question was asked calmly, but Wilcox's eyes were dancing with anticipation.

"Phillip," Katherine said, "maybe we should wait until you feel better before you—"

"No, I'm afraid I owe Agent Wilcox an apology. I owe all of you an apology." Phillip stood up and took a deep breath, waiting for the dizziness to cloud his thoughts, but his head was surprisingly clear. "All of you deserve to hear the truth of what really happened that night, the night the Barbara farmhouse burned to the ground." Wilcox had an expectant look on his face, as if he had been waiting more than three years to hear what Phillip was about to say.

"I shot Paolo Cataldi," Phillip said bluntly and then told them everything, determined not to leave anything out about the series of events—how Bailino had contacted him to help locate Jamie Carter, how he had smuggled the antique gun from his office to meet Bailino, and how he had used that gun to shoot Cataldi after Bailino had learned of Jamie's whereabouts. "It wasn't Bailino. It was me. I didn't intend to be there, but found myself driving there. For Jamie? Bailino? Myself? I don't know." He motioned toward the photos in Wilcox's hands. "And, with regard to the bullet hole, I was aiming for his chest, not the eye. That's it. That's the whole truth." He inhaled deeply and felt a weight lifted from his shoulders. "Katherine knew nothing about this, for obvious reasons …" He reached out for his wife's hand. "Samuel O'Connell seemed to stumble upon the scene at the end, when I was coming out of the building. For three years, I worried if he knew that there was more to the story. Now he's gone, and I guess I'll never know."

The room was quiet for what seemed like a long time until Wilcox broke the silence. "I don't appreciate being lied to, Mr. President," he said.

"I know, and I'm sorry for that. I meant what I said earlier this week, that I trust the three of you implicitly and—"

"Apparently, not implicitly enough." Wilcox crossed his arms.

"Things aren't always so black and white," Phillip said. "There was more going on, Agent Wilcox."

"Yes, you were aiding and abetting a fugitive," Wilcox said.

"Don't be ridiculous," Katherine scolded. "I think you know that whatever Phillip did he did because he believed it was the best course of action."

"The law is the law, Mrs. Grand," Wilcox said. "I would assume the person who established a legal roundtable would know that what he was doing was not only illegal, but wildly unethical."

"All right, *enough*," Brandon said in a voice that took Phillip by surprise. The young agent had been quiet but now appeared flustered. He rocked gently on his heels. "This is getting us nowhere. Whatever happened before happened before, and it's not helping us take care of the present situation." He took the photos from Wilcox and placed them into the briefcase. "I think we all have enough respect for one another to accept our judgments as to what is the best way to get the job done." Brandon's eyes moved from Wilcox to Phillip. "Sometimes that involves keeping others in the dark—whatever our reasons ... I understand that, as should you, and we can't let that divide us. We need to find whoever it is that is trying to bring down the presidency of the United States. Whether you believe that person is Don Bailino or not, we need to work together to find out."

Again, the room was quiet, and a wave of embarrassment seized Phillip, but he also felt pride for his young agent who had not only become an estimable member of his security detail but also, it seemed, quite the mediator. "Brandon's right," Phillip said. "We need to move on."

"Agreed," Wilcox said with a nod. "One question, first ... Did you know he was alive?"

"Who?" Phillip asked. "Bailino? Of course not."

"So the message you left for Jamie Carter wasn't some kind of warning? We couldn't have missed them by more than an hour."

"Absolutely not," Phillip said.

Wilcox sat back in his seat, appearing satisfied, but also troubled. "Jamie Carter is still a missing puzzle piece. You realize that."

"Any ideas on where she is?" Katherine asked.

"We received a tip from a hotel manager in South Dakota," Brandon said. "We received it just after Edward Carter filed the Missing Person report." He took another photo out of the briefcase and handed it to Phillip. He and Katherine peered down at the grainy photo of a woman and man. "It was taken at about one o'clock this morning eastern time. It's a still from security camera footage."

"What is she pointing at?" Phillip asked.

"Can't be sure," Wilcox said.

Phillip brought the photo closer to his eyes. It was Jamie, for sure. He would have recognized her anywhere. "Maybe she's in trouble, and she's telling the hotel clerk that there's someone after her?"

"I don't think so, judging from the expression on her face and her body language," Wilcox said, and Phillip was inclined to agree. "Clerk says she paid for a night's lodging, but left before he came in the following morning."

"Was she with anyone?" Katherine asked.

"Not that he could see," Wilcox said. "And she wasn't with a child."

"And there's more," Brandon said. "Only hours after Edward Carter filed the Missing Person report for both his sister and his niece, he *retracted* it. Said it was a mistake."

"That's curious," Katherine said, and Phillip could tell his wife was sifting through the information in her mind, a function of her years as a PR strategist and media spokesperson. "Had he heard from Jamie?"

Wilcox nodded. "She called him, and although we were unable to get a location on her, we were able to get a general region on the call, and that hotel is smack-dab in the middle of it."

"What does that mean?" Phillip asked. "She's on her way back?"

"With Bailino?" Katherine asked.

"We don't know," Wilcox said. "Unfortunately, there's only one person who can answer all these questions." He crossed his arms. "And for some reason no one—her brother, her employer, anyone—knows where she is."

22

Bailino merged onto I-395 toward Washington, D.C., the nation's capital looming in the distance—a bunch of white buildings with pretty domes and regal columns, most of them filled with dirty politicians. He thought perhaps being out in the sticks for more than three years with a bunch of lumberjack barflies—for whom red was a color on a flag, a complexion, and a mind-set—would change his outlook on government. It hadn't. The twenty-four-hour news cycle had taken care of that. He thought of Phillip Grand dealing with these clowns, most of whom would sooner see their own mothers die of lung cancer than lose their income from the tobacco lobby. Still, he felt a sense of hope. Despite all that had happened between them, Bailino knew Phil was one of the good guys. Bailino would have voted for him if he hadn't been dead.

"Are we almost there?" Faith asked from the backseat.

"Almost, cupcake," Bailino said, glancing in his rearview mirror. The little girl was such a trouper. Even after more than twenty hours in the car, she never complained or whined, spending most of the time staring out the window or patting Lucky's belly. That sense of patience would serve her well in her life.

Jamie had been sitting quietly in the passenger seat for the last few hours, ever since he told her about ToniAnne Cataldi. He could tell she was in her head, trying to figure shit out. He meant what he had said. He had more than enough places for them to hide out—for the rest of their lives, if need be. He just had to talk some sense into ToniAnne first. And that could take a while.

"It's going to be all right," he said. "Whatever happens."

"What if it's not her?" she whispered suddenly. "What if someone else is trying to hurt the president?" As she leaned toward him, the top of her shirt fell slightly away from her skin, revealing a hint of cleavage. "Or Faith?"

"It's her. Trust me." He had the urge to reach for her hand but held back.

"Couldn't anyone have shot him in the eye?" she asked.

"It's possible, but ToniAnne could do it without thinking twice, and would do it out of habit. People usually go for the head or chest. You have to want to shoot someone in the eye and do it before they realize you're going to do it, because they'll move and you'll miss."

"You've seen her do it?"

Bailino nodded. "She used to bring Joey upstate from time to time, even though my preference was to pick him up. That woman never listened." He glanced in the rearview mirror at Faith, who was still looking out her window. "We used to go hunting—deer, bears, rabbits. Most hunters shy away from the head so they can have a pretty trophy for their wall. ToniAnne aimed straight for the eyes. That girl was a born hunter, but she was born in a family that thought women belonged either on a pedestal or in the kitchen or bedroom." He shrugged. "I guess now that Gino and Paolo are gone, she thinks she needs to do something. She thinks it's her time. And I know she has a hard-on for Phillip Grand—she blames him for the death of her father, Gino. And, probably, for mine."

"But it's more than just being a good shot, isn't it? You have to be sure not to leave evidence at the crime scene. All that."

Her face had developed a slight hardness—there were small lines around her eyes and mouth—but it was as sweet as when he had seen her in Bryant Park for the first time. "I stopped underestimating women about five years ago." He smirked.

She twisted a strand of hair behind her ear, revealing the delicate curve of her cheekbone. The scent of her freshly washed hair had diminished, but he could still smell it, and it reminded him of being on top of her, the feel of her dry skin.

"The Feds wouldn't even think to question ToniAnne—her father kept her out of things—for the most part," he said. "She was barely a blip on their radar, which used to piss her off ... As far as they know, she runs some kind of home haircutting business, but trust me, she's a far better shot than any hairdresser."

He took the U.S. 50 exit toward downtown and drove along Constitution Avenue, eventually making a few turns and pulling into a parking spot just across from the International Spy Museum. He reached into the glove compartment, put on a baseball cap, and handed Jamie a pair of sunglasses.

"We're there?" Faith asked.

"Yes, sweetie," Jamie said, reaching for her handbag.

Bailino put his hand on hers. "You know what to do, right?" he asked.

Jamie nodded, letting his hand cover hers. "Yes, I know. It'll be okay. I trust Phillip."

He ignored the wave of jealousy that flooded through him and put his hand back on the steering wheel as Jamie reached back to unbuckle Faith's seat belt. Lucky, who sensed something was happening, was alert and sitting on the backseat, her paws on the back of Bailino's headrest.

"Be careful, sweetheart," Bailino said.

"I will," she said, opening the passenger's-side door. "You too."

"I'm fine."

"How are you going to contact me?"

"When you get the signal, you'll know."

She nodded, looking as though she were going to say something but decided against it, and stepped onto the sidewalk. When she opened the back door, Faith sprang out of her car seat, while the dog stayed seated, waiting to be told what to do.

"Okay, honey, let's go, but be careful," Jamie said. "Don't step in the puddle."

"I saw the white buildings. That means we're near home, right, Momma?"

"Almost," Jamie said, tying the laces of one of her new sneakers and pulling their luggage out of the car.

Faith peered into the front seat. "Aren't you coming?" she asked Bailino.

"Not right now, cupcake," he said, "but go with your momma."

"When will I see you?" A look of disappointment spread across her face.

"I'm not sure, but I'll come as soon as I can. I didn't forget what we talked about."

"We have to go, sweetie," Jamie said, putting her hands on the little girl's shoulders. She was inspecting everyone around her, the strange bodies brushing by, and moving Faith if they were too close. *Good girl.*

"But," Faith said, "wait …" She climbed into the passenger seat, sitting on her knees. She reached under her shirt and pulled out her necklace with the gold cross. "Here," she pointed the cross in Bailino's direction, "I want you to have this."

She stared at him with seriousness, and for the first time he recognized his own eyes looking back at him. "But I thought it was your favorite thing," he said.

"It is." She smiled.

"Then you should keep it."

"But you're my favorite thing more," she said.

Bailino didn't know how to argue with that. He reached behind her neck, unclasped the necklace, and placed it around his own neck, the coldness of the gold rope chain familiar against his skin.

"Now, you'll remember me," she said, satisfied. She turned to get out of the car, but Bailino gently placed his hand on hers.

"Wait, I have something for *you*," he said.

"You do?"

He whistled, and Lucky's snout came into the front

seat. The dog licked Bailino's face.

"Now I'm giving you *my* favorite thing." He put the dog's leash in her tiny hand.

Faith's face lit up. "Really? For myself?"

"Yep, she's all yours. After all, you have the same last name."

"You're kidding, right?" Jamie asked, sticking her head into the car. "She's bigger than our apartment."

"She needs love more than mountains. Walk her once or twice a day, she'll be fine. She'll watch *her*," Bailino said, motioning to Faith.

"Oh, Momma, can we please keep her?" Faith clasped her hands together and closed her eyes. "Please, please, please, please, please—"

"All right, all right ..." Jamie said. "But we have to hurry." She stuck her head back out, and Bailino could see she was looking for security cameras. "I have no idea how I'm going to get Lucky into Uncle Edward's car. What else do we need?"

"I already put the dog's stuff in your luggage," Bailino said.

Faith bounced out of the car and went into the backseat, wrapping Lucky in a hug. When she tried to get the leash on the dog's collar, she couldn't latch it, and Bailino held the collar still until the little girl could snap it closed.

"You're coming home with us, Lucky!" Faith squealed. The dog licked her face.

"Look at that ..." Bailino said. "She really is lucky, after all." He winked at Jamie.

Faith lunged at Bailino and wrapped her arms around his neck, squeezing him hard, her body arched across the well of the backseat. Before she let go, she put her mouth near his ear and whispered, "I love you." Then she zoomed back out of the car. "C'mon, Lucky," she said, holding her mother's hand. "We're going home."

Lucky's single eye followed the little girl out of the car, but the dog sat dutifully on the backseat.

"Goodbye, friend," Bailino said, scratching the dog behind the ears. "Take care of them."

Faith poked her head back into the car. "Come on, Lucky! You want a treat?"

At the word *treat*, the dog jumped toward the little girl, out of the car, and onto the sidewalk.

"So much for loyalty," Bailino said as Jamie closed the front and back doors.

"Drive safely," Jamie said. "And thank you."

Bailino nodded. "I'll be in touch."

Jamie took hold of the luggage, two stacked bags, with one hand and covered Faith's hand and the leash with the other, and the two of them walked in the direction of Union Station, Lucky trotting beside them. Images played in Bailino's mind of a life that could have been, and he remembered something Gino once said to him when Bailino had returned from the Army: "Don't get all hoity-toity on me, kid. Those pins might make people think you're some kind of war hero, but I know who you really are."

As Jamie and Faith disappeared into the crowd of tourists, Bailino believed he was watching two of only three people in the world who knew who he really was. The third was living only a couple of miles away in one of those pretty white buildings.

23

P hillip sat at his desk in the Oval Office, reading the tax bill for the third time—a bill that had received overwhelming support in Congress and that he knew had senators eagerly awaiting his signature—but his mind was elsewhere. He looked at his watch. Jamie would be arriving anytime.

Phillip had been surprised and relieved to hear from her. All she said was that she and Faith were fine, that she needed Phillip to have both her apartment and Edward's home cleared by security, which made sense, given they still didn't know what was going on, and that she needed to speak with him—and she needed to do it in person.

For a moment, Phillip considered not telling Katherine or Wilcox, but after he had finally come clean and confessed his involvement in the events of spring 2014, he didn't want to start again on the wrong foot. He promptly reported the call to Katherine, Brandon, and Wilcox, asking them to give him some time with Jamie to sort through what had happened before any official inquiry. Katherine and Brandon were kind enough to comply. Wilcox wasn't.

"She's late," Wilcox said from one of the sofas. He

clipped his cell phone back onto his belt when there was a knock at the door.

❂

Although it was Saturday evening, Jamie Carter had the unremarkable look of business, wearing a plaid skirt that ran just above the knee and a black V-neck sweater that was neither too tight nor too loose. Her long brown hair was tied into a neat ponytail, and she held a clipboard in her hands along with her cell phone, as if reporting for duty. If Wilcox hadn't known better, he would have assumed she was in the middle of a routine day in the Oval Office rather than having just returned from a rendezvous with a wanted felon.

Jamie smiled warmly at Phillip Grand and looked as if she were about to give him a hug before noticing Wilcox standing there. She nodded in Wilcox's direction and stuck out her hand.

"Agent Wilcox," she said. "It's been a long time. It's good to see you."

"It has." Her handshake was firmer than he remembered. "How was your trip?"

The question was intentional, to catch her off guard, and he thought he would have caught the slightest facial tick or body gesture, but there was neither. Either Jamie Carter had nothing to hide, or she had learned a lot about the psychology of deception in the past few years.

"Please, let's sit down," Phillip said, motioning to the sofas.

Jamie sat on the sofa across from Wilcox, which put them face to face, while Phillip Grand positioned himself in a chair between them, forming the third point of the human triangle. They sat quietly for a few moments, a palpable tension hanging in the air, until Jamie broke the silence. "I think Collins is happy to see me." She smiled.

"I think that's an understatement," Phillip said, also smiling. "He's been working round the clock."

Smiling, Wilcox thought. *Everyone is smiling*.

"How's Faith?" the president asked.

"She's good," Jamie replied. "She just—"

"If we can cut short the small talk," Wilcox said. He leaned forward and put his elbows on his knees. "Jamie, I would like to know where you've been for the past few days." If Wilcox had had any delusions that Jamie would be startled by the interruption, he was wrong. Her penetrating calmness remained.

"Faith and I took a drive out west," she said.

"To Wyoming?" Wilcox asked.

Jamie glanced at Phillip Grand, who appeared like he wanted to protect her as much as question her. "Yes," she said, "we stayed in Cody, Wyoming."

Wilcox hesitated. His professional instincts were to treat Jamie as a possible suspect in a crime, to grill her as if she were in an FBI interrogation room. However, he had grown fond of the Carters and had gotten to know both Jamie and Edward quite intimately in the years following her abduction. And, yet, the woman sitting in front of him seemed like a stranger. "Why Wyoming?" he asked.

"I wanted to get Faith as far away from Washington as I could."

It wasn't quite the answer Wilcox had been hoping for. "And you happened to end up in Cody, Wyoming, Ms. Carter?" he asked, realizing he hadn't called her *Ms. Carter* in years.

"No, I didn't just end up there," Jamie said. "I went to a

place that Bailino had told me about three years ago when we were on the run from Paolo Cataldi."

"*We?*" Wilcox asked. "When *we* were on the run?"

"Yes," she said. "At the time, he said it was a safe place, a place that no one knew about. I took a chance that it was still there and still available to us."

"You're telling me that, in this entire country, you believed that was the only safe place? Thirty-three Cooper Court?" Wilcox blurted the address with authority. He wanted her to know that he knew *exactly* where she had been. Again, she was unrattled.

"To be honest, Agent Wilcox, I wasn't thinking straight. I just knew I needed to get away—to get Faith away—from the White House, from D.C." She looked at the president. "Please forgive me for abandoning you, sir, when you might have needed me most."

"Please," Phillip said with a wave of his hand. "It's nothing. You did what you thought was right." He got up, put his hand on Jamie's arm, and sat beside her on the sofa—a clear indication, in Wilcox's mind, of what side he was on.

"So I drove there, and when I got there, well ..." She looked directly at the president now. "He was there."

"Who was there?" Wilcox asked, wanting her to say the name.

"Bailino," she said plainly.

Phillip sat back on the couch, appearing astonished, as if Wilcox's earlier pronouncements weren't enough to have him believe Bailino was alive and that he was finally coming to terms with the truth.

"He had been hiding. He had," Jamie lifted her left

arm, "no hand on his arm. He cut it off back in 2014, at the Barbara farmhouse, to escape and to throw off law enforcement."

Wilcox's blood was pumping so hard it pulsed in his ears. "Where is he?" he asked, standing up.

"I don't know," she said, maintaining eye contact with Wilcox.

"Think very carefully about how you answer, Ms. Carter," Wilcox said, leaning toward her and placing his hands on his hips. If Jamie Carter was playing the body language game, so would he.

"I don't know," she said again.

"Ms. Carter, why didn't you contact law enforcement the moment you realized that Don Bailino was alive?" Wilcox had begun pacing in front of the sofa like a tiger in a cage.

"Because I was afraid."

"Of Don?" Phillip asked.

Jamie shook her head. "No, of whatever was happening here. I didn't know what was going on. Neither did he."

"Really?" Wilcox unsuccessfully tried to hide the sarcasm from his voice. "Why do I find that convenient?"

"Agent Wilcox," Phillip Grand said, standing up so that they were eye to eye. "This isn't an inquisition."

"Nor is it a reunion," Wilcox said. "Mr. President, do you really think it's a coincidence that in the same week we find an explosive device in the White House we also find out that one of the world's deadliest criminals is still alive?" He peered down at Jamie. "Where is he?" he asked again, trying to keep his voice calm.

"I don't know." She placed her clipboard on the sofa

and stood up, the three of them in a tight circle. "And if you know Bailino in the way you say you do, you'll know that he wouldn't tell me where he was going."

"How did you get back to the East Coast?" Wilcox asked.

"I'm assuming you know my rental car is back in Wyoming."

"Don't worry about what I know. Please just answer the question."

"Bailino drove us and dropped us off," she said.

"He was *here*? In D.C.?" Wilcox asked. "Where?"

"Around 800 F Street Northwest."

"Near the International Spy Museum ..." Wilcox said, unclipping his cell phone from his belt. "How poetic." Presumably, it had been hours since Jamie and Faith had allegedly been dropped off, so any lead on Bailino would have already fizzled. Jamie Carter had managed to dutifully report to the president as soon as she was back in town, but she had also dutifully given Don Bailino enough time to escape. "What kind of car was Bailino driving?"

"It was a black truck with a flatbed," Jamie said. "Something nondescript. I'm not sure of the make or model."

"You drove cross-country in the damn thing, and you don't know the make or model?"

"Agent Wilcox ..." the president warned.

"Mr. President, look, if what Ms. Carter is telling us is true, it means she had every opportunity to contact the authorities and turn Bailino in. She didn't. That makes her guilty of ... let's see," he ticked each off on his fingers, "aiding and abetting a fugitive, obstructing justice, and we can throw in accessory to the attempted assassination of the president of the United States."

"Agent Wilcox …" Phillip Grand was getting more and more agitated. "Why on earth would—"

"He told me he knew who did it," Jamie said, "who placed the explosive device in the White House and also in Bethesda, near Walter Reed."

The words sent Wilcox's brain into high gear. "Who?" he asked. "Who is it, Ms. Carter?"

This was the first question for which Wilcox detected a slight pause before Jamie's answer. "I don't know," she said.

Wilcox threw up his hands. "This is ridiculous. Ms. Carter, you realize the amount of resources that were spent on you by the federal government to keep you and your daughter safe from the man you are apparently trying to protect?"

"Agent Wilcox," Jamie said, her tone and her expression even but sincere. "Please try to understand. We are on the same side."

"And what side is that?" Wilcox said.

"He told me to tell you—to tell both of you—that he will take care of it."

It was as if a jolt of electricity shot through Wilcox. "He told you to say that to *me*?"

"You, specifically," she said. "He knew that you had been reinstated and that you would be working the case."

Wilcox imagined an underground room in Bailino's log cabin with FBI investigators adorning his walls in the way that organized crime members dotted Wilcox's.

"And just what are we supposed to do? All go on vacation while Bailino takes care of everything?" Wilcox asked.

"He said he would get word to me when things were safe," she said.

"How?" Wilcox asked, quickly adding. "Don't answer that. Let me guess ... You don't know." Wilcox swiped his phone.

"What are you doing?" the president asked.

"I'm going to tell my men to check out the surveillance video outside the Spy Museum. Maybe we can get a plate number, and we'll take it from there." He glared at Jamie. "Do me a favor and stick around," he said. "No more road trips."

Without another word, he left the Oval Office and strode through the White House, past the staff members and agents, and out the front door toward FBI HQ at the J. Edgar Hoover Building. The streets were empty, the nighttime air cool and calm and in stark contrast to the heat being generated in Wilcox's body. *Why is everyone protecting this man*, he thought to himself, *this cold-blooded killer with an apparent heart of gold*. Despite the revelation that Bailino was alive and possibly in the D.C. area, he felt like he was no closer to catching the damn guy. Yet, he *was* sure of one thing: if this man who had charmed a president, and perhaps even a nation, was ever going to be apprehended, Wilcox was going to have to do it himself.

❁

"You all right?" Phillip asked Jamie once Wilcox had left.

Jamie sat back down on the sofa to pick up her clipboard

and cell phone. She had done everything Bailino had asked, but was having second thoughts. On the road, on the run, with survival instincts kicking in, it had all made sense, but now that she was back at the White House, beside the president, and on the side of law and order, she wondered if she was making a mistake.

"I'm fine," she shrugged. "It was to be expected."

Phillip sat down on the sofa next to her. "It's going to be all right, you know," he said, in that fatherly way, the same words Bailino had said to her only hours ago. "Although," he motioned to her cell phone, "I'd be careful when making or receiving calls with that thing, if you know what I mean."

"I do." She gave a small smile.

"How's Faith?" he asked.

His kind eyes were so different from Bailino's and yet filled her with a similar sense of comfort. "She's fine. We're going to be staying at Edward's for the time being." Jamie pressed the clipboard against her chest. "I really meant what I said. I'm so sorry I wasn't here." The swelling on the president's forehead filled her with guilt.

"Oh," he said, touching his bruise, "this old thing? I'm all right. Katherine has me on bed rest. She made me promise I'd go straight upstairs and to bed after meeting with you." He motioned to her clipboard. "Are you planning on working tonight?"

Jamie nodded. "If it's all right. I need to focus on something else for a while. I won't be long."

"Understood," he said, and they both stood up and made their way toward the Oval Office door. Phillip opened it. "How is … *he*?" he asked.

"Okay, considering." She stepped over the threshold. "Seeing him was like seeing a ghost."

"Does he really think he can stop this thing?" he asked, closing the door behind them. The outer offices were dark and muted; the president's soft-spoken voice echoed across the corridor.

"That's what he says."

"And you believe him?"

Jamie shrugged. "Wouldn't you?"

24

ailino sat down in the empty train car, slipping the train ticket and fraudulent credit card into his pocket, and pulled the lid of his baseball cap down. He didn't expect the authorities to find his truck in the Amtrak station parking lot for another few hours, and his plan was to try to get some sleep. He pushed his duffel bag under his legs as the train pulled out from the station and checked his phone for any news updates as a woman wearing a tight skirt slid into the seat across from him and pulled out a tablet. She smiled.

"The train's empty tonight," she said as she placed her things on the seat next to her. "I guess everyone's already gotten where they needed to go."

He nodded politely and shifted in his seat away from the camera lens of her tablet, which was adorned with various cartoon stickers. She caught him looking.

"These are my son's. He's two. Do you have any children?"

Bailino nodded. "A daughter," he said.

She smiled. "There's nothing like it, right? Being a parent."

She glanced at the end of his left arm, presumably

looking for a wedding ring, but he had his arm tucked into his pocket. He had a feeling that she would be surprised to know that not only didn't he have a wedding ring, but he didn't have any finger to put one on. Her left ring finger, on the other hand, was intact—and unadorned.

"Are you from New York?" she asked, and Bailino knew that for the next two hours he wasn't going to get to sleep at all.

❂

By the time the train reached Manhattan's Penn Station, Bailino knew just about everything there was to know about Deidre, the girl on the train—the area of Manhattan she lived in, how her brother was in rehab for a prescription drug addiction, how she feared her son had autism because he wasn't talking yet. It always fascinated him how much information people divulged to a perfect stranger. Bailino, of course, had said very little, but Deidre didn't seem to notice. He found that most people didn't nowadays—they seemed to want to talk more than listen.

"Well, it was nice talking to you," Deidre said when the train stopped.

"You too," Bailino said, wrapping his duffel bag over his head with his right hand and keeping his left arm artfully out of sight. "Which way are you heading?"

She perked up when he showed interest. "Thirty-Fourth Street."

"So am I," Bailino lied. "We can walk together."

As they passed the police officers and National Guardsmen patrolling Penn Station, he kept close to Deidre and put a smile on his face as she told him about her sister's colonoscopy for some digestion problems she was having. Smiling couples didn't attract the attention of law enforcement the way single people—particularly men walking alone with duffel bags—tended to. They crossed into the Long Island Railroad station, where a saxophonist had attracted a sizable crowd, and then up an escalator to the street level where the Saturday evening noises and smells of New York City greeted them with the excitement of a frat party.

"Are you going cross town?" she asked.

"No," he pointed the other way, "I'm going west, but it was nice traveling with you." She lingered a moment, waiting, he knew, for him to ask for her telephone number. After quickly weighing the pros and cons, he decided it would be best to leave on a positive note. "Do you mind if I take your number?" he asked.

"Sure," she said excitedly. "Should I text it to your phone?"

"Nah, I'll remember it," he said, and she dictated it to him. "Until we meet again."

"I look forward to it," she said as he turned west on Thirty-Fourth Street, slipping into the pedestrian traffic and expecting never to see Deirdre or hear about her medically challenged family again.

The city was alive with youth and booze, and Bailino's lungs inflated with New York's palpable atmosphere. He had missed the hurrying, the having to be somewhere, the anonymity that came with being in a crowd. He turned left on Eighth Avenue toward the post office, whose lobby, it turned out, even at that late hour, was crowded. As he navigated through the large space, he reached into his duffel bag and pulled out a key ring, flipping to a key adorned with a crescent moon. He stuck it into a post office box, pulled out a large brown envelope, shoved it into his bag, and locked the box again.

Outside, young people were sitting on the concrete steps in pairs. He sidestepped them, checking his watch, and returned to Eighth Avenue, walking uptown with the tourists toward the theater district. At Fortieth Street, he turned east until he got to Sixth Avenue, Bryant Park stretching out before him.

It was the first time Bailino had been back at the park since he first saw Jamie Carter wandering around for a place to eat her lunch. It was quieter, more at peace, without the weekday lunch crowd. He adjusted his duffel bag and kept walking until he got toward the middle of the block and made a left toward a tiny eatery that was closed; a few young people lingered at the nearby tables. He leaned his back against a large potted plant, pretending to look at the buildings, until a group of kids stood in front of him to take a selfie. Quickly, he dug his fingers into the dirt of the plant, sticking close to the sides, and fished around until he found a small plastic bag. He pulled it out and continued walking. When he exited on Forty-Second Street, he made a left and then a right to continue down Sixth Avenue. About a block away, he looked inside the bag. It was sealed, but empty.

Fuck, he thought. *Well, someone got a nice windfall.* He had never been a fan of the dead-drop system in Manhattan—too many prying eyes and prying fingers, unlike upstate New York—but Gino had done things the way he wanted to.

He made a few more stops in midtown, having a

bit more luck this time, and continued walking until he reached the southeast corner of Central Park, which was filled mostly with couples in fancy dresses and suits and a few young families. He kept walking along the park's curvy paths until he reached the statue of Balto, which had been one of his favorites ever since his father told him about the famous sled dog delivering medicine to sick kids in Alaska in the 1920s. He thought of Lucky.

A little boy and girl were climbing on Balto's back, which was glowing bronze from all those tiny hands caressing it over the years. Bailino sat on a nearby bench pretending to be busy with his phone until the children's parents called to them and they ran off. Then he got up and moved closer to the dog, kneeling down to read the statue's inscription while placing his right hand into a hidden crack in the rocky base. The plastic baggie he retrieved was damp but intact, and he stuck it in his duffel bag with the other hauls of cash and IDs.

That should do it, he thought. *For now*.

He left the park, crossed Fifth Avenue, and descended into the subway station. He purchased a MetroCard from one of the machines and took the W train downtown to the last stop, Whitehall Street, for the Staten Island Ferry.

When he arrived, the crowds were already walking toward the boat, which was set to leave in a few minutes. Bailino followed along, keeping his distance from two law enforcement officials holding police dogs. On the ferry, he took the stairs to the bridge deck and stood outside as more and more people gathered. He was surprised how many passengers were aboard. Most of them appeared to be tourists—the ferry was free, after all, and provided an excellent view of downtown Manhattan and the Statue of Liberty. Most of them probably had no intention of staying on Staten Island and would take the next ferry back. He didn't blame them.

As the boat crossed New York Harbor, he spotted Ellis Island, the place his grandfather had first arrived in America to make a better life for his family. Bailino wondered what his grandfather, whom he had met only when he was a baby, would think about all his hopes and dreams resting on the shoulders of tiny Faith Carter. A gambling man, or so Bailino was told, he probably would have liked the odds.

Staten Island neared, and most of the tourists left their posts along the railing, since there was little to see out on the water now, and gathered near the front of the ferry in order to exit. Bailino stood with them, keeping his eye on a pair of Department of Transportation workers, who were busy talking sports. Once the ferry docked, the crowd surged forward onto the island borough of New York City, with more than half of them making an immediate U-turn to leave.

As Bailino walked through the familiar neighborhoods, new construction seemed to be everywhere—tall, unfinished structures lining up like dominos. He imagined few of the people who would inhabit these buildings, living on top of one another, would ever know that there was a place in this country where a man could live alone on acres of land and never see another soul for months.

He kept walking, zigzagging along, until he reached the front gate of an old Victorian. He stood before it and looked directly into the lens of the security camera that he had helped to install. He was only there for a few seconds when the intercom clicked and a tinny voice exclaimed, "Holy fucking shit!"

As the metal gates swung inward, Bailino stepped onto the property and walked toward the house as the plump, petite figure of ToniAnne Cataldi came rushing toward him.

25

ToniAnne would have recognized that walk anywhere. She ran barefoot, the deep red of her toenails catching the glare of the streetlights, across
the paving stones and jumped right into Bailino's arms,
wrapping him in a four-limbed hug.

"Hi, Ton," Bailino said flatly.

She plastered his face with kisses, leaving the final kiss
for his lips. "You fuckin' maniac," she said, squeezing the
back of his neck. "I knew you were alive all this time. I said
it, didn't I, Lorenzo?"

Lorenzo emerged onto the porch and placed his hands
on the railing. "Yeah," he said with obvious contempt.
"Right again."

"Oh, don't be such a poop." She grabbed Bailino's hand
and pulled him toward the house. "Come inside."

"Listen, I can't stay long," Bailino said.

"Don't be silly." ToniAnne pulled him into the kitchen
and unwrapped his duffel bag from his body, placing it on
the floor. "Stay as long as you like."

"If the Feds haven't been here already, they'll probably
be here soon."

"Here?" She laughed. "They haven't been here in

years. Plus, the world thinks you might be in Wyoming, or Washington, or fuckin' Timbuktu. And I wouldn't worry about any of my neighbors getting a glimpse of you ..." She waved her hands dismissively. "They stopped looking to see what went on in this house years ago, and for their own good. But enough about that. Let me look at you ..." She unbuttoned his overcoat and stared. "Man, that country air agrees with you." She felt his abs.

"Knock it off, Ton," Bailino said and pushed her hands away.

"Since when are you so shy? Take off your coat. Stay a while." She pulled his overcoat off and held up his left arm, eyeing the charred skin at the end of his forearm. "Holy shit. This is the fuckin' sexiest thing I've ever seen."

Lorenzo, who had moseyed into the kitchen behind them, peeked over ToniAnne's shoulder. "It's fuckin' disgusting," he said before leaving down a hallway.

ToniAnne leered at him. "Don't you have some chest hair to shave?" She pushed Bailino into a chair. "You want something to eat? I'll make you something."

"You don't have to go to any trouble."

"It's no trouble at all," she said. "I have leftover eggplant parm in the fridge. I'll heat it up." She unwrapped a pan of food, carved out a large portion, plopped it onto a plate, and shoved it into the microwave oven, adjusting her hair in the reflection of the microwave oven door.

"How's Anna?" Bailino asked.

"Good, good, busy." ToniAnne grabbed utensils and a napkin and made a place setting in front of him. "Her husband's a pig, but you know that ..." She pulled a piece of paper held by magnets off the fridge and held it up. "Gina got Student of the Month in her class last month."

"Very nice," he said.

The microwave oven beeped, and ToniAnne placed the warmed dish in front of him, mixed it quickly with a fork, and grabbed a bottle of Cabernet Sauvignon. "I'm outta scotch, Donny, but will this do?" she asked.

"It's fine, whatever," he said and took a bite of the parm. "Thanks, Ton. It's as good as I remember."

"Anything for you, baby." She got two wine glasses from the cabinet, poured the wine, and placed his glass on the table. She sat across from him and raised her glass. *"Salute."*

"Salute," Bailino replied and drank a mouthful. "I need to talk to you," he said, putting his glass down. "Alone, without Mr. Big Ears listening."

"Lorenzo," ToniAnne called, "make yourself scarce."

"You've gotta be fuckin' kidding me," Lorenzo said from somewhere out of sight. He started muttering, but then a few doors slammed, and it was quiet again.

"Okay," ToniAnne said, pulling her chair closer to Bailino. "Where were we?"

"That putz treating you nice?"

"Nice enough," ToniAnne said. "Not all men are gentlemen, like you, Donny boy, you know that." She rested her hand on his arm, and its familiarity shot through her like an electric current. "So what brings you to my humble abode? What do you need to talk about?"

"You need to call this off, Ton."

"Call what off?"

"Don't be cute with me. You know what I'm talking about."

ToniAnne walked her fingers up his arm. "What's with all this talking? You never used to talk so much." She pulled his handless arm toward her mouth and slowly sucked on the end of it. "I'd love to see what you can do with this thing."

"Enough, already." He pulled his arm away. "I need you to be serious."

ToniAnne took a deep breath. "All right. What do you want to know? How I'm going to fuck up that goddamn Phillip Grand?"

"What does Anna have to say about it?"

"You know Anna—she never had the stomach for this stuff," ToniAnne said.

"Yes, I know, she was always the smart one."

"Very funny."

Bailino took another bite of food. She could watch him eat all day. "Seriously," he said, "what do you need to stir up trouble for? Grand isn't a problem."

ToniAnne's cheeks got hot. She jumped out of her seat and grabbed a picture frame from the wall next to the back door, and held it in front of Bailino's face. "Have you forgotten? Has all that damn fresh air made you forget what happened to our baby?"

Bailino gently pulled Joey's high school graduation photo from her and placed it on the table. "I think about him every day, Ton. *Every fucking day*. So, no, I didn't forget, but Grand isn't the problem."

"Oh, no? Are you fucking kidding me? The next thing you're going to tell me is he didn't kill my father." She chugged her glass of wine and poured another.

"Gino was on death row, Ton. What did you expect?"

"I expected him to get out." She gave him a hard look.

"Don't give me this shit now." Bailino pushed the plate away. "You're changing the subject, which is your specialty."

She ran her fingers through his hair. "You, for one, should know I have many more specialties than that."

"Listen, what happened to Joey is because of your father, not Phillip Grand."

She rubbed the tops of his ears. "We're going to have to agree to disagree on that, my friend," ToniAnne said, reaching for another sip of wine. "And, frankly, I don't see how this is any of your concern. Why is Phillip Grand always such a sore subject with you?"

"Not my concern?" Bailino rubbed at his five o'clock shadow. He looked tired—sexy as hell, but tired. "Do you know how they found your explosive device?"

"My hope is it was while the president was sucking the First Lady's cock."

"My kid found it."

ToniAnne studied him. "So it's true? I would have bet money that skank was pregnant already and was just saying it was your kid to try and cash in on the publicity."

The creases in Bailino's forehead became rigid, and, for a minute, she thought she saw the burnt skin at the end of his left arm tighten. She put her arm around him. "You sure it's yours, Donny? It's stupid to get all worked up for someone else's kid."

"She's mine," he said flatly.

ToniAnne dropped the subject. She knew him well enough to know when he didn't want to talk about something. She bent down in front of him. "I don't want to fight … I tried to visit you in the hospital, you know. Fuckin' Feds wouldn't let me near you."

He shook his head. "It's no big deal."

Something was different about him, and she couldn't place what it was. She peeled back the neck of his T-shirt, revealing the ragged scar along his clavicle, and ran her fingers across it. "You can hardly see it."

He pulled her hand away and held it. "End this now, Ton."

She sighed. "All right. For you, I'll think about it." She lifted her right leg and sat on his lap, straddling him.

"How did you get to O'Connell?" he asked.

"How did you know it was me?"

"Yeah, an eye for an eye—O'Connell's for Paolo's. Next time, why don't you just draw the Feds a diagram?"

"The Feds didn't figure out nuthin'. You did. You know me too well …" She threw her head back and laughed. "It was too easy. Started talking to the kid online after he uploaded the video of Grand three years ago—telling him what a great cameraman he was, yadda yadda. You know how stupid boys are—he probably thought immediately that I was some lonely housewife looking for attention. As if …" ToniAnne waved a dismissive hand. "I wanted to feel him out, see if he had anything else, so I started blasting Grand, saying I didn't trust the guy, yadda yadda. The kid totally took the bait, told me he had something on Grand that he was holding onto, said it was something 'big,' and I said, 'Bullshit,' and he said there was more to the video, and I said, 'I'd do anything for that.'" She smiled thinking of how she reeled him in. "For, like, two years, the kid held out on me … I practically had to blow him over the phone until finally he invited me over, thinking that I was going to fuck him, I'm sure. I was thinking more along the lines of a bullet in the eye." She shrugged. "You know what they say, men are from Mars …"

She put her hands to his face, but he pushed them down with his left arm. "Is there anything that can tie you to that device or to Samuel O'Connell?" he asked.

"You know me better than that, Donny." She ran her hands through the gray hair at his temple. "But, shit, I wasn't kidding when I said I want to release that video. Getting Grand impeached or watching him resign would be the highlight of my life."

Bailino shook his head. "Listen to me … The only reason I'm here right now talking to you, Ton, is *because* of Phillip Grand. Fuckin' Paolo went off the deep end."

"He was mourning my father."

"Please …" Bailino leaned back. He wiped his mouth with the napkin and threw it into his plate. "That sick fuck wasn't mourning anything but his own miserable life. He was going to slice up a little girl."

"Your kid, right?"

"That's right." The skin around his eyes tightened again.

"You're getting all hot and bothered again." She put her arms around his neck. "Why don't we just go upstairs, and I'll help you get out of these clothes and relax."

"What will make me relax is if you quit this shit."

ToniAnne sighed loudly. "I'll tell you what … If I release the video, I promise to quit with the pyrotechnics. How's that for a compromise?" She leaned in to whisper in his ear. "How about a quickie?"

"Nah."

"Why, you tired?" She inched closer to him. "Don't worry, baby, I'll do all the work. Lorenzo's got me in spinning classes four times a week. My thighs are rock solid." She squeezed her inner thighs on his legs. "You can just lay there and look handsome."

He grabbed her chin and looked her in the eye. "I gotta go."

"What's with you?" she said, starting to get angry. "It's not like you to turn down a good fuck. And, frankly, it's the least you can do for me not getting rid of that no-good Phillip Grand."

Bailino leaned back and let out a long exhale. "So if I go upstairs, you'll end it now? I can't be worried about this shit."

"I'll release the video, but no more bombies. You've got yourself a deal, big guy."

"And Lorenzo?"

"Lorenzo?" ToniAnne laughed. "Please ... I'll send him out for some cigarettes. He's fucking the girl who works at Walmart, so he won't give a shit anyway."

"Nothing's changed, I see." Bailino reached down and looped his left arm through the straps of his duffel bag. ToniAnne hopped off him and put the plate and utensils into the sink. She grabbed the two glasses of wine from the table and hurried up the stairs past Bailino and put the glasses on her bedroom dresser. When he got to the door, she lunged at him.

"Still like it rough?" ToniAnne asked, running her long nails down Bailino's arms.

"You have no idea," he said.

"I knew you missed me," she whispered and closed the bedroom door.

✪

ToniAnne pulled the sheet off her and rolled out of bed. She walked toward the window where the setting moon was peeking out behind two buildings across the street and leaned her naked body against the cool glass of the window. "I'll say it again … That West Coast air did you wonders, Donny."

By the time she turned around, Bailino was up and getting dressed.

"Where you running off to?" she asked.

"Errands," Bailino said. "I told you, I gotta go."

"What kind of errands?"

"Does it matter?"

"Well, maybe I want to come."

"That's not a good idea," he said.

ToniAnne ran her hand across the top of her dresser, grabbed her hairbrush, and began running it through her knotty hair. "Are you coming back?" she asked.

"Does it matter?"

She slammed the brush down on the dresser. "Of course, it matters."

"Ton, you got a nice life here." He slipped on his shoes. "You've got the grandkid, you've got Anna, you've got the putz down at Walmart, you don't need me. In fact, I'm the last thing you need."

She walked toward him, jiggling her large breasts. "So why did you come here? To tell me to lay off Grand? That was it?"

"How many more of those explosive device parts do you have lying around?"

"Why? What am I, a supply store now?"

"Do you have any of the parts or not?"

"Maybe."

He pulled the strap of the duffel bag over his head and plucked one of her father's old flat caps from a pile next to her Communion photo.

ToniAnne folded her arms. "Apparently, that's all I'm good for—food, clothing, and a quick fuck."

Bailino slipped the cap onto his head. "C'mon, where's the stuff?"

ToniAnne sighed. "Basement. Back room."

He nodded. "I'm going to take Gino's old Corolla," he said and ducked out the bedroom door.

"Knock yourself out." She watched him go down the stairs. "So that's it? Wham, bam, thank you, ma'am?" she called as he disappeared around the bend. She heard a set of keys jingle, the door to the basement unlatch, and his footsteps on the wooden basement steps.

She pulled on a T-shirt, thong, and jeans and stood by the bedroom window. Something was up. She could feel it. Maybe he was in some kind of trouble, and not with the Feds, and he didn't want her to know—typical Donny, wanting to take care of things by himself.

Outside the window, Bailino emerged from the house, zipping up his duffel bag. She buzzed the gate open for him using the bedroom remote control and waited for him to look up and wave, but he kept on walking. He strode straight through the open gate and around the fence toward the Corolla parked on the street, the iron bars making him disappear and reappear like a character on a film strip. When he was out of sight, ToniAnne picked up her cell phone and wrote a quick text:

You got him?

The reply was immediate.

Yeah.

26

Bob rang the top doorbell of the brownstone and took one last assessment of his wardrobe. It had taken a visit to three vintage clothing stores to find just the right tweed jacket with elbow patches to go with his jeans and loafers. He imagined the jacket was worn by some unknown but prolific author or professor from the late 1970s.

An inside door opened and then the front door, and Nadia appeared. She was wearing a peasant blouse that was off the shoulders and tight skinny jeans.

"You're here!" she said, her perfect smile wide. "At my house. I can't believe it."

"Well, believe it," Bob said, turning on the charm. "Here, this is for you." He handed her the small bouquet of flowers he was holding.

"Oh, they're beautiful. Come in!" Nadia said. "Everybody's here, so it's perfect timing."

As the door closed behind them, she hurried up the stairs, tiny hops on the balls of her bare feet, and the strings of her blouse flapped onto her butt as if she were being spanked.

She led him inside a second-floor apartment and into a large living room that was filled with women of all ages and sizes, just about all of them wearing those peekaboo-shoulder tops that had become popular in the middle-aged-mom clothing stores. A half-circle of chairs had been arranged to line up with a sofa, love seat, and armchair, and several of the women were seated.

"Everybody, this is Robert Scott, the *author*," Nadia said as a way of introduction. "Mr. Scott, this is everybody." She fanned her arms out.

"Please," Bob said, "call me Bob."

"Oh, okay." Nadia giggled like a schoolgirl who had been told to call her principal by his first name. "*Bob.*"

The women stared at him admiringly, as Nadia offered him something to drink.

"I'll have whatever you ladies are having," he said, and the women laughed for no reason.

Oh, this is going to be a piece of cake, Bob thought. "Is that seat taken?" he asked, pointing to the armchair.

"Oh, not at all," said an older woman who looked like Mrs. Doubtfire and was sitting on one of the chairs. "That is the seat of honor. For you."

"That's my mother," Nadia said, handing him a glass of wine. "She's a big fan."

"Ah, I thought it was your sister," Bob said, and the old woman blushed.

"Ladies, ladies, let's find our seats," Nadia said, clapping her hands, and a group of women who had been standing near a spread of cakes that was bigger than most of the bakeries Bob had been to moseyed over to the living room area.

As the ladies took their seats, arranging glasses, plates, and purses, Nadia stood in the center of the room. "Thank you all for coming," she said, "and a special thank you to our guest of honor, author Robert Scott."

A round of applause, and Bob smiled with gratitude. *He could get used to this.*

"I know we read a different book this month, but," she said with that delightful smile, "it was just serendipity that I ran into … *Bob*," she smiled wider, "and I knew it was just meant to be, so … We're all familiar with Bob's book, *A Lust for Lies: The True Story Behind the Kidnapping of Charlotte Grand* …" She held up the book, turning to Bob. "We read it when it came out in paperback, but I know some of us, me included, read it again, special for tonight." She beamed. "Oh, and, ladies, our guest of honor has offered to sign our books at the end of the discussion!"

"This way, you can make more money off them on eBay once I'm gone," Bob said, and the ladies chirped with laughter.

"All right, let's get started." Nadia took her seat on the sofa, next to Bob's armchair. "Normally," she explained to him, "the host will facilitate the meeting, but so many of us have lots of questions that I thought we would just do a Q&A format. We can go around the room, if that's all right with you … *Bob*."

"Sure, that's fine by me," he said, taking a sip of his drink. "Fire away."

"Mom, do you want to start?" Nadia asked.

Mrs. Doubtfire appeared flustered but gathered herself and unfolded a piece of paper that was on her lap.

"Gosh, I have so many questions," she said. "I don't know where to start."

"That's all right. I have all night," Bob said with a smile.

"Well, I guess my first question is … What is Don Bailino like in real life?"

Bob's smile was on the verge of collapse as all eyes focused on him. "Well … as I say in my introduction, I didn't really ever meet Don Bailino. I—"

"He's just so dreamy," said a woman sitting on one of the dining room chairs, waving at her face with a paper plate.

"You think everyone is dreamy, Brigid," Nadia said, and the women laughed.

"He reminds me of a young Robert De Niro, doesn't he?" said another woman, a schoolteacher type with heavy black bangs and large-framed eyeglasses.

"Definitely," said an Asian girl who looked college-age. "I'm not into old guys, but I would do that guy in a heartbeat."

"Honey, when you're my age," Brigid said, "you'll do anyone," and the women laughed again.

"Do you think he's alive?" someone asked, and all eyes were on Bob again.

"Honestly, I really don't think so. I mean, how could the guy survive a burning building? That shit … I mean, *stuff*, excuse me … only happens in books. He would have to—"

"I don't know," said Asian girl. "I think that guy could do anything."

"And to protect the woman he loved?" Mrs. Doubtfire added, her eyes aglow. "Certainly."

The conversation continued bubbling until it reached a boiling point and finally splintered into two- and three-person chats. Bob downed his glass of wine.

"Would you like another?" Nadia asked, and Bob

nodded, handing her his glass. "Isn't this great?" she added. "It's always such a lively discussion."

"Yes, great." Bob suddenly had the urge to knock out one of Nadia's perfectly white teeth. "Ladies, ladies ..." he said as Nadia handed him his freshened glass of wine. "You all do realize that this guy—Don Bailino—is, you know, a psycho."

They all stared at him in silence.

"I mean, he's *killed* people," Bob said. "*A lot* of people."

"Yeah, but that's the world he was born into," the schoolmarm said.

"He can't help it if his father dragged him into that business," said another, and several women nodded.

"A cop, though?" Bob asked. "He killed a cop."

"That's true," Nadia said with a nod, and Bob wanted to kiss her right then and there.

"That's the way life was back then ..." Mrs. Doubtfire said with authority. "It was us versus them."

"Do we know for a fact that he killed a cop?" asked the Asian girl, looking skeptical.

"Yes, and then some," Bob said. "It's been docu—"

"I don't know if I believe it," offered a wrinkly woman with blond hair sitting next to Mrs. Doubtfire. "They mess up those DNA things all the time."

"Ladies, is anyone interested in the actual writing of the book?" Bob asked, hoping to change the subject. He chugged the rest of his wine and placed his glass on the coffee table, his head already becoming a bit cloudy.

"Yes, yes, enough about that," Nadia said. "Let's talk about you, Bob. Tell us, when did you decide to write the book?"

"Well, I—"

"Yeah, were you ever afraid?" Asian girl asked. "Of Don Bailino, I mean."

"Yeah, like, that he would come and get you for spilling all his secrets," schoolmarm asked, and the women nodded.

"Afraid?" Bob rolled his eyes. He didn't know if he was feeling the effects of the wine or of their undivided attention. "The guy's a paper tiger. Really, I'm not sure what the big deal is about him. All that stuff has really been blown out of proportion."

"Well, your ex-wife fell for him, right?" Asian girl said. "At least, that's what you wrote in your book."

"He must have had *something*," said the girl next to her, and Bob didn't realize until that moment that the two women were holding hands.

"How did you feel about the baby?" Doubtfire wanted to know.

"That must have hurt," schoolmarm said.

"Had you tried before?" asked a woman eating a large piece of chocolate cake at the far end of the circle. "Did you want kids?"

Nadia picked up his glass for another round as Bob settled into the armchair. He didn't know how long book clubs were supposed to last, but even if it was only an hour, he knew it was going to be a long night.

27

Phillip sat in the darkened White House kitchen, a half-eaten package of Oreo cookies on the counter in front of him. He had promised Katherine that he would go right back upstairs after his meeting with Jamie; she was probably in the bedroom suite waiting for him. He had also promised her that he would cut down on the late-night cookie binging after his first presidential physical showed an uptick in his cholesterol—the bad kind. He was killing two promises with one Oreo.

Cholesterol was the least of his problems. Phillip popped another cookie into his mouth. Wilcox had been upset, and Phillip couldn't blame him. Over the course of twenty-four hours, the longtime agent had found out that two of the people he trusted the most had been in cahoots with the one man he had spent most of his professional life trying to bring down. That certainly didn't bode well for Phillip's chances of Wilcox taking the position of FBI director once all of this was over—if it ever was over. As much as Phillip feared for the bomber's next target, he was also afraid that whoever it was might go underground, popping up one day when everyone least expected it. Like Bailino.

He scanned the still-unfamiliar kitchen, which somehow, despite all the foot traffic and constant eating by the kids, appeared showroom-new at the end of each day. He missed his late-night walks through the Albany Executive Mansion. Even after ten months, the White House wasn't quite home for him yet, and he wondered if it ever would be, when he could look upon the men in the presidential portraits as a peer rather than as an interloper.

He reached for another cookie and wiped the crumbs from his mouth and the kitchen counter, returning the box to the pantry. He hid it under some granola bars, even though Katherine knew all of his hiding spots. When the family first moved in, Charlotte and Philly had marveled at the size of the walk-in pantry—which was about three times bigger than the one they had at the Albany Executive Mansion. Phillip fingered the tiny signs his daughter made designating which shelves belonged to which members of the family, including a small area for Faith Carter. Charlotte was organized like her mother.

Still feeling hungry, Phillip took a small apple from a fruit basket, rubbed it on his pants until it was good and shiny, and placed it on the kitchen counter. He fumbled through a few drawers, the implements and utensils all resembling one another in the dark, until he found an apple slicer and then two others. Why anyone, even the president of the United States, needed three apple slicers, he didn't know. He pulled one of them out and pushed it through the apple, quickly eating a slice and then finishing the rest. Then he lingered over the kiwi and the bananas in the fruit basket but soon found himself back in the pantry, eyeing the box of cookies. *Just one more*, he thought and reached for the box when something rattled in the next room.

Phillip immediately shut the pantry door, closing himself off from the kitchen. He wasn't sure why, only that the sound seemed muted and isolated—a noise made by someone trying not to make any noise. His first thought was that it was an intruder. *The bomber?*

He peeked through the levered pantry door and scanned the kitchen. No one was there, although the apple slicer on the counter caught his eye.

Dammit, he thought. If it was Katherine, she would know he had been there. *How will the children learn to clean up after themselves if their own father doesn't*, she always asked when he left paperwork on the bed and empty cereal bowls on the nightstand. It was a question that Phillip would probably never be able to answer.

He stood there, watching and waiting, but the longer he did, the more foolish he felt. Perhaps it was a rodent. Or the building settling. Certainly, a house as old and big as the White House would have its share of creaks. He imagined the next episode of *Saturday Night Live* parodying a U.S. president trying to stand up to terrorists when he couldn't even stand up to his wife or a White House mouse—the sketch practically wrote itself.

He was about to open the pantry doors when there was a flicker of movement. Then the kitchen door swung open, and a Secret Service agent began walking through the room. Even in the dark, Phillip could make out the precise cut of the federal agent's suit, but it was not light enough to identify who it was. Because the agents rotated the round-the-clock security detail, it could have been any one of them.

At this point, Phillip feared he had waited too long to make himself known—if he made any noise at all the agent might accidentally shoot him, since the bombings had the entire White House on high alert. He stayed perfectly still as the agent picked up the apple slicer, and that's when Phillip saw it—the pink plastic ring on the agent's finger.

Agent Summers.

Phillip hadn't seen him since the day of the attempted assassination in Bethesda. Summers had gotten Phillip back to the White House in record time and then returned to the command center to work with the agents on the scene. Phillip never got the chance to thank him for helping to save his life. He was about to call out when, to his astonishment, Agent Summers placed the apple slicer in his jacket pocket and promptly left the kitchen.

Phillip remained perfectly still inside the pantry, Brandon's words returning to him: *The IED was composed of found objects.* An apple slicer—something ordinary, not likely to be missed. A cold sweat broke out across his skin. Had this happened a week ago, Phillip would have thought nothing of it, but now he knew that with time, patience, and the right know-how, an apple slicer could be as lethal as a Hello Kitty watch.

28

Bob inserted the coffee pod into the Nespresso machine when what he probably should have been having was a Bloody Mary. That was the first and last book club he would ever do, a decision he made after the three-hour mark of last night's Q&A marathon. It was like those ladies didn't want to ever go home.

He pressed the button, causing the machine to whirl, and sat down on the sofa, putting his feet on the coffee table beside a pile of consulting work, which he pushed to the side with his leg, and turned on the television. That rinky-dink side work he was doing was taking up more time than it was worth, and that didn't even include the invoicing and re-invoicing he needed to do—prying money from some of these slobs was like getting blood from a stone. At least when he worked at Worcester, Payne & Leach he could let accounts receivable handle that crap. He surfed the Sunday morning political shows, but not one of them was talking politics—they were all consumed with Don Bailino.

What the hell is going on, he wondered. *It's like an epidemic.*

He muted the set and took out his cell phone, but it wasn't any better. Bailino features and opinion pieces were clogging up his news feeds. Rogue accounts and Bailino hashtags were sucking up all the chatter on Twitter. With only three scrolls, he had spotted at least three T-shirts that read *Save Bailino*. And the FBI hadn't even confirmed that the guy was alive yet.

Bob tossed his cell phone back on the sofa. Four years ago, that thing had practically vibrated itself to death with all the requests he was receiving for talk show appearances and book signings, and now here he was sitting alone in his apartment on a Sunday morning like every other sap. He raised the volume on the television when he saw a graphic at the bottom of the screen that read *Bailino: At Large or At Rest*. In a split screen, an old woman with the title of *organized crime historian* was blathering on about something.

"We must reiterate for those just joining us," said a CNN anchor Bob didn't recognize, as if for Bob's benefit. "The FBI has not confirmed any information regarding a hunt or a search for Don Bailino …" *Yeah, no kidding*, Bob thought. " … although sources tell CNN that such a hunt or search is, indeed, underway, and there seems to be many people who are ready to believe it."

"Well, I'm a believer," the old woman said, raising her hand as an affirmation. She was wearing a turtleneck sweater—*probably to cover up her neck wrinkles*, Bob thought with a smile. He made the volume louder. "Think about it: There was never a body, just a body part—that right there should have tipped off the Federal Bureau of Investigation, which, in my opinion, was much too eager to put this case to bed. Don Bailino has always been a force to be reckoned with, and it seems he has, for about three years, had the upper hand—so to speak." She smiled for the camera.

Ugh, Bob rolled his eyes. *Where do they find these people?*

"It really isn't that difficult for someone to hide, even in this technologically driven age," the woman continued. "If Don Bailino had hidden enough money, he could certainly live a modest lifestyle off-grid for many years. Most fugitives ..."

Bob turned off the set. He was tired of so-called experts prattling on about things they knew nothing about. He was the one who should have been appearing on CNN. He was the one who had real insights into the matter—after all, hadn't he penned a bestselling book about the guy? As far as Bob was concerned, Bailino was about as alive as Bigfoot or the Loch Ness Monster or the boogeyman hiding under his bed. Not that it mattered. All that mattered was that people *thought* Bailino was alive; the rumor that launched a thousand T-shirts. What did Bob care? His book sales were up again, and he could use the royalties.

He got up and practically lunged at his filled cup in the cradle of his Nespresso machine, gulping the coffee down as his head started to clear. Maybe it was worth calling some of the press contacts he had acquired during the book tour to see if they needed a sound bite, he thought, letting the last sip of coffee pool at the bottom of his mouth before swallowing. Why sit around and wait for people to contact him when he could start making calls, get his name out there again? Anything beat doing paralegal work. He knew editors and producers had short memories when it came to their contact lists. They probably needed a little prodding.

He leaned against the counter. Maybe he could try Jamie, whose name was also making the social media rounds after Edward mistakenly filed a Missing Person report. What a boob. Sure, Jamie had made it clear that she wanted nothing to do with him, but that had been a long time ago. Maybe she had softened—or come to her senses.

Yeah, the more he thought about it, the more he knew Jamie was his way in, but how could he appeal to her? Talk about a tough nut to crack. The woman didn't have an interest in money, or so she said. *Lord knows, she didn't dress like she did.* He'd have to appeal to her sense of ethics. He'd tell her that if Bailino was alive, it was her duty to talk about it publicly, ferret him out, how it would be a public service. The Carter siblings were all about public service. And that could be his ticket back to CNN. *Would that work?* he wondered. Maybe. He'd have to make his plea in person, though. He did his best work in person.

He pulled out his cell phone and checked his calendar. He wasn't due in court until Thursday. Nothing but damn consulting work for the next few days. That could wait. He did an online search for flights to Washington; there was an 11:10 out of Kennedy. He looked at his watch. He could make it, if he hurried, so he booked it and called for an Uber. Then he ran into his bedroom, plopped a suitcase onto his bed, and quickly packed some underwear and toiletries, along with a few suits.

As he zipped his suitcase shut, he felt a rush, starting to feel like his old self again. He should have done this a week ago. It was only a matter of time until he was on CNN instead of that cretinous organized crime historian.

He thought about texting Jamie to let her know he was going to be in town and would like to have dinner—maybe he could persuade her over a few glasses of wine—but he thought it better to wait. He could go straight to the White House first thing tomorrow morning, now that she was back from vacation, or wherever she was. Just walk right up to the front gate, like he did five years ago when he marched into the governor's Executive Mansion in Albany. They had let him in then, so Grand was bound to let him in now, wasn't he? One of his former legal roundtable lawyers? It was a no-brainer. And even on the off chance that he was refused entry, there would be press roaming around that would notice him, and that meant air time.

His Uber app pinged, notifying him that his ride had arrived, and Bob rolled his suitcase toward the apartment door. He turned off the coffeepot and the lights, and wrote a quick message for Mrs. Estabauer to take in his mail for the next few days—it would give the old landlord something to do.

He pulled his keys from the counter and turned the knob of his apartment door when the door suddenly swung open, startling him and knocking his luggage and keys to the floor.

"What the fuck?" Bob said, reeling backward as a man pressed him against the wall, his massive arm pushing against his windpipe. "Take whatever you want," he gagged, trying to fight back, but the guy was quick and like a tank. He couldn't make out the man's features—it was dark and he was wearing some kind of hat—but suddenly the overhead light flicked on, and Bob was staring into dark eyes he had never seen before in person but knew instantly. He looked at the open door.

"She's not home," Bailino said, his voice reeking of coffee, the cheap kind. "She got into a car about a half hour ago with some kids. Looked like grandchildren. It's just you and me, Mr. *New York Times* bestselling author."

Bailino's grip loosened on Bob's neck, but he kept him locked against the wall. "You gonna be a good boy?" he asked, taking out a pistol.

Bob eyed the handless arm pressing against his windpipe and put his hands up in the air. A small part of him still wanted to believe Bailino was dead. "What do you want?" he said in the deepest and most dangerous voice he could muster.

"Well, what I want is irrelevant right now. It's what I *need*."

Bob tried to swallow but couldn't gather enough saliva. "What do you need?" he asked.

"I need you to text Jamie Carter." Bailino slowly let go of Bob, who took in a huge gulp of air.

"Jamie Carter?" Bob's voice sounded hollow. "We're not married anymore. I wouldn't even know how to—"

In an instant, Bailino's arm swung up and knocked Bob's head into the wall, and he fell to the floor.

"Let's try this again," Bailino said.

"All right ..." Bob said, covering his head with his hands, his ear ringing with pain. "Give me a minute ..."

"Where's your phone?"

Bob tried to gather his thoughts as well as some kind of strategy, but he was still hung over. Absently, he dug his phone out of his pants pocket, and Bailino knocked it out of his hands and onto the floor.

"Relax …" Bob stood up carefully. "I'll do whatever you want. You don't have to hit me again."

"Are you kidding? Hitting you is the most fun I've had in years." Bailino looked around the apartment. "Nice place. What's with the suitcase? Taking a trip?"

Bob was quiet.

"I asked you a question."

"Yes, I'm taking a trip."

"Where are you going?"

Bob hesitated, and Bailino straightened his arm holding the gun. "I knew it. You're as dumb as you look."

"Washington."

"For what?"

Bob's instinct was to hesitate again, but he pushed the words out. "The president needs to see me."

Bailino leaned toward him, watching him closely. "Is that right?"

"I mean," Bob said, "I need to see the president."

"The president? Or the president's press secretary?" Bailino asked.

Bailino looked as if he was going to hit him again when Bob's phone, which was lying on the floor, pinged.

"What's that?" Bailino motioned toward the phone's screen.

"My Uber."

Bailino seemed to consider this. "Don't want you to miss your ride, so let's make this snappy. Pick up the phone, unlock it, and then face it toward me. Very slowly, so I can see the screen, and open your contact list."

Bob reached down and did as he was told, and Bailino watched him carefully, although he took a slight step back in order to see the phone screen, as if he needed reading glasses. Bob scrolled to Jamie's phone number, wondering if he could somehow get the jump on the guy when Bailino placed the barrel of the gun against his temple.

"You gonna be a tough guy?" Bailino asked.

"No," Bob said.

"Wow, you're not so tough when the cameras aren't rolling," Bailino said. "Now, click *Text Message*."

"Wouldn't you rather do it?" Bob held out the cell phone for him.

"Nah, I like ordering you around." He pressed the barrel of the gun against his temple.

Bob clicked the app, opening a new message.

"Now, press *Send*," Bailino said.

Bob hesitated. "But there's no message."

"I'm a man of few words." Bailino smirked.

Bob pressed *Send*.

"Now, if you're smart, you'll put that phone away, pick up your bag, and go get into your Uber," Bailino said. "Are you smart?"

"Yes," Bob said, and before he could stop himself, added, "Very."

"I doubt that." Bailino put the pistol away. "Have a nice trip," he said. With his foot, he pushed Bob's luggage toward him, and as Bob picked it up Bailino darted out of the apartment. In the hallway, Bailino slung a duffel bag over his shoulder and walked down the stairs like he lived there, even straightening one of Mrs. Estabauer's picture frames on the way out.

Bob stood there, stunned. He rubbed the front of his neck, which felt raw, his touch making the skin sting. He began dialing 911, but stopped. He didn't see the point. By the time they got there, Bailino could be anywhere in the city, and the last thing he needed was some Italian maniac after him. Still, having police on the scene might fetch some media coverage and an opportunity for Bob to make the news. He decided not to chance it.

He looked at the weird blank message Bailino sent to Jamie. There was no reply. Was there supposed to be? Would she think it was weird that Bob sent her a blank text? Or was Jamie *expecting* a blank text?

He remembered an assault case he had tried when he was at Worcester, Payne & Leach several years before. One of his clients had been accused of stalking his ex-wife, but because the legal definitions of stalking varied from one jurisdiction to another, Bob had been able to convince the jury that his client's behavior—he had only sent a series of blank texts to the woman—would not cause a reasonable person to feel fear, and he had gotten the guy off. Turns out, the texts were some kind of warning or signal, and two weeks after his client went walking out of the courtroom as a free man he wound up strangling the woman to death in front of their two-year-old daughter.

Was Bailino sending a warning or a signal to Jamie?

Bob grabbed his luggage from the floor, slammed his apartment door closed, and ran down the stairs, his suitcase bumping behind him. He shoved the landlord's note under her apartment door and hurried down the stoop onto the sidewalk.

"Did you call for an Uber?" asked a kid standing in the street next to a double-parked Chevy. He looked annoyed. "I asked that other dude who came out, but he just kept walkin'."

"Yeah, that was me," Bob said. He wheeled his luggage toward the trunk of the car, put it in, and got into the backseat.

"You're lucky," the driver said with a huff after he closed the trunk and slipped into the driver's seat. "I was just about to leave." He put the car into drive and pulled into traffic.

Lucky, Bob thought. Five minutes ago, he wouldn't have used that word for what had just happened, but Bailino's unexpected arrival had been exactly the thing he had been looking for.

"Where you headed?" asked the kid, who had calmed down. "I mean, once you get to the airport, where you going?"

"Washington," Bob replied absently.

"What, do you have a meeting with the president or something?" The kid laughed.

Bob smiled. "Or something."

Actually, the White House no longer held an interest for Bob. He leaned back against the seat of the car. By this time tomorrow night, he not only expected to be featured on the evening news, he expected to be the main story.

29

Jamie Carter kissed her daughter good-bye, patted the head of a big dog that Wilcox had never seen before, and then slipped into Edward's car. He looked at the clock on his dashboard: 10:07 a.m. As she eased onto the road, Wilcox followed from a few car lengths behind. Jamie had gotten pretty savvy when it came to both stationary and moving surveillance, and he had a feeling she'd be able to spot his car, which is why he borrowed his brother's. He found it ironic—both of them driving their brother's cars, both of them not wanting to take their own, perhaps for similar reasons. Still, he kept his distance.

Jamie was the last person Wilcox ever thought would be under his surveillance, but he had to treat her as he would any other person of interest. Her song and dance in the Oval Office—if that, indeed, is what it was—had to be sussed out. That was his job, whether or not Phillip Grand was in agreement. And if Jamie was telling the truth, then she would be vindicated. It was as simple as that.

He followed her to I-95, which, since it was a Sunday, was moving pretty steadily, and onto the north entrance ramp. When she merged into the middle lane, he stayed in the right lane and then after a few miles maneuvered behind a moving van, which provided additional concealment. Wilcox turned on the radio to pass the time, but wasn't listening. The moving van in front of him changed lanes, and Wilcox changed along with him, keeping Jamie's vehicle within eyeshot.

Signs for Maryland appeared in the distance, and soon the two cars were crossing the state border. *Son of a bitch,* Wilcox thought. *She's ignoring the request to stay put.*

They drove past Baltimore, and after the moving van took the exit ramp, Wilcox stayed behind a blue SUV in the middle lane. Fifteen minutes on I-95 turned into a half hour and then into an hour. *Where the hell is she going?* When Jamie put on her indicator and took an exit in Delaware, Wilcox's pulse quickened.

Bailino's car had been found at the Wilmington, Delaware, Amtrak train station earlier that morning. Agent Fuller had spent most of the night watching surveillance footage and had been pretty sure he spotted Bailino getting onto a train headed to New York City. He had sent a video still to Wilcox to confirm, and although Wilcox couldn't be sure, since a baseball cap covered much of the target's face, he was inclined to agree.

What did that mean, he wondered. He looked at the street signs. Jamie was heading toward the University of Delaware in Newark, which was about a half hour from Wilmington. Had Agent Fuller IDed the wrong guy? Wilcox didn't think so. It made sense that Bailino would get the hell out of Delaware since that was where he left his car. Or did that make it the perfect spot for a meeting?

He followed Jamie off the exit ramp, letting several

vehicles get between them. As they drove for a few miles, the streets grew narrower and more congested, old homes turning into frat and sorority houses. Finally, she parked her car on a block near campus, across the street from a green quad. Wilcox made a right-hand turn and parked in between two cars on a similar side street. He reached onto the passenger seat for a pair of sunglasses and a baseball cap and put them on, and then he quickly got out of his car, pumped a few quarters into the meter, grabbed a backpack from his trunk, and walked toward the corner of the block.

It was a beautiful fall morning, and students, most of whom probably didn't have class on the weekend, were out and about—having breakfast and lounging on the grass. The campus was surprisingly crowded, with groups of students and adults touring the grounds, perhaps for Parents' Weekend—a perfect time to visit for someone who wanted to get lost in a crowd.

He looked for Jamie, who, he remembered, was wearing a white T-shirt and jeans—an outfit he assumed was intentional and would make it difficult to track her among the students—and, for a moment, he couldn't locate her, but then he spotted her. While most of the people on campus were strolling casually, someone wearing a T-shirt and jeans was walking with purpose away from campus.

She was crisscrossing streets, as if trying to lose a tail, although she didn't look behind her. She strode past the university's dormitories and toward the main street of the college town. Wilcox pulled down his baseball cap and followed from a half block behind. When she got to the main street, she ducked into a Starbucks, and Wilcox kept walking, shielded by a student and a lecturer-type whose relationship looked more than professional. He crossed the street with them and walked into a nearby Panera Bread, which, with its large windows and crowded restaurant, offered a solid place to conduct his surveillance.

Wilcox stood in the vestibule, inside the door, watching the front of Starbucks closely. He couldn't imagine she had driven nearly two hours for a cup of coffee. Lots of people were seated at the outdoor tables, and the front door was opening constantly, with patrons filing in and out. It dawned on him that perhaps she was simply meeting an old school friend or colleague, but that still wasn't enough to explain why she had defied his request to stay local. Some of Panera's patrons began to eye Wilcox suspiciously, so he took out his phone, pretending to speak with someone so he didn't arouse any more suspicion.

After about ten minutes, Jamie emerged from the coffee shop with a duffel bag slung over her shoulder. She stood on the sidewalk, looked left and right, and started walking back in the direction of her car when a man came out of Starbucks and called to her. Wilcox pressed his nose against the cool glass of the front door.

Could it be, he wondered, resting his hand over the gun under his jacket.

The two talked briefly, and as they parted the man put his hand on Jamie's shoulder, and Wilcox's mind drifted back to his interview with Paolo Cataldi at the FBI field office in Albany three years before:

"Do you recognize this person?" Wilcox had asked, showing Cataldi a photo of Jamie Carter.

"Yeah," Paolo had answered. "That's Donny's girlfriend."

Quickly, Wilcox opened the front door, but a troop

of students and parents were idling on the sidewalk, and when he managed to push his way through them, both Jamie and the man were gone. He stood there, trying to catch his breath, when his cell phone buzzed. As he put the phone to his ear, surprised by the name on his screen, he didn't notice that a man, just inside the glass of Panera Bread, had also been watching the scene, and was doing the same.

30

"What's that?" Edward asked, as Jamie placed the bulky duffel bag on the floor. As she did, Lucky came charging through the open back door into the kitchen and started sniffing it, her tail wagging. "Geez, please tell me it's not dog food?"

"No," she said, giving the dog a pet on the head. She reached onto the counter where she had left her car keys earlier that morning so she could transfer the duffel bag to her car.

"How did it go?" Her brother was standing near the kitchen cabinets, pulling out boxes of microwave popcorn. "Your meeting with the vice president."

"Fine," Jamie said. She didn't want to keep lying to Edward, but she had had to tell him something—the text from Bob had taken her by surprise—and after leaving for a week with no notice or information, he wouldn't have settled for radio silence again. Despite the long drive, the meeting with Bailino at Starbucks had been quick, and if what he said was true, that ToniAnne Cataldi had been behind all the attempted assassinations, what was in the duffel bag was enough to put her away for a long time.

"The meeting went well," she added, a comment she hoped wasn't another lie.

"So what's in it?" Edward asked. "The bag?"

"Oh, just stuff for the president," she said, which, technically, was true. Whenever Jamie said things were "for the president," she knew Edward wouldn't snoop or ask any more questions. He was too respectful of the office—and the man. "Where's Faithy?"

"She's with Trish, Sara, and Peter in the yard. They were all taking turns rubbing Lucky's belly last I saw."

At the sound of her name, Lucky sat attentively, watching Edward, probably hoping for a treat, although Edward didn't notice. He was busy humming to himself while removing frozen turkey and veggie burgers from the freezer. Although he had been angry with her for going MIA for nearly a week, the anger hadn't lasted. It never did. Their relationship sometimes reminded her of a parent and child—the parent punished the child the night before for some infringement, and then the next day, when the sun came up, all was forgiven and forgotten.

"Do you need help with anything?" Jamie asked.

"Nah, you know me, James. I love barbecuing, although not as much as I like making breakfast in the park." He smiled.

He was smiling more these days. At first, Jamie hadn't been on board when Edward told her he would be moving down to Virginia after she accepted the White House press secretary position. There had been no reason for him to uproot Trish and the kids simply because she had decided to relocate, but he ended up finding a good job at an environmental law firm in Alexandria, and he and Trish were able to buy a much larger home with what their house had been worth on Long Island. Edward seemed content here, more relaxed, and that made her happy.

"Momma, is that you?" Faith called from outside. She stood in the back doorway, her little body dark against the sunny backdrop. "Come out, we're playing with bubbles."

"C'mon, Lucky, let's go play with bubbles," Jamie said, and the dog walked beside her toward the back door.

Outside, Faith was already on the move, running with the bubble wand, and Lucky charged after her, trying to eat all the soapy liquid slipping into the wind. Was that dog ever *not* hungry, Jamie wondered. The two of them ran in widening circles, Faith laughing and calling to the dog to follow her and Lucky obeying like a good little soldier. It was only when Jamie saw Faith running free—the way she was now, the way she was in Wyoming—that she felt truly at peace. Being cooped up in the house, even if it was the White House, was no life for a child. Her daughter carried so much baggage, because of who her mother and father were, that it was nice to see her behaving like an ordinary nearly five-year-old.

Jamie wondered what their lives would look like now that Bailino was lurking in the background again. She saw the way he had looked at her at Starbucks, the way he had always looked at her. She didn't feel afraid; she didn't know what she felt. Safe, maybe, but did this mean that she and Faith would never really be free?

The front doorbell rang, and Jamie heard Edward yell, "Coming!" as Faith returned to the backyard deck to reload her bubble wand.

"Momma!" she said, dunking the wand three times. "I missed you."

"I missed you too, sweetie, but it looks like you've been having some fun."

"They've been asking me for a dog," Trish said, motioning toward Peter and Sara. The three of them were sitting at the table playing cards. "See what you started."

"Please, Mom," Sara said. "Do you have any sevens, Peter?"

"Go fish," Peter said before turning to his mother. "Aunt Jamie has a dog, and she works all day, too."

"Guys, Lucky will be spending lots of time here. She's everyone's dog," Jamie said as the back door opened, and Edward emerged.

"Oh, Edward will love that," Trish said with a wink. "Right, hon?"

"James?" Edward said. He had a strange look on his face.

"What is it?" asked Trish, her expression changing. She too could sense something was wrong.

"Trish, keep the kids here, okay? Jamie, can you come inside?" Edward opened the door wider.

"Sure," Jamie said. She followed her brother into the house, and he closed the back door behind them. She was about to ask what was going on when she realized two people were standing in the kitchen. As she got closer, she saw the first was Special Agent Wilcox and, much to her surprise, the second was Bob.

"Agent Wilcox?" Jamie asked. "What are you doing here?" She ignored Bob, who looked so excited he might burst.

"I'm afraid I'm here on official business," Wilcox said.

Jamie glanced at the duffel bag on the floor and then at Edward. She knew she was going to have to come clean eventually, but she hadn't planned on doing it in front of her brother. "Special Agent Wilcox, I have something—"

"Jamie," Wilcox said, "you are under arrest."

"What?" Jamie took a step back. She checked behind her to make sure the back door was closed and Faith was still outside. "Under arrest?"

"What on earth for?" Edward asked. "Is this a joke?" He glared at Bob.

"I'm afraid not," Bob said.

"Mr. Scott, please," Wilcox said, motioning to Bob to remain quiet. "Jamie, you're under arrest for conspiracy, aiding and abetting a felon, and the attempted assassination of the president of the United States."

"You can't be serious," Edward said, stepping in front of Jamie.

Wilcox took out a pair of handcuffs. "I'm afraid I am, and I suggest that you move, Edward, before you too are arrested. For obstruction."

"This is ridiculous," Edward said, standing firm. Edward's lawyer face was emerging, the one Jamie had seen displayed in many courtrooms, both as a defense lawyer and prosecuting attorney.

"Is it?" Wilcox said. "Have you asked your sister about Don Bailino?"

"What about him? Are the leaks true? Is he alive?" Edward asked. "If you know that to be true, Agent Wilcox, why the hell don't we have any protection?"

"You should ask your sister that too," Wilcox said, crossing his arms.

Edward turned around, and all eyes went to Jamie. "What's going on, James?"

Jamie took a breath. Edward's pleading eyes made her hesitate.

"What would Reynaldo Rodriguez's family think about you protecting the man who killed him?" Wilcox said.

"Bailino didn't kill Reynaldo," Jamie said.

"*Protecting?*" Edward asked. Now *he* took a step back. "What is he talking about?"

Jamie focused on Wilcox. She would have to deal with Edward later. "Agent Wilcox, you know me ..."

"I *don't* know you," Wilcox said. "I thought I did, but I don't." One of the handcuffs was dangling from his crossed arms like a pendulum. "I followed you today, I followed you all the way to Delaware."

"Delaware?" Edward said, putting his hand on the counter next to a bowl of freshly popped popcorn as if to hold himself up. "I thought you were heading into the office for a meeting with the vice president?"

"The plot thickens ..." Bob said with a smile.

"Shut up, Bob," Jamie said. "Why are you even here?"

Wilcox looked as if he were about to explain, but Bob cut him off.

"I got an unexpected visitor last night," Bob said. "I think you know who it was." Jamie could feel all their eyes on her again, but she said nothing. "I thought it was my duty as a citizen of the United States to report it to the FBI."

"You son of a bitch," Jamie said. "You don't give a damn about the United States."

Edward put his hand on Jamie's shoulder, his eyes no longer shocked, but concerned. "Jamie, what is going on?"

"Edward, I don't know where to start," she said when Wilcox stepped forward with the handcuffs.

"Wait," Jamie said. She reached for the duffel bag, but Wilcox pushed her back surprisingly rough.

"No sudden movements, please," Wilcox said.

"It's why I was in Delaware. It's evidence that ToniAnne Cataldi was behind the assassination attempt."

Wilcox didn't even glance at the duffel bag. He wrapped the cold metal around her wrist. "You have the right to remain silent," he said, locking the first and then the second handcuff. As he recited the rest of her Miranda rights, Bob's smile nearly broke his face, as if he were going to plunge his hand into the popcorn and start eating it.

"Is that really necessary?" Edward asked.

"I'm afraid that it is," Wilcox said. "What's in the bag, Ms. Carter?"

"It's parts used by Cataldi for the explosive device."

Edward turned pale. "You brought that into my *house*, James?"

"There's nothing lethal in it," Jamie said. "Just parts like—"

"It doesn't seem like you're making good decisions these days, Ms. Carter." Wilcox got behind her and began ushering her forward.

"Edward," Jamie pleaded, "it's a long story ... Please look after Faith." As confused and angry as her brother was, he nodded, and relief washed over her.

"Did she tell you she was in Wyoming?" Wilcox asked Edward as they reached the front door.

The look on Edward's face told Wilcox that she had

not. "At that log cabin?" Edward asked Jamie. "Where they think Bailino is?"

"*Was*, Mr. Carter," Wilcox said. "He seems to be wherever your sister is."

"Edward," Jamie said quickly before she was out the door. "I needed to bring Faith somewhere safe, and that was—"

"Bailino's arms," Bob said smugly as Wilcox pushed her outside.

"Edward," Jamie cried, "you know that's not—"

"I suggest you don't say any more without a lawyer present," Wilcox said and moved her down the front steps as several knocks came from the back door, followed by Faith's muffled calls. "Momma? Momma?"

"Agent Wilcox," Jamie said, trying to see his face, but he was holding her arms firmly in front of her. "There's got to be another way. Let me say good-bye to my daughter ..."

"I'm afraid not," Wilcox said, pushing her toward a car she didn't recognize in Edward's driveway. Neighbors were out on their front porches now and peeking over backyard fences, their cell phones raised high. On the street, cars were pulling up and double-parking, as men and women with video cameras rushed in their direction.

Wilcox opened the back door of the car and, in contrast to his earlier handling of her, pushed her somewhat gently inside, although he slammed the door behind her. Then he went back into the house and returned with Bailino's duffel bag, Bob trailing behind him. He placed the bag in the trunk of the car without even opening it, got into the driver's seat, and locked the car doors. When Bob tried to get into the passenger side, Wilcox rolled down the window.

"You'll have to grab an Uber, Scott," Wilcox said. "I appreciate the help."

Bob appeared dumbfounded as Wilcox threw the car into reverse and skidded out of Edward's driveway, as more and more neighbors flooded the street in front of Edward's house, flashes popping and videographers trailing the car for half a block.

When they had driven for a few minutes, Wilcox stared at Jamie through the rearview mirror. She stared back.

"You didn't have to do that, you know," she said. "You could have called me to the White House or to FBI headquarters. I would have come. You know that. My daughter has been through enough."

"What's happening now is because of *your* actions, not mine, Ms. Carter," Wilcox said, shaking his head. "What happened to that nice girl I met five years ago? The one who knew the good guys from the bad guys?"

Jamie glanced out the window, as Wilcox merged onto I-95 going north. "She's gone."

31

"Are you out of your mind?" Phillip asked when Wilcox entered the Oval Office.

It had been more than an hour since Phillip summoned Wilcox for a meeting and interrupted Sunday dinner with his family—the first dinner they had had in more than a week, a celebration of sorts after Agent Summers had confessed to the attempted bombings. He thought it all might be over. Instead, it turned out to be the calm before the storm. "Why wasn't I informed of this?"

"Mr. President, time was of the essence ..." Wilcox said.

"Bullshit," Phillip said. "You knew I'd never go for it. Arresting Jamie for ... What was it?" He picked up his cell phone, which had been practically glued to his hand for the past hour, and scrolled. "Conspiracy, treason, and aiding and abetting a known felon," he read from the news website, "and who the hell knows what else? Where is she?"

"She's being held in an undisclosed location," Wilcox said coolly.

"There's no such thing as undisclosed. I'm the goddamn president—*president*—of the United States," Phillip said, slamming his cell phone on the desk and cracking the screen. "For Chrissakes, Wilcox ... You really think that Jamie Carter is trying to assassinate the president? *Me?* That she was trying to harm her own daughter?"

"We'll leave that for a jury to decide."

"I need to speak with her."

"I'm afraid that's not possible."

"Not possible?" Pain shot through Phillip's temples, and the dizziness that he had managed to keep at bay returned. He rubbed the corners of his eyes with his thumb, rendering the room blurry for a few moments. How did it all seem to get out of control? "Are you kidding me?" he said. "Do I really need to pull rank here? Why are you following around Jamie Carter? Agent Fuller got a full confession from Agent Summers early this morning."

"I've been fully apprised on what is going on with Agent Summers."

"And is that not enough? Summers confessed."

"We may know the executioner, but we don't yet have a mastermind. Or motive."

"What does that mean? You think the mastermind is Jamie Carter?"

"No, but Jamie knows more than she's letting on."

"Summers said he acted alone," Phillip said.

"According to Jamie Carter's so-called evidence, I wouldn't be so sure."

"Evidence?" Phillip remembered seeing Wilcox drag a duffel bag from Edward's house into a trunk of a car on one of the news sites. "And that's reason to drag her in front of television cameras like a criminal? Not to mention the additional damage that was done to my administration, which is already in turmoil. Did you see the video that was released a half hour ago?"

Wilcox appeared uncharacteristically taken by surprise. "Video?"

"O'Connell's video. The *whole* video. It's gone viral. He's back from the dead, apparently, with the director's cut of that little video he took of me three years ago sneaking around the Barbara farmhouse like a spy, shooting an antique pistol, and then running inside moments before the farmhouse burned down to the ground."

"With you saving Jamie and Faith Carter at the end," Wilcox said.

"Yeah, well, that's old news, and no one cares." Phillip paced behind his desk. "Speculation has already begun about what the hell I was doing there, in the same place as Bailino, in the same place as Paolo Cataldi when—as the media reported—I told the FBI that I was on my way to my housekeeper's …"

Wilcox looked as if he were about to say *I told you so*, but Phillip didn't give him the chance.

"There's talk of corruption," Phillip continued. "MSNBC is apparently pulling my old military records looking for any clues as to my ties with Bailino, how I may have secretly been funding his exile in Wyoming. As you know, all it takes is a whiff of corruption these days— nothing concrete—and government officials are *finished*. Just before you arrived, Collins gave his notice." Phillip held up an envelope that was on his desk and threw it back down. "The guy couldn't get out of here fast enough. And rumor has it that Rudy Ray Mitchell—kind, good-hearted, soft-spoken Rudy Ray Mitchell, my friend to the end—is thinking of stepping down and running against me in the next Republican primary. That's if they don't impeach me. And you know who might run with him? Josef Clark—if you can believe that." Phillip raked his hands through his hair. "I have good people working for me, Agent Wilcox— *good people*—who, in a single week, have feared for their own safety, been interrogated by federal agents, been ridiculed by late-night television, and discovered that the president they trusted is a liar. And on top of all that, I have a country to run and a special agent who is running around playing cowboys and Indians with Bailino ..." Phillip came around his desk and stood before Wilcox who, even seated, appeared tall. "You've got Bob Scott talking up a storm on every news show that will have him. He practically gave a play-by-play of Jamie's arrest to Wolf Blitzer ... It's a goddamn media frenzy." Phillip's eyes searched Wilcox's face. "Do you really have nothing to say?"

"It was necessary," Wilcox said simply.

"Necessary? To embarrass Jamie? For what? Stumbling upon Bailino?"

"Well, that's her story ..."

"And you think there's more to it? Based on what? What purpose could—"

Phillip caught himself. "Wait a second ... You *don't* think Jamie is trying to hurt me, do you? You're trying to ferret out Bailino." Phillip threw his hands into the air. "*Jesus ...*"

"I told you before," Wilcox said. "If the cat can't find the mouse, then we need to get the mouse to go to the cheese."

"Yes, we've played this game before. Have you

forgotten how it turned out? Innocent people died," Phillip said. "What is this vendetta you have with Bailino? You realize you're no different than Paolo Cataldi—using an innocent woman to get what you want."

"Jamie Carter is far from innocent," Wilcox said. "Bailino saw to that."

"And that whole charade, parading her out in front of her brother's home handcuffed in front of all the press. Who leaked to the press that you'd be there? Let me guess … Bob Scott." Phillip shook his head. "You do realize that Edward Carter and his family are private citizens who have been dragged into the spotlight. You're playing a very dangerous game, Agent Wilcox."

"If that's all, Mr. President?" Wilcox said, standing up.

"Like hell, it is," Phillip said, returning to his desk. "You're off the case, Wilcox. I want Jamie Carter out of jail, or wherever the hell she is."

"You're not going to do that, sir."

"I am, and I will." Phillip picked up the office telephone as his cracked cell phone lit up and vibrated on the desk. He picked it up and stared at the number, which he had memorized by now. He looked at Wilcox. "It's Bailino."

In a flash, Wilcox was at Phillip's side, examining the phone screen in Phillip's hand as if he had just received the phone call he had been waiting for his whole life. He picked up his cell phone.

"Answer it, Mr. President," Wilcox instructed, plugging in a number and holding his own cell phone to his ear. "On speaker. We should be able to get a location immediately, but try to keep him on the phone as long as you can …"

Phillip knew it was useless to try to keep Bailino on the

phone, and he knew that Wilcox did too. Bailino would stay on the phone as long as Bailino wanted to. He swiped the screen, pressed *Speaker*, and held the phone in the air between himself and Wilcox like a hot potato. "Yes?" Phillip said.

"Is that schmuck Wilcox there?" asked Bailino's unmistakable growl. There were street sounds in the background. Wherever Bailino was, he was outside.

After a beat, Wilcox replied, "Where are you, you son of a bitch?"

"Right across the street, asshole," Bailino said. "Come and get me."

32

By the time Wilcox got to the D.C. Central Detention Facility, Bailino had already been photographed and his one hand fingerprinted. It hadn't taken much effort for him to be detained, according to the agents Wilcox had dispatched once Bailino gave away his location. Wilcox would have liked nothing more than to see Bailino on his knees, up close and personal, but he had been held up by Phillip Grand, who had insisted on accompanying him to the facility until Wilcox talked him out of it.

True to his word, Bailino had been standing across the street from the White House, a stone's throw from the backs of television producers, editors, and camera people focused in the opposite direction on their on-air personalities, all of whom had had their weekend disrupted by the release of the Phillip Grand video and arrest of Jamie Carter. Apparently, the only tricky part had been handcuffing Bailino—detaining a one-handed person required some finagling—but Wilcox's men said he complied and probably would have gotten into the back of their sedan by his own volition if they had let him.

Wilcox rode the elevator to the lower level of the building, where Bailino was being held. When the elevator doors opened, two armed agents appeared, beginning a long line of paired agents. Wilcox wasn't taking any chances this time. They nodded at him as he approached when suddenly the adjacent elevator door opened and Phillip Grand emerged, ringed by Secret Service agents.

"Mr. President, I thought we went over this," Wilcox said, striding down the long corridor.

"We did, and I'm coming in with you," Phillip said, charging down the hallway beside him. "You just didn't agree."

"Fine, but with all due respect, don't get in my way," Wilcox said as one of the agents opened the holding room door, which clanked as if they were entering a bank vault, and the two men stepped inside.

Bailino was seated at the long side of a rectangular table, facing them. He was wearing a brown jumpsuit, a leather belt cutting across his midsection to which his right hand had been secured, his handless arm chained behind his back.

"Agent Wilcox," Bailino said with a smirk upon seeing him. "It's been a long time." When Phillip Grand came into the room, Bailino simply said, "Hey, Phil."

The man Wilcox had been chasing for years appeared older and grayer, with a deep tan covering the lines on his face, but Wilcox knew that, despite appearances, he was every bit the ruthless criminal hanging on his office wall. "Did you really think we'd never find you?" Wilcox asked. "Did you really think you'd live out the rest of your life up in the mountains? That you'd never have to pay for all you've done."

"*You* found *me?*" Bailino said. "Talk about fake news. If

I'm not mistaken, I just turned myself in. In fact, I think I saw that on CNN about a half hour ago."

Even though Wilcox's agents were able to take down Bailino in a matter of minutes, as soon as the news media got wind of what was going down right behind them on Pennsylvania Avenue, they turned their cameras and started rolling. Wilcox was sure that it hadn't been by chance that Bailino had chosen that particular location for surrender.

"I was there, at the house ... the log cabin in Wyoming," Wilcox said. "Inlaid Boon? An anagram for Don Bailino. Very clever."

"Just keeping it interesting." Bailino smirked.

"You're running out of places to run. It's over."

"Is it?" Bailino asked. "Tell me more, Agent Wilcox."

"Cutting your own hand off. Using the sewers for whatever twisted purpose you had—to escape a burning building, to grab Charlotte Grand, to get in and out of the Little Yellow Hotel. It's done. You're done."

"I see you've done your research," Bailino said. "Impressive."

"It's my job to know about you," Wilcox said. "Now ... Where's ToniAnne Cataldi? She's wanted for questioning."

Bailino shrugged. "Beats me. Isn't she home?"

"No, she's not."

"Did you try the mall?"

A heat flared within Wilcox's body and roared through him like an engine. "This can be difficult, or this can be easy," he said.

"It's never easy," Bailino said. "You know that. And, just so you know, we don't swim in the same school,

ToniAnne and me. You've been watching too many fishing shows."

The comment caught Wilcox off guard.

"It's my job to know about *you*," Bailino said.

"I wouldn't play games if I were you." Wilcox pressed his palms onto the table. "You might have no problem going back to prison, but I don't think Jamie Carter is looking forward to it."

The mention of Jamie's name caused the corners of Bailino's eyes to tighten. "Who's playing games here? You never intended to send her to prison. This whole charade was to get me here, and now I'm here. And you're going to let her go."

"Really?" Wilcox let out a small laugh and sat down opposite Bailino at the table as if they were going to play a round of poker. "This may come as a surprise to you, but your magical powers and your charm don't work with me."

"Is that right?" Bailino asked. "You're hurting my feelings."

"We don't need you."

"I'm afraid you do—if you want ToniAnne, for questioning or custody, whichever it is. I prefer the latter. I know you have the bag. I saw you put it into your trunk on CNN."

"Are you referring to that duffel bag of junk that I got from Jamie Carter?"

"ToniAnne's fingerprints are all over those explosive device parts."

"And so are yours," Wilcox said. "Maybe you're trying to frame her. We already have someone in custody."

"Who? Summers?"

Against his will, Wilcox hesitated again. He refused to think that Bailino was a step ahead of him.

"There are two things that ToniAnne likes to do most: fuck and talk," Bailino said. "I got a heap of both the last time I saw her."

"You're telling me Agent Summers and ToniAnne Cataldi are working together?" Wilcox asked. "Why?"

Bailino shifted in his seat, although the chains prevented him from moving much, and turned his attention to the president, who had been noticeably quiet. Phillip Grand had been standing to the side, watching and still looking astonished that Bailino was even sitting there at all. "The guy had nothing against you, Phil," Bailino said.

"Then why did he do it?" Grand asked, his soft-spoken voice muffled to nearly a whisper in the soundproof room.

"You're right," Bailino said. "It makes no sense. A bright-eyed, up-and-coming agent with an impeccable record and a beautiful family? What would make a man do something so out of character? What would make a peaceful man turn violent?" He waited for the president to answer, but Phillip Grand stood there quietly. "Think about it, Phil. Think of those young boys we saw over in Iraq—lobbing grenades at the American soldiers who had just given them some candy and a basketball. Why? Why does anybody do anything?"

Wilcox could see the president was thinking—his eyes were unfocused, lost in thought. He couldn't afford to let Bailino get into Phillip Grand's head. "Enough with this," Wilcox said, "I—"

"To protect his family," Phillip blurted, his eyes

regaining clarity. *"Jesus,"* Grand ran his hands through his hair, "ToniAnne Cataldi killed Agent Summers's daughter."

Bailino smiled like a doting teacher as if a student had come up with the right answer. "How did his daughter die?" he asked, as if it were a reminder.

"Hit-and-run," Phillip said. "She ran the little girl down."

Bailino shook his head. "More likely one of her flunkies. She didn't say, but it was probably her main flunky, Lorenzo Cavetti. ToniAnne prefers bossing people around from her couch than getting her hands dirty, unless she's standing behind the barrel of a gun." He shifted again in his seat, a short grunt escaping from his lips. "And Summers has another one at home, right? Another daughter? He has to protect what's left. That's why he's not giving up ToniAnne, and he's taking the heat. He can't, not without risking her life."

"That's a lovely theory," Wilcox said. "But Summers knows we could have protected him."

A small chuckle escaped from Bailino's lips. "I think what Summers *knows* is that you cannot," he said. "She would have gotten to him eventually. They always do. You're bound by the law. They're not."

"Is that what you people do?" Wilcox said with a sneer. "Go after people's kids."

"You gonna lump me in with them?" Bailino said with a shake of his head. "Whatever. I don't give a shit. I'm trying to help you here ... ToniAnne Cataldi has no problem killing kids. *Other people's kids*. His. Yours. Especially yours," he said to Grand. "She blames you for the death of her son. *Our* son. That's why I left Wyoming, to get her to stop this nonsense, and I did."

"Really?" Wilcox asked. "Wow. How? Let me guess … You asked her nicely?"

"In a word, yes."

"Did she release that video, Don?" Phillip asked.

Bailino nodded. "That dumb fuck O'Connell was a pawn in a game that he had no idea he was losing."

"She killed him for a video?" Wilcox asked incredulously.

Bailino shook his head. "She killed him for fun. The video was just an excuse."

"So you're saying a fifty-something-year-old woman— from a criminal family, yes—but with no priors and no criminal record just decided to go on a killing spree?" Wilcox asked. "I'm not buying it."

Bailino smirked again. "How was O'Connell shot?"

"Is this a rhetorical question?" Wilcox asked.

"He was shot in the eye, right?" Bailino said.

"I see you can read the papers. *Impressive.*"

"Is there nothing familiar about that, Agent Wilcox? Have you not seen that before?"

A flicker of a memory appeared in Wilcox's mind. "I'm not here to be quizzed," he said.

"I can tell from your face that you *have* seen that before. About twenty years ago, am I right?"

Wilcox crossed his arms and leaned back in his chair, his eyes steady on Bailino.

"Agent Wilcox?" Grand asked.

"Okay, I'll play," Wilcox said. "In the late '90s, NYPD recovered two bodies off the Belt Parkway in Brooklyn. Each had been shot in the eye. So?"

"The official word was that those homicides were

unsolved, right? But you thought you knew who did it, didn't you?"

"I still do," he said. "I'm staring at him."

"Wrong," Bailino said. "It was ToniAnne."

"Why don't we pin 9/11 on her too, while we're at it," Wilcox said.

"I don't understand," Grand said. "Why did she even bother with O'Connell? How did she know there was more to the video than O'Connell was letting on?"

"She didn't," Bailino said, "but she had a hunch, and she stalked that kid like a sniper, buttering him up until he spilled the beans—and then she spilled his blood all over his off-campus housing."

The room was quiet, and Wilcox was trying to figure out Bailino's angle. He was sure he was up to something. "So you say that—somehow—you got ToniAnne Cataldi to stop the bombings, but you couldn't get her to *not* release the video?"

Bailino shrugged. "That was the compromise, unfortunately. Phil's integrity for his life. But now ..." He motioned toward his chains. "All this nonsense? Me here? Scott shooting his mouth off to anyone who will listen? I mean, will that guy just go home already? There's no telling what she's gonna do until she gets what she wants."

"And what is that exactly?" Wilcox asked.

"Me," Bailino said simply. "It was poorly played, Wilcox."

"Fuck you, Bailino," Wilcox said, pushing back in his chair, its legs scraping along the concrete floor with a screech. "I've heard enough of your bullshit. Jamie Carter is going to rot in a prison cell, and she'll have you to thank for it."

"No, she won't," Bailino said. "Phil won't let that happen. Will you, Phil?"

Phillip Grand continued to stand there silently, and it was clear that they all knew Wilcox was bluffing. The president would never allow Jamie Carter to go to prison. It was written all over his face and was exactly why Wilcox didn't want him taking part in the interrogation.

"If you really thought the president would pardon Ms. Carter," Wilcox asked Bailino, "then why go through all the trouble of turning yourself in? It makes no sense."

"Wow, you are pretty smart, after all," Bailino said with a smirk. "Here's the thing …" He got down as far as he could to the table, as if he were about to reveal a secret. "She's been through enough, more than any decent human being should go through in this lifetime, and I'm not about to see her, or the kid, harmed anymore—not if I can do anything about it, and right now I can. These are my terms …"

"Terms?" Wilcox said. "You're joking, right?"

"Let him speak, Agent Wilcox," Phillip said, a reprimand that Bailino seemed to enjoy.

"In addition to letting her go," Bailino said. "I need the FBI to say that incarcerating her was a mistake—a mistaken identity, a mix-up at the DMV, whatever you can come up with works for me. I need to know that she can go on and live her life without this black mark on top of everything else. She has enough baggage to carry."

"Let me get this straight …" Wilcox said. "Jamie Carter aids and abets, and in the end it's my career that gets tarnished? You can't be serious."

"I am. Very."

It amazed Wilcox how a man who could barely move on a chair because he was wrapped in chains could have such a look of authority.

"Don ..." Grand said, finally coming forward. "This has to stop—my children, my family, *your* daughter, Jamie ... They are in danger."

"I know," said Bailino, his expression softening slightly. "I feel responsible."

"Is that a confession?" Wilcox asked.

The softness vanished, and a look of impatience replaced it. "For the last time ... I had no idea what ToniAnne was up to, but, frankly, I should have."

Wilcox leaned forward on the table until he and Bailino were inches apart. "But you *do* know where she is," he said.

"Release Jamie Carter, talk to the press, and then we'll chat," Bailino said, leaning back in his chair as much as the chains would let him, as if he were calling an end to a meeting he had arranged. "I'll tell you everything you need to know to apprehend her. You have my word. Once that's done, I can get down to the business of spending the rest of my life behind bars."

33

ToniAnne videotaped her granddaughter feeding bread to a dirty white duck that had lost most of its feathers. It was just the kind of duck she expected to see in the middle of New Jersey, a stone's throw from the black smog of one of the burgeoning industrial sectors. For all she knew, they were being bombarded with radiation at that very moment.

"Grandma, look, it's taking it from my fingers," Gina said with a giggle.

"Not too much bread now," she said, zooming in. "We don't want the duck to get too fat."

"Then no man-duck will want her, right?" the little girl said.

"That's right."

The park lights blinked on as the sun continued its descent behind a spattering of trees, and ToniAnne clicked off the camera and placed it on her lap. She couldn't think of a better way to celebrate the release of O'Connell's video than by spending it with her granddaughter, but the truth was she was exhausted. Gina was a ball of relentless energy. She looked at her watch. Lorenzo was late. Again. She was about to call him when she spotted a lone figure coming toward them from the path leading to the parking lot.

"Well, it's about time," she said when Lorenzo reached them.

"Goddamn traffic on the Turnpike," he said, flopping onto the bench beside her.

"Oh, please. When is there ever *not* traffic on the Turnpike? You stopped at Walmart, didn't you?"

Lorenzo ignored the question and called to Gina. "Hey, Gigi!"

"Hi, 'Zo," Gina said, skipping over. "We were waiting for you."

"Did you have fun with Grandma today?" he asked.

Gina nodded, her face lined with dirt and red streaks from the icicle pop ToniAnne had bought her earlier. "Yep, we went for a walk. We collected leaves. Here, look," she said, showing him the folded and crinkled colored leaves in her pocket. "And ate and walked again and went on the monkey bars and had an ice and fed the ducks ..."

"All right, kid," Lorenzo said, already appearing bored. "Not too many of those treats, though, because then you'll have an ass like grandma." He tried to pinch ToniAnne's butt, but she swatted his hand away.

"Ready to go, Gina?" ToniAnne asked. She held up the little girl's jacket, and Gina slipped her arms through the sleeves.

"Going? Already?" Lorenzo said. "I just got here. I've been sitting in the car all fucking day, following Bailino on his errands—Brooklyn, Delaware. Do you know how long it takes to get to Delaware? It's a fucking long drive."

"Language, please," ToniAnne said, covering Gina's ears. "Sweetie, go play on the swings for a bit longer, okay?" she said, zipping up the little girl's sweatshirt, and Gina ran toward the playground.

"Guy drives three hours to hand a woman a duffel bag," Lorenzo said with a shake of his head. "Couldn't he do it in Jersey?"

"Yeah, and it got her arrested," ToniAnne said with a smile. She had been concerned when Donny had left that morning—he didn't seem like himself. When Lorenzo called to say he had seen Donny hand that Jamie woman the duffel bag with the IED parts, ToniAnne thought that all that fresh Western air had messed with Donny's head, but she should have known better. Over the last few hours, as Gina walked, played, ate, and frolicked with dirty ducks, ToniAnne had been happily reading all the news on her cell phone about that slut getting arrested and getting what she deserved. ToniAnne should have never doubted him. "Genius," ToniAnne said, putting the tips of her fingers to her lips and kissing them. "Where's Donny now?"

"How the fuck should I know? I came home after I called you."

Gina came running back, her arms spiraling around like a windmill. "Grandma, there are bugs by the swings."

"That's okay, Lorenzo's rested enough. We're leaving."

"Back into the car …" Lorenzo said with a huff, getting up from the bench. "Why don't I just live in the car, since I'm in there all the time anyway?"

"Good idea," ToniAnne said, wrapping the video camera strap around her shoulder and taking Gina's hand.

"This way, I won't have to pick up your dirty underwear from the floor. You can just toss it out the window as you drive on the Expressway." Gina giggled.

They hurried along the path to the parking lot, since, as Gina had rightfully reported, the mosquitoes, gnats, or whatever they were, were out in full force, and ToniAnne strapped Gina into the backseat of her daughter's SUV and got into the passenger's side, placing the camera in the well of the seat.

"You really should get a new one of those things," Lorenzo said, motioning to the video camera. "They sell ones now that you don't have to carry on your shoulder, you know. Why don't you just use your phone?"

"This one was my father's, and it works fine enough," she said.

"Suit yourself, old-timer." He put on his seat belt. "Do you mind stopping at a McDonald's? I'm starving."

"Didn't you get enough to eat at Walmart?" she asked with a laugh.

Lorenzo rolled his eyes.

"Is there a McDonald's around here, Geen?" ToniAnne asked, turning around to look at her granddaughter. Although Anna had been living in Jersey for nearly ten years, ToniAnne had never really bothered to familiarize herself with the area. All the jug handles confused her.

"Ummm …" Gina tapped her index finger against her bottom lip. "I'm not sure."

"Let me check my phone," Lorenzo said. "I know there's a McDonald's around here somewhere …" He swiped his phone and poked around.

ToniAnne turned on the radio and, after a few minutes

of watching Lorenzo stare at his screen, said, "What's taking so damn long? Are you having a seizure?"

Lorenzo looked up at her, his tired eyes wide.

"What's the matter?" she asked.

He turned the phone in her direction, and a photo of Donny appeared. "What the fuck?" she said, grabbing the phone and raising the volume. Lorenzo tilted it so he could watch with her.

" ... notorious Don Bailino—rumored to have been alive and in hiding for more than three years—was taken into custody by the Federal Bureau of Investigation today after surrendering in front of the White House."

"What the fuck is he doing?" Lorenzo asked.

"*Shhhh ...*"

"I can't see!" Gina called from the backseat.

"Sources close to the FBI tell us that Bailino turned himself in in order to have Jamie Carter, who had been arrested earlier this afternoon, released. Carter—whom you may remember was abducted by Don Bailino more than five years ago and gave birth to his child—was arrested while visiting her brother, Edward Carter, in Virginia," the news site displayed a photo of the house and street, "by retired FBI Special Agent Paul Wilcox, who is working on the investigation into the attempted bombings, reporting to the president. However, Jamie Carter was released not long ago, and the FBI issued the following statement: *The investigation into the attempted assassination of the president of the United States is a massive undertaking involving the work of hundreds of agents. Conducting an investigation of this size— having to chase down every lead and thoroughly examine every detail—can sometimes lead down erroneous paths. The Federal*

Bureau of Investigation was given incorrect and misleading information with regard to Ms. Jamie Carter, and, after a thorough interview, it was determined that Ms. Carter is in no way a person of interest in this investigation, nor is she a suspect. To be clear, she has committed no crime. The FBI apologizes for any distress or embarrassment this incident may have caused. We now have a live interview with a Mr. Robert Scott, who ..."

ToniAnne pushed the phone away and sat back in the passenger seat.

"Wow ..." Lorenzo said. "The guy went to jail for her ... I told you your ass was too big."

ToniAnne hardly heard him, the stock image of Donny that the media had a habit of using remaining in her mind's eye like a camera flash. It was one of her favorites. She had been with him at the Knights of Columbus the night the Feds had taken it fifteen years before. She had been with him when they had gotten home that night too.

"Holy shit, Ton, look ..." Lorenzo tilted the phone toward her again. This time, an image of her house on Staten Island flashed on the screen showing FBI agents stationed outside the gate. Lorenzo read from the screen: "Sources say ToniAnne Cataldi is wanted as a person of interest for a crime they are investigating. Whether that crime is related to the attempted—" ToniAnne grabbed the phone and tossed it out the window.

"What the fuck?" Lorenzo said. "I just got that one."

"I'll buy you a new one," she said, digging into her purse and throwing out her phone as well. The events of the past twenty-four hours were circling her mind like puzzle pieces—Donny not telling her where he had been for more than three years, the duffel bag of explosive parts landing in the hands of Jamie Carter and then the Feds, the way he reacted when she brought up the kid, *his* kid, the way he recoiled from her touch the night before, the way Lorenzo said Donny reached for Jamie's shoulder in Delaware, him kneeling on the ground in front of the White House, turning himself in to save … *her*. How could she have been such a fool?

"Grandma, are we going to McDonald's?" Gina asked.

"Not tonight, honey. I'm going to have to drop you off at your friend Makenna's house, and Mommy will pick you up from there later, okay?" ToniAnne couldn't risk going anywhere near Anna's house. If the Feds weren't there by now, they would be soon. She put her hand on Lorenzo's shoulder. "You up for another ride?" she said, and Lorenzo placed his hand on top of hers.

"With you?" he said, giving her hand a squeeze. "Anytime. What do you have in mind?"

"Looks like we're heading south," ToniAnne said, buckling up her seat belt. "The Feds want to play cat and mouse? Well, two can play at that game."

34

As soon as the taxi turned onto the block around the corner from Edward's house, Edward was already waving it down in the middle of the street, standing with a man Jamie didn't recognize. Her brother handed a fistful of bills to the driver through the open car window before opening Jamie's door. "You okay?" he asked, helping her out.

Jamie nodded. "Is Faith all right?"

"Yes, she's fine," he said as the cab pulled away. "James, this is Chester, our neighbor." Chester and Jamie shook hands. "Let's hurry and get you inside before the press sees us."

He took Jamie's hand and guided her into a handsome Colonial-style house that was presumably Chester's. The three of them walked through the front door and then in and around three large rooms in various paint colors until they reached a back door, which was open. Once outside, Edward shook Chester's hand.

"I owe you one, man," Edward said.

"Anytime," Chester said. "Nice meeting you," he said to Jamie and disappeared inside the home.

As Edward and Jamie crossed the backyard, Jamie

wondered if Chester would have thought it was so nice to meet her had the FBI not made a big to-do and apologized for her arrest. The organization had released a convincing statement, which she had learned about only once her phone, purse, and pistol had been returned to her and she watched the news on the way to Edward's house; at the detention facility, the agents who had been assigned to her had simply uncuffed her and said, "Go," without any fanfare. She hadn't even seen Wilcox again.

When they reached the four-foot chain-link fence that separated Edward's and Chester's properties, Edward got down on one knee. "C'mon, I'll give you a boost," he said.

"That's okay. I can do it." Jamie dug the toe of her shoe into one of the metal holes and climbed her way up. As soon as her feet landed on the grass on the other side, Faith was running across the yard. "Momma! Momma!" she called as Trish stood behind the screen door, watching her. When the little girl reached them, Trish went inside the house.

"Faithy!" Jamie said, picking her up and squeezing her. "How can you possibly look like you've grown in only a couple of hours?"

"Where did you go?" the little girl asked as Edward landed beside them.

"I had to take care of a few things, but it's all over now. I'm back."

The three of them walked toward the house, Faith holding both Edward's and Jamie's hands, and Jamie noticed a hole in the side fence just behind a trio of shrubs.

"Is that new? What happened?" she asked, worried that perhaps the press had damaged the property.

"Don't ask," Edward said.

"Lucky didn't mean it," Faith said, looking up at Jamie with her big brown eyes. "She was chasing a bunny and tried to squeeze through. She's sorry."

"Did she get hurt?" Jamie asked Edward.

"She's fine, although I nearly broke a rib trying to get her back."

A fire was roaring in the metal firepit, and a box of graham crackers, an open bag of marshmallows, and various utensils lay on the table near it.

"We're making s'mores!" Faith said, letting go of their hands and reaching for one of the roasting sticks for the marshmallows.

"Not yet," Edward said, gently taking the stick from Faith's hands. "We have to wait for Sara and Peter."

"Sara! Peter!" Faith called, charging up the deck stairs.

"I'm trying to keep things as normal as possible," Edward said, going up the stairs behind her.

"I appreciate that," Jamie said, walking up next to him as Edward opened the screen door, and they went inside.

Before Jamie made it past the threshold, Lucky was on her hind legs, pressing her big paws onto Jamie's shoulders and licking her face, nearly knocking her over.

"She missed you too," Faith said with a smile before running farther into the house.

Trish and Sara were sitting on the sofa in the living room, and Peter was standing near them, carrying Faith, who had jumped onto his back, piggyback-style.

"Aunt Jamie, did you see all the news cameras outside?" Sara asked.

"No, I must have missed it," Jamie said, giving Trish a wink.

"We did too," Peter said sadly. "Mom wouldn't let us look out the window."

"I'm so mean." Trish stood up and mussed Peter's hair. "It looks like most of them went home, finally. You okay?" she asked Jamie.

"Trish, why don't you take the kids outside and get started on the s'mores," Edward said.

"Yay!" Faith cheered, climbing down from Peter's back, but then her face turned serious. "What about Lucky?" she asked. "Can she come too?" Again, at the mention of her name, Lucky sat up and stared at Faith and then Edward.

"I think Lucky is going to stay in for a while," he said.

"*Awww!*" Faith grabbed Lucky by the neck and hugged her. "I'll save you a s'more, Lucky, I promise," she said as Trish escorted the children to the backyard. Lucky followed behind them anyway.

"I'll pay for the fence," Jamie said, putting her purse and cell phone down on the coffee table. Her pistol holder was digging into her calf, and she had the urge to take it off, but Edward didn't like seeing it around the house, so she left it on.

"It's fine. Please, one problem at a time." He peeked out the window. "Trish is right. They're just about all gone, although it's hard to see in the dark. What's going on, James? I had been on the phone with my firm trying to get someone to get you out—I know it's environmental law, but they've got lots of connections. But no sooner had I found someone than you called to say you were coming home. Why? Is it true what they're saying? Bailino surrendered to get you out?"

Jamie shrugged. "I don't know." She sat down on the sofa, suddenly feeling tired. It had been a long day.

Edward sat beside her. "They used you to get to him, right? Great ... And now they're looking for someone named ToniAnne Cataldi. Cataldi ... I assume she's one of them?"

Jamie nodded. "A daughter, niece. Bailino told me she was behind the whole thing."

"Why?"

"Revenge, I guess."

They sat there quietly until Edward put his hand on her shoulder. "James, I don't think you're going to like me saying this ... but maybe you should think about changing jobs."

"Changing—?"

"Hear me out. I know being the press secretary of the president of the United States is amazing and—"

"I won't do that," she said. "I won't quit."

"I think President Grand will understand. It looks like everyone is jumping ship."

"All the more reason," Jamie said. "I will see this out and be with the president as long as he needs me."

"James," he said in a voice that was probably meant to be comforting but came out condescending, "that's commendable, but do you really want to risk putting your daughter in more danger? For your career?"

"It has nothing to do with my career," Jamie said. "It has to do with my friend, Phillip Grand."

Edward took in a deep breath and leaned back on the sofa. She could tell he didn't agree, and that was fine. He didn't have to.

"Once they find this ToniAnne person, will it be over?" Edward asked. "Finally?"

Jamie didn't know what to say. Edward had asked her that several times before, and she had asked herself that same question far more. *Would it ever be over?* "I don't know," she said again.

"All right." He stood up. "Enough of this ... We have to live our lives or else they win, right? Let's go stuff our mouths with marshmallows."

Jamie smiled. "Sounds good to me," she said when she heard something. "What's that noise?" she asked. It sounded like it was coming from the back of the house.

Edward craned his neck toward the back door. "No!" he shouted and charged down the hallway.

"What's the matter?" Jamie asked, following him.

Lucky was on her hind legs and scratching at the back door. With every push of her large paws, the mesh screen was bending in.

"The damn dog is going to ruin my screen," he said, "in addition to my fence." He was about to tug on the dog's collar when Jamie stopped him.

"I'll take care of it," she said as Lucky let out a big howling bark, her head thrown back like a wolf, and then she continued clawing at the screen.

"What's the matter with Lucky?" Peter asked, peeking in from outside.

"Well?" Edward shouted to Jamie as Lucky let out another howl. "I thought you were taking care of it."

The second howl was more intense than the first, and the hairs on the back of Jamie's neck stood up. "Something's wrong," she said.

"Dogs bark, James," Edward shouted.

"Not this one." Jamie opened the screen door as Lucky went charging into the yard and down the deck stairs, startling Trish who was helping Sara with her s'more.

"What are you doing?" Edward asked, following Jamie outside. "What about the hole in the—"

"Where's Faith?" Jamie asked Trish.

"She's playing on the swing set," Peter said, pointing toward the empty playground equipment at the side of the yard. "Wait, she was there a minute ago."

"Faith!" Jamie screamed. She ran down the stairs. "Faith!"

"Faithy!" Edward called, right behind her.

"I swear, Jamie, she was *just* here." Trish said, leaning over the deck fence, a panicked look on her face.

Jamie was running in the direction of Lucky's barks. The dog was at the front of the house, pushing on the fence with her large paws, her strong hind legs bending against the ground as if she were going to try to jump. Jamie came up next to her, the dog as tall as she was, the two of them peering over the fence.

"Faith!" Jamie called. It was dark and hard to see. The block, unlike earlier that day, appeared empty, most of the cars off the street and parked in their respective driveways. She scanned the area as Lucky continued to bark and lights were turning on in the neighboring homes. Under a streetlight, down the block near a fire hydrant, two teenage girls were walking a small dog, and farther down a person with a video camera was walking across the street.

"Edward, call the police!" Jamie yelled and opened the front gate. "Stay here, girl," she said to Lucky, "I'll be right back," and closed the gate behind her, flagging down the two teenagers.

"Have you seen a little girl?" Jamie asked when she reached them, startling them. They looked at one another and shook their heads, their little dog yapping at Jamie's ankles.

She kept running, screaming for the cameraman, who had reached the sidewalk on the other side of the cross street. "Excuse me! Sir!" she called, and he turned around. "Have you seen a little girl?" She could still hear Lucky barking in the distance.

The man studied her and swung his video camera in her direction. "Hey, you're—?"

"Yes, I know, Jamie Carter. Did you happen to see a little girl, by any chance?"

"A little girl?" He thought for a moment. "Did she have dark brown hair and dark brown eyes?"

"Yes!" Jamie said.

"And she was wearing black leggings and a pink sweater?"

"That's her!" Jamie said. "Do you know which way she went?"

"I do." He leaned down to whisper in Jamie's ear. "She's in the trunk of that car over there," he said, pointing to a black SUV on the next block. "And if you don't come with me right now, you'll never see her again."

35

Phillip watched Bailino crack the knuckles of his right hand one by one against the table's surface. His fingernails were uncharacteristically dirty and chipped, and he wondered if that was from his three-plus years of living on the land out west, but it seemed unlikely. Even in the army, in the middle of the deserts of Iraq, Bailino had been meticulous about his manicure.

Wilcox had been gone only a few minutes to finalize the release of Jamie Carter and gather the paperwork needed to process Bailino into the system, but Phillip knew it was too long as far as Wilcox was concerned. He had handled most of the facilitating from the holding room, and his eyes probably would have never left Bailino at all if some bigwig upstairs hadn't asked to see him about the deal—the Bureau didn't take kindly to mea culpas. Phillip eyed the young agent Wilcox placed inside the holding room in his absence. The agent had been instructed to *shoot Bailino if he moves at all* but looked as if he had never fired his gun at anything other than a paper bull's-eye.

"What's your name, young man?" Phillip asked.

"Agent Hansen, Mr. President," said the young man,

his eyes shifting away from Bailino for a moment. "Agent Richard Hansen."

"How long you been with the Bureau, Agent Hansen?"

"Going on two years, Mr. President."

"Well, I appreciate your desire to serve your country. I see too many young people spending their days idly on their phones. It's nice to see someone showing some initiative."

The agent gave a small smile but kept his attention focused on Bailino.

"Agent Hansen," Phillip continued, "are you familiar with the eighth amendment of the Constitution?"

"Yes, Mr. President. It prohibits the United States government from imposing excessive bail, fines, or cruel and unusual punishments," he said proudly.

"Well ..." Phillip motioned to Bailino. "This man has been handcuffed in this position for hours. Would you agree that this could be categorized under cruel and unusual punishment?"

Agent Hansen examined Bailino's restraints. "Yes, Mr. President, but Agent Wilcox said—"

"The Constitution is the Constitution, Agent Hansen, and this is not acceptable. I think you would agree that it's important to follow the letter of the law here. We wouldn't want Bailino released on a technicality. Not on *our* watch." Phillip returned the small smile. "I believe you may uncuff his wrist and arm, and he will still pose no threat. His legs are shackled, he is unarmed, and there is a line of agents outside ready to shoot him on sight. He's not going anywhere."

The young man hesitated, appearing conflicted,

but then nodded and circled the desk until he was behind Bailino. After a few clicks and maneuvers, the back handcuff was off and dangling to the ground, and Bailino's left arm came forward to rest on the table, and for the first time Phillip saw the jagged stump where his left hand had once been. When the other handcuff had been removed, the young agent collected both handcuffs, nodded at Phillip, placed them in a pocket, and returned to his post.

"Thanks," Bailino said, rolling his shoulders as Phillip sat down in the seat across from him. Despite all his bravado, all the back and forth with Wilcox, Bailino looked tired.

"Why are you here, Phil?" Bailino asked, rubbing his wrists.

"What do you mean?"

"Judging by our friend Wilcox's expression, it's clear he doesn't want you here. He's afraid I'll work my magic"—he waved his right hand in the air for emphasis—"on you. And I don't need a babysitter. I can take care of myself. I'm a big boy. You don't need to worry about me."

"I never worry about you."

"You've always worried about me," Bailino said. "That was your problem." He leaned back in his chair and brought his shoulders up to his neck and then released them, leaning his head to the left and then to the right, each time followed by a crack. "Are you here because you're hiding?"

"Why would I be hiding?" Phillip asked, glancing at the young agent whose eyes were still fixed on Bailino.

"You tell me. Remember when we were in that little

dive bar in South Carolina—Pete's, was it?—just after basic training and that shy girl with the big tits and the red hair asked you to dance to some Garth Brooks song? You excused yourself to the bathroom, and I found you ten minutes later hiding in one of the bathroom stalls."

"She wasn't my type."

"I know. You like 'em bossy." He smirked.

"Katherine was the best thing that ever happened to me."

"I know she was. And I was the worst."

Phillip shrugged. "Not really … If we're being honest, it's probably because of you that I'm here."

"I could have told you that."

"Not *here* here," he said, motioning to the holding room. "The White House. That video of me at the farmhouse is what got me reelected as governor and what carried me into the White House. And now, ironically, it will be what gets me impeached …"

"Give me a break, Phil. That video didn't get you elected, and you know it."

Phillip pressed his thumb and forefinger on the bridge of his nose to stem the headache he felt coming on. "Maybe it's for the best. Maybe I should just step down."

Bailino leaned forward. "Look at me, you big dummy," he said, his dark brown eyes, while older, still possessing that same intensity. "How you've handled yourself got you where you are. In the army. In the Governor's Mansion. In your *life*. Not some fuckin' video. You always worried too much." He crossed his arms, and the stump of his left arm stuck out of the sleeve of his jumpsuit. "You'll figure it out. I knew from the first minute I saw you in that baggy military uniform that you were going to do some good in this world. Lord knows, we need some."

A quiet settled upon the room. "Can I ask you a question?" Phillip asked.

Bailino looked around. "I'm not going anywhere."

"Why Charlotte? There were dozens of ways you could have gotten the stay of execution for Gino Cataldi. Why put her in danger?"

"She was never in danger."

"C'mon … You know as well as I do that things happen, things we never expect. You can't control everything. That was *your* problem. You always tried to." Phillip fingered the peeling vinyl at the edge of the table. "So why kidnap Charlotte?"

Bailino shrugged. "It got your attention, didn't it?" he said. "Maybe I just wanted to see you."

The door opened, and Wilcox entered holding a file folder. Phillip leaned forward to get up from the chair, but Wilcox motioned for him to stay and placed the paperwork on the table. Wilcox glanced at Bailino's handcuff-less wrists, but didn't say a word. He nodded at the young federal agent, who excused himself and left the room.

"She out?" Bailino asked. "I'm not signing shit until I know she's out of this place."

"She's out. Took a cab home," Wilcox said. He spread the paperwork on the table.

"And was I right? Was there anyone matching the description of Lorenzo Cavetti in front of Walter Reed."

Phillip could tell immediately that Bailino was right. Wilcox seemed to wince every time Bailino scored a point, and he was doing it now, which is probably why Bailino liked to rub it in. "Yes, we IDed him from security camera footage a block away," Wilcox said nonchalantly, as if it weren't a big deal. "He was on the scene."

Bailino smirked. "You know, I would have made a pretty good FBI agent. I missed my calling."

"Let's get on with it," Wilcox said, pushing the paperwork toward him. "You want a lawyer?" he asked.

"Nah ... Believe it or not, Wilcox, I trust you," Bailino said. "Got a pen?"

Wilcox pulled one from his shirt pocket when his cell phone rang. He pulled the phone from the clip on his belt and checked the caller ID. "One second," he said, stepping into the corner of the room as Phillip's private cell phone rang as well. He looked at the screen, which read *Edward Carter*.

"What's the matter?" Bailino asked, watching Phillip's expression.

"It's Edward Carter," Phillip said.

"Answer it, Phil," he said with urgency.

"Wait," Wilcox said, pulling his cell phone from his ear. "I have Brandon Fuller on the line. Patricia Carter called 911 a few minutes ago to report Faith Carter was missing."

"What?" Phillip said as his cell phone stopped ringing and Edward's call went to voice mail.

"But now they *both* are, Jamie and Faith. They disappeared from the house." Wilcox glared at Bailino.

"Could Jamie have taken off again?" Phillip asked no one in particular, but Bailino answered.

"She wouldn't do that," he said. "Not again."

"What could have happened then?" Phillip asked.

"I'll tell you what happened," Wilcox said, slamming

his fist onto the table. "This is all part of your plan, isn't it? You son of a bitch." Bailino's usual poker face gave away nothing, prompting Wilcox to start pacing in front of the table. "I almost fell for it … Getting me to release Jamie Carter—how noble of you—only to have ToniAnne Cataldi, who we can't find and whose whereabouts you haven't told us yet, abduct her so that she could trade to get you out."

"And why would I do that exactly?" Bailino said. "Think about it. The minute Jamie's released, you'd just arrest her again, and we're right back where we started."

"So what then?" Phillip asked, placing his cell phone on the table.

"I think Wilcox is right," Bailino said. "This has ToniAnne written all over it, and I have a feeling I know where she's taken them."

"Of course, you do," Wilcox said. "Why am I not surprised?"

"Get over yourself, Wilcox," Bailino said.

Phillip could feel the tension building in the small room, which, with little ventilation, had grown quite warm. "What's going on, Don?" he asked.

"My guess is that, because of Agent Double O Wilcox's performance for the cameras this afternoon at Carter's house, ToniAnne figured out how to get to them."

"Where are they?" Wilcox demanded.

"My guess? Jersey."

"We've already been to her daughter, Anna's, house," Wilcox said.

Bailino shook his head. "Not Anna. She has nothing to do with anything."

"Where then?" Phillip asked.

Bailino hesitated, and before Phillip realized what was happening Wilcox was around the table and pushing Bailino's chair back against the wall, Bailino's handless arm acting as a barrier.

"Give it your best shot, you prick," Bailino said, landing a quick punch into Wilcox's side with his fist when Phillip lunged between them.

"Enough," he said and pulled the two men apart. "Agent Wilcox, this is not the way."

Wilcox, his face flushed, walked toward the far corner of the room and took a few deep breaths as Phillip helped Bailino rebalance the chair on the concrete floor.

"Don," Phillip said, putting his hand on Bailino's shoulder, "we need to know where they are."

"I can't tell you that," Bailino said, still glaring at Wilcox. "Why?"

"Phil, if I tell you, and the Feds and the SWAT team go in, they're dead."

"So let me guess ..." Wilcox turned around, his arms across his chest. His face was still flushed, but his breathing had calmed. "You have more terms?"

"ToniAnne wants me, and she'll do anything to get me."

"Tell her to get in line," Wilcox said.

"She's just playing your game, Wilcox. How does it feel being on the other side?"

Wilcox started toward him again, but Phillip held up his hand, and he stopped.

"Phil," Bailino said, "if you don't let me take care of this, you know what will happen. You and your family will be next. That's not a threat, that's a fact. I'm their—and your—only chance. I think you know that."

"And what are you going to do?" Wilcox asked Bailino. "Go and ask her nicely again to stop?"

"I'll have to figure it out once I get there."

"Great plan," Wilcox said with sarcasm. "And once you figure out how to save Faith and Jamie Carter, then you'll just march right back into prison?"

"Yep."

"Bullshit," Wilcox said, and, based on what had happened at the Barbara farmhouse, Phillip was inclined to agree. "Once you get there, it'll be you and Cataldi with two hostages, and we're exactly where we are now, except you're free."

"Wire me up," Bailino said. "Do whatever you have to do. Just get me in the same room with ToniAnne, and I'll do the rest."

The two men looked at Phillip, who sighed and leaned against the wall, which felt cool even under his suit.

"You can't be seriously entertaining this, Mr. President," Wilcox said.

"It's not your call, asshole," Bailino said.

"Gentlemen, *please* …" Phillip said, trying to think. "Do we have another option?"

"Yes," Wilcox said. "We have a lot of options."

"There are *no* other options, Phil," Bailino said. "This is it, if you want Jamie and Faith Carter alive. If ToniAnne doesn't see me, it's over."

Phillip stepped away from them to find some air in the small room. He had built his career on putting and keeping criminals behind bars, not letting them go, and he knew that there was a very good chance Bailino, if given this opportunity, would manage to escape, one way or another. He also knew that Jamie and Faith Carter's best chance at getting out of this thing was Bailino. He ran his hands through his hair. The media would have a field day if they found out Bailino was on the loose, even under FBI supervision, but with ToniAnne's volatility, there was a strong likelihood that many more people would be in danger if he didn't seriously consider Bailino's offer. He thought of Charlotte and Philly when his cell phone rang again on the table. He looked at the cracked screen.

"It's Edward Carter again," he said, picking up the phone. "I have to take this." He headed toward the door.

"Mr. President?" Wilcox asked, motioning toward Bailino.

Phillip opened the door, a wave of cool air hitting him in the face. "Let him go," he said and left the room.

36

It had been years since Bailino had been to the Hydeman old folks' home off Exit 2 in Jersey, only now it was called the Hydeman Assisted Living Facility. Back then, the property consisted of about fifty or so acres of grassland—old Gino used to joke that the place was "really putting its residents out to pasture"—but, according to the signage at the front of the parking lot, it looked like the grounds had been expanded to at least double that size.

Business must be good, Bailino thought.

Normally, a bunch of haggard-looking figures would be wandering about and trying to escape, but instead the place looked like a ghost town. Old Hydeman's son, with the help of local PD, managed to clear the property pretty quickly after a resident-care assistant placed a 911 call reporting that four visitors—two women, a man, and a child—had entered the building just around the time Phillip Grand was leaving the holding room at the D.C. detention facility. Lucky for her, the assistant had been near a vending machine, out of view, when the elderly front desk clerk started asking the group questions, and one of the women took out a pistol and shot the clerk in the eye before the group headed for the stairwell. The authorities presumed that the guests were inside Room 343, old Mary Cataldi's room, and Bailino presumed they were right. There was probably more ammunition in that room than in the local police department.

The rising sun was low in the sky as Bailino walked through the empty parking lot. Wilcox hadn't been too happy with him after the clerk had been killed—"just another death to add to your list of accomplishments, Bailino," he had said—but letting Wilcox get the jump on ToniAnne would have only put Jamie and Faith in more danger. ToniAnne was many things, but she wasn't stupid. She could spot a sting operation a mile away. The death of an elderly clerk? Bailino could live with that.

He pulled at the collar of his shirt. He was wearing so many wires he was surprised that he didn't glow: GPS, microphone, camera. It had taken hours for Wilcox's people to string him up, although Bailino thought it was a waste of time. A live video feed wasn't going to save Jamie and Faith Carter any more than a fleet of FBI agents would, but Wilcox had made it clear—if any transmission was interrupted, even for a second, then his agents would break down the doors. Bailino hoped a plane didn't fly overheard.

He crossed the threshold into the empty building and tried to get his bearings—the old circular stairway that he remembered had been replaced by three elevators, and the dumpy lobby looked like something from a five-star hotel with an ornate crystal chandelier that was bigger than his living room at the guesthouse. To the right was a long, colorful tropical fish tank that probably got more attention than the facility's residents. Next to that was an emergency stairwell, and Bailino took the stairs to the third floor and followed the signs to Room 343.

When he got there, the door was closed. He knocked, and it opened immediately.

"I knew you'd know where to find me. You always did," ToniAnne said with a wide smile.

"Yeah, well, you didn't make it too difficult."

"You alone?"

"Very funny," he said and walked into the small apartment toward the large window overlooking the grounds, which resembled a crowd shot during the Macy's Thanksgiving Day Parade. Outside the front gates, swarms of law enforcement agents covered the acres of carefully mowed green grass like agitated bees. "Where are they?" he asked, looking around.

He spotted Jamie sitting on a chair in the next room, rope tied around her wrists and her legs, which were tied to the legs of her chair, similar to the way he had found her in the old Barbara farmhouse three years before. She looked tired and a bit bruised, but okay.

"You all right, sweetheart?" he asked.

"She's fine," ToniAnne said, rolling her eyes.

Across from Jamie, on the other side of the room, sat an old woman hunched over a desk. "You remember my Aunt Mary, Donny, right?" ToniAnne asked, walking over to her.

Paolo Cataldi's wife, Mary, glanced at Bailino, the hump on her upper back preventing her from sitting up straight. She was holding an envelope. She raised it and slid her brown tongue across the adhesive before folding the flap down and setting it on a stack of mail.

"Aunt Mary," ToniAnne shouted into her ear, "you remember Donny Bailino, right?"

Mary looked up and stared into Bailino's eyes, and Bailino thought there was a flicker of recognition, but then it was gone.

"She has dementia, poor thing," ToniAnne said. "Happened right after her sister, Fran, died last year." She gave her aunt a peck on the cheek. "I hate seeing her like this."

"Where's the kid, ToniAnne?" Bailino asked.

"They won't let me see her," Jamie blurted.

"Shut the fuck up, you," ToniAnne said, running her hand along Mary's course gray hair as if she were petting a dog. "What's the rush, Donny? You just got here. Let's talk …"

"Stop being cute. I need to get the kid out of here and to the Feds, and then we can talk."

ToniAnne huffed her displeasure. "That wasn't my plan."

"Well, that's the new plan," Bailino said. "If that kid doesn't leave here unharmed, and soon, things will go very badly."

"*Your* kid," she said. "Right?"

"That's right. She's my kid."

"You had another kid, you know. His name was Joey."

"Yeah, I know, and your fuckin' lunatic uncle had him killed."

"Po*tay*toes, po*tah*toes …" ToniAnne waved a dismissive hand and picked up the cell phone on Mary Cataldi's desk.

"Who are you calling?" he asked.

ToniAnne blew him a kiss and then spoke into the

phone. "Lorenzo? … It's me, *idiot* … I need you to bring the kid to the lobby and let her walk out." She smiled at Bailino and hung up. "Satisfied? Let's talk." She motioned toward Jamie. "This one's not too talkative. Between her and Aunt Mary, I'm bored to death."

Bailino stood next to a wall unit housing a small television and porcelain knickknacks and peered out the window. "I need to see the kid walk out of here, and then we can chat."

"I need to see too," Jamie said, standing up, but ToniAnne smacked her across the face, and Jamie's head hit the wall.

"Sit the fuck down, I said," ToniAnne shouted.

"Ton, relax …" Bailino said as Jamie sat back up. When she looked at him, her cheek was red, and her eyes were wet.

"Girl was packin'," ToniAnne said, picking up Jamie's pistol and holster from the floor. "I think Lorenzo enjoyed frisking her."

A twinge of anger flared up inside Bailino, but he casually glanced out the window again. "I'm waiting," he said.

For a few minutes, it was quiet in the room, the only sound coming from Mary Cataldi's soft rolling of a ballpoint pen across a piece of paper, which she shoved into an envelope.

"Who is she writing to?" Bailino asked.

"No one." ToniAnne shrugged. "She's been doing Publisher's Clearing House to keep busy since she got here. Isn't that right, Aunt Mary?" The old woman looked up at her absently and then returned to her work. "These piles just seem to get higher and higher until I come to mail them for her. She said she wants to get a haircut this week in case that nice man knocks on her door with the balloons and the TV cameras for the big grand prize. Isn't that what you said, Aunt Mary?" Mary didn't bother looking up. "The old bat couldn't bother to visit the beauty parlor for my granddaughter's Communion, but she'll pretty herself up for a dead Ed McMahon."

"How come I don't see any kid out there, Ton?"

"Relax, things take time."

"What things?" Bailino asked when he spotted movement in the parking lot. Faith's tiny body emerged from the building and was walking across the white lines of the vacant parking spots toward the gate and the street.

"She looks like you, you know," ToniAnne said to Bailino. "She has your eyes. Joey's eyes."

Faith was moving awkwardly—not in a straight line, but in a zigzag—like she was off-balance. She left Bailino's view for a few seconds when she walked underneath an awning, but she popped back out on the other side and got about a third of the way through the parking lot when she stopped as if to catch her breath.

"What's the matter?" Jamie asked, watching him.

"I told you to shut the fuck up," ToniAnne said and pulled Jamie's pistol from its holster.

"Would you relax, already, Ton?" Bailino said and glanced at Jamie, who was searching his eyes for answers.

"Nothing's the matter, sweetheart," he lied. "Everything is fine."

37

Wilcox watched the little girl tread lightly through the empty parking lot toward him and his men. Some of the facility's residents, who had had no family to pick them up and were standing off to the side, were moaning, and Wilcox motioned to the staff to quiet them. He hadn't expected Faith to come out so quickly based on the video and audio they were receiving. He had to give Bailino some credit.

"Easy, everyone," Wilcox said, motioning with his hands for his men to stay back as he moved slightly forward.

Faith, who appeared to have a gag in her mouth, was moving in measured steps, placing one foot gingerly in front of the other. She was gazing into the crowd as if looking for a friend or someone she recognized, and Wilcox took another few steps forward, trying to get her attention. He passed the automatic gate, which was in the open position and marked the entry to the assisted living facility's parking lot; his eyes scanned the barren concrete, the empty spots making the ground look like a giant gameboard.

"Here, Faith," Wilcox said, putting his hand in the air in a stiff wave. "It's all right. My name is Agent Wilcox. Do you remember me?"

The little girl stopped and narrowed her eyes at him.

"I'm here to help you. Come." Wilcox slowly reached toward her.

Faith pivoted slightly and started walking again, this time in Wilcox's direction. As she got closer, he could see her face was puffy, tears coming down the sides of her cheeks. He extended his arm farther, and she slowly held up her hands, which were bound together with rope. When she reached him, he wrapped her small hands in his palm and gently guided her away from the building, but he could feel her resisting.

"You're safe now," Wilcox said. "Come with me."

Faith made a noise, and Wilcox realized she was trying to say something, but the gag in her mouth was preventing her. Her cheeks were blowing in and out as she struggled for air.

"*Shhh* … It's okay." Wilcox crouched down and slowly pulled out the small dishrag with the facility's logo that had been stuffed inside her mouth. "You're going to be okay."

Faith whimpered as Wilcox again tried to guide her out of the parking lot and toward the crowd of FBI agents behind him, half of whom were watching them intently while the other half continued watching the building, weapons at the ready.

"Faith," Wilcox said, a little more firmly this time, "I need you to keep walking, okay?"

She gently pulled down on Wilcox's hand, and he crouched closer to her.

"What is it?" he asked.

"No-peanut emergency," Faith said in a tiny voice.

"What do you mean? I don't understand," Wilcox said

and suddenly saw a small wire at the base of the little girl's neck, just under her pink sweater, and he felt the blood drain from his face.

Across the parking lot on the third floor, in Mary Cataldi's room, there was movement in one of the windows. A figure had come into view—the unmistakable silhouette of Don Bailino.

From behind him, Wilcox heard one of his agents approach. "Stay back," he ordered in a low, firm voice.

"Sir, we have eyes on the target. Should we take him out?" the agent whispered.

Wilcox had instructed his men that Bailino, once released, was to be treated as an enemy of the state, regardless of whatever the president had in mind. However, they still didn't have Jamie Carter. Whatever her nebulous role was in what was happening here, she was still innocent in the eyes of the law.

"Stand down," he whispered. "And I need you to get me Agent Barracks."

The agent's eyes opened wide at the mention of Agent Barracks who headed up the bomb squad team. He glanced at little Faith Carter, backed up slowly, and disappeared into the crowd.

Wilcox put his hand on Faith's cheek and wiped away a tear. "Now, I don't want you to move, Faith, okay?"

"Is my momma all right?"

Wilcox furrowed his brows. "You didn't see her inside the building?"

The little girl looked as if she were about to shake her head but thought better of it. "No," she said instead.

Wilcox glanced up at the third-floor window. Bailino

was still there. Watching. Had that son of a bitch double-crossed Wilcox and strapped up his daughter with an explosive device to save his own skin? Had this whole plan of his—the concern for Jamie Carter, for his daughter—been some kind of charade? If it was, he was wasting his time. Wilcox's men had surrounded the facility's property and were stationed throughout the area—he had men at every port, every bus and train station, *even in the local sewer system*. There was no getting out this time.

"I'm just going to lightly touch the front of your sweater," Wilcox said.

Despite the tears, Faith appeared resolute and calm. The little girl had gone through so much in her young life, all because of who her father was and, perhaps, what her mother had become. Wilcox gently felt the front of her sweater. Underneath was something hard and pointy. He peeked and saw the antenna of an old cell phone.

Someone came up behind him. Wilcox turned around to see the large, imposing figure of Agent Barracks, who had the foresight not to communicate with him through his earpiece. There was no telling what might set off the IED.

"I have an IED," Wilcox whispered. "Possible remote trigger."

"We have the bomb robots on standby, sir," Barracks said.

"I don't think we have time. I need you to block all cell-phone transmissions."

Agent Barracks hesitated. "Then we lose our eyes and ears on—"

"Do it now," Wilcox ordered in a strained whisper. He

would be damned if he was going to let another innocent person die today. "And slowly—and quietly—move everyone behind me back about seventy feet."

The crime scene reports at both the White House and Walter Reed noted that the primary blast radius of each of the IEDs had been short. Wilcox had to assume the radius of the device strapped onto Faith Carter was the same, because he had no time to assume otherwise. If this one blew, it wouldn't make much of a blast. It was clear that whoever rigged it didn't care about killing a lot of FBI agents—only killing Faith Carter.

"Roger that," Agent Barracks said and disappeared in the crowd.

Wilcox had disarmed bombs in the field before, but that was long ago and while wearing a protective suit. The device that had been found at the White House and at Walter Reed had been primitive, and, based on Wilcox's quick estimation, so was the one strapped to Faith Carter. He knew he wasn't dealing with experts, and, frankly, he didn't know if that was a good thing or a bad thing— homemade explosive devices required very little technical knowledge, but for that reason they were highly unstable.

He wiped the moisture from his brow. He had only minutes to either dismantle the device or get it off Faith Carter before Bailino or whoever was up there decided he or she had had enough of waiting and activated it before Barracks had the chance to cut cell-phone transmission. It occurred to him that the device was some kind of decoy, but he couldn't be sure, so he had to work fast.

He gently examined Faith's sweater, careful not to disturb the wires that had been wrapped around each button. If Wilcox had had any thoughts of trying to slip the thing off the little girl, they vanished once he got a closer look. Whoever had put it on had wrapped and wrapped the wire around her like a yo-yo.

"I want my momma," Faith Carter said softly.

"I know," Wilcox said, "but please don't move, okay."

Wilcox traced the wires of the mechanism to where they connected, just below Faith's right armpit. The unit was identical to the one his team had found at Walter Reed. If he was correct, it was just a matter of gently pulling off the second wire, but it would be difficult to manipulate in its current position. He carefully reached his hand under Faith's sweater.

Faith's big brown eyes stared up at him, and he hesitated. What if the wires had been switched? What if whoever had done this knew that Wilcox would go for the second wire and had reversed the charge? Would the mechanism really be an exact replica of the first?

Wilcox thought about the files he had stacked on his desk for the Cataldi family and all that he had learned over the years about their methods and their habits. Then he carefully snaked his hand around the first wire and wrapped his palm around the second, and with his other hand, he held the back of Faith's head, pulling her close.

"It's going to be okay," Wilcox whispered into Faith's ear, and, before he could change his mind, he pulled out the second wire.

38

"What are we waiting for, Donny?" ToniAnne asked.

Out the window, Bailino watched Agent Wilcox lift Faith Carter into his arms, carry her back behind the police barricade, and disappear into the crowd of smiling FBI agents. "Nothing," he said and stepped away from the window.

"You always were a horrible liar, Donny," ToniAnne said with a smile, "which is probably why you never lied much."

"She's okay?" Jamie whispered.

"No one's talking to you, girlie," ToniAnne said.

"So we're hurting little girls now, Ton?" Bailino asked.

"You never were any fun, Donny. Always so serious." With Jamie's pistol in her right hand, ToniAnne ran her left along Jamie's hair as she had done with Mary Cataldi. "How is it that someone is always saving your ass?" she hissed, grabbing a handful and giving it a yank.

"Ton, c'mon, stop the nonsense and put the gun down."

"Wow, you really like her, don't you, Donny? Enough to go to jail for her?"

"I've been in jail all my life," Bailino said.

"So you say," ToniAnne said, releasing Jamie's hair and picking up her cell phone. "So you've always said … Shit, I have no cell service."

Bailino realized that Wilcox must have shut down cell-phone transmission when he discovered the bomb. He opened up his jacket and ripped the wires from his body.

"What the fuck?" ToniAnne said.

"You think they're just going to let me waltz in here alone?" Bailino said. "But it looks like the cell service is down. The old tunnels still accessible?"

"You bet your ass. At least, most of them. We lost a few after the new construction when they converted this place into the palace that it is."

Bailino imagined Wilcox had the property surrounded, but if the tunnels were still intact they could get ToniAnne and Lorenzo into the Pine Barrens of New Jersey, which is why the illegal tunnels had been built in the first place—so old man Hydeman could supplement his retirement home income with an illegal wildlife trade. With more than a million acres, the Pine Barrens offered plenty of places for the two of them to hide. Maybe Bailino would get lucky and they would get eaten by a coyote. "You need to go," he said.

"You're not coming?" she asked. "What the fuck did I go through all this for?"

"I appreciate it. I do. But, I told you, you're better off without me."

"Fuck the baby mama," ToniAnne said, swinging the gun in her hand and leering at Jamie. "Let her rot in jail or wherever. Come with us."

"Take Lorenzo and get out of here," he said. "There's not much more they can do to me."

ToniAnne sighed. "Always the gentleman ..." She lifted Jamie's face up by the chin and said, "You must be somethin' real special, honey," and then she picked up her purse, wrapping the strap around her shoulder. "You know, Jamie, Donny and I used to do it right here in this bedroom. Remember that, Donny? When Nonno and Nonna went to Bingo? *B-4 and O-yes ...*"

"We don't have time for this shit, ToniAnne," Bailino said. "Once the cell service is back up, this place is going to be filled with Feds."

ToniAnne rolled her eyes. "You're always in such a rush." She held up Jamie's gun. "You don't mind if I take this, do you, *sweetheart*? Something to remember you by? I leave you my man. I take your gun. Not really a fair trade, but it will have to do."

Bailino could tell that Jamie was watching ToniAnne closely, but she said nothing.

ToniAnne kissed the top of Mary Cataldi's head. "Good-bye, Aunt Mary," she said. The old woman looked up at her grandniece as if seeing her for the first time.

"Well, I guess that's it," ToniAnne said, looking around the apartment, her eyes landing on Bailino. "I'll always love you, you know, Donny," she whispered with a sad smile.

"You need to go," he said again.

"I know ..." ToniAnne picked up a bulky bag that Bailino assumed was filled with additional firearms and cash. "Oh, I forgot one thing," she said, and she aimed the pistol and fired at Jamie, who fell to the ground.

39

"What the fuck was that?"

Wilcox slammed the door of his sedan, where he had just buckled Faith Carter into the backseat, and Agent Barracks appeared at his side holding the dismantled IED. "We don't know," Barracks said. "Feed's gone."

"Stay with her," Wilcox said, motioning to Faith Carter, and pulled out his gun as another gunshot went off. He gave the sign to a group of agents stationed closest to the facility, and they slowly made their way into the parking lot.

The window of Room 343 was still open, but Bailino was no longer there. Wilcox was reasonably sure the shots, judging by their timbre and volume, had come from that room. By the time he got to the front door of the building, his men were already in and swarming the lobby, checking behind the front desk and along the seating areas.

"Upstairs," Wilcox said, pivoting right and heading for the emergency exit. He stopped when he reached the stairwell door, expecting Bailino, or whoever it was, to be ready for them inside. In a narrow stairwell, it would be like shooting federal agents in a barrel.

Wilcox motioned for his team near the elevator to follow when the closest elevator door opened with a beep, and a blast shook the room, knocking three of his men back.

"Get down!" Wilcox shouted as the next elevator dinged, the door opened, and another explosion rocked the room.

As smoke filled the lobby, Wilcox located two of his men and pointed them toward the stairwell, and the three made a break for the stairwell door. Slowly, he opened it and peered inside; it looked clear. As he and his men filed up the stairs, a hand came over the banister and threw an object down.

"Get down!" Wilcox called again, crouching into a corner as the device hit the floor and an agent dove through the door back into the lobby as the explosive device detonated with a loud boom, black smoke filling the stairwell. When the smoke began to clear, Wilcox saw one of his men had been hit and was crawling toward the exit, his leg torn at the calf.

"Man down," Wilcox said, charging up the stairs. He hopped over the handrail before he reached the next landing to save time and leapt up the next flight to the third floor, hiding behind the emergency exit door just as it opened. The bomber threw his arm back to lob another device down the stairwell, but Wilcox grabbed him from behind, and as the man turned around, Wilcox saw that it was Lorenzo Cavetti. Cavetti was about to shove the IED at Wilcox, who shot him in the chest, and Cavetti went tumbling down the stairs, the device exploding in his hands and filling the stairwell with more black smoke.

"Agent Wilcox!" a voice called from below.

"I'm all right," Wilcox shouted, peering down at Cavetti's still and ravaged body.

He opened the door to the third floor and glanced out, clear air filling his lungs. A long hallway ran the length of the facility; it was quiet and appeared empty. Slowly, he made his way toward Room 343, checking inside each open apartment door, and as he got closer he heard movement and a familiar voice shouting.

Bailino.

Wilcox raised his gun and went charging down the corridor.

40

Jamie saw it coming.

When ToniAnne Cataldi turned back from the apartment door, Jamie's body—after years of constant vigilance, constant awareness—shifted for cover, and she fell backward as the bullet, probably aimed at her eye, whizzed past the side of her face and landed obliquely into her shoulder. She hit the floor hard beside Mary Cataldi who, despite all the activity around her, continued filling out her paperwork undisturbed.

Jamie tried to scramble for cover but the chair that was attached to her was hindering her movement. ToniAnne raised her gun again, this time at Bailino, but he barreled into her just as the shot when off, hitting a nearby lamp, and slammed her against the wall, batting Jamie's pistol from her hand.

"How do *you* like it when someone you love hurts, you son of a bitch?" ToniAnne screamed as Bailino threw her to the floor. "Doesn't feel so fuckin' good, does it?"

"You like it rough, right, Ton'?" he roared. "Yeah, I remember." He got on top of her, straddling her body, and clasped his one hand around her neck, pressing into her chest with the other. "Let's see how you like it now."

ToniAnne was swinging her arms wildly, slapping Bailino, who seemed undaunted and continued squeezing as her face became puffy and red.

A series of blasts from somewhere below shook the building. Jamie's shoulder was on fire, but her eyes zeroed in on her pistol, which was lying on the floor only a few feet from her. Using her legs, she pushed herself toward it, reaching for it with her bound hands and trying to ignore the pain in her shoulder, the blood warm as it oozed into the fabric of her shirt.

"You fuckin' cunt," Bailino was shouting.

ToniAnne's arms were limp now, her face discolored and bloated, her eyes bulging from their sockets, but Bailino kept squeezing until it looked as though ToniAnne Cataldi's head would pop off. Finally, as he released his hand from her neck and searched the room until his eyes found Jamie, there was a noise at the apartment door.

Fearing it was Lorenzo Cavetti, Jamie gave one last push toward her pistol, but Bailino reached it first and swung it toward the door as another gunshot ripped through the room. Bailino fell back to the floor as Agent Wilcox rushed inside, his gun still pointed at Bailino.

"*Nooooo,*" Jamie screamed, pushing herself forward.

"Jamie, get back," Wilcox ordered, keeping his gun on Bailino, who was lying with his back arched, his right hand groping his chest as if to pluck out the bullet.

"Where's Faith?" Jamie asked, holding up her bound arms.

"She's fine," Wilcox said, but hesitated before reaching for Jamie's wrists, as if debating whether or not it was a good idea to set them free, but then he reached into his pocket and sliced the ropes with a switchblade. Wilcox glanced at Mary Cataldi before examining Jamie's shoulder. "What happened?" he asked, reaching for her hand, but Jamie pulled away and continued to crawl toward Bailino, using one side of her body, the chair dragging behind her.

"Get back, I said, Jamie," Wilcox shouted, picking up her gun, which Bailino had dropped to the floor as two more agents entered the room.

Jamie reached Bailino's arm, latched onto it, and pulled herself up onto his waist. His chest was heaving and covered in blood, which was trickling down the sides of his shirt and onto Jamie's hand, the fabric turning a deeper and deeper red. Jamie pulled the bottom of his shirt up and onto his wound to try to stem the bleeding. He groaned.

"Fuck," he whispered, looking down.

"Don't move," Jamie said. "We need an ambulance," she said to Wilcox.

"Don't bother, sweetheart," Bailino said, his breathing coming in ragged bursts. He tilted his head toward her, his red face beaded with sweat. "Your shoulder," he said and tried to reach for it.

"It's okay," Jamie said. "I saw it coming."

"At least …" His throat sounded full, and he coughed, a gurgle that refused to clear. " … one of us did," he said between ragged breaths and coughed again. "Damn country living."

A loud siren filled the air, the volume increasing until it sounded like the ambulance was just outside the open window.

"Step back, Jamie," Wilcox ordered again. An agent Jamie didn't recognize came up next to him.

"The building's clear, sir," the agent said, and Wilcox nodded.

Bailino's eyes were trying to find Jamie, but they couldn't focus.

"It's all right," she said. "I'm here."

"I ... I ..." Bailino's lids began to flutter. "I ... I ..."

She tilted his face so she could see the dark brown of his eyes, Faith's eyes.

"I ... I ..." he said again, raising his head from the floor.

"I know." Jamie placed her hand behind his head. "Me too," she said, and his breathing eased. She reached for Bailino's hand and squeezed, and his hand slightly tightened on hers. Then Bailino's eyes closed, and he let out a long breath as his head fell back into her hand and the EMTs rushed into the room.

41

Phillip stared at the cover of *The American Conservative* magazine, his large face taking up most of the page. With all that had gone on in the past week, he had forgotten about the article and would have had it retracted had he remembered.

He flipped to the cover story, which consisted of a two-page family portrait of him, Katherine, and the kids on the White House lawn flanked by blooming cherry blossom trees. He looked so much younger, he thought; the interview and photo shoot had been conducted only six months prior, during his first hundred days in office, but it felt like a lifetime ago. Against his better judgment, he began reading the story:

Not since the days of Theodore Roosevelt—and, arguably, the father of our nation, George Washington, before him—has the United States had a true hero at its helm. Statesman and war veteran Phillip Grand rode into the White House on a wave of awe and gratitude from a populace not often privy to selfless acts of honor and courage, and he has brought a new energy to the White House and to many Americans' view of the future ..."

"Such a handsome man," Katherine said, coming up

behind him and putting her arms around him. "Although with the way people are gaga for the damn cherry blossoms around here, I'm not sure anyone will notice. If only they had the same excitement for what goes on in the big white house behind the trees …"

"I assume people will be lining birdcages with this issue." Phillip closed the magazine and placed it on his desk.

Katherine sighed. "From what I hear, the issue has been very well-received. I doubt the magazine will be losing readership."

"The video is out, Katherine. I'm not the man who saved Jamie and Faith Carter anymore. I'm not the *hero*. I'm the man who helped Don Bailino escape and lied to the FBI. The Republicans who read this magazine," he motioned to the publication, "want to skin me alive. Forget about losing readership. We'll lose the Senate in the midterm elections."

Katherine reached for his hand, pulled him toward to the sofa, and sat down beside him. "Phillip, you know as well as I do that people will believe what they want to believe, whether it's true or not. And I believe they want to believe in you, even with everything that's happened." She looked into his eyes. "And if they don't? And if they vote you out? If Clark, Mitchell, and the entire Republican Party turns their back on you? Who cares. Fuck 'em."

Against his will, Phillip gave a small smile.

"And I know you couldn't care less about this magazine interview. That's not what's really bothering you, is it? You're upset because you couldn't save him."

It had been more than twenty-four hours since Phillip had received the call from Wilcox that Bailino was dead. Phillip's instinct was not to believe it, since Bailino seemed to be able to evade death all his life. He insisted on visiting the morgue to see for himself, and Wilcox knew better than to argue. It was only when Phillip had seen Bailino's lifeless body inside the body bag that he realized it to be true.

The thought of a world without Don Bailino seemed surreal. He had been lurking in the shadows of Phillip's life way before he ever stepped into the nursery to kidnap Charlotte. It's a strange thing to have a man be so absent from your life and yet make such an impression. On the surface, Phillip would go on as he had, but, inside, he would be forever changed.

"You gave him what he wanted in the end," Katherine said, as if reading his mind. "If you ask me, that was more than he deserved."

"A person can't help who his parents are, Katherine."

"You think that gives him a pass? There are plenty of people out there with shitty parents who find their way. You and he may have started in the same place, in some respects, but you are far from the man that he had become."

"I will never be the man that he was," Phillip said.

"You are that and more," she said, cupping his chin in her hand. "And I think he knew that, too. Now …" She put her tablet on his lap. "I was looking over the agenda for tomorrow's press briefing. Have you spoken to Jamie?"

Phillip nodded and rubbed his eyes. He had been able to squeeze in a few hours of sleep after he and Katherine had returned from the hospital after Jamie's emergency surgery. Although the doctors had told him that the bullet had penetrated the soft tissues surrounding her shoulder joint and assured Phillip that there was no permanent damage, he knew there were probably months of physical therapy in front of her, and possibly additional surgeries. Phillip was thankful it hadn't been worse. "Spoke to her about an hour ago," he said. "She seems to think she'll be back to work in six weeks. I told her not to worry, that she should take as much time as she needs."

"Well, until she's back, who would you like to lead the daily press briefings? At this point, with all the resignations, our choice is between the sous chef and the custodian."

"I'll do them until we get someone up to speed," Phillip said.

Katherine wrinkled her nose. "Only if you promise me you're not thinking of doing something crazy, like announcing your resignation."

Phillip shook his head. "I thought about it," he said, "if I'm being honest, but I decided against it."

"Why?"

Phillip thought of Bailino's pep talk in the holding room. "What was that you said? Fuck 'em." He smiled. "I'll stay as long as the American people want me, whether that's one term or two."

"You know, if there's one way that you and Bailino were the same, it was that you both knew how to fight for what you want—and what you believe in," Katherine said when there was a knock at the door.

"Yes," Phillip said, and the door opened. Brandon stood at the threshold.

"Agent Fuller," Phillip said. "Come in. Is everything all right?"

"I was just about to leave for the day, Mr. President,"

Brandon said. Phillip knew the young agent had been working through the night to tie up any loose ends of the various investigations. Although his eyes were still characteristically bright, his posture showed fatigue. "I thought I would check to make sure you're all right."

"That's kind of you, Brandon, but not necessary. You should go home. Enjoy a little downtime. You've earned it."

Brandon smiled and turned to go, but stopped. "For the record, Mr. President. I just want to say that, despite … well, everything … I've never been prouder to serve as a member of our nation's law enforcement than I am serving your administration. I'm here for whatever you need, for as long as you need," he said. He bowed his head and left the Oval Office, closing the door.

"Now," Katherine said, "does that sound like someone who wants you to step down?"

Before Phillip could answer, there was another knock on the door, this one softer. Before he could say *Come in*, the door opened, and Charlotte's bright face appeared.

"Daddy!" she said, running toward him, her backpack swishing behind her.

"How was school, cookie?" he asked as she jumped onto his lap.

"We learned about Thanksgiving, about the Indians and the Pilgrims. We're doing a secret project to hang on the bulletin board for the month of November."

"Thanksgiving? That's one of my favorite holidays," Phillip said.

"Mrs. Rienecker says that when the Pilgrims were really, really cold that the Indians gave them seeds and food." Charlotte was rushing her words, as if to get all the information out in one breath. "And then the Pilgrims invited the Indians who helped them to dinner."

"That's right. From the start, our country was founded as a place where people could live and pray freely, and they learned how to help each other and accept each other's differences."

"And they had broccoli for lunch today. *Ewww.*" Charlotte tossed her backpack onto the floor. "Is Faith coming home soon?"

Phillip loved that Charlotte felt that the White House was Faith's home as well as hers. He felt that way too. "Pretty soon," Phillip said. "Where's your brother?"

"He's with Grandmother. When? When is Faith coming home?"

"Well, that's hard to say." Although Phillip hadn't told his daughter the exact circumstances surrounding Jamie's absence, that didn't stop her from asking—when she woke up, during breakfast, on her way to school. She was as persistent as her mother. "It looks like she's going to take some time off."

"Again?" Charlotte said with a huff. She folded her arms.

Phillip smiled. "Yes, this time probably for about a month or so, so we'll have to remember all the fun things we do so we can tell Faith when we see her again." He kissed her cheek.

"Come, Charlotte. Let's let your father do his job, while you do yours. *Homework,*" Katherine said, picking up her tablet.

"*Awww!*" Charlotte pouted. She picked up her backpack

and reached for her mother's hand, and the two of them left the Oval Office as Phillip returned to his desk.

The office was strangely quiet, perhaps the calm before the new storm. There was much to do—new staff to hire, postponed meetings to reschedule, briefings to study. He reached into the bottom drawer of his desk and pulled out an old book he once kept in the bookcase of his office at the Executive Mansion in Albany. He opened to a middle page marked by an old Polaroid photo, taken during Family Day, of him and Bailino the day before their graduation from army boot camp. The two men had their arms around one another, their smiles wide. It was the last photo they had taken together, and one of the only.

He stared at the photo, which sparked the same memory of him and Bailino sitting in his hospital room at Walter Reed, watching *Roseanne*:

"Why do you like this show if you don't think it's funny?" Phillip had asked.

"There's more to life than just laughs, Phil," Bailino had said. "Why do I like it?" He shrugged. "It's a reminder that shit ain't perfect, but we do what we can."

Phillip smiled at his young self and his best friend before closing them back inside the book for safekeeping and returning it to the drawer. The desk phone rang, and he answered it. "Yes, Janice."

"Mr. President, I have the ambassador to the United Nations on the line."

"Put her through," Phillip said.

"And don't forget your four o'clock with Mr. Walker from the Global Institute. He likes to arrive early."

"I won't, Janice, thanks," he said, putting the phone

receiver to his ear and leaning back in his chair. *Shit might not be perfect,* Phillip thought, *but we do what we can.* And, at least for now, that meant getting back to the business of being the president of the United States.

42

Wilcox lifted the last box onto his desk and surveyed the walls of his home office. All that
remained were a few files and the hanging
mug shots of the men he had spent his life hunting down.
He circled the room and, one by one, ripped them from
their thumbtacks, placing them in the box. When he got
to Bailino's, he stared into the eyes of the man he had
seen die before him at the assisted living facility, before
removing the poster and laying it on his desk. He took
a black Sharpie from the box and drew a big X through
Bailino's face. Then he put the poster inside the box with
the others, taped the flaps of the box closed, and placed
the box near the trash bin. Case closed.

He walked into the kitchen and opened the
refrigerator. He reached for a sparkling water, thought
for a moment, and then opted instead for one of the
bottles of beer his brother had left for him when he
moved in. He twisted off the cap and took a slug, while
surveying the boxes of candy and bottles of wine his
colleagues at the FBI had sent him upon learning that
Bailino had finally been taken down—the crowning
jewel of a decades-long career and almost guaranteeing

Wilcox's unanimous confirmation by the U.S. Senate for FBI director.

He glanced out the window at Arlington's bustling downtown. A neighboring building partially blocked the late-day sunlight, which cast a long shadow across Wilcox's window, and he was reminded of Bailino's dark silhouette inside the window of Room 343. Wilcox had been sure that Bailino had been taunting him, after managing to trick Phillip Grand into setting him free under the guise of saving Jamie and Faith Carter, but over the last twenty-four hours he had started to consider an alternate interpretation: that Bailino had been trying to *help* in some way—perhaps by maintaining visual contact with Wilcox, by helping to determine the whereabouts of ToniAnne Cataldi, or by ensuring the safety of little Faith Carter. Why else stand there, a bull's-eye on his chest from more than a dozen rifle scopes? Wilcox tilted the bottle up, polished off the rest of the beer, and placed the bottle on the kitchen counter.

The truth was that after decades of playing psychological games with criminal minds, Wilcox didn't know the answer. For all the hours, days, and weeks spent on surveillance, on listening in on other people's lives, on building massive profiles for those who would harm others, the answer came down to an educated guess. And what if Bailino had been trying to help? Does one act of justice undo a lifetime of crime? Does it bring back the innocent people that Bailino had killed? *Things aren't always so black and white*, Phillip Grand had told him. Maybe so, but, as a law enforcement agent, shouldn't they have to be?

Wilcox opened his laptop on the kitchen counter. He clicked one of the icons at the bottom of the screen, which maximized his email client, clicked on *Write*, and started typing:

Dear Mr. President,

I am honored that you are considering me for the post of director of the Federal Bureau of Investigation. I have spent my professional life protecting the United States from all enemies, foreign and domestic, whether by terrorist attack, high-technology crime, or corruption at all levels. I know our relationship has been complicated at times, but I have the highest regard for you both as a man and as the leader of the country that I love. However, after much deliberation, I am going to have to decline your generous offer. These responsibilities are no longer my business. They belong to the future. Simply stated, I'm going to try retirement for a while.

Sincerely, Paul Wilcox

He sent the email and closed his laptop. Then he picked up his cell phone, dialed, and placed the phone next to his ear.

"Do my eyes deceive me?" Randy said as soon as he picked up the other end of the line. "Is this the phone number of my long-lost brother, the toast of the FBI?"

"Very funny," Wilcox said.

"What's up, Paul?"

Wilcox hesitated. "I was wondering if the offer for dinner still stands."

There was a pause. "Of course, it does," Randy said. "It's open-ended."

Wilcox leaned against the window and looked out at the people on the ground below who were hurrying out of office buildings and getting into taxis, walking into clothing stores, and bars, people living their lives. "Great," he said. "Now, tell me about this Bev person. Does she like fishing?"

43

It took three tries for the old German lady to get her landlord key into Bob's door before it opened. Her hands shook so much that they were rattling his patience, and he was about to ask her if she needed carpel tunnel surgery when the metal key slid into its grooved sleeve, and the lock opened. He rushed inside, pulling his wheeled luggage behind him.

"Next time, you remember your key, eh?" she said, handing him his mail. She looked around the place as if she were inspecting it. She frowned when she saw the brown, wilting leaves of the ficus tree in the corner of his living room.

"Yes, yes, I will, Mrs. Estabauer," Bob said, dropping the mail on a side table. He couldn't remember what he had done with his keys. He had left his apartment in such a rush after that bastard Bailino cornered him. Last he remembered, they were in his hand.

The old woman pointed to the kitchen counter. "Dere day are," she said, with a shake of her head.

"Ah, yes, that's right," Bob said with a dismissive wave as if remembering they were there but actually had no recollection of putting them there. He put down the

Chinese food he was holding, picked them up, and put them in his pocket, tapping them lightly with his hand. "Won't forget 'em next time … Oh, and before you go …" He dug his hand into his back pocket and pulled out his wallet. "I have this month's rent."

"'Bout time," the old woman said, holding out her palm.

Bob had the urge to throw the money at her pinched expression, but now that he was back in the news and the money would be rolling in again, he planned on leaving this rent-controlled shithole and buying something in Manhattan. Until then, he needed this rent-controlled shithole, so he placed the bills gently into her palm. When he was finished, the old bat had the nerve to start counting them.

"It's all there, no worries," he said, ushering her out the door and closing it with a soft click. The old kraut would probably be out there for another twenty minutes with those arthritic fingers of hers.

Bob stood with his back against the door as if bracing for impact and glanced around his apartment. The last few days had been a whirlwind, and if he played his cards right the days ahead would continue to be. Heading down to D.C. on Sunday had been an even better idea than he thought. He opened the brown paper bag he put on the table with the chicken lo mein from the Chinese place down the block, and his cell phone rang. Bob looked at the caller ID and picked up on the second ring. He cleared his throat.

"Robert Scott," he said, adding, "*Esquire.*"

He held the phone to his ear with his shoulder and

locked the apartment door, before Ms. Estabauer had any thoughts about coming back in.

"Yes, I was with the FBI when the arrest was made of Jamie Carter …Yes, I would be happy to speak to that … Yes … A bestseller … Yes, it was … I am thinking about it … Yes, I was on the inaugural roundtable. How did you get my number again?"

Bob listened as the woman on the other end of the line detailed their first meeting nearly five years before, when his first book had gone to auction. "Ah, yes, I do remember," he said, even though he didn't. "The roundtable? Yes, the president and I are very close … Shaped lots of new legislation together … Yes, that would be an interesting perspective … All right, when would you need me? … Let me check my calendar. Would you mind emailing me the request so I have it in writing? … Perfect. Thank you … And I look forward to seeing you again as well."

He hung up the phone and pumped his fist into the air. That had been the third call that day alone from a large publisher looking to work with him on another book. What a bunch of sheep these publishers were—all of them scouring the same news feeds for the latest natural disaster or murder spree. Not that Bob cared. Things couldn't have gone better if he had planned them—the consultation with Wilcox, the arrest of Jamie, the arrest of Bailino, the kidnapping, and, finally, the death of Don Bailino, the pièce de résistance. And with Bailino out of the way, Bob could *really* write whatever the hell he wanted in the next book about their interaction—who would dispute it?

He reached for a fork from the dishrack, twirled it into a lump of lo mein, and smiled. He had managed to outfox one of the most wanted criminals in American organized crime. After the book tour, Bob was sure he'd be asked to lecture and even teach a course. He imagined an entire wall devoted to him at the Mob Museum in Vegas, right next to Eliot Ness.

"Thank you, you fuckin' prick," he said, hoisting his fork into the air. He remembered the way Bailino had barged into his apartment, thinking he had the upper hand, the smug look on his face, the damn bully. "May you rot in hell, you son of a bitch." He shoved the loaded fork into his mouth.

He wolfed down the rest of the lo mein, threw the container into the garbage, picked up his carry-on, and wheeled his suitcase into the bedroom. He unzipped the suitcase, swooped up his dirty clothing with his hands, and dumped it into a pile onto the floor, making a note to himself to start interviewing for assistants. He rummaged through his closet, found his lucky purple suit, which still had the dry cleaning plastic over it, and laid it over a chair. He pulled out a pair of shoes, clean socks and underwear, and placed them neatly beside the suit. He had to be at the *Good Morning America* offices at the crack of dawn for hair and makeup—the car that the producers were sending for him was supposed to arrive at 4:00 a.m. He looked at his watch; he had exactly four hours to get some sleep before he had to take a shower.

He ran into the bathroom, turned on the cold-water faucet, and looked in the mirror. *Damn, he looked good.* That's what triumph did for a guy. He felt so good that he thought he might even give Jamie a call this week, maybe give her a chance to get back with him. That was the last thing he wanted, but the pairing would make for a great story: Two heroes reunited following the death of the villain. The publicity might be worth the boredom, and plus her kid needed *some* kind of male role model. Edward was too much of a dud. He would think it over.

He took off the clothes he was wearing and tossed them on the floor with the rest of his laundry and stood naked in the center of the room, wondering if he had time to call the book club chick for a quick romp in the hay. He decided against it—he didn't want to look flushed for the cameras—and turned on the television, thinking maybe he could catch the replay of his CNN appearance. A commercial was playing. He reached into his carry-on, set a 3:30 alarm on his cell phone, and placed the phone on his nightstand. He sat on the bed just as the news anchor appeared on screen and began talking about the end of the American organized crime scene, a photo of Bailino appearing on screen.

"*Good riddance, you son of a bitch,*" Bob said with a satisfied smile and threw his head back onto his pillow, setting off the explosive device stowed under his bed.

44

J amie placed the shovel and gardening gloves into her tote bag. She rotated her shoulder, which ached, and rubbed the bandage with her hand.

"I think this needs more water, Momma!" Faith called. The little girl was pawing at the dirt where Jamie had planted the daffodil bulbs.

"Okay, you can give it a tiny bit of water, Faithy, but not too much."

The little girl grabbed the handle of the watering can and poured a few more drops. "There, perfect," she said as Lucky sniffed around the dirt. "When will they grow, Momma?"

"In the spring, sweetie. We'll come back to check on them."

The little girl stared at the mound of dirt with concern. "Will he be cold?" she asked.

"No, I don't think so," Jamie said with a smile. "I think he'll be happy here."

Jamie surveyed the acres of land that had once housed the Upackk facility. Over the past six weeks, people had been trickling onto the property to wrap trees with yellow ribbons. Jamie assumed they were the people Bailino had helped over the years—to find a job, get out of prison, go to rehab. They were the people who didn't see him as a criminal, or if they did they didn't care, and because there had been no public funeral, as per Bailino's wishes, perhaps people needed a place to mourn. "I think this is the perfect spot," she said.

Faith put her hand on her hips and gave the area a once-over. "Me too, and I think Lucky thinks so too." The dog curled herself into a ball and sat on the mound of fresh dirt.

Jamie had thought long and hard about where Bailino's final resting place should be. He had amended his last will and testament in 2014, just before he had been shipped off to Stanton Federal Correction Facility. His only stipulation was that he be "cremated with his remains to be buried near his children." At the time, Joey Santelli had been alive and well and attending MIT, instead of where he was now—buried in a plot beside his mother and grandfather in Queens. Had Bailino died in prison, perhaps it would have been ToniAnne Cataldi making the decision about his final resting place, but that wasn't to be, and if Jamie hadn't intervened, Bailino would have probably ended up in a pauper's lot or public cemetery—or in a dumpster somewhere, if NYPD had had its say. Often with the death of a criminal—particularly one as well known as Bailino— there was worry about vandalism or a public backlash with the remains. Ironically, the only people looking to desecrate Bailino's grave were probably the ones who were supposed to protect it—law enforcement officers, who had no love for the man who had killed some of their own. Although Jamie had considered burying Bailino near Joey Santelli, she chose instead to lay his remains on the property near the factory he had loved. Only she—and perhaps Lucky—would know the location of the unmarked grave. Even in death, Don Bailino would be evading the police. He would have liked that.

Faith was twirling around a large oak tree, the pink tutu that Rosalia Garcia had given her that morning lifting as she spun, making her appear like a tiny bird. Her daughter appeared unscarred by what had happened in New Jersey, perhaps compartmentalizing the bad things that had been done with the bad people who had done them, not unlike her father. However, Jamie knew looks could be deceiving. She would continue to monitor Faith as the months and years wore on.

Below them, down the hill, the hollowed-out structure of the Upackk facility, which had been left abandoned for nearly four years, stood defiantly like a modern-day Colosseum, much of the concrete and lumber taken either by local builders or hoodlums.

An unseasonably warm breeze wafted up the hill, blowing Faith's pigtails and the taffeta of her tutu and rattling the tree branches. It was easy to see why Bailino loved the upstate New York area—Jamie had learned to love it herself while she served as press secretary for Phillip Grand when he was governor of New York. Only a four-hour drive from New York City, the area offered a respite from all the noise and clatter. The slower pace had taken some getting used to, but she had found a pediatrician that she loved and had met some people who might one day become friends, which is why she had decided to return to the Albany area after President Grand's tenure as president was complete. She would build a new home.

"Momma, look!" Faith called, twiddling Bailino's gold chain that was hanging from her neck. She pointed north toward an open patch of grass where a deer was standing still, its ears twitching.

"It's okay, honey," Jamie said. "It won't hurt you."

"What's it doing?"

"Maybe it hears something like a wolf or a coyote and wants to be ready in case they decide to chase it."

"They always do," Faith said and pet the top of Lucky's head.

The deer scampered off into the woods, and Jamie surveyed the wide expanse of land that belonged to her daughter. She once thought it would be best to let Faith decide what to do with all she had inherited from Bailino—including the two thousand dollars in hundreds he had stuffed inside Lucky's collar. Yet, something that he had said in his Wyoming greenhouse had resonated with her, how he had hired veterans to help with some of the odd jobs around the property: *Gives them something to do. Makes them feel useful.*

When she returned to Albany, Jamie planned to clear the remnants of the old factory and establish a foundation for military veterans and their families who had been physically wounded or had struggled with the aftermath of deployment or their service. If her plans came to fruition, the hollowed-out Upackk facility would house a large camp for military families to come and spend time together. She had already gotten the seal of approval and pledged support from the president, for whom, like Bailino, caring for the military had always been an important cause. And the First Lady had already started wrangling people for donations.

"Who knows?" Katherine Grand had said to Jamie. "One day, I may be working for you."

Jamie's phone rang. She looked at the caller ID and swiped the screen, not surprised to see the displayed name. "Hi, Mr. President," she said.

Phillip Grand had been checking up on her often for the past six weeks, even more than Edward, which Jamie would have thought was impossible.

"Everything all right up there?" he asked. Jamie could hear Charlotte in the background clamoring for the phone. "Not now, Charlie," the president whispered. "You'll see Faith tomorrow."

"Yes, we're fine, Mr. President," Jamie said. "We'll be leaving in just a few minutes."

"Good. Did you take care of everything you needed to take care of?"

"I think so," Jamie said, picking up the watering can and looking back at Bailino's grave. Phillip Grand hadn't asked her what her plans had been involving Bailino's remains, but she could tell he wanted to know. Perhaps, one day, he would be the only other person she would tell.

"Did you visit with Rosalia?" he asked.

"Yes."

"How is she?"

"Good," Jamie said, although the old woman was showing signs of age. The death of Reynaldo had been hard on her. "I have four loaves of banana bread and two trays of homemade cookies in the trunk of my car with your name on them. She wanted to give more, but that was all I could fit."

"Ah, a productive trip, indeed," the president said. "I

haven't had Rosalia's banana bread in years." The president paused in his usual, thoughtful way. "Anything else worth mentioning?"

Jamie thought for a moment. "No, not really. I think that's it."

"Well then, have a safe trip, Jamie. We're looking forward to having you back home."

"I will, Mr. President. See you tomorrow."

Jamie clicked off the call as Faith and Lucky played what looked like hide-and-seek around a large tree. "Come on, you two," she called. "It's time to get going."

"Let's go, Lucky," Faith cheered as she ran past Jamie with the dog jumping beside her.

The two of them ran down the small hill toward the road, where Jamie's car was parked on the pebbled shoulder. As soon as Jamie opened the back door, the two of them clambered inside, and Jamie strapped them into their respective seats and closed the door. She dumped the excess water from the watering can, placed it in the trunk, along with the tote bag, and slammed the trunk lid closed.

She took one last look at the tiny mound of dirt that was barely noticeable from the road, before circling over to the driver's side and getting behind the wheel. She removed her ankle holster and placed it in the well of the passenger side. Eventually, she hoped to stow it someplace where she would never have to use it again. She had had her fill of bullets.

"You two ready back there?" Jamie asked, looking into her rearview mirror. Lucky's head was lying in the little girl's lap.

"We're ready!" Faith cheered.

Jamie started the engine. The sun was shining in her eyes, and she pulled down her visor, which displayed the two photos she had clipped there earlier that day. She ran her finger along the glossy invitation that Rosalia had given her to Pedro Rodriguez's wedding that spring. The photo showed Pedro and his fiancée seated in an old Cadillac in front of Santiago's Garage with their arms outstretched wide and their smiles even wider. Jamie thought of Reynaldo, who probably would have been astounded that his little brother had gotten his act together and was finally settling down, but she also knew how very proud he would have been.

Then Jamie ran her finger along the surface of the second photo, which was smaller and grainier. She had thought of telling Phillip Grand while they were talking on the phone, since she had already told Rosalia, but decided to wait. Everyone would find out soon enough. Although it was too soon to know if the child would be a boy or a girl, Jamie told Rosalia that she planned on naming her baby Reynald or Reyne in honor of Reynaldo—her lover and her friend—and the old woman's eyes lit up in a way that Jamie hadn't seen in a very long time.

Jamie caught a glimpse of Faith's dark eyes in the rearview mirror and as always saw in them the eyes of the man who had upended her life, for better and for worse. She put her hand on her belly. Edward would balk, but Jamie was thinking about giving her baby a middle name of Don or Donna, also in memory of a lover and a friend, but that was a decision for another day. She put the car into drive. For now, she would get back to the work and the family she loved, and her unborn baby would go by the name scribbled in black ink on the side margin of the ultrasound photo: Baby Carter.

ACKNOWLEDGMENTS

The final book of the Baby Grand thriller series is more than just the end of a trilogy. It's like saying good-bye to old friends. I have lived with these characters for more than twenty years—they've followed me around, whispering dialogue in my ears while I was driving, cooking dinner, lying in bed—and I will miss their company. As always, I want to thank my family, my friends, and all the fans of this series for their tremendous support—every kind word you've said to me, every comment you've posted on social media, every author event you've attended has meant so much. While it's true that authors write alone, I never felt alone. And, finally, a big thank-you to actor Robert De Niro, whose film work, particularly in the 1990s, inspired the character of Don Bailino. As Phillip Grand thinks to himself in *Baby Carter: It's a strange thing to have a man be so absent from your life and yet make such an impression*. I may be leaving behind this cast of characters, but there are many more ready to take center stage. I'm off on my next literary adventure. I hope you will join me.

ABOUT THE AUTHOR

 Dina Santorelli is an award-winning, best-selling author of thriller and suspense novels. She was voted one of the best Long Island authors for two consecutive years. *Baby Grand*, her debut novel, became a #1 Political Thriller, #1 Kidnapping Thriller, and #1 Organized Crime Thriller on Amazon Kindle and reached the Top 30 in the Paid Kindle Store. Additionally, Dina's novel *In the Red* was awarded first place in the genre fiction category in the 28th Annual *Writer's Digest* Self-Published Book Awards. Dina also lectures for Hofstra University's Continuing Education Department.

Follow Dina on social media:

 Facebook: @dinasantorelliwriter

 Twitter: @dinasantorelli

 Instagram: @dinasantorelli

 Goodreads: @dinasantorelli

Join Dina's newsletter and get a free short story titled "A Baby Grand Story: Bailino," a companion piece to the Baby Grand Trilogy! You'll also receive regular updates on Dina's various books and author events, as well her popular 3 Things I Love: http://www.dinasantorelli.com/subscribe

Coming in 2019!

A new thriller by Dina Santorelli!

IN THE RED

When Kirk Stryker, a respected certified public accountant, is brutally murdered in his office in the Long Island village of Gardenia, all eyes are on rival Marty Benning, the handsome newcomer whose high-tech firm has been stealing Stryker's business and attention. Muriel Adams, a middle-aged mom who has given up on love, falls head over heels for the charming yet enigmatic Benning, despite the warnings of friends and family, and when Benning is arrested for Stryker's murder, she is the only one to believe in his innocence. Is Muriel blinded by love? Or is Benning playing her for a fool? *In the Red* is an emotionally charged contemporary thriller that follows the police investigation, media coverage, and political and economic fallout surrounding this high-profile crime, and, ultimately, uncovers a dark underbelly that reveals the dangerous places the heart can lead.